MORRIS AND CHASTAIN INVESTIGATIONS

PLAY WITH FIRE & MIDNIGHT AT THE OASIS

JUSTIN GUSTAINIS

SOLARIS

First published 2013 by Solaris
an imprint of Rebellion Publishing Ltd,
Riverside House, Osney Mead,
Oxford, OX2 0ES, UK

www.solarisbooks.com

ISBN: 978 1 78108 082 5

10 9 8 7 6 5 4 3 2 1

A CIP catalogue record for this book is available from the British Library.

Designed & typeset by Rebellion Publishing

Printed in the US

PLAY WITH FIRE

For Linda
and a rainy night in Salem.

"If you love God, burn a church."

– Jello Biafra

"Deliver me, O Lord, from eternal death
on that awful day,
when the heavens and the earth shall be moved:
when you will come to judge the world by fire."

– Catholic prayer for the dead

"Some men just want to watch the world burn."

– Alfred the Butler

One

Author's note: the events in this story take place shortly after those described in the most recent Morris and Chastain novel, Sympathy for the Devil.

On the day that Quincey Morris got out of jail, Libby Chastain was waiting for him.

Gate four of the Metropolitan Detention Facility in Brooklyn is nothing more than an iron door set in a big stone wall. There is a small parking lot nearby; Libby sat there, behind the wheel of a black Lincoln Town Car. She kept the engine running for the heat, and waited for that door to open. There was nothing to look at apart from the wall, the door, and some paper cups and other trash that blew around in the erratic wind.

Monday, January 16th, Morris's lawyer had told her. *Eleven a.m.* And here it was eleven sixteen, and still no Morris.

Libby had noticed on her way that the parking lot adjoining the intake gate was much larger than the one in which she now sat. *It's as if this place is eager to lock people up, but in no big hurry to let them go.*

Still, things could have been worse. Federal prisoners awaiting trial, like Morris, were kept here, but those under the jurisdiction of the city were sent either to the Tombs (the Bernard B. Kerik Detention Complex in lower Manhattan, which earned its morbid nickname a long time ago), or, even worse, Riker's Island – an overcrowded hellhole that has generated more horror stories than Stephen King.

Morris had been incarcerated since July, following certain events that took place at the Republican National Convention, which had been held in the city. Given the charges against him, a list which even John Dillinger would have found impressive, Morris's judge had denied bail.

Libby had heard that Mal Peters, who had been arrested along with Morris, was also due for release today, but later. She wondered if Peters would be met by someone called Ashley, who looked like a beautiful woman but was in fact something else entirely. The word was that Father Paul Finlay, who had also conspired with Morris and Libby and some others to save the world, would be sprung tomorrow, or the day after.

Libby had not visited Morris in jail – at least, not officially. As a known associate of the prisoner, she had been fairly sure that both the Secret Service and the FBI were interested in talking to her. They had no evidence to connect her with the dramatic business at the Republican Convention, but she might well be held for questioning – maybe for days. So Libby had kept a low profile. She temporarily moved out of her apartment, leaving behind some faked correspondence to show that she was going to be hiking in the Adirondacks for an extended period, exact location unknown.

But she had visited Morris secretly, using a spell for spirit transference. She had appeared in his cell on several occasions, her translucent form looking like a stereotypical movie ghost, while her body remained, behind locked and warded doors, in the bed where she had lain while casting the spell. Morris was familiar with the phenomenon and so had not freaked out when she showed up.

Her last visit had been four nights ago.

"You're looking more cheerful than usual," Libby said to Morris. "Considerably moreso, in fact. And I bet I know why."

Morris grinned at her. "Gloomy Gus paid me a visit yesterday."

Gustav Volmer, attorney at law, was known by that nickname because of his perpetually lugubrious expression. Volmer tended to take on cases that no other attorney would touch, and consequently rarely had good news to deliver to his clients.

"The old bastard was smiling so broadly when I walked into the visitors' room, I thought he was having a stroke," Morris said. "Turned out he had good news for me. I figure the last time something like that *happened was when he told Sir Thomas More that Henry VIII had decided to forego the drawing and quartering, and just have him beheaded."*

Libby, or rather the projection of her spirit, nodded. "The government's dropping all the charges," she said. "Lack of evidence. All a big misunderstanding. Turns out that Stark had actually been abducted by a bunch of terrorists, who escaped in the confusion. You and the other two guys were just caught in the middle."

"I assume you had something to do with that," Morris said.

"Well, not directly. The orders came straight from the Attorney General, I understand. He in turn, was acting on very specific instructions from the White House."

"So our new President decided I had no involvement with the conspiracy to kidnap his former political rival, Senator Howard Stark? What led him to that happy conclusion?"

"Stark did, actually. He's mostly recovered from the bullet wounds, you know. And no longer being possessed by Sargatanas has done wonders for his morale, even if he didn't get to be the Republican nominee this time around. He paid a call on President Leffingwell the day after the inauguration – and brought a couple of friends with him."

"And those friends were...?"

"Me and Ashley," Libby said. "Of course, there was no way we were going to get official clearance to visit the President – especially Ashley. So we made ourselves invisible. At least, until we were in the Oval Office."

Morris shook his head slowly. "Damn, I wish I could have been a fly on the wall for that *little meeting."*

Libby nodded, smiling. "Stark led into it pretty well, but, still – the expression on Leffingwell's face when we appeared out of thin air..."

"Priceless doesn't describe it, I bet."

"A bet you'd win. Up to that point, things went pretty much as you'd expect. Stark told the whole story, beginning with the night he was possessed by Sargatanas, right up to the point where Mary Margaret Doyle put two bullets into his chest. Naturally, Leffingwell decided that Stark had gone completely insane. He was about to ring for the Secret Service when Ashley and I made our rather dramatic entrance. That lent Stark's account a certain verisimilitude, you might say."

"So I get to walk," Morris said. "Peters and Finlay, too? Gloomy Gus doesn't represent them, so he didn't know anything about their cases."

"Yep – their charges are being dropped, too, with apologies all around."

Morris was quiet for a moment, frown lines creasing his face. "It just occurred to me – why just drop the charges, instead of a full pardon for each of us?"

"I looked into that," Libby said. "It seems a President can only pardon somebody who's already been convicted of a crime. Your trial's not even due to start until March at least. Anyway, we figured you'd rather not have the conviction on your record."

"Yeah, you're right about that, for sure."

"Anyway, pardoning the three of you would lead to a lot of embarrassing questions – the kind that Leffingwell would really prefer not to answer. Telling the truth about what happened would be out of the question, of course."

"Isn't it always?" Morris said.

Two

The door that constituted gate four swung open, finally, at eleven twenty-four. Quincey Morris walked through and Libby caught a glimpse of the uniformed corrections officer who pulled the door shut again after Morris was outside. Morris hunched his shoulders against the cold – unsurprising, since he wore only the lightweight suit he'd been arrested in last July.

Libby blinked her lights once to be sure he saw her, and then put the big car into gear. By the time Morris reached the end of the sidewalk that led to the parking lot, Libby was parked there waiting for him.

He got in, pulled the door shut, and turned to look at her.

"How you doin', cowboy?" Libby asked.

A grin split Morris's lean face. "Better now. A hell of a lot better now."

Libby touched the gas and headed the car toward the parking lot exit. After a moment Morris said, "Nice wheels."

"It's rented, of course. You know I can't afford to keep a car – especially one like this – in New York. But I thought the occasion warranted something a little special. In fact, I don't know what happened to the

brass band I hired. They were supposed to be here at eleven, and I've had them practicing 'The Yellow Rose of Texas' for weeks." Libby shook her head in mock disappointment. "You just can't count on anybody, these days."

As Libby turned into the street, Morris looked at her thoughtfully. "I don't know, Libby," he said. "I'm pretty sure there are a few people who can be counted on. Like your own self, for instance. Thank you – for everything."

"Heck, you're the one who just spent six months in the slam – courtesy of an ungrateful nation, who doesn't appreciate what you saved it from."

"You did as much of the saving as I did, if not more. Anyhow, you can't expect gratitude from people who don't know what really happened."

"I suppose. But a few people *do* know. And some of them actually *are* grateful."

Libby's big purse was wedged between the bucket seats. After a quick glance down, she reached in and removed an envelope, which she handed to Morris. "This guy, for instance."

Morris looked at the envelope. The return address was listed simply as "The White House, Washington, D.C." In the center, Morris's name was written, in ink.

Libby saw his look out of the corner of her eye. "A big envelope, containing that and another one with my name on it, was delivered to my place yesterday by a couple of large gentlemen in suits. They did not, I suspect, work for FedEx – although the 'Fed' part might well apply."

Morris opened the envelope to find a single sheet of expensive looking paper with the same simple address as the envelope. The letter was written by hand, in black, spider-thin ink.

Morris looked at the sheet for a lot longer than it should take to read the brief contents. Finally he asked Libby, "Wanna hear what it says?"

"Sure."

Dear Mister Morris,

I used to think that I understood this world we live in reasonably well. But in the last few days I have learned some things that I once could never have imagined, let alone believed. However, the evidence I have seen is impossible to deny. It would seem that a small group of heroic people – led, I understand, by you and Ms. Libby Chastain, have saved the United States, indeed the world, from unimaginable catastrophe. You, and the others, undoubtedly deserve the Medal of Freedom, a ticker tape parade, and a generous pension for life. But if I tried to bestow upon all of you these just rewards, one of two things would happen. Our fellow citizens would not believe my reasons for doing so, and I would be judged insane. Or, perhaps worse, they would *believe me, and the entire nation might well go insane.*

Having the Attorney General drop all charges against you and your colleagues is the very least I can do. Your arrest records will also be quietly expunged.

On behalf of a nation that will never know the invaluable service you rendered it, please accept my thanks.

Sincerely, Robert J. Leffingwell.

"Well, that's nice of him." Morris said. "Pity I can't have it framed to put on the wall."

"I can see how that might cause awkward questions," Libby said. "So what *will* you do with it?"

"Remember that fireproof safe at my house – the one

you put the aversion spell on, so nobody but me could open it?"

"Sure I do."

"Inside, there's a good-sized metal box that holds what I think of as the 'Morris Family's Memorabilia Collection.' Been in the family for something like eighty years. The letter's going in there."

"Now that's a collection I wouldn't mind seeing, sometime," Libby said.

"I'd say you've earned the right, quite a few times over. Just remind me, next time you're down in Austin. You might be interested to see that this isn't the first presidential letter that'll be in there."

"I can't say I'm surprised at all. There's another one, huh?"

"There's two of 'em, actually. One's got FDR's signature on it. The other one's from Lyndon Johnson."

"I can hardly wait," Libby said. "But what would you like to do now?"

"For starters, jail food being what it is, I'm lookin' to get myself on the outside of the biggest, juiciest steak to be found in this town."

"I thought you might have something like that in mind. Our reservation at Peter Luger's is for twelve thirty. We should just make it."

"Bless you. Then, after reminding myself what real food is like, I wish to consume a large quantity of very good bourbon, preferably someplace private so I won't make a drunken fool of myself. Be kind of ironic to get arrested for drunk and disorderly my first day out of jail."

"That had occurred to me, too. I've got a suite reserved at the Plaza, and in its living room you will find two bottles of Jack Daniel's finest aged bourbon."

"Christ, Libby – this is all fantastic, but must be costing you a fortune."

She shrugged. "The Sisterhood came through with a fat check – your half's in the bank, by the way."

"The Sisterhood?"

"They *did* hire us, remember – even if they had no idea at the time just how high the stakes really were. And they felt morally obligated to keep us on the payroll as long as you were locked up."

The Sisterhood was a loose affiliation of female practitioners of white witchcraft. Many of its members, with successful careers outside the magical world, contributed generously to the organization's contingency fund.

"That's good of them."

"Well, shit, Quincey, all we did was save the United States from a demon-possessed president last summer."

"Arguably. I mean, Stark might not have won the general election."

"*Arguably* still counts with the Sisterhood," Libby said.

"Well, I hope you're planning to help me put away some of Mister Daniel's finest, later."

"Not my intoxicant of choice. But I'm pretty sure we'll find a bottle of Grey Goose vodka next to the ice bucket, too. The suite's got two bedrooms, in one of which I plan to be nursing a *massive* hangover tomorrow. But it'll be worth it."

Morris smiled. "Hope you still think so in the morning."

Libby drove a few more blocks before speaking again. "So, we're going to get you the best steak in town, and then go on the biggest private one-night bender in town–"

"Arguably."

It was her turn to smile. "Arguably. Then what?"

"Well, now that I'm out of durance vile, I assume the Sisterhood is going to cut off the funds."

"I expect so. Their gratitude, like most people's, has a short half-life."

"In that case, maybe it's time to go back to work."

"Cowboy, I couldn't agree more."

Three

JANUARY IN DULUTH, Minnesota, and cold as the proverbial witch's tit – although that scurrilous claim about magic practitioner's mammary glands has never been explained, or proven. But it was warm inside the big Caddie – too warm, really, for people already wearing winter coats. That might have explained the sweat on the face of the young man sitting in the passenger's seat, but it didn't. The man behind the wheel knew it, too. The perspiration meant that Jeremy was losing his nerve.

"I'm not sure I can do this, Theron."

The one who called himself Theron Ware looked at the younger man, showing none of the impatience he felt.

"It *has* to be you, Jeremy, we've been over all that before. More than once. And you *agreed* with me, remember?"

"Yeah, but I'm not sure–"

"He has to come out unsuspecting, and that fresh-faced look of yours is just the thing to get him there."

"It's not just that, it's all of it. The whole fucking ritual."

Ware slowly ran his hand through his thick, black hair – a sure sign that he was getting angry. It was a sign that Jeremy should have heeded.

"Need I remind you," Ware said, "of the stakes involved here, or of the glory that will be ours – the power *and* the glory – if we have the fortitude to take the knowledge we have gained and *use* it?"

"I'll do it, Theron, if you want," Elektra said from the back seat. Ware did not turn around to see the look of scorn she was giving Jeremy, but he knew it was there.

"I've already considered that, Elektra, as you know. In some ways, it's tempting. A female might cut a more pathetic figure than the average male, and win the priest's sympathies more readily. But I'm afraid your years on the streets have left their mark on you, my dear. The *shaman* would be on guard the moment he saw you."

Mark, the big, slow one sitting next to Elektra said, "Want me to do it? It's cool, I don't give a fuck."

"Thank you for your willingness, Mark," Ware said, "but I don't think your ... talents are a good fit for this. No, it has to be Jeremy."

He turned back to the man in the front seat. "There's a term that those civil rights idiots used to use, decades ago. 'Keep your eyes on the prize.' Do you know what that means?"

"I – I guess it means to focus on the reward to come, no matter how–" Jeremy swallowed "–no matter how bad things are at the time."

"Very good," Ware said, keeping the sarcasm out of his voice. "It's important to stay focused. And you might also focus on the consequences of letting me down in this endeavor. Do you wish to experience those consequences?"

"No, Theron – no, of course not."

"Are you *quite* certain?" Ware made an unobtrusive

gesture with his left hand while muttering two words in a language that none of the others would recognize, even if they heard it clearly.

A thin stream of blood began to flow from the corners of Jeremy's eyes.

It seemed to take Jeremy a moment to realize what was happening. Then he put his hand to his face, took it away, and gaped at the blood that smeared it.

"No, Theron, please. Make it stop. I'll do what you want, all of it, just make it stop!"

"You agree to lure the priest, and take your full part in what is to follow? Do you?"

"Yes, yes, anything. Please!"

Ware made another gesture, and the blood disappeared as if it had never been there at all.

"Then I suggest you get moving," Ware said.

Four

LeBron James faked left, went right, then seemed to defy gravity as he blew past the defender and went for the basket. He made the emphatic jam, and managed to get himself fouled in the process.

Father Joe Middleton shook his head in disgust and wondered if it would be blasphemous to ask the Lord to grant the Knicks something that resembled a defense. Although his vocation had brought him to Minnesota, he was a New Yorker born and bred, and had been a Knicks fan most of his life, heartbreaking though such devotion could often be. After a moment, Father Joe concluded that God probably had better things to do than get involved in a basketball game, even though players and fans of every sport seemed to call upon His intervention with great regularity.

Then the doorbell rang. Father Joe was alone in the rectory tonight, which meant it was up to him to both answer the door and minister to the needs of whoever was on the other side. He assumed ministering of some sort would be called for – it was too late for deliveries to the church, and Father Joe hadn't ordered a pizza. He clicked the TV off and gave a small sigh. Well, at least he would be spared the aggravation of watching the Knicks go down in defeat yet again.

Opening the door revealed a fresh-faced young man in his twenties who was plainly agitated about something.

"Father, you gotta come," he said rapidly. "Please Father, it looks bad."

"Take a deep breath," Father Joe told the young man. "I mean it – a deep, deep breath."

The visitor complied, perhaps tamping down his adrenaline a bit in the process.

"Now tell me what's happened," Father Joe said.

"Guy's been hit by a car, just two blocks from here. I saw it happen. The son of a bitch that hit him didn't even slow down – just kept on truckin'."

"Come in," Father Joe said. He quickly opened a nearby closet, put on his black overcoat, then picked up the small leather satchel that contained everything he would need to perform the Anointing of the Sick sacrament at the accident site. "Did anybody call 911?"

"Yeah, my buddy did. He said he'd stay with the guy while I ran over here. We better hurry, Father – the guy that got hit, he was bleedin' real bad."

Father Joe grabbed a set of keys from a hook near the kitchen door. "Come on. My car's out back." A few seconds later, as he was fumbling to get the black Oldsmobile's door open, two thoughts skittered across the back of his mind, like errant leaves in the wind. One was the absence of sirens. Duluth Emergency Services was very efficient – there should have been sirens wailing by now. The second thought was that the young man who had followed him out to the driveway hadn't gone around to the passenger side, waiting for Father Joe to unlock the door. Which meant he must be standing right behind ...?

That was the last coherent thought Father Joe had for quite a while. He heard rather than felt the sound of something hard impacting the back of his skull, briefly filling his brain with a brilliant fireworks show, before everything went to black.

Five

Father Joe woke up with a headache that dwarfed any he'd had in the past, and the priest had known more than his fair share of headaches over the years.

Then he opened his eyes, and realized that the throbbing in his skull was the least of his problems.

He was naked, lying on his back atop something that was smooth, hard and cold. A quick glance around told him that he was in the sanctuary of his own church, Saint Bartholomew's, and his position relative to other objects he knew well – the pulpit, statue of Saint Bartholomew and the rank of offertory candles – meant that he was atop the altar, devoid of the ceremonial cloth that usually draped it. He tried to move, and found that his wrists and ankles were somehow tied to the marble slab with rope. He was trying to wrap his mind around his predicament and figure out both how he'd got here and what it meant, when a pleasant male voice said from behind him, "Welcome back to the land of the living, Father – although I don't think you'll be staying."

Father Joe strained his neck in an effort to get a look at the speaker, but the man was already moving. He passed through the periphery of the priest's vision and a second later was standing at his feet, gazing down at Father Joe with an expression of amused contempt.

The man appeared to be of average height and build. His midnight-black hair was brushed straight back, and a well-trimmed goatee encircled his mouth. His shirt and slacks were of the same color as his hair.

Father Joe took all this in within an instant, then his attention was riveted on the knife the man was holding. It was more of a dagger, really, at least a foot long from the ebony hilt to the tip of a blade that glinted briefly in the ceiling lights. The man toyed with it as he spoke, allowing Father Joe to see that the hilt was intricately carved, with small jewels worked into the wood.

The man's face briefly split into a grin. "You like the getup? Like something out of a bad horror movie, isn't it? And the facial hair adds a nicely Satanic touch, don't you think? Personally, I prefer a nice gray Armani, or even a sweatshirt and jeans for casual wear. But my *disciples* expect this kind of image, and in this age image is everything, or very nearly. Don't you agree, *Father*?"

The man tilted his head a little, not waiting for a response. "Do you know, I don't believe I've called anyone 'Father' since the old man died, lo those many years ago." A dreamy expression briefly appeared on the man's face, but it was the kind of dream from which you'd wake up screaming. "What I wouldn't give to have *him* trussed up there, in your place. I could keep him alive and screaming for hours, I expect."

"In any case, you're far more appropriate for my purpose."

Father Joe tried to speak, and failed, his voice box constricted with fear. He cleared his throat and tried again. "And what purpose *is* that, exactly?"

The man raised an eyebrow. "I would have thought that was obvious. Where are you now, Father? I mean specifically."

After a few seconds, Father Joe was able to croak, "On the altar."

"Very good. And what purpose does any altar serve, hmmm?"

Father Joe didn't try to speak this time – but he didn't have to.

The man in black smiled, as if at a prize pupil. "Exactly – a sacrifice. A more meaningful one than that charade you go through here every weekday and twice on Sundays."

He raised his head and looked toward the back of the church. "Stop dragging your asses and get it finished, people." His voice echoed in the near-empty building. "I'd rather not explain what we're about to the half-dozen old bags who show up for six o'clock mass!"

Looking back at the priest he said, more conversationally, "Actually, it might be rather amusing to have them here and make them watch what we're going to do to you. But we need to be done and gone before the cock crows, more's the pity."

"Done – with what?" Father Joe croaked.

"Why, the ritual, of course, the final step of which will require us to burn this place to the ground. That's what my minions – I just *love* that word – are doing, however slowly. Setting incendiaries at strategic points, to make sure this holy shithole burns hot and fast. We can't have the fire department saving any of it – it just wouldn't do, you know."

He peered at Father Joe for a moment. "I see the prospect of burning alive has just occurred to you. Don't worry, Father – we'll be finished with you before the incendiaries go off. You'll be spared the experience of the flames – which is more than your church did for many of my brethren, back in the old days. The Burning Times, they call that period now, did you know? Well, guess what – the Burning Times are *back*. Only this time, we'll be doing the burning. And when we're done, all of you will burn."

"You mean... all... priests?" Father Joe had to force the words out.

"Oh, no, my dear man. You're thinking on too small a scale. I have something rather... Ah, but it seems that the minions are done, at last. Come on, children – gather 'round!"

Soon Father Joe was surrounded by three more people. He recognized one of the men as the one who'd lured him out of the rectory. He'd been joined by a red-haired woman with a hard face, and another man with a large build and vacant expression. The first two produced sheets of paper with words typed on both sides and held them expectantly. The man in black looked at the third. "Don't tell me Mark, that you've forgotten your copy of the ritual. For your own sake, don't you tell me *that*."

The large shoulders lifted and fell in a shrug. "I already got it memorized, Ware. I'm good to go."

"I don't *care* if you think you know it by memory. The invocation has to be done *precisely* as written, and I don't want you getting all excited and forgetting something once things start to get messy. Now get out your copy!"

"Okay, okay. Be cool." Mark produced a folded sheet of paper and opened it out.

"That's better." The man in black looked at Father Joe. "It may occur to you to try disrupting the proceedings with some of your holy mumbo-jumbo. Be advised at the first word from you – the *very first* – I will cut out your tongue. Understood?"

Father Joe nodded.

"Very well." The man in black looked at the others. "Let us begin."

The four of them began to chant, in a language that had already been old when Christianity was young. The priest prayed silently – not for deliverance, but for God to receive his soul on the other side, despite what Father Joe regarded as his many sins and shortcomings. He was distracting himself by considering the theological question of whether what was about to happen to him constituted martyrdom when the voices ceased.

"Very good," the man in black said. I'm sure our Master will be pleased. Now let's *really* make him happy."

He picked up the big knife and stepped forward.

Over the next few minutes, Father Joe tried very hard not to scream. But his resolve lasted less than thirty seconds.

Six

"I CAN'T SAY I'd be surprised to see somebody from the Civil Rights Division drop by for a look at this case," Byron Cummings said, "but I don't see what interest Behavioral Science has in a church burning."

Cummings was Special Agent in charge of the FBI's small Duluth field office, and he didn't much appreciate agents from Washington – or, in this case, Quantico – trying to tell him how to run an investigation. Of course, the FBI hadn't been called in yet, and neither of his visitors had tried telling him to do anything at all, but Cummings figured it was just a matter of time.

Especially these two – Fenton and O'Donnell (who Cummings, both a racist and sexist, privately thought of as "the black guy and the redhead with the tits"). He'd heard about this mismatched pair before. Rumor was they'd got in some kind of trouble in Idaho or Iowa last year, but nobody in the Bureau's extensive gossip stream seemed to know what kind of trouble it was, or why these two hadn't been fired over it.

One story said that they'd been involved in the death of Walter Grobius, a secretive *uber*-billionaire who'd been killed in a massive fire at his Midwest estate. A variation of the rumor held that Grobius had been some kind of devil worshipper or something, and that Fenton and O'Donnell were trying to hang a bunch of ritualistic child murders on him.

But none of that shit mattered to Cummings. The death of Father Joseph Middleton and subsequent torching of St. Bartholomew's church might or might not call for federal involvement – the Duluth PD hadn't put in a request, so far. But if they did, the local field office, led by Byron Cummings, was going to handle it – not a couple of affirmative action poster kids from serial killer central.

"Father Middleton's death had certain… ritualistic elements to it." That was from Fenton, the black guy. He had short hair, a thin mustache, and a suit that probably cost more than Cummings' last paycheck.

"What gives you that idea?" Cummings asked. "The autopsy report hasn't been made public yet. Hell, even *I* haven't had a look at it."

"Someone at DUPD sent us a copy," O'Donnell said. "Thought we might be interested."

"And who the hell was that?" Cummings wasn't particularly upset that one of the local cops was leaking info about the case – he was pissed because they hadn't leaked it to *him*, first. He noticed that O'Donnell hadn't even used a pronoun to identify the gender of the leaker.

"It doesn't matter," O'Donnell said. "The fact is we've seen the report, and we'd like to find out more about the case." Consistent with the red hair, she had a dusting of freckles across her nose. Cummings wondered if they were also sprinkled across those nicely formed tits of hers.

"It seems likely that whoever torched the church expected to destroy all evidence of how Father Middleton had died," Fenton said. "This was no nutjob with a five-gallon can of gas and a Bic lighter. The arson squad's initial report says that professional-level incendiary charges were used, placed strategically around the church."

"Strategically, huh?" Cummings thought that was a pretty fancy word coming from somebody who looked like every third word out of his mouth should be *motherfucker*. Cummings had grown up in a bad part of the Bronx, where he'd learned to hate and fear the black gangs who continually battled for control of the local drug trade. He tended to view every black male he met as either a present, former, or potential gangbanger.

"Even if that's true," Cummings went on, "all it means is that somebody went on the internet and did his research. What's that got to do with those 'ritualistic elements' you're talking about?"

"Because, despite all their elaborate efforts," O'Donnell said, "the arsonists fucked up." Cummings loved it when attractive women talked dirty – possibly because his own wife never said anything nastier than "fudge."

"A section of the church's ceiling fell over the altar area before the building was fully engulfed. It partially protected Father Middleton's corpse from the flames," Fenton said. "It was still pretty badly burned – but it wasn't reduced to ashes, which is what we figure the arsonists had in mind."

"So, there was enough of him left to do a half-decent autopsy, I get you," Cummings said. "How did the poor guy die, then, if he didn't burn to death?"

"The killers used a knife." O'Donnell's voice, fairly expressive to this point, had become flat and emotionless. "A large one, from all indications."

"More important was the way the knife was used," Fenton said.

"You mean multiple stab wounds?" Cummings asked him. "Nothing unusual about that, unfortunately."

"It was more than that. Several occult symbols were carved into the body, probably *ante-mortem*," Fenton said.

"That was before Father Middleton was castrated, eviscerated, and had his heart cut out of his body," O'Donnell said. "All while he was still alive, most likely."

Cummings, who was cursed with a vivid imagination, felt his stomach perform a slow somersault. His office dealt with a few bank robberies, the occasional kidnapping, and a parade of terrorist suspects who always turned out to be innocuous – but nothing like this. The cases of real butchery were outside his jurisdiction, and handled by the police. He swallowed a couple of times and said, "Why in the name of God would somebody do that? I mean, what were they trying to *achieve*?"

"Well, for one thing, it wasn't in the name of God – at least not the same one you and I worship," O'Donnell said grimly. "As to their precise motive – I look forward to asking them about that someday – preferably through the bars at a maximum security prison."

"All right," Cummings said. "So, what can the field office do to assist you?"

"There's nothing we need from you right now," Fenton said. "Bureau procedure says we're supposed to check in with the local field office, and we always follow proper procedure." Cummings thought he detected a light touch of irony at the end of that sentence, but wasn't certain.

"However, we need to talk to some of the detectives at DUPD about the case," O'Donnell said, "and there's no way to tell in advance how much cooperation we're likely to get. If somebody starts digging his heels in, we may ask you to make a phone call or two, to smooth the way." She stood up then, and her partner followed suit. "I'd like to think we can count on you for that, should the need arise."

Cummings had a full bottle of Pepto-Bismol in his desk, and he wanted to get these two out of there so he could down about half of it. He could not stop focusing on the mental image of what father Joe Middleton must have looked like, once those crazy fuckers had finished with him. "Yeah, sure," he said hastily. "I'll grease the wheels for you. Whatever you need."

"Thank you, Agent Cummings," O'Donnell said.

"We appreciate it," Fenton chimed in, and then the two of them turned and left.

The door had barely closed behind them when Cummings was reaching into the bottom drawer of his desk.

Seven

RON SHUMAKER, THE lead detective on the church arson/murder case, had a beat-up desk in the detective's bullpen at Duluth police headquarters. Around the big room other detectives, men and women, were typing, drinking coffee, checking e-mail, or reading the paper – when they weren't throwing covert glances toward Shumaker's two visitors, who were said to be a couple of feds from out of town.

With his button-down shirt and tweed sport coat, Shumaker came across more like a college professor then somebody who'd been a cop for nineteen years. The black-rimmed glasses he wore didn't hide the bags under his eyes, however. Ron Shumaker looked as if he hadn't had a good night's sleep in a long time.

He pushed a thick manila file across the desk toward Agents Fenton and O'Donnell. "You're welcome to look it over, but I can't let you take it out of the building or copy it – the chief would have my ass. If you want to spend some time on it without being disturbed, I can probably find you an interrogation room that nobody's using."

Unknown to Shumaker, agents O'Donnell and Fenton had already seen a copy of the case file. But that had been three days ago, and a lot can happen in an investigation during that length of time.

"Maybe it'll save us some time if you can just answer a couple of questions," Fenton said.

Shumaker gave a tired shrug. "Ask away."

"For starters," O'Donnell said, "the forensic evidence about the perps currently amounts to shit, right?"

"Yeah, pretty much. Of course, they *did* burn down the fucking building, which makes it kind of hard to identify hair, fiber, fingerprints, all that. The arson squad wrote up a report about the stuff they used to create the blaze – that's in the file, for what it's worth."

"There's no shortage of snow around here, this time of year," O'Donnell said. "Any useful footprints?"

"Not one. We hadn't had any precip for a couple of days before this all went down, so the stuff on the ground was hard-packed into ice."

"Eyewitnesses?" Fenton asked.

"At five in the morning? Not likely, in that neighborhood. Nobody even knew there was a fire, until a passing patrol car saw the flames coming through the roof."

"How about nuts calling up after the fact, taking credit, if that's the word," O'Donnell said. "Any of those?"

"Yeah we had a couple of confessions. None of them could answer questions about the means of ignition, the mutilations, or anything else that wasn't on the news. Nuts – like you said."

Fenton leaned back, the chair he'd borrowed creaking in protest. "What do you think, Detective?

Were these locals? You guys must keep tabs on the local hate groups."

"Yeah, we worked our snitches among the local skinheads and KKK types. Came up empty."

"You've got the Klan, way up here?" Fenton asked.

"Oh, sure – the local Klavern, if that's what they call it, consists of four guys and two of their girlfriends. Those clowns couldn't organize a barbeque, let along something like what happened at St. Bart's. And besides–" Shumaker hesitated.

"Besides, what?" O'Donnell asked him.

"I'm trying to think how to put this," Shumaker said. "If it had happened at a local synagogue, or the one mosque we have in town, I could kind of understand it. I mean, there's assholes who hate Jews – everybody knows that. Other idiots hate Moslems, especially since 9/11. But nobody around here's pissed off at the Catholic Church. Not *that* pissed off, anyway."

"But as you've suggested, they might not be locals," O'Donnell said. "Which raises the question – why Duluth? There's Catholic churches in pretty much every city and town in the country."

"A better question," Shumaker said, "is why *anybody* would do that to a priest before burning the church down around him. Somebody's got a lot of hate going – and before you ask, we checked to see if Father Middleton had any enemies. Didn't find a thing. The guy was a priest, for cryin' out loud – and not the kind who fucks altar boys, either."

"Maybe it wasn't personal at all," O'Donnell said slowly. "Maybe any Catholic priest in Duluth would do."

Shumaker stared at her. "What the hell's that supposed to mean?"

"I'm not sure yet," she said. "Just something that needs thinking about. Forget it for now."

"If we assume the perps weren't local," Fenton said, "then how did they get there? To the church, I mean."

Shumaker shrugged. "Drove, I suppose, but it doesn't matter. Nobody saw a car parked near the church – we asked that when canvassing the neighborhood."

"But you're assuming there *was* a car, right?" Fenton said.

"Either that, or they walked. But being on foot means it takes too long to clear the neighborhood, once the fire's started. So, yeah – they probably drove. So what?"

"So, if they're not local, and they had a car," Fenton said, "where'd they get it?"

Eight

"SINCE WHEN DOES the FBI care about stolen cars?" Axel Swenson asked. "It ain't a federal offense, last I heard."

Swenson didn't look at all like a Viking type, Fenton thought. Short black hair, brown eyes, and a Fu Manchu mustache that had gone out of style with bell-bottom pants. His construction company must be pretty successful, since he could afford the Cadillac El Dorado that was parked in his driveway. The police report said Swenson had reported it stolen Tuesday morning. On Thursday, the manager of a supermarket, clear across town, had reported to police what seemed to be an abandoned vehicle in his parking lot. The license number and description matched one on the police hot sheet, and the following day Swenson was invited to pick up his car at the police impound lot.

"You're right, Mister Swenson – it isn't a federal crime," Fenton told him. "But it's possible that the people who stole your car have been involved in a series of bank robberies across three states – and that *is* the FBI's business."

Swenson's thick eyebrows headed toward his hairline. "Bank robbers? Jeez Louise! I figured it was just some fuckin' kids, out joyriding, or something."

"You're lucky it wasn't," O'Donnell said. "Joyriders almost always trash the car once they're done with it – especially when it's a nice ride like yours. They're probably resentful that the owner can afford a fancy car, and they can't. But from what I understand, your car wasn't damaged, at all."

"Yeah, thank God. Didn't have so much as a scratch on her."

"And if a professional had been involved," she went on, "you'd never have seen your car again. The thief would either be filling a specific order – usually from somebody in another state – or he'd have sold it to a chop shop, for the parts. That's why we think this might have been the people we're interested in."

"But there wasn't no bank robbery around here," Swenson said, frowning. "Not that I heard of, anyway."

"You're right," Fenton said. "Something must have scared them off, or caused them to change their minds."

Swenson may not have gotten past high school, but that didn't mean he was stupid. "So what makes you think it was bank robbers, if no bank got robbed?"

Fenton was ready for that one. "Because the M.O. of the car theft was the same as the cases where there were bank robberies. M.O. means–"

"I know what it means," Swenson said. "I watch TV." He sounded slightly offended.

"Of course – sorry," Fenton said. "But, to get specific – you've got a car alarm, right?"

"Sure – factory installed. The dealer said it was the best there is."

"But it didn't go off, did it?"

"No – if it had, I'd have been out there with my gun faster than a scalded cat." After a second he hastily added, "I got a permit."

"I'm sure you do," Fenton said. "You've also got a steering wheel lock on your Caddie. The wheel's not supposed to turn unless the ignition's turned on, right?"

"Yeah – that didn't stop them either. Bastards."

"And the police report said that none of the ignition wires were loose. The thieves didn't hot-wire it."

"Christ, what'd they do, then?" Swenson asked. "Use magic?"

Fenton glanced at his partner before saying, "No, of course not. But however they did it, somebody did something similar to three other cars that were used in bank robberies within the last six months. That's why we'd like to take a look at the car, if you don't mind."

"It's okay with me, but what are you expectin' to find that the cops didn't?"

"Uh, we brought a mass spectrometer with us," Fenton said. "The Minneapolis P.D didn't use one when they went over the car."

"Mass spectrometer, huh? Yeah, they use those on *CSI* all the time," Swenson said. "Let me get you the keys."

Nine

Colleen O'Donnell, FBI Special Agent and practitioner of white witchcraft, pulled the Caddy's door closed and looked at her partner, one eyebrow raised.

"*Mass spectrometer?* For goddess's sake, Dale."

"Best I could come up with," Fenton said. "Anyway, it worked, didn't it?"

"We should count ourselves lucky he didn't ask to see it."

"If he had, I was counting on you to work some hocus-pocus and convince him that we'd showed it to him."

O'Donnell just shook her head. Then she said, "Speaking of hocus-pocus, I might as well get on with it."

"Right."

O'Donnell closed her eyes and began to breathe very slowly, very deliberately. After five such breaths, she began to speak softly in a language they don't teach in any university. Fenton wasn't conversant in the language, but he'd heard these words before and knew what they meant.

O'Donnell continued in the arcane language for perhaps two minutes. Then she took a deep breath and expelled all the air from her lungs in a vigorous exhale. After a slow count of three, she inhaled loudly. Again that slow, silent count of three before she let the air out and began to breathe normally again. With her eyes still closed, she said "Yessss. Oh my, yes."

She opened her eyes half a minute later to find Fenton looking at her. He did not appear happy. "Black magic," he said.

"Undeniably. And fairly fresh – it certainly could have been conjured five days ago, when the car was stolen."

Fenton nodded glumly. Making a slight gesture toward the house, he said, "I don't suppose it's possible that Swenson in there is a practitioner?"

"No – I'd have known the moment we walked inside."

"Figures – our luck never runs that good."

The two of them sat quietly for a few moments. "So a black magician rolls into town and ritualistically murders a priest," O'Donnell said.

"Uh-huh. Then burns the church down around him. Just to hide what they did to the poor guy?"

"No, that's too... elaborate," she said. "If that's all they wanted, it would have been a lot simpler to just take the body away and bury it someplace."

"In Minnesota? In January? Somebody around here dies this time of year, they either cremate 'em, or keep the body on ice until the ground thaws in April."

"That's a point, but not a huge one. There's lots of ways to hide a corpse that don't involve that kind of arson, Dale. Burning the church – that was part of the ritual. I'm sure of it."

Fenton shifted in his seat. "You're pretty well versed in what black magicians do, and how they do it. It's part of your witch training, right?"

"Yes, of course."

"You ever hear of the bad guys using a ritual like this?"

"No. Nothing that even comes close," she said.

"Well, shit."

They got out of the Caddy making sure to lock it behind them. By prior agreement, Fenton went to their rental car parked at the curb while O'Donnell rang Swenson's doorbell.

When he answered she said, "Here are your keys, Mister Swenson. We want to thank you for your cooperation."

"That's okay," he said. "Where's your partner?"

"Oh, he's putting... our equipment away." O'Donnell did not trust herself to say "mass spectrometer" with a straight face.

"Did you find what you were looking for?"

"No, I'm afraid not," she lied.

As Fenton pulled the car into traffic he said, "I'm trying to get my mind around this mess. Somebody conducted a black magic ritual at the church, but it's one you never heard of."

"Correct, unfortunately."

"People do black magic in order to *get* something, right? Power, riches, revenge – something they can't achieve on their own."

"Uh-huh."

"So what does this fucker *want*?"

O'Donnell looked out through the side window, at all the innocent, unaware people who went about their lives oblivious to the darkness that was all around them.

"I don't know," she said. "And that's what frightens me."

Ten

YOU HEAR THE word "monastery," and, if you're like most people, the image in your mind's eye is of a cold, forbidding structure of stone, where oddlooking men live out their lives copying manuscripts and dreaming up new ways to torture heretics.

St. Ignatius Monastery, in the Rocky Mountains overlooking Missoula Montana, isn't like that. The pleasant-looking buildings are mostly wood and brick, and they were all built to include central heating, which comes in handy during the Montana winter. The monks are quiet, friendly, studious guys who aren't interested in torturing anybody. There's nothing scary about the place – with one exception. The basement of St. Thomas Aquinas Hall has a room whose contents might well frighten you, if you knew they existed. Most people don't – including about eighty per cent of the monks who spend their lives at the monastery. Quincey Morris and Libby Chastain hadn't known what was in that room, either – until they were told that it wasn't there anymore.

The abbot who ran the place, Father Theodore Bowen, had bushy black eyebrows that were an odd contrast to his pure-white hair. He was tall and broad, wearing a long brown robe cinched at the waistline by a plain white cord. Bowen's cincture may have been a little longer than average; his waistline offered plain proof that monastery dining halls no longer rely upon gruel as a staple.

Bowen was normally a genial man, but as he led Morris and Chastain along the basement corridor that led to room nine, he wore the somber face of someone whose doctor has just told him that the X-rays have come back, and there's a problem.

Morris noticed surveillance cameras mounted on both sides of the corridor, each one pointed at the door they were now approaching. On each camera a small red light burned to show that it was operational.

Unlike most of the doors at St. Ignatius, which are made of wood and hollow in the middle, the door to room nine was steel, and solid all the way through. It had two locks, each requiring a separate key, as Father Bowen demonstrated. The click of a light switch revealed that room nine was in fact two rooms. The one where they stood was sparsely furnished, with a long table, four chairs, some religious paintings on one wall, and a large crucifix on the wall opposite.

"This, as you can see, is the reading area," Father Bowen said. "But we keep the books in here."

They followed him to another solid looking door with a keypad next to it. "Burglar alarm," Father Bowen said over his shoulder. He used his body to block the keypad from their sight while he tapped in a series of numbers, then he inserted a third key into yet another lock.

"You take wise precautions, Father," Libby Chastain said. "Not all of them based in science, I see."

Father Bowen looked at her. "Excuse me?"

"Above the door," she said. Morris followed Libby's gaze and saw a complex symbol drawn on the wall in red and black. It was enclosed in a circle no bigger than a dessert plate. "That *is* a magical ward, isn't it?"

Father Bowen cleared his throat, which hadn't sounded husky a moment earlier. "Yes, it is, Ms. Chastain. I should have known that someone of your reputed talent would recognize it. Father Richie, who is a member of our community, has been given training and permission to practice abjuration magic – but only when strictly necessary."

Libby nodded approvingly. "It's a good one you've got there."

"Not nearly good enough, it seems." Father Bowen opened the second door and reached inside to flick on a light. "Come in – please."

The windowless room was about twenty feet by thirty, and unremarkable in every way, except for the bookcases that covered every foot of wall space. Many of the books contained there were very old, judging by their bindings. Walking slowly along the shelves, Morris saw several books that he recognized and one whose existence he had always doubted.

The shelves of the bookcases were packed tightly, except for one about halfway along the left wall, which showed a gap of about two feet. Morris nodded toward the space. "Does that represent what was taken?"

"Yes," Father Bowen said. "Nothing else appears to have been touched, even though several of these works would fetch a good price on the antiquarian market. It would seem the thief knew exactly what he wanted."

"When did he take it?" Morris asked.

Father Bowen frowned. "Sorry?"

"When did this burglary of yours take place?"

Father Bowen blew breath out between pursed lips. "That's rather difficult to say, precisely. This room isn't in use every day, or even every month. The theft was discovered three days ago when Brother Armand came in here, to do some authorized research. The last person before him to use this room was Father Palmer, just over seven weeks ago."

"So the theft could have occurred anytime over the last seven weeks?" Morris tried to keep the incredulity out of his voice. He almost succeeded.

"But you've got surveillance cameras trained on the outer door," Libby said. "They would have recorded the break-in. Doesn't the video have a time and date code?"

"Someone appears to have, uh, tampered with the video system," Father Bowen said. "It has apparently been operating on a feedback loop, playing the same footage over and over, instead of showing what was happening in real time."

Morris snorted. "Has anybody checked to see if Danny Ocean is still in jail? Or maybe Tom Cruise and the IMF boys passed through town."

Father Bowen looked confused. Apparently popular culture was not his strong suit.

Libby looked pointedly at the empty space on the shelf, and then asked Father Bowen, "What is it that was taken, exactly?"

The priest seemed relieved to receive a question he could answer. "Marsilio Ficino's 1484 translation of the *Corpus Hermeticum*," he said. "Five volumes. Original binding, if it matters."

Morris blinked a couple of times, all sarcasm forgotten. "That's the Latin version, right? Can't be that many copies of *that* still around."

"Two others, as far as we know," Father Bowen said. "One is locked in a secure room in the Vatican and the other, interestingly enough, is believed to be in the Kremlin."

"You two lost me about a minute ago," Libby said. "I've never heard of this *Corpus*..."

"*Hermeticum*," Morris said. The Latin translation of an even older work in ancient Greek by... I forget his name."

"Hermes Trismegistus," Father Bowen said. "One of the most brilliant men of his age, or so we're told. He wrote it in Egyptian-Greek, somewhere in the Second or Third Century A.D. There are no known copies of the original in existence." He looked at Morris. "Although parts of it are said to be even older, with Trismegistus merely acting as translator."

Morris nodded slowly. "Yeah, I've heard that rumor."

"Older?" Libby said. "How much older?"

"As old as Solomon, perhaps – although that's never been proven to the satisfaction of all the experts," Father Bowen said. "Some believe it, though."

"Solomon? It was written by *Solomon*?" Libby's incredulity was clear in her voice.

"Like the man said, it's never been proven," Morris said. "But if it's true, it would be very powerful stuff."

"Solomon was said to have been given power over demons, especially the demon Asmodeus, who is believed to be high in the councils of Hell," Father Bowen said. "According to legend, Solomon was able to both summon and banish demons at will."

Libby glanced again at the empty space where the *Corpus Hermeticum* had been kept. "So that's what was in there – Solomon's instructions for calling and expelling demons?"

Father Bowen wiped a palm across his face. "I don't know, for certain – I've not read it. No one in the community has ever been given permission to read it.

It's possible that there's no one still alive who has – not counting whoever stole it, that is."

"So what's it doing in a library, even a very exclusive one like this," Morris said, "if nobody's allowed to read it?"

"This archive serves two functions," Father Bowen told him. "One is, of course, research. Many of these books *are* available to scholars – although the number of those allowed access has traditionally been quite small, and they are required to obtain permission from an office in the Vatican. But its other function is protection. Some of the works kept here are intended *never* to be read – by *anyone*."

"Then why not just destroy those, so you don't have to worry about them anymore?" Morris asked him.

Father Bowen seemed to choose his words carefully before he spoke. "That approach has, in fact, been recommended by a number of people – including myself. As a solution it has, I think, a certain elegant simplicity."

"But they won't let you," Libby said. "*They* being whoever in the hierarchy you report to."

"No, they won't. The reason behind that decision is logical, even if some of us regard it as morally bankrupt."

"Why morally bankrupt?" Morris said. "If you don't mind my asking."

Father Bowen walked slowly along a wall of bookcases. He removed a book, seemingly at random, glanced at its cover, and replaced it. He looked at Morris. "I was trying to think of the best way to explain their viewpoint, and perhaps an analogy will help. The United States is a benevolent, peace-loving nation." Father Bowen produced a brief, rueful expression. "At least, that's the image most Americans have of our country. Correct?"

Morris and Libby both nodded.

"And yet it is a poorly kept secret that the U.S. government, in addition to its large nuclear arsenal, has a considerable stockpile of chemical and biological weapons, every one of which is banned by the Geneva Convention and a host of other international agreements. You're aware of this, yes?"

More nodding.

"Now, a succession of presidents, and other high government officials, have sworn that the United States will never, ever make use of such horrible weapons. And yet we have refused to destroy them."

"Because, in a hostile world, nobody who's got a weapon that powerful is going to just throw it away," Morris said. "It would be like one of my ancestors, who was a Marshal in Dodge City, locking away his guns before going out into the street. Could be nobody would take a shot at him – but somebody *might*."

Father Bowen looked at Morris. "I see you're a man who understands the value of analogy, yourself."

"So the upshot of all this analogy-making," Libby said, "is that the church wants to keep dangerous books like the *Corpus Hermeticum* around – just in case."

"Succinctly but admirably put, Ms. Chastain," Father Bowen said. "And whether I personally agree with that decision or not, I have taken a vow of obedience. It was my responsibility to safeguard that book – and in this I have failed." He looked from Libby to Morris and back again. "I would like you to help me atone for my failure by restoring the *Corpus Hermeticum* to its proper place of safekeeping."

"Why was it here in the first place?" Morris asked. "The Vatican's got a well guarded collection of occult books – you said so yourself, although I already knew about it. Why weren't *they* looking after it?"

"They're following the principle of not keeping all of one's eggs in a single basket," Father Bowen said. "If something should happen to that collection in Rome – through fire, explosion, natural disaster or terrorist attack – having backup copies at other secure sights offers some insurance that the information will not be lost, even if some of us believe that it should be."

"So the Vatican's backup location is a monastery in Montana?" Libby asked. "I'm sorry, I don't mean that the way it sounds."

"No offense taken, Ms.Chastain. I would say in our defense that this facility has had an excellent record of security for almost a hundred years." Father Bowen made a face. "Until recently, that is. And we are not the only such location to house dangerous materials – there are others."

"Where are they?" Morris asked him.

"I'm sorry, but I am not permitted to say how many other secure facilities there are, or where they are located. I hope you understand."

"Sure, I do," Morris said. "But it might not be a bad idea for you to check with the hierarchy to see if any of those other locations have been hit, or if an attempt has recently been made."

Father Bowen frowned. "Why?"

"It would be useful to know whether the focus of the thief, was this particular facility, or whether he's tried and failed to get into one of the others. Or even succeeded."

Father Bowen nodded slowly. "All right. I'll see what I can find out."

"Good," Morris said. "In the meantime–"

"*No, you won't.*"

Both of the men turned their heads to stare at

Libby. Before either one could speak, she went on, "I'm sensitive to deception, Father – that's part of my training, too. And what you said just now was a flat-out lie, although I don't know what your motivation was."

Father Bowen's face began to grow red. "Ms. Chastain, I'm afraid in this instance, your vaunted abilities have let you down. I have every intention of doing what–"

"You're covering your ass, aren't you?" This time, it was Morris who interrupted him.

"Mister Morris, I don't know what you think you're–"

Morris went on as if the priest hadn't spoken. "I've known Libby a long time, and she's never wrong about things like this. So, if I accept as a fact that you're lying, it isn't hard to figure out why. You haven't even reported this to your superiors, have you?"

Father Bowen just stood there, looking at him.

"I'd been wondering, if this set of books is so damn dangerous," Morris said, "why there wasn't a team of investigators from the Vatican crawling all over this place. Now I think I know the reason – you didn't tell them, did you? You're hoping that Libby and I can recover the *Corpus Hermeticum* without causing a lot of fuss that anybody in Rome would notice. Then you can just put it back on the shelf and act like nothing ever happened. Nobody at the Vatican would even know that you fucked up. That's it, isn't it?"

Father Bowen held Morris's withering gaze for perhaps three seconds longer, then dropped his eyes. He took in a breath and let out a long sigh that seemed to come from deep within him.

"There is some truth in what you say," he told them. "I have not reported this theft to my superiors, even though we have very specific protocols that say I must do so immediately. And it is possible that concern for my position here, as well as plain, sinful pride, played a role in my decision."

Father Bowen paced the length of the room, which didn't take him long. "But there is more to it than that," he said. "Informed of the theft, the order would almost certainly close this place down. That would have serious consequences – and not just for me. There are several men in our community who have lived here most of their adult lives. They would find life outside, even in another monastery, difficult at best and impossible at worst. Furthermore, many lay people from all around the area – to meditate, and pray, and find some peace in their lives. If this monastery were not available to them..."

Morris seemed unimpressed. "Yeah, sure. And during the Watergate scandal, Richard Nixon argued that the investigation should stop because it was hurting the presidency and the country, by preventing him from focusing on the job he was elected to do – keeping us all safe from harm."

"I resent that comparison, Mister Morris," Bowen said with a scowl. "I am a man of God, not a... a–"

"Crook?" Morris said mildly.

"Precisely. It may be that I cannot alter your opinion of me, but in future I will thank you to keep it to yourself – unless it affects your willingness to accept this assignment."

"No," Morris said. "The job needs doing – regardless of who I have to do it for."

Eleven

It was snowing lightly as Morris headed their rental toward the motel.

"You were pretty hard on him, Quincey," Libby said.

"Not as hard as I should have been. He's just a fucking bureaucrat, and they're all the same, whether they wear a three-piece suit or an outfit like Bowen's. All they care about is covering their asses."

"But, as you said, it's the assignment that matters, not the employer."

"Keep reminding me of that, will you?"

"Getting a line on this *Corpus Hermeticum* isn't going to be the easiest job we ever took."

"If the jobs were easy, they wouldn't need us to do them," Morris said. "But you're right – this could be pretty complicated. Tell me – did you get a whiff of black magic down there in the book room?"

"No, not a trace."

"I was afraid of that," he said.

"Afraid? The absence of black magic isn't usually a bad thing, Quincey."

"No, but if you'd found some, it might help narrow the list of suspects. There are a few practitioners we both know who might be very interested in that book, if Bowen's right about what it contains."

"And yet, the thief got past the ward above the door – and as I told Father Bowen, it was a pretty good one. Some civilian who just fell off the turnip truck isn't going to be able to do that."

"Yeah, but a non-magician can carry magic with him, to a limited extent. Remember those guys who tried to kill you last year?"

Libby had been the target of professional assassins while in her New York condo. Although the killers were not themselves magic practitioners, they had been given a magical device that, when activated by a word of power, allowed them to get past the complex system of wards that guarded Libby's home.

"I'm not likely to forget," Libby said, with a shiver.

"Maybe that's who we're looking for," Morris said. "Somebody who isn't a practitioner but can work a little magic in specific situations if a professional prepares it for him."

"Which means you've just narrowed the field of suspects to all humans who don't practice magic. That's a pretty large group, I understand."

Without taking his eyes off the road, Morris grinned at her. "Sarcasm does not become you, Ms. Chastain."

"I was trying for irony. But, either way – we'd better have some way of narrowing the field a little more, or we're going to be at this a *long* time."

"I actually had some thoughts on that," he said.

"Please do share."

"Well, clearly, this job wasn't done by just any civilian. In addition to the magical feat of getting past that ward, he – or she – was able to get in there, diddle with the video surveillance system somehow, get past these sets of locks, and get out again, without being seen by anybody. Sounds like professional work to me."

"Professional, as in burglar," she said.

"Yep."

"Professional, in the sense of somebody who's for hire."

"That's what I'm thinking."

"Somebody who's good at breaking and entering, and also skillful enough to overcome magical defenses," Libby said. "That's a pretty unusual skill set."

"Offhand, the only one I know who's good enough is me, and I've got an alibi."

"I've never heard of anybody like that either," she said. "But maybe I know somebody who has."

"You're thinking of the Sisterhood?"

"As one possibility, yes. And it occurs to me that you probably know a few people who might've done business with somebody like that. Assuming he or she exists."

Morris could see the sign for the Best Western up ahead. "So maybe we ought to spend time making some phone calls tonight," he said. "And if that doesn't turn up anything, maybe I should go back to New York with you tomorrow, so we can have a word with a guy who doesn't like to talk on the phone."

"You mean Barry Love," she said.

"That's the fella. But first, I figure we ought to attend to more important matters."

She looked at him. "Such as what?"

"Such as dinner," he said. "That steak house across the street from the motel looked pretty good. Care to give it a try?"

Twelve

ALBUQUERQUE, NEW MEXICO does not have a large Jewish population, but their numbers are sufficient to support a single synagogue, Temple Beth Israel. The synagogue's congregation was just big enough to afford the services of a single Rabbi, and David Feldman had that honor – and all the responsibility that went with it.

This Tuesday evening, Rabbi Feldman was tired. This was not unexpected, since his day had started at five thirty a.m. and here it was approaching ten at night and he was still in his office, working.

He had promised his wife that he would start getting home at a decent hour – at least early enough to help her tuck their two children into bed at nine, but what can you do when people need you? He had taught two classes at the Hebrew school this morning, visited a member of the congregation too old and frail to attend temple, counseled a young couple contemplating marriage, had long phone conversations with three potential donors to the Building Fund, interceded on behalf of a congregant who was having trouble getting an auto loan, and here he was working on Saturday's sermon when what he really wanted was a comfortable chair, a decent meal, and a few hours spent in the comfort of his family. Was that too much to ask?

For a second, he fancied that he could hear the voice of God in his head answering, *Yes, David, some days it really is*.

Feldman's fanciful conversation with the Creator brought a smile to his lean face. He shook his head and returned to work on the sermon. He had just figured out a good way to develop his theme of "serving God often means serving each other" when there was an urgent knock at his office door.

He looked at the clock: ten fifty. Whatever the knock on his door might mean at this hour, it wasn't likely to be anything good. Feldman sighed, put down his pen, and went to find out just how bad the news was going to be.

Thirteen

ENGULFED IN GREEDY flames, the building that had once been Temple Beth Israel burned like a Nazi wet dream. About a dozen nearby homes were evacuated, and the black swirling smoke made the air virtually unbreathable for a radius of three blocks. The flashing red lights of the responding fire trucks and police cars combined with the flames and smoke issuing from the synagogue to produce a hellish vision that Hieronymus Bosch might have envied.

Lieutenant Ramon Gutierrez, commander of AFD Fire Response Unit number six, clambered into the cab of one of his team's fire trucks and pulled the door shut behind him. Only then did he remove his helmet, then the oxygen mask. Gutierrez spent a few seconds savoring the experience of breathing air that had not been processed through a filter, then opened the snap pocket in his yellow slicker to produce his two-way radio. Within moments, he was talking to his boss.

"We've got it under control now, sir." He spoke loudly, so that Captain Benson on the other end could hear him – there was plenty of competing noise coming from outside. "It won't spread beyond the building – but the synagogue itself is a total loss. It was fully involved by the time we got here."

With his free hand, Gutierrez pulled a bandana from his pocket and used it to wipe away some of the sweat and soot that covered much of his face. "I'm thinking that some kind of accelerant was used, Captain, but we won't know for sure until the fire marshal's guys make their report, and my guess is they won't even be cleared to get in there until sometime tomorrow."

He listened for a few seconds, then said, "Yes, sir. The rabbi in charge of the place is named David Feldman, F-E-L-D-M-A-N. I asked HQ to locate him, but nobody seems to know where he is. They called his wife, and she says he hasn't come home yet. He was expected several hours ago, I gather. The wife says she called him a bunch of times, starting around ten o'clock, but he never answered. She's pretty hysterical at this point, I understand. Hard to blame her."

Gutierrez listened some more. "Yes, sir, we'll know for sure in the morning, once the structure is safe to enter – or what's left of it is. But if the Rabbi's in there, my guess is we won't find much left. It's a damn hot fire, sir, with no chemicals or other hyper-combustibles to explain it. That's why I'm thinking it was arson."

He listened briefly and said, "Yes, sir, I'll keep you informed, and I'll bring the day watch commander up to speed when he comes on duty. Gutierrez out."

Lieutenant Ramon Gutierrez slipped the radio back into his coat pocket, replaced his oxygen mask and helmet, and went back to fight the conflagration engulfing what had once been Temple Beth Israel.

Fourteen

"COULD BE A coincidence, I suppose," Colleen O'Donnell said.

"Because last time it was Catholics, and this time it's Jews." Dale Fenton nudged a piece of charred wood with his foot. "That what you mean?"

"The differences in faiths, yes," O'Donnell said. "Then there's the geographical factor. Duluth, and then Albuquerque? If they wanted to burn down a synagogue, there's plenty of them closer to Minnesota than this one. Seems like a lot of trouble to go through."

"Assuming that's all they had in mind, I'd have to say you're right," Fenton said.

"Which means, either it's not the same guys..."

"Or it is, and there's a common factor that we don't know about yet."

"I hate it when that happens," O'Donnell said.

"Yeah, me too, and besides – uh-oh."

"Uh-oh what?"

"Look yonder," Fenton said, pointing with his chin.

O'Donnell turned and saw that an ambulance had pulled up as close to the wreckage as it could get. Its red light was not flashing – apparently nobody was in any hurry.

The FBI agents watched as two EMTs brought out a stretcher from the back of the ambulance. A man in a fire marshal's uniform went over and spoke to them briefly, then they followed him, toting the stretcher, into the ruins of Temple Beth Israel.

A few minutes later they emerged. There was something on the stretcher now, covered by a sheet and the EMTs moved gingerly through the ruins in the direction of the ambulance, where Fenton and O'Donnell were waiting for them. The men and their burden were about fifty feet away when Fenton sighed and said to O'Donnell, "Odds or evens?"

"Evens." O'Donnell counted out loud "One, two..." On "three" each of them stuck a hand out. O'Donnell was displaying two fingers. Fenton showed two, also. "Damn," he said softly. "Well, guess I get the nightmares this time."

When the EMTs reached the ambulance, Fenton was waiting for them. He displayed his ID, nodded toward the stretcher and said, "Mind if I take a look?"

The EMTs looked at each other, and then one of them shrugged and pulled back the sheet to reveal what lay underneath it. Fenton had his look, swallowed hard and said "Thank you." He returned to his partner as the stretcher was being loaded into the back of the ambulance.

"Burned beyond recognition," Fenton said. "If anything was done to the poor guy before the fire got him, the M.E. is going to have a hell of a time proving it."

O'Donnell nodded slowly. "That leaves the incendiary devices, assuming there were any."

"I'd say the chances are pretty good," Fenton said. "I talked to one of the firemen who was here last night, and he said the fire burned hot and fast. Too fast for accidental ignition, in his opinion."

"So if there were incendiaries, and they've got the same signature of the ones used in Duluth, we could be onto something."

"Yeah," Fenton said. "But what?"

"That's a question for–" The phone in O'Donnell's pocket made a beeping sound. She pulled it out and looked at the screen. "Text from Sue. She wants us to call in." O'Donnell used her thumb to scroll down the rest of the text message, her lips flattening into a thin, straight line as she read. Then she shut the phone down and looked at her partner. "Looks like we've got a problem."

Fifteen

Private investigator Barry Love could usually be found, when he could be found at all, on Ninth Avenue just off Forty-Eighth Street. His office was on the fifth floor of a brick office building that had probably been built when America still liked Ike. Love specialized in cases involving what he called "the weird shit," so it was inevitable that he would cross paths with Morris and Chastain sooner or later. A couple of years ago, they had sought Love's help on a case, and in the process had helped him out with a small demon infestation.

Love's work had made him twitchy and paranoid, perhaps with reason. Consequently he rarely would talk on the telephone, and never made use of email or text messaging. He'd once said that such technologies made it too easy for "them" to find out what he was up to. So Morris and Chastain had to come to him.

They were trying to identify someone with a skill set that would have allowed him to steal the well-guarded *Corpus Hermeticum* and get out again undetected. Their phone calls from Montana had produced nothing useful – but if anybody would know such a person, it would be Barry Love.

Making an appointment was, of course, out of the question, which explains how Morris and Chastain found themselves outside the heavy wooden door that read "Barry Love Investigations."

The door had been plain, unadorned wood the last time they'd visited, but since then a number of designs had been drawn on the door in various colors. Some others were actually carved into the wood.

Morris stared at them. A few of the designs looked familiar to him, but he couldn't remember from where. Pointing with his chin, he said to Libby, "Think Barry's got him some vandalism problems?"

Libby looked at the door for a few seconds. "Not unless there's a gang of witches in the neighborhood, and we tend not to go in for tagging much." She shook her head. "Those are wards. Pretty sophisticated, too."

"If he's home, we can ask about them," Morris said, and knocked on the door. He waited, got no response, and knocked again, with the same result.

"Well, shit," he said.

Libby Chastain shrugged. "We knew it was a toss-up as to whether he'd be in or not."

"Yeah, it always is, with Barry."

"Let's go find dinner someplace close by," Libby said. "Then we'll come back and see if he's here. If he's still not around, you can crash on my couch tonight, and we'll try again tomorrow."

"If there's a better idea than that, I can't think of it," Morris said. "I noticed an Italian place down the street that might–"

The clanky old elevator that had brought them to the fifth floor was moving again, the sound of its operation was loud in the quiet building. The arrow above the elevator shaft showed that the car had been summoned to the ground floor.

"Could be Barry's about to save us some trouble," Morris said.

Libby was watching the floor indicator. "Seems likely," she said. "I don't imagine this building sees a lot of traffic after five – or even before five, for that matter."

They both jumped a little when the door from the stairway burst open to reveal Barry Love, who began to walk rapidly along the hall toward them.

"Haven't seen you guys in a while," he said by way of greeting, while still thirty feet away.

"We figured you were on the elevator," Morris said.

"I sent it up here," Love said. "Misdirection."

Morris and Libby exchanged looks, without being obvious about it. *Same old paranoid Barry*.

Barry Love was just under six feet tall, and wiry. There was quite a bit of gray in the brown hair, even though Love had not yet reached forty. His face had the careworn look of a man who doesn't sleep much, and who has bad dreams when he does. His arms were not visible under the sport coat, but Morris knew that they were covered with tattoos designed to be sigils against demons.

Love unlocked the two deadbolts that kept his office secure, flicked on a light, and motioned them inside. Then he closed the door behind them and relocked it. "I don't mean it the way it sounds," he said, "but I wish you hadn't come. Not now, anyway."

The two windows in Love's office had their shades drawn. He went to the nearest one and used a finger to move the curtain aside a couple of inches, allowing him to look out and down. What he saw didn't seem to reassure him.

"Are you having trouble with demons again, Barry?" The last time they'd been here, Love's office was being attacked by a trio of demonic creatures. Morris and Chastain had helped him handle the situation.

"Yeah but not like last time. Sit, if you want."

While they eased into the visitors' chairs, Love sat down at his desk, which was covered as usual by books, files, random sheets of paper, and fast food wrappers.

"What's your problem now, Barry?" Morris asked.

Love shrugged his bony shoulders. "Apologies to Robert Johnson, but... I've got a hellhound on my trail."

Libby sat up a little straighter. "Do you, now?"

Love nodded wearily. I've been catching glimpses of it for the last week or so. I think it's waiting to catch me alone, at night, in an unprotected place."

"Is that what the stuff on the door is for?" Morris asked. "Wards against the hellhound?"

"They've worked pretty well," Love said. "So far, at least. It can't get through the door – I've heard it trying. But I can't live my whole life in this office. I've got work to do."

"Who set it after you?" Morris asked.

"Don't know for sure. I can think of at least three people in the city with the skill – and the motivation. I tend to piss off a lot of left-hand path types in my job, know what I mean?"

They both nodded. Love was probably the city's foremost occult detective – as such, he made a lot of enemies.

"But that's my problem, and I'll deal with it," Love said. "Meantime, what can I do for you guys? I assume this isn't a social call."

"No, afraid not," Morris said. "We wanted to–"

"Wait!" Libby held up a hand. "I'm trying to think."

She sat with eyes closed and brow furrowed for half a minute or so. Then she looked at Barry Love and said, "I may be able to help with your hellhound problem."

She picked up her big purse and began to sort through its contents. Without looking up she said to Morris, "I'm not exactly tooled up for complicated working. Got anything on you, Quincey?"

Morris carried a switchblade, which made him a criminal in New York State. But this weapon had a silver plated blade that had been blessed by the Bishop of El Paso. It had saved his life, and Libby's, more than once. He pulled the knife from his pocket and clicked it open. "Only this. Sorry."

"Um," Libby said. She looked around at Love's office, whose shelves were covered with books, religious icons, and all manner of occult bric-a-brac. "Maybe you've got what I need here, Barry."

Love spread his hands. "Try me."

Libby closed her eyes in concentration.

"Sea salt," she said.

"Absolutely," he told her. "Regular table salt, too."

"Honey."

"Hmmm. Yeah, I think I've got some packets left from that breakfast takeout last week."

"Sulphur."

"Got a box of wooden matches. Will that do?"

"Yes, I think so. And some kind of flammable liquid."

After a moment's thought, Love opened a drawer and placed a half-empty bottle of cheap Scotch on top of his desk. "Guess I'll have to make the sacrifice," he said.

"Excellent," Libby said. "Now, if you'll assemble those other items for me, please, I believe I can cast a spell that will have a very satisfactory outcome."

Twenty minutes later, she had just finished using the first two fingers of her right hand to apply the concoction she'd created around the entire perimeter of the office door. As she did so, Libby had recited an incantation in ancient Greek. Morris had studied enough Greek in high school to realize that he had absolutely no idea what she was saying – but this was Libby Chastain, white witch *extraordinaire*, so it didn't really matter.

"Oh, I'll need a reliable ignition source," she said. "A wooden match takes too long to flame up, and there's always the chance it'll blow out. I know Quincey doesn't smoke, so Barry, can you...?"

Barry Love produced a plastic disposable lighter and handed it to her. "I smoke like a furnace," he said. "Lung cancer is the least of my worries, and tobacco helps me relax."

Libby tested the lighter, then adjusted the flame to make it higher. "Very good," she said. "Now comes the tricky part."

Barry Love gave her half a grin. "Figured there was gonna be a tricky part, sooner or later."

"Is the hellhound out there now, Barry?" Libby asked.

"I don't know for sure, but I figure it'll show up pretty quick if it thinks I'm vulnerable."

"You mean, if the wards on the door weren't protecting you."

"Exactly."

"All right, then. What I'm about to suggest involves an element of risk," Libby said. "But if it works, it should rid you of this creature, once and for all. Of course, there's no guarantee that whoever called up this hellhound won't send for another one someday."

"*Someday* sounds like a pretty good deal to me right about now," Barry Love said. "Let's do it."

"And, if something should go wrong," Libby said, "Quincey is our backup."

Morris held up the knife, its silvered blade glinting in the light. "If it jumps you, try to keep it away from your throat long enough for me to stick it with this."

Love looked at the blade, then at Morris. "Will that thing destroy a hellhound?"

"Can't say for sure," Morris said, with an embarrassed shrug. "I never tried it on one before."

"Then maybe we'd both better hope Libby's spell does the trick."

"Amen to that, podner."

Sixteen

It was just past midnight when the Dodge Caravan rolled past the sign that read, "Welcome to Decatur – Alabama's Friendliest City!"

"Wonder how friendly they'd be if they knew what we had planned for them?" Jeremy said from the passenger seat. After taking part in two sacrifices, he had lost any uncertainties that had plagued him in the beginning. He was a true member of the team now.

From the rear seat Mark began to breathe loudly and rapidly and a moment later groaned, "Oh, my God!"

Jeremy glanced at the driver. "Does it piss you off, hearing him say that name?"

Ware gave a small shrug. Without taking his eyes off the road he said, "In other contexts, it very well might – which you would all do well to keep in mind. But it seems to be almost universally uttered at the point of orgasm. Atheists and agnostics say it, too. Hell, even *I* say it."

There was a spitting sound from the back, then Elektra appeared, wiping her mouth and chin with Kleenex. "How come we always have to travel at night, Theron?" She was careful not to say that in anything like a whining tone. Polite questions were permitted, but whining was punished.

"We can hardly have you back there performing fellatio on one of the boys in broad daylight, can we, Elektra? Some righteous citizen might see, and tell the police – and we are carrying things in the back that I would rather not explain to the authorities."

"The thermite bombs, you mean?" Jeremy said.

"Those especially, yes. Besides, I enjoy the night – it seems to give me strength, whereas I often find daylight saps my energy. It's psychological, I'm sure – since I haven't joined the ranks of the bloodsucking undead."

"Vampires are real?" Elektra asked.

"Most certainly."

"I always thought it was just one of those things they use to scare kids at the movies."

"Elektra, my dear – how can you believe in the power of black magic, which you have seen with your own eyes, and doubt the existence of other dark things?"

"Well, when you put it that way..."

"Are we gonna be stopping soon?" That was Mark who had apparently recovered from Elektra's oral ministrations.

"As soon as I find a motel that looks small enough for the clerk not to process my credit card if I show him a great deal of cash."

"What good is a credit card, if you never use it?" Jeremy asked.

"I do use it, frequently – but not on this trip," Ware said. "I don't want any record of our passage through town to appear on some database. It's possible that the FBI might have seen a pattern in our sacrifices, and one of their tactics is to see if the same credit card has been used in the vicinity of more than one so-called crime scene. I don't want to make things easy for them."

"Oh, yeah," Jeremy said. "They do stuff like that on TV all the time."

"I don't plan to be as careless as those morons in the cop shows. Although I suppose it's possible that someone, official or not, might get on our trail, eventually."

"You don't sound too worried about it," Elektra said.

"I'm not. I have various contingency plans to deal with interference, if and when it comes our way."

"How about this place?" Jeremy pointed to a large neon sign coming up on their right. "It says 'Vacancy.'"

"Looks like it might be suitable," Ware said. He turned into the motel's parking lot. "Let's see if anybody is still awake at the registration desk – yes, I believe I see a light. Good."

Ware parked their vehicle and slid out from behind the wheel. In five minutes he was back and handing Jeremy a key with a big plastic tab attached. "This is your room. I'm next door."

He started the engine and drove slowly down the line of motel rooms, peering at room numbers as he went. "When the three of you are doing whatever it is you do in bed tonight, try to keep the noise down. I want to get some sleep."

"Yeah, we got a busy day tomorrow," Mark said, with a snigger.

"Exactly," Ware said. "A town like this ought to be just full of Baptist churches. I'm sure we'll have no problem finding exactly the right one."

Seventeen

Barry Love received a nod from Libby Chastain, took and expelled a deep breath, and opened wide the door of his office. As instructed, he took a few steps back, but remained squarely framed in the doorway. Morris stood a few feet behind Love and to the side, the blessed switchblade open and ready in his hand. Libby Chastain knelt to the right of the door, out of sight from the corridor. She held Barry Love's lighter in one hand and was softly reciting the ancient Aramaic words of a spell that she hoped she remembered correctly.

From Love's office, the hall ran for perhaps two hundred feet before turning a corner to the left. Love stood looking down that corridor like a Christian in the arena waiting for the lions to appear, fear and resolution alternating in his expression.

It was very quiet there on the fifth floor of the old office building, especially after Libby stopped chanting. The battery-powered clock on Love's wall clicked off the seconds audibly. Once the door was opened, it did so twenty-eight times before Love said, tightly, "There it is."

Looking over Love's shoulder, Morris saw the hellhound as it slowly rounded the corner at the end of the hall. A year or so earlier, Morris had encountered a black dog that was being used to guard a sorcerer's estate, but this was a different creature entirely.

Mate a bull mastiff with a black panther and raise the resulting progeny on growth hormones, and you might have something resembling the creature that stood in the corridor, staring at Barry Love's open door and growling. Its eyes glowed crimson over a gaping mouth equipped with the kind of fangs a lion might envy. Even from a couple of hundred feet away, Morris could smell the odor of brimstone that clung to the creature.

The hellhound, muzzle dripping, stood for a few seconds, as if mentally thanking Satan for leaving its prey unguarded at last.

Then it charged.

"It's coming!" Morris snapped.

Libby Chastain began softly chanting again as she raised the lighter and sparked it into a two-inch high flame.

Barry Love stood in place, as he'd been instructed to do, but he apparently couldn't stop his hands from clenching and unclenching, over and over.

Morris's stomach felt as tight as one of the detective's fists. He *really* hoped Libby's spell would work as planned, because the closer that monster got – and it was closing rapidly now – the less confidence Morris had that his knife's six-inch blade would do any good, silver plate and Bishop's blessing notwithstanding.

The hellhound was fifty-feet away and closing fast. Libby touched the lighter's flame to the doorframe where she had smeared her hastily-assembled magical concoction. The alcohol in the Scotch worked like a charm, as it were, and within a couple of seconds the doorway was surrounded by flame – but there was only enough fuel to keep the fire going for a few seconds, so Libby'd had to wait until the last possible moment.

The hellhound was, understandably, not deterred by fire, but as it stormed through the open door she finished her chant by shouting "D'Neenad!" which is ancient Aramaic for "Depart!"

An instant after crossing the threshold, the great beast disappeared, leaving nothing behind but the stink of sulphur and its final howl of frustration and rage.

Barry Love slowly took his arms down from where he had crossed them to protect his throat if the beast attacked. "What... what did you do to it?" he asked.

"All systems... tend toward... equilibrium," Libby said. She sounded a little out of breath. "Even supernatural ones. The beast was not native to this plane of existence – it *belonged* in Hell. I just gave enough of a magical shove to send it back to its natural environment."

Morris folded his knife and put it away. "As nice a job of impromptu spellcasting as I've ever seen you pull off. Well played, Libby. Well played."

"I don't know how I can thank you," Barry Love said. He offered the Scotch bottle to his guests, had no takers, and so took a long pull from the bottle before putting it away. "That thing was making my life a living hell, if you'll excuse the expression. It feels like I can take a deep breath for the first time in a week."

"Think of it as professional courtesy," Libby said with a smile. "After all, we're both in the same business, broadly speaking."

"Well, I sure appreciate it," Love said. "And if there's ever anything I can do to repay the favor..."

"As a matter of fact," Quincey Morris said, "there

probably is. Do you reckon maybe we could all sit down again?"

Once they were seated, Morris said, "We're trying to get a line on a guy – and I use *guy* just for the sake of discussion. The one we want may well be female."

"Assuming such a person even exists," Libby said.

Barry Love leaned forward, the old leather chair creaking beneath him. "Now you've got me intrigued. Just who – or *what* – are you looking for?"

"I suppose the shorthand description is," Libby said, "we want an occult burglar."

Love's head tilted a little to the side. "You mean, something like a vampire who steals stuff? I know quite a few of *them*."

"No, we're talking about somebody who steals *from* occult types – I mean, folks who can use magic to protect their property."

"Hmmm," Love said. "Are we talking about white or black magic here?"

Libby and Morris looked at each other before Libby said, "Either one, probably. I don't think it matters."

Love leaned back again. "Maybe you guys better tell me *exactly* what you have in mind."

After a brief hesitation, Libby said, "All right, we will. I'm sure we can rely on your discretion."

The detective gave her a crooked grin. "You could, even if you *hadn't* just saved my life. Go on."

Libby and Morris took turns explaining to Love about the burglary at St. Ignatius Monastery.

When they were done with the story, Morris said, "Ordinarily, I'd be inclined to say that any practitioner could be a suspect. But Libby says there was no scent of black magic anywhere around the book repository."

Barry Love looked at Libby. "What about traces of white magic?"

"Couldn't tell," she said with a headshake. "I'm too close to it. It would be like trying to smell myself."

"But some kind of magic was certainly used," Morris said. "Whoever it was, he got past that ward over the door – which would have stopped any run-of-the-mill sneak thief."

Love sat there for a while, staring off into the middle distance. Then he said, "I don't know anybody like that personally, but I know a guy who just might."

He went to one of his battered filing cabinets, pulled open a drawer that squeaked in protest, and came up with a small, ring-bound book. When he brought it back to the desk it was clear that he was holding a battered address book, its bent plastic cover decorated with coffee rings. Several scraps of paper had apparently been tucked between the book's pages.

Love thumbed through the book for a few moments, finally coming up with an old three-by-five index card that seemed to have the information he wanted. He peered at the card as if the writing on it was in a language he didn't know very well. Then he said, "Either of you guys got a phone I can use for a local call?"

Libby was closest, and handed him her Samsung Galaxy S. "You have to press the–"

"I know what to do, thanks. I'd call him on my own phone, but you never can tell who – or what – might be listening in, you know?"

Love glanced at the card again and began to tap numbers on the phone's keypad. Then he put the phone to his ear. He sat there placidly for a few seconds, but then apparently heard something that did not please him. "Pick up, Raoul," he said, frowning. "It's me."

A few moments later, his voice was louder. "I said *pick the fuck up*, Raoul!"

The elusive Raoul must have answered, because Love said, "You know better than to blow me off, man. Or you damn well ought to."

There was a pause, and Love said, "All right, forget it. Listen, remember the guy you were telling me about a couple months back – the one who supposedly got Karen van der Hoeven's spell book back from the witch who stole it from her? You said the story was, he got past a shitload of magical protection, then cracked her safe besides?" Pause. "Yeah, that's the one. Tell me, do you remember the dude's name, or did you even know it in the first place?" Pause. Love grabbed a pen and began writing on the index card. "How do you spell that? Uh-huh. Where's he live, do you know?" Pause. "Okay, well thanks for the name, Raoul. I owe you a favor. No – *not* a big one."

Barry Love terminated the call and handed the phone back to Libby. "Here you are. You know, I'd appreciate it if you wouldn't hang on to the number I just called."

Libby looked down at the phone, pressed the touchpad a couple of times, and said, "Already deleted."

"Thank you," Love said. "Now, about the guy you're interested in – who *is* a guy, by the way – I've got good news and bad news."

"The good news being that you got his name," Libby said, "and the bad news is that you don't have an address for him."

"Aww, you were listening," he said with a grin. "Yeah, that's pretty much it. Well, at least I got the name. Anybody wanna do a drumroll?"

"We'd rather just have the fella's name," Morris said.

"Okay," Barry Love said. "His name is Robert Sutorius."

Eighteen

During the cab ride to Libby's condo, Morris and Chastain kept their conversation discreet. If they spoke openly, it was unlikely that the driver would understand anything he heard, or know whom to tell about it even if he did. But a lot of small, unnecessary risks eventually add up to the big one that kills you.

"So, I guess we'll have to find this fella," Morris said. "Any ideas?"

"I'll ask my Sisters, for a start," she said.

"Didn't you try that route once already?"

"Yes, but all I had then was a job description. Now we have a name."

"Maybe we should start the way everybody else does these days, and Google him," Morris said.

Libby gave vent to a rather unladylike snort. "You think somebody like him has a website? Or maybe a blog?"

"Probably not, although he's got to drum up business *somehow*."

"I'm guessing in his case, it's mostly by word of mouth."

"Maybe, but have you noticed – these days, most things that start out as word of mouth end up on the internet sooner or later."

"You have a point," Libby said. "Anyway, it can't hurt–"

Music began to issue from Libby's purse. People of a certain age might have recognized the light, bouncy ringtone as the theme from the nineteen sixties TV series, *Bewitched*. Libby liked her little jokes, sometimes.

She plucked the phone out of her purse and checked the Caller ID. She looked at Morris. "It's Colleen."

Morris didn't need a last name. As far as he knew, the only "Colleen" he and Libby had in common was Colleen O'Donnell – white witch, member of the Sisterhood, and Special Agent for the FBI.

Libby brought the phone to her ear. "Hey, Colleen." She listened, then said, "I'm not at home at the moment, but I will be, as soon as the cab, Quincey and I are in, gets us there... Yes, he's here, too."

Libby listened some more, then checked her watch. "Ten o'clock should be good, if you want to come over then... Okay, see you soon. Bye."

She put the phone away and turned to Morris. "She and Fenton are in New York, and they want to talk to us. I hope you don't mind that I invited them over."

"It's your home, after all," he said. "But no, I don't mind. Maybe they'll even have some ideas about how we can track down the guy we're looking for."

"Can't hurt to ask."

They were silent for a couple of blocks, and then Morris said, "It'll be just like Old Home Week, apart from Hannah, who may or may not still be among the living."

"Have you heard from her?"

"Not since that weird Christmas card I told you about. If she was coming over too, we could have a reunion of the whole crew from Iowa."

"Idaho. It was Idaho," Libby said.

"Right. I'm always getting those two confused."

Nineteen

LIBBY CHASTAIN'S CONDO was painted in earth tones, and her taste in furniture ran toward Scandinavian modern. FBI Special Agents O'Donnell and Fenton sat on a couch from Denmark, sipping Jamaican Blue Mountain coffee and waiting for Libby to sit down so that the four of them could have a conversation.

Eventually, Libby quit bustling about and took a seat in a chair across the glass coffee table from the two agents. Morris sat in a matching chair ten feet to Libby's left.

Libby looked at Fenton and O'Donnell and said, "I assume this is official business?"

"Well, it is, and it isn't," Fenton said. Libby thought his lean brown face had more lines in it than she remembered from two years ago, when the four of them had done battle against the very forces of Hell.

"We're not here on official business, but we're here *about* official business." O'Donnell frowned. "That was about as clear as mud, wasn't it?"

Morris nodded at her. "Pretty much."

"Maybe we ought to start at the beginning," Fenton said. "Somebody is burning churches – well, houses of worship – and black magic is involved, but in a way that we don't understand."

Morris leaned forward, frown lines creasing his forehead. "There was a Catholic church someplace in Minnesota that burned down a few weeks ago," he said. "One of yours?"

Fenton nodded. "That was the first, far as we can tell."

"Where else?" Libby asked.

"A synagogue in Albuquerque, New Mexico, three nights ago," O'Donnell said. "That's it – so far."

Libby added milk to her coffee and stirred, slowly. "Those are pretty disparate examples," she said. "Minnesota and New Mexico, Catholics and Jews. Are you sure they're connected?"

"Connections exist on two levels," O'Donnell said. "One is the means of ignition used."

"The perp – or perps – are using multiple thermite devices, to make sure the buildings burn quickly and completely," Fenton said. "That's what was used in Duluth, for sure, and the preliminary fire marshal's report in Albuquerque says it was probably the same thing. This isn't a bunch of kids running around with a can of gas and a box of matches."

"Thermite's pretty unusual for amateurs, all right," Morris said. "What's the other connection?"

"In each case," O'Donnell said, "a clergyman affiliated with the place of worship was found dead inside."

Morris whistled softly, then asked, "Cause of death the same?"

"That's where it gets tricky," O'Donnell told him. "By a fluke of luck, the body of the priest in Duluth was not consumed by the flames completely. So, in his case there's no doubt homicide was the C.O.D."

"Not just homicide," Fenton said, "but ritual murder. The poor bastard was disemboweled, castrated, a bunch of other stuff. And occult symbols were carved into the body."

"What kind of occult symbols?" Libby asked.

"We had drawings made," Fenton said. "I've got a copy in my briefcase that I'll leave with you. But it's just the usual Satanic stuff."

"And what about the one in New Mexico?" Libby asked. "The Rabbi."

"The fire got him," Fenton said. "The body's just a charred lump of meat. They're going to try for an autopsy, but..." Fenton suddenly sounded tired.

"And there's other evidence of black magic in the Minnesota case," O'Donnell said. She briefly explained how she had come to sniff out the vestiges of black magic in the undamaged stolen car.

"Until you got to the last part, I thought it might just be a gang of psychopaths," Libby said. "But black magic in the car – that changes everything."

"Yeah, it sure as shit does," O'Donnell said.

Morris refilled his coffee cup from the pot Libby had put on the table and said, "Which raises the question – what do you want from us?"

"We want you to take over the investigation," Fenton said. "Unofficially, of course."

"Why?" Libby asked. "Quincey and I probably couldn't do a better job on this case than you could, and you've got the FBI behind you, to boot."

"That's kind of the problem," Fenton said. "We *don't* have the Bureau behind us any more – not this time."

"What Dale means is, we've been taken off the case," O'Donnell told them. "Somebody in Washington decided that these church burnings constitute hate crimes, and are thus to be properly handled by the Civil Rights Division."

"And you can hardly report to the bureaucrats that you've uncovered evidence of the use of black magic, can you?" Libby said.

"Not hardly," O'Donnell said grimly.

"But we've explained what we found to Sue," Fenton said. Susan Whitlavich was the head of the Behavioral Science Division. Surprisingly open-minded for an FBI administrator, she had accepted the existence of the supernatural and often sent Fenton and O'Donnell out to investigate it. "She says that there's enough money in the contingency fund to hire you two as consultants, reporting directly to her – well, through Colleen and me."

"Sue had to assign us to another case," O'Donnell said. "Fortunately, it put us close enough to New York so we could talk to you guys in person."

"What other case?" Morris asked. "If you'll pardon me for being nosy."

"Aw, we've been over in New Jersey all day," Fenton said. "Half a dozen homeless people have been killed and partially eaten over the last few months, and some genius thinks it might be the Jersey Devil. It's bullshit."

Morris gave him half a smile. "You don't figure it really *is* the Jersey Devil?"

"It'll probably turn out to be some other homeless guy who thinks he's Hannibal Lecter," O'Donnell said. "But, in the meantime, we got these civil rights agents investigating the church bombings as just another series of hate crimes. It's more than that – it *has* to be – but they'll never see it, because they're not trained to see it."

"So, what do you say, guys?" Fenton asked. "The Bureau can meet your usual fee, unless it's gone way up since the last time." He looked at Morris. "I'd have thought you, in particular, Quincey, would be eager for some work, after six months in the slam. Congrats, by the way, on getting the charges dropped."

"I am eager," Morris told him. "Or rather, I was – until Libby and I found a gig out west recently."

Fenton's eyebrows went up. "You're working already?"

"Afraid we are," Libby said. "I think we'd be happy to take on this job for you–" she looked at Morris, who nodded "–but our first obligation is to the people who've hired us."

"Well, shit," Fenton said.

"For what it's worth," Morris said, "the job we've taken on has got some pretty serious implications. Or, rather, they could become serious, if we don't do what we've been hired to."

"This job's got some serious implications, too," O'Donnell said. "These churches aren't being chosen at random. As Dale pointed out, if you've just burned a Catholic church in Minnesota and decide your next target is a synagogue, there are plenty of them closer than New Mexico."

"I suppose you've checked for connections between the two congregations, the clergymen, and so forth," Morris said.

"'Course we did," Fenton said. "We haven't found anything that looks like a common factor." He shook his head slowly. "There's a black magic ritual being carried out here. We don't know what it is yet, but somebody's going to an awful lot of trouble. You've got to figure he's expecting a pretty big payoff."

"And since black magic is involved," O'Donnell said, "it's a reasonable assumption that the payoff is going to be something pretty horrible."

"You're probably right," Libby said. "But we have to finish the job we've got before we take on another one. I'm really sorry."

"Why don't you talk to Barry Love, in New York?" Morris said. "He's pretty good at this kind of stuff."

Fenton shook his head again. "Too erratic. The guy's just not dependable."

"We gave him a job last year," O'Donnell said, "and he let us down pretty badly. Maybe it wasn't his fault – we still don't have all the facts, but..."

"But he's poison with Behavioral Science, whether he deserves to be or not," Fenton said. "There's no way that Sue would hire him again."

After a few seconds' silence, Morris said, "Have you talked to John Wesley Hester? I know he's British, but he's worked in the States quite a few times. And he's good, too."

O'Donnell was looking at Morris strangely. "Oh – you didn't know."

Morris stared at her. "Didn't know what?"

"Hester's dead, Quincey," she said. "I'm sorry to bring you bad news. I assumed you'd have heard, but I guess you were pretty busy last year, with one thing or another."

Morris was staring into his coffee cup, as if the answer to all of life's questions might be found there. Without looking up, he asked, "What happened?"

"Way we heard it," Fenton said, "last year, Hester was involved in that hinky business at Scion House, outside London. There were rumors that Jeffrey Scion, or maybe his brother, had let loose a trapped demon that had been discovered while doing some excavations for a new wine cellar."

"I remember seeing something online about that," Libby said, "although Hester's name didn't come up in the story. Wasn't there some kind of fire?"

O'Donnell nodded. "A huge one, by all accounts. Destroyed Scion House and killed a bunch of people, the Scion brothers included." She shrugged. "Maybe there was demonic activity, after all."

"Hester's body was found among the dead," Fenton said. "Positively identified. Sorry, man. Didn't know you two were close."

"We weren't blood brothers, or anything," Morris said. "But, still... he was a good man."

"And so are you, Quincey," O'Donnell said. "And Libby is a damn fine witch. That's why we need you."

"And you can have us, too," Morris said. "As soon as this job is done."

Fenton and O'Donnell looked at each other, and seemed to mutually acknowledge that further entreaty was useless. Fenton looked at Morris, blew a breath out through pursed lips and asked, "Any idea how long this thing you're doing is likely to take?"

"Impossible to say," Libby told him. "Although..." She looked at Morris, who thought for a moment then nodded. Libby went on, "It might be possible for you to help us speed the day."

"By doin' what?" Fenton asked.

"Have either of you ever heard," Morris said, "of a guy named Robert Sutorius?"

Fenton frowned then looked at his partner. Colleen gave him a small headshake. "Doesn't ring a bell," he said. "But hum a few bars, and we'll see if we can fake it."

"Sutorius is supposed to be, for lack of a better term, an occult burglar," Libby told them. "And I don't mean by that a magician who steals, although he may have magical training. I'm talking about someone who steals *from* magicians."

"And probably from other people in the supernatural world, too," Morris said.

Fenton grinned at Morris. "The only fella I know who's really good at that stuff is you."

"Guilty as charged," Morris said. "But not this time."

"What do you want to know about this guy?" Fenton asked.

"Principally, where to find him," Morris said.

O'Donnell had seemed to be staring off into the middle distance. She said, slowly, "You know, I think I read something in a report last year..."

She looked at Libby. "Does this building have Wi-Fi?" Upon receiving a nod, O'Donnell picked up the briefcase she'd brought with her, opened it, and brought out a Dell laptop. Then she produced a power cord. "Is there someplace where I can plug this in? My battery's running pretty low."

"No problem." Libby took the end of the cord and found an open outlet. Straightening up, she said, "I'm afraid I can't guarantee you a secure connection."

"Doesn't matter," O'Donnell said. "My computer's encrypted, and so's the one at the other end."

O'Donnell worked the keyboard for a while. "Seems to me there was mention of a guy like that in something I got from Monica Reyes, in the New Orleans Field Office."

"Other people in the Bureau know what you guys... really do?" Morris asked.

"A few of them," O'Donnell said. "Monica's cool – she's seen her share of the weird shit." She kept working.

"Looks like we may be due for another trip to New

Orleans," Libby said, and made a face.

"What's the matter?" Fenton said. "You don't like the Big Easy?"

"It's a nice town," Libby said. "But Quincey and I had a couple of bad experiences there a couple of years ago."

"I didn't say I thought the guy was in New Orleans," O'Donnell said without looking up from the keyboard. "I only said that's where – aha!"

"You found him?" Morris asked.

"Found the report I was thinking of, anyway. Give me a second."

She scrolled down the document, her eyes moving back and forth rapidly. Then she said, "Bingo!"

"What have you got?" Libby said.

"Listen to this: *The missing talisman was later traced to Robert Sutorius, a professional thief who specializes in matters involving the occult. Sutorius was found to be residing in Brooklyn, New York. Agents from the New York Field Office tried to interview Sutorius, but found him uncooperative. In any case, Sutorius is believed to work for hire, so it is unlikely that the talisman remains in his possession.*"

Morris and Libby looked at each other. "*Brooklyn?*" Libby said.

"That was true when the report was written," O'Donnell said, "which was a little more than two years ago. No guarantee he's still there."

"Well, let's find out," Libby said, and stood up.

"Going to go work a little magic?" Fenton asked.

"I may have to," Libby said, "but I thought I'd try the easy way first – with the phone book. Excuse me."

When Libby had left the room, Fenton asked Morris, "You think a guy like that is actually gonna be listed?"

"Hell, people who want a magic wand or a spell book stolen have got to find him somehow," Morris said. "Anyway, we'll know in a minute."

It was more like two minutes before Libby Chastain returned, carrying the phone directory for Brooklyn.

"The Goddess be thanked, he's actually in here," she said. "Court Street, in Cobble Hill. We could even give him a call, but I think it might be better if we arrived unannounced." She looked at Morris, who was grinning, and asked, "Tomorrow?"

"Yeah," Quincey Morris said. "Tomorrow."

Twenty

Go to YouTube. Type "church burnings" in the search box, then click on the little magnifying glass icon.

On the first page (of the more than thirteen thousand results), scroll down. About halfway along the page, you'll find a clip labeled "Decatur, AL Church Burning." Click on it, and this is what you'll see:

A high-tech graphic reading "News Alert" appears on the screen, then disappears in a flurry of animated motion to reveal a pretty blonde with long, straight hair seated at a news desk. In the same shot, to the left of her face, is a graphic reading "Developing Story."

The blonde points her good looks at the camera and says, with no trace whatsoever of a Southern accent, "Good Evening. At this hour, a fire is raging at the Sacred Word Baptist Church in Decatur. Randall Carlson, from News Channel 43's Decatur Newsroom is at the scene. Randall?"

Cut to a well-dressed black man in his late twenties, who is looking squarely at the camera, a grim expression on his round face. He holds a microphone with a clearly visible "WAFE News 43" logo on it and he is standing just in front of a line of yellow police tape.

Behind him is a scene of chaos – flames, flashing lights of several colors, and men, some in yellow slickers and others in uniforms, running about and shouting. As the young man begins to speak, a graphic reading "Randall Carlson – Decatur Bureau" briefly appears at the bottom of the screen.

"Sharon, I'm here at the scene of the immense fire which seems destined to destroy the Sacred Word Baptist Church, which has been a popular center of worship in Decatur for over forty years." Unlike the anchor, his accent suggests that he has lived in the south at some point in his past.

Pre-recorded video now fills the screen with images of the fire, which is about to engulf the church steeple, and the cross atop it, in hungry flames. The reporter's voice can be heard off-screen.

"Witnesses say the fire broke out somewhere between eleven thirty and midnight, and that the fire spread so quickly, much of the building was aflame when the first fire trucks arrived, although they, of course, responded very quickly.

The video of the burning steeple fades out and is replaced by another prerecorded segment, which shows the reporter interviewing a local resident.

"Can I have your name, please?" He pushes the microphone toward the face of a woman in her sixties, stopping about an inch from her ample chin. She wears tightly-permed white hair, a print dress, and horn-rimmed glasses.

"Mary Rose Carteret," she says, clearly nervous to be on television.

"And you were a member of the congregation here at Sacred Word Baptist?"

"Oh, yes. For over thirty years. I never missed a

Sunday service, except for that time when I had the flu."

With the tact and sensitivity of journalists everywhere, the reporter asks her, "And how did you feel when you saw the church in flames?"

The woman seems at a loss for words at first, but then manages to get out, "Terrible, just terrible. How could God allow something like this to happen?"

Cut to the reporter, live again in front of the yellow tape. He says, "I'm here with Captain Travis McNeal, head of the Decatur Department of Public Safety." The camera operator adjusts for a two-shot that includes a tall heavy man with a red face and a blue uniform. Unlike the men and women under his command, it is clear from his clean face and clothing that Captain McNeal has been nowhere near the fire tonight. When he answers questions, he looks at the camera, not the reporter. Captain McNeal has done this before.

"Captain," the reporter says, "What kind of progress is your department making in controlling this immense blaze?"

"We have evacuated all houses in this block, and the block behind it, for the safety of the residents." The Captain's accent shows that he, at least, is a local boy, born and bred. "The roof of one house briefly caught fire, but an alert hose team extinguished it quickly. Unfortunately, there isn't much we can do for the church building itself."

"So you would say that the church itself is a total loss," the reporter suggests.

"Unfortunately, yes. Fire response units arrived very quickly, once the fire was called in. But, as you said, the building was fully engulfed by the time they arrived."

"Do you suspect arson as a cause of this blaze, Captain?"

McNeal thinks about this for a moment before responding, his voice careful and deliberate. "The fact that the blaze spread so quickly is suspicious to my way of thinking, but that's just an opinion. The State Fire Bureau's people will investigate, once it is safe for them to enter the scene. They will make a determination as to cause."

"One last question, Captain. Have you spoken to–" the reporter consults his note "–Reverend Puddy, the pastor of Sacred Word?"

"I haven't seen him so far. I assume he is among the... onlookers." The chief says the last word the way Sitting Bull probably said, "Custer." "I expect I'll be speaking with him before the night is over."

"Thank you, Captain McNeal." The camera moves to center the reporter in the shot again. "There you have it, Gail. A beautiful church, beloved by many in Decatur's Baptist community, has been destroyed by this blaze, its exact cause unknown. From Decatur, this is Randall Carlson reporting."

The blonde at the anchor desk reappears on the screen. "A terrible fire, down there in Decatur. News Channel 43 will of course, continue to bring you details as they emerge. I'm Gail Chandler, coming to you from Huntsville. Now back to 'Pee Wee's Big Adventure.'"

Twenty-One

ROBERT SUTORIUS HAD a turn of the century brownstone on a corner lot in the Cobble Hill section of Brooklyn.

Quincey Morris paid off the cabbie and joined Libby Chastain on the sidewalk that fronted the place. Looking at the house he said, "Nice, but not what I expected. The occult burglar business must not be doing so well these days."

"This is Brooklyn, Quincey, not Beverly Hills. Maybe he doesn't want to live an ostentatious lifestyle that will draw attention to himself."

"Maybe not. But if I were a potential client, this place wouldn't exactly inspire confidence."

"It might, if you knew something about the real estate values around here. That," she said, gesturing toward the modest looking structure, "is what two million dollars will buy you in this part of town."

Morris's eyebrows went up. "Two million? Seriously?"

"That's what he paid for it, four years ago – well, just under two. I looked it up."

"Well, then, let's go in and ask the man about how he's been earning his money recently," Morris said.

"Think he'll tell us?" She produced a small smile.

"I was kind of hoping, that you'd make him an offer he can't refuse."

A black wrought-iron gate was part of the five-foot high fence that surrounded the property. It opened without resistance, although Morris thought he heard a "click" that didn't come from the lock mechanism.

"You notice that?" he asked Libby.

"He knows we're here. But then I wouldn't have expected otherwise."

Six broad concrete steps led up to a tiny porch and a heavy looking carved wooden door. It had no lock or keyhole anywhere on it that Morris could see. A doorbell button was set into the wall nearby, so Morris pushed it a couple of times. He couldn't hear if anything was ringing or buzzing inside the house.

"He's either got a real quiet doorbell or damn good insulation," he said to Libby.

"I'd bet on the insulation, and not just the kind that keeps the heat inside during winter." She touched the wall next to the door. "There's something… strange about this place."

The door was opened by a man whose height was closer to Libby's 5'8" than to Morris's 6'2". He had quick green eyes and a cap of tight ginger curls that fought a losing battle against a receding hairline. The tweed sport coat he wore had the kind of fabric and fit that cost a great deal of money.

"Robert Sutorius?" Morris asked.

"Yes I am," the man said. He studied them for a few moments. "And I imagine you two are Quincey Morris and Libby Chastain." He stepped back, opening the door further. "Do come in."

Morris and Libby found themselves in a large living room painted in pastels of orange and brown. The furniture, which looked new, was in Regency style which Morris had never much cared for. The floor was covered with a series of overlapping Persian rugs that looked like they might be genuine.

"Very nice carpets," Libby said. "Do any of them fly?"

Sutorius gave her a broad smile and a wink. "Not so far, but then maybe I just haven't asked the right person to fly one yet." He gestured toward an open door. "This way, please. We can talk in my office."

The door to Sutorius's office was a perfect circle, perhaps eight feet in diameter, made of a rustic looking wood construction. It was a door that Bilbo Baggins would have loved at first sight.

The office itself seemed vast – although, given Sutorius's limited ability to use magic, that might have been an illusion. But Morris noted that each of the three walls was crammed with full-size bookcases, many of which actually contained books. The other shelves held some simple magical tools and a number of odd-looking electronic devices whose function Morris could only guess at.

Morris thought this was the sort of study that Barry Love might have, if the detective only possessed money, good taste, and a more relaxed temperament.

Part of the room was given over to a conversation area – presumably where Robert Sutorius interviewed prospective clients. Four comfortable-looking chairs surrounded a large coffee table with magical symbols beautifully carved into the surface and legs. Sutorius led them over, saying, "It might be most comfortable if we talk here. Do sit down."

After everyone was seated, Sutorius said, "I normally only see people by appointment, but for such distinguished guests I don't mind making an exception."

Libby looked at him closely. "I never object to being called 'distinguished,' on those rare occasions when it occurs," she said. "But I'm fairly sure we haven't met before."

"Oh, no, we haven't," Sutorius said. "I'm sure I'd remember."

"Then I can't help but wonder how you knew who we were – have you seen photos of us?"

"Well, Mister Morris here had his picture in the papers, and everywhere else we now call the media, quite a few times last Summer."

"That's true," Morris said. "Unfortunately."

"Congratulations, by the way on getting the charges dropped – however you managed it," Sutorius said. "I've wondered more than once what all that brouhaha at the Republican Convention was about. I don't suppose you'd care to enlighten me."

"No," Morris said, "I don't think I would."

"To be expected, I suppose. Anyway, once I saw that Quincey Morris was standing on my doorstep in the company of a white magic practitioner, it didn't take Sherlock Holmes to conclude that she must be Libby Chastain."

"I can't fault your logic," Libby said, "but how did you know that I'm a white witch?"

"I have been trained, by experts, to recognize the presence of magic – both white and black. It has come in handy in my work."

"I can imagine," Libby said.

"Now," Sutorius said, spreading his hands briefly, "How can I help you? If the job involves something that is beyond your own considerable capabilities, it must be interesting, indeed."

"Actually," Morris said, "we're here to talk about one of your *past* assignments."

Sutorius's pleasant expression disappeared faster than a mouse at a cat show. "Have you now?" The warmth in his voice had dropped several degrees.

"We have reason to believe," Libby said, "that you, um, liberated something called the *Corpus Hermeticum* from its place of safekeeping."

"A very secure room at St. Ignatius Monastery, that would be," Morris said.

"Did I really?" Sutorius's voice showed only polite interest, and not very much of that.

Libby said, "Since you're not a practitioner yourself – in the strictest sense – we assumed you'd have no real use for the book yourself."

"That's why we figure you were hired to acquire it for someone else," Morris said. "We'd very much like to know who your client was, and where we might find him – or her."

All Morris got from Sutorius was a chilly smile.

"Okay, look," Morris said, leaning forward in his chair, "we understand that you're a businessman." He waved one hand back and forth, as if dispersing cigarette smoke. "Nobody's expecting you to give the information away. The book is the property of the Vatican, and they want it back badly – all five volumes of it."

Sutorius looked as if he were watching a TV weather report for a place he'd never visited, and never intended to. But he was giving his attention to Morris, which means he did not notice Libby Chastain's hand slip into her big leather purse, which she had kept on her lap during the conversation.

"There's a lot the guys in Rome are prepared to offer," Morris said, while Libby's fingers identified the vial she had placed at the top of her purse's contents, and quietly thumbed off the lid.

Morris's voice grew louder, and he began to count off on his fingers. "One, money – more than you'd ever get for one of these burglary jobs of yours, or even ten of them. Two, information. The Vatican has sources you can use–"

Libby Chastain's right hand came out of her purse, a small quantity of blue powder in her fist. She opened the hand, quickly extended it toward Sutorius, and blew on it, hard.

While most of the powder was still in the air, Libby said three words of power in ancient Chaldean. Then she sat back to observe the effect. She got one almost immediately, but it wasn't what she was expecting.

Sutorius *laughed* at her. He did not chuckle, or chortle, or snicker. He roared, as if Libby had just told him the funniest joke he'd heard in years.

Morris turned to look at Libby. She sat quietly, her face expressionless. But her gray eyes were blinking rapidly, a clear indication that she was profoundly shocked. Nothing like that had ever happened to her before. Nothing like that was ever *supposed* to happen.

Sutorius finally regained his composure, and began to brush the blue powder off his jacket and the coffee table's polished surface. "I'll have to vacuum later, I suppose," he said, as if to himself.

Then he sat back and looked at Libby. "Is *that* what this was all about?" He did not, quite, sneer. "Morris distracts me with silly patter, while you hit me with – what? Some kind of truth spell?"

Libby nodded mutely.

"And then I was supposed to blithely tell you everything you wanted to know, betraying the trust of a valued client *and* ruining my reputation completely, after which you two would simply go on your merry way, laughing about how easy it had been?"

Morris sighed. "I wouldn't have put it in those precise words, but – yeah, that's about the size of it."

Sutorius's expression became indulgent. Perhaps he felt sorry for them. "Not a terrible scheme, in its conception. And the execution, while a little clumsy, was good enough to get the job done. But I'm afraid you lacked one vital piece of information."

He waved his arm in an expressive gesture that took in the whole room, if not beyond. "Within this house, magic does not work – neither white, nor black, nor gray. No matter how experienced or skilled the practitioner, no matter what materials or spells are used. It. Will. Not. Work."

Libby's eyes were wide. "How on earth did you achieve *that*? Or is it another one of your secrets?"

Sutorius gave a miniscule shrug. "I won't go into specifics, of course, but the short version is – I hired one of the most powerful magicians in the country, and he spent two months constructing a magic-dampening spell, and the better part of a week putting it into operation and adding safeguards."

"Magic to prevent magic," Libby said wonderingly. "I wouldn't have thought it possible."

"Nor I, at first," Sutorius said, and chuckled. "But clearly it *is* possible. The practitioner has promised to refund his considerable fee if anyone ever succeeds in performing magic within these walls. That was over a year ago, and I haven't asked for my money back, so far."

"What if, instead of magic, we'd come with a couple of Colt .45s?" Morris said. "Your anti-magic spell wouldn't stop those, would it?"

"No, you're right – it wouldn't," Sutorius said. "But if you'd been armed, I'd never have opened the door to you. Did you happen to notice the fence surrounding the property? In addition to keeping out the neighborhood dogs, it's also a scanner. State of the art. By the time you reached my porch, I knew you weren't carrying anything more lethal than that knife in your right pants pocket. And if you'd been unwise enough to attempt such a gambit–" Sutorius reached under his coat and produced a slim automatic pistol "–I would have checkmated that, as well. Fatally, I'm afraid."

He stood up, the gun still in his hand but pointed at the floor. "Well, this has been very entertaining," he said, "but I'd like you both to leave now. And, needless to say, don't come back."

Morris and Libby stood, careful to avoid anything that might be interpreted as a sudden move. As they walked ahead of Sutorius to the front door, Morris said over his shoulder, "What if someday we had a real job for you? Not telling us your secrets, but the kind of thing you do best, and paying top dollar. Just for the sake of discussion, would you be interested in talking to us then?"

Sutorius thought for a moment. "If you *were* serious, and not planning to waste my time – again – I might consider it. But that scenario seems rather unlikely, don't you think?"

He opened the door and used the gun to usher them through it and out onto the small porch.

"You folks have a very good day, now." He gave them an unpleasant smile. "You've certainly made mine."

They walked back past the elaborately disguised scanner and through the gate. At the sidewalk, Morris gestured toward the nearest corner. "We can probably get a cab over there."

He was right. Five minutes later, he and Libby were being driven back to her condo.

"Well," Libby said, "*that* was certainly a humbling experience."

"For you and me both, kiddo," Morris said. "You and me both."

"And, embarrassing though it will be, I think I have to tell the Sisterhood about this, just so they know that such things are possible. It flies in the face of everything we're taught."

"Maybe once you tell them, they'll figure out a way to get past it. One of these days."

"Not soon enough to do us any good on this job," she said.

"No, I reckon not."

"What was that you said in there, at the end–" She glanced toward the driver, who seemed only interested in the traffic and the Middle Eastern music playing softly on his radio "–about hiring him for a legitimate job sometime? You weren't serious, were you?"

"Not about that, no," Morris told her.

"What, then?"

"Just an idea I had. I'll tell you about it at home." He made a small head gesture in the driver's direction, and Libby nodded.

"Anyway," Morris said, "it'll only work if I can get in touch with a couple of friends of ours, and that may prove difficult."

"Why – what's the problem?"

"You never know – somebody might have told them both to go to Hell."

Twenty-Two

"WELL, IF THEY won't fucking do it, then they won't fucking do it," Sue Whitlavich said. Colleen O'Donnell's boss was one of the smartest women she had ever met, and the one with the filthiest mouth – both considerable achievements, considering the number and variety of people Colleen knew.

While an agent at the FBI's Chicago field office two decades ago, Whitlavich had gone to graduate school part time. The fact that she had excelled at both was a tribute to her intelligence, ambition, and the fact that in those days she had very little that could be construed as a life. Her Ph.D. from the University of Chicago was in Abnormal Psychology, but it was her dissertation, "Rethinking the Monster: A Jungian Perspective on Serial Murder," that had brought her to the attention of the Behavioral Science Section.

She'd transferred into Behavioral Science and spent the next nine years chasing (and mostly catching) serial killers before being promoted to Assistant Section Chief. Three years later, when her boss, Jack Crawford, had suffered his fatal heart attack, the top job went to Sue by virtual acclamation. But beginning a couple of years ago, the reports of her two best field agents had begun showing Sue Whitlavich that the world was an even darker place than she'd realized. Her vulgar paraphrase of *Hamlet* had been, "There's more weird shit going on in the world than even *I* ever thought was fucking possible."

TV and the movies notwithstanding, the FBI didn't have anything like an "X-Files Division." But when a Bureau investigation stumbled across something that appears contrary to the generally accepted view of reality, it usually got dumped in the lap of Behavioral Science, and Sue Whitlavich almost always gave it to O'Donnell and Fenton. The work of those two agents was rarely discussed even within the Behavioral Science Section, and never discussed outside, if Whitlavich could help it.

"It's not like Morris and Chastain *won't* take the job," Colleen O'Donnell explained. "They just *can't* – not right now. They've taken on another assignment, and they feel obligated to finish that one before getting involved in something else."

"I guess you'd have to say their sense of ethics is kind of admirable," Fenton said, grudgingly.

"It would be a lot more admirable if it wasn't being such a fucking pain in the ass," Whitlavitch said.

She slapped both palms lightly on her desk. "All right, we'll hope Morris and Chastain find that book they're looking for sooner rather than later, and in the meantime I'll keep quietly nagging the AD to let us take the church burning file back from Civil Rights."

"There was another one, night before last," Fenton said. "Baptist church, down in Alabama."

"Looks like the same signature on the ignition devices," O'Donnell said, "and the body of the pastor was found in the rubble, next day."

"Yeah, I saw the news," Whitlavich said. "Whether

that's gonna make it easier or harder for me to change the Assistant Director's mind remains to be seen. He can be a stubborn motherfucker, sometimes."

She opened a drawer, pulled a file from it, and tossed it on top of her desk. "Meanwhile, looks like a couple of women in Vegas have turned up dead, drained of all their blood. The local law's trying to keep a lid on it, as you can imagine – don't want to scare the old ladies away from the slot machines."

O'Donnell picked up the file and began to page through it. "Vampire, you're thinking? Or garden-variety psychopath who wants to be Bela Lugosi when he grows up?"

"That's what you're going out there to find out," Whitlavich told her. "I've smoothed things over for you with Bernie Jenks at the Las Vegas Field Office – nobody should give you a hard time. If they do, let me know, and I'll cut somebody a shiny new asshole. Now take the file, and scoot."

They scooted.

The main office for the Behavioral Science Section contained desks for two secretaries and an intern, an ancient Mister Coffee that nobody ever drank from more than once, an unreliable photocopier, and the agents' mailboxes. The Bureau still had not embraced the digital age completely, so some official correspondence still came out on paper.

Fenton had pulled several sheets of paper from his box and was glancing through it is as O'Donnell said, "I hope we can get Morris and Chastain working on the church burnings pretty damn soon. All those guys in Civil Rights ever do is write legal briefs – they've got no clue what's really going on." She did not speak loudly – but, then, it was not a very large office.

"Maybe that guy whose name we gave them in New York will move things along," Fenton said. He tossed everything that had been in his mailbox into a nearby trash basket. "Let's get some lunch," he said. "I hear the canteen's got fried chicken, with watermelon for dessert. Yum."

She looked at him. "It's winter, Sachmo – remember? Watermelon's out of season."

He grinned at her. "Hell, I'm just jivin'."

"Yeah," O'Donnell said as they turned toward the door. "I be down with that."

Ten feet from where they'd been standing, intern Walt Duran unobtrusively made a note and stuck it in his shirt pocket. Then he went back to the arrest reports he'd been given to sort.

Walt planned to apply for the FBI Academy next year, when he finished college. He was a Criminal Justice major at George Mason, an avid gamer, and one more thing worth noting – Walt Duran was an occasional stringer for the Branch Report.

Twenty-Three

The Branch Report is an online gossip column with delusions of self-importance. This undue self-regard has been fed by the fact that the publication very occasionally stumbles upon a story with actual news value, and breaks it hours before what publisher Frank Branch likes to call the "lamestream media."

Mostly, the Branch Report consists of nothing more than links to items appearing in various "news" sites on the web – most of which are of the right-leaning variety. But occasionally, Frank Branch puts in an item that hasn't appeared anywhere else in cyberspace – yet.

Walt Duran had barely spent the $100 fee that Branch had sent him through PayPal when this item appeared in the Branch Report:

Sources inside the Justice Department have revealed that "occult investigator" Quincey Morris, who was mysteriously freed from prison after facing a slew of federal charges stemming from the last RNC convention, has been hired by the FBI to investigate the series of fire bombings of churches and synagogues that have occurred over the last six weeks. Morris's "partner," one Elizabeth Chastain, calls herself a "white witch."

Maybe she can use some magic to keep Morris out of jail this time.

A great many people followed the Branch Report, some of whom would never have admitted as much publicly. One of its regular readers, who found the item concerning Morris and Chastain to be of great interest, was a man known as Theron Ware.

Twenty-Four

"I MUST SAY Mal, you're looking well," Libby Chastain said. "I was about to add 'for someone who's been through hell, but then...' " She let her voice trail off, with a smile.

"You'd be right, too," Mal Peters told her. "When you've actually *been* in Hell, six months in a federal detention facility is a piece of cake, by comparison. Besides–" He laid his hand briefly on the thigh of the beautiful, thirtyish woman next to him "–I had regular conjugal visits, even if the correction officers never knew about them."

Malachi Peters had once done "wet work" for the CIA, spending a number of years all over Europe killing people whom somebody in Washington regarded as a threat to national security. That had lasted until 1983, when Peters, on a mission in Budapest, had been betrayed – and shot dead.

As James Bond would have been shocked to learn (if he really existed), killing for patriotic motives is still considered murder in the eyes of the Almighty. Peters' soul had been judged and consigned to Hell, where it had remained until last year.

That had been the year that one faction in Hell – demons being as prone to quarrels and cliques as humans, if not more so – had decided to have Republican Presidential candidate Howard Stark secretly possessed by one of their number and continue his campaign. With demonic assistance, the thinking went, Stark could become President, then use the powers of the office to carry out Hell's longtime agenda – the destruction of the human race.

But another group of demons, some of them quite important in the hierarchy, had decided that if the plot succeeded, it would bring on the long-predicted battle between Heaven and Hell called Armageddon. The faction opposed this, because they had no faith (unlike some of their kind) that Hell would triumph in this ultimate confrontation. And if there was a worse punishment than the miseries of Hell, that group of demons was not eager to find out what it might be.

So their leader, Astaroth, had sought out a hitman. Peters had been given flesh again and sent back to Earth, with instructions to assassinate Senator Stark before he could win the White House. What would happen to Peters afterward had never been made clear.

Things had not worked out quite as either side had planned. But the election had come and gone, and Howard Stark, although still alive, was neither possessed by a demon nor President of the United States. Morris and Chastain had played a vital role in bringing about that outcome, as the new President, Robert Leffingwell, was well aware.

And now Peters, who had been released from prison the same time as Quincey Morris, sat on Libby Chastain's couch next to the most beautiful woman that either he or Morris had ever seen. She could, at will, become the image of *any* man's ideal woman, but her usual human form was tall, blonde, slim, and quietly elegant.

"I wondered whether you'd use your powers to visit Mal secretly. I guess I'd have been surprise if you didn't."

The woman sitting next to Peters called herself Ashley when on this plane of existence. But in Hell she had been a demon of the fourth rank called Ashur Badaktu, given human form by Astaroth and sent to assist Peters in his task of murder. She was also instructed to keep him happy, orders she had carried out by fucking him stupid at every opportunity.

"Almost every night," Peters said. "Sometimes the toughest part of prison for me was getting out of bed in the morning."

"Libby and I were glad to learn that the two of you are still among us," Morris said. "Us humans, I mean."

"We were afraid that you were both going to be called back to Hell," Libby said, "once the matter of Senator Stark was resolved satisfactorily."

"You're not the only one," Peters said. "It's pretty stressful knowing that every time you go to sleep, you could wake up to find yourself in Hell – forever."

"I keep telling him not to worry," Ashley said. "I'm pretty sure I've got it figured out. When I was allowed to leave Hell, there was a big division among the hierarchy over whether to put Stark, and the demon possessing him, in the White House. The whole Armageddon thing, you know?"

Morris and Chastain nodded. They already knew this part of the story.

"Well, the way I figure it," Ashley went on, "things got worse after I left, especially once the Stark plan went to shit. My best guess," she said, "is that there's a civil war raging in Hell right now. Astaroth and the others are too busy with that mess to worry about a couple of pawns like Peters and me who've been left over on this side of the board. With luck, they'll forget about us for centuries, maybe longer."

"I was very glad that you were still here in January, Ashley, to pay that call on President Leffingwell with me," Libby said. "Presenting him with one living example of supernatural power might have been enough, but both of us together…"

"Yes," Ashley said with a smile, "that did seem to seal the deal, didn't it?" She gave Libby a very direct look – the kind that would have brought almost any man literally to his knees, panting with lust. "Is that the only reason you were glad to see me back then, Libby? *Are you glad to see me now?*"

Libby was using magic to guard herself, but even so she felt her body responding to Ashley's succubus-like power. Being a demon, she was unconstrained by such human baggage as sexual morality. Ashley knew that Libby was bisexual and, some time back, had invited her to frolic. Libby had declined, provisionally.

"Cut it out, Ashley," Libby said, not quite severely. "This isn't the time, or the place."

In that same throaty alto, Ashley said, "That implies that there *will* be a proper time and place, doesn't it?" A wicked smile curved her full, red lips. Libby was aware that Morris, seated in a chair to her right, was shifting his weight uncomfortably.

Peters put a gentle hand on Ashley's shoulder. "Come on, honey. Not now, okay?"

Peter's relationship with Ashley, both before prison and since, was the kind that a man might have with a pet leopard. He did not give orders, but polite requests were usually complied with. Both leopards and demons, after all, are capable of affection for humans – up to a point.

Ashley rolled her eyes. "Oh, all right," she said, in mock annoyance. "There goes my plan for the orgy I was going to suggest later. Okay, so what *shall* we talk about?"

"Well, the thing is," Morris said, "we'd like to ask a favor."

Ashley raised an elegant eyebrow. "Indeed? Well, since we've already established what kind of favor you're *not* asking for, I'd be very interested to hear what I *can* do for you."

"It's something along the lines of the way you helped us at the Republican Convention last summer," Libby said.

"Oh, you mean '*Now you see me, now you don't?*'"

Libby nodded. "Yeah, pretty much.

"Well, that's always fun. I *love* the way they scream when I do the big reveal. When and where is this party of yours going to take place?"

"The *when* is tomorrow, if you're free," Libby said. "Assuming the man we want to... impress is home, that is, and will open the door to us. There's a tricky aspect to that, which I'll explain to you later."

"And the *where* is Brooklyn," Morris said. "Just across town."

"Brooklyn, huh?" Ashley pretended reluctance, "Well, I guess that'll be okay." She glanced at Peters. "To paraphrase something lover boy here once said to me – I've been in Hell, so I guess I can handle Brooklyn."

She looked at Libby then. The gaze was not lustful, as it had been before, but speculative, instead. "So, if I do this job in Brooklyn tomorrow, that means you two will owe me a favor. *Each* of you. Are we agreed on that?"

Libby took a deep breath and said, "Yes, Ashley. I, personally, will owe you a favor. And if you want to cash that in by having me jump in the sack with you afterwards – then, okay, that's what I'll do."

Ashley held the look, but there was some amusement in it now. "Gracious me," she said. "You must want to impress this guy in Brooklyn pretty badly."

"I *said* I'd fuck you, Ashley." Libby sounded tired. "Let's not talk it to death."

After a moment, Ashley said, "Nah – that makes it too easy. I may ask you for a favor someday, Libby, but it won't involve you getting naked and letting me wrap my thighs around your head."

Libby's voice was steady as she said, "Fair enough, then."

Ashley stood up to leave, and Peters followed suit. At the door, Ashley turned and gently rested her hand on Libby's cheek. "But the day will come, my dear – and so will you, over and over." Ashley took her hand away and grinned. "Afterwards, you'll be asking yourself why you ever waited so long to say 'yes.'"

After their guests had gone, Morris returned to the living room. Realizing he was alone, he turned and looked back. Libby Chastain was resting her back against the front door, her face a trifle flushed. Morris thought he heard her say, very softly, "Maybe I will, Ashley. Maybe I just will."

Twenty-Five

THERON WARE AND his crew had rented a house in Billings Montana. The contract he'd signed was for a year, but they would be gone inside two weeks. Cheap motel rooms were all very well most of the time, but now Ware had some magic to work, and he needed space and privacy.

Billings was over one hundred miles from Sheridan Wyoming, which was to be the site of their next sacrifice. But all the towns anywhere near Sheridan, on both sides of the border, were tiny – certainly small enough so that a group like Ware's might be noticed, and remembered later. The Billings metro area, on the other hand, contained over half a million people. It was easy to disappear in a place that size.

Ware had set up his equipment in the basement, and the scrying spell he'd been preparing was almost ready to go. He heard footsteps thumping down the stairs, and a moment later Elektra came into view, wearing the flannel shirt and ancient jeans that were her standard attire.

He had found Elektra Hamilton in a girls reform school two years ago, when she was seventeen. She'd been in the children's prison (for that is what a reform school is) for a year already, sent there for starting the fire that burned down her house, killing her parents and baby sister. When she turned eighteen, the court had decreed, she was to be transferred to a women's correctional facility, there to spend the next twenty to thirty years contemplating the enormity of her crimes.

Elektra had protested volubly at her trial that the fire was a terrible accident, and that she'd had no intention of hurting anybody. But once Ware had helped her escape and she had joined his little band, her explanation was considerably more terse: "The fuckers deserved it." Even her nine-year–old sister, Ware had asked, who'd suffered from spina bifida? "Especially her, the whiny little cunt."

Reaching the bottom of the basement stairs, Elektra asked, "Whatcha doing?

"Preparing to do a little scrying," he told her.

"Yeah? Who you lookin' for?"

"That man and woman I told you about. The ones we read about online last week."

"Oh, yeah. That investigator guy and his buddy, the witch. Think he's fucking her?"

"I wouldn't presume to know, or care, my dear. But if the scrying should reveal any intimate details of their lives, I'll be sure to share them with you."

"Yeah, okay. Um, the guys and me were gonna take the van and check out some of the strip clubs downtown. That okay?"

"Fine – just don't do anything stupid. If you get yourselves arrested – *for any reason* – you will cease to be of use to me. Understand?

She brought up her hands in a placating gesture. "Yeah, sure, don't worry. We even got a designated driver – Jeremy. I promised to buy him a lap dance from some cunt in one of the clubs, if he just drinks coke all evening."

"Very wise, I'm sure."

"Yeah, well, you want anything before I go – a blowjob, or maybe a quick fuck? I could bend over that workbench thing there, if you want."

"No thank you, my dear. You run along with the others and have a good time. But be back by sunrise, or I shall become quite *vexed* with you, understand?"

Elektra unconsciously took a step back. She knew what "vexed" could mean with this man. He sometimes scared her worse than her father ever had. "Sure, we'll be back long before then – I promise."

"All right then, I'll see you in the morning."

"Okay – see ya."

He was glad the children, as he sometimes thought of them, were leaving for a while. Scrying took a great deal of concentration, and that required silence.

Ware filled the dark blue basin he'd bought at Target with water, within an inch of the brim. Then he dropped in small amounts of rosemary, belladonna, and earth from a baby's grave that he had harvested himself the day before, being forced to use a blowtorch on the frozen ground.

He closed his eyes, gradually cleared his mind of extraneous thoughts, then addressed the one he thought of as his spirit guide.

O Lord Asmodeus, give me sight.

O Lord Asmodeus, give me vision.

Give me the power to see beyond these walls.

Give me power to see your enemies, who are also my enemies.

Let me see the dwelling places of your enemies, the man Quincey Harker Morris and the woman, Elizabeth

Catherine Chastain. Let me know their whereabouts and their movements.

Then let me destroy them.

Ware slowly passed his left hand, palm down, over the water five times, then waited. Slowly, images began to appear on the surface of the water. Images of a city at night. Images that moved. He stared at what was being revealed to him, glancing occasionally at the photos he'd downloaded from the internet of a man with black hair and a heavy beard, and a woman with brown hair and eyes the color of arctic seas.

In a few minutes, he saw what he was looking for.

He had found them. And they were together.

Twenty-Six

IT WAS JUST after seven in the evening when Robert Sutorius opened his front door, already alerted by his security system about what he would find there. Morris and Chastain had brought another woman with them this time – a woman, he had to admit, of amazing beauty.

But he still managed a dour tone as he said, "Back again so soon? I must say I'm surprised."

"You said you'd be willing to discuss a straight business proposition – an assignment involving the work you specialize in. Well, we've got one – or more precisely, this lady has."

Morris turned to the beautiful blonde. "Ashley Stone, let me present Robert Sutorius, the man I told you about."

Sutorius said, "How do you do?" then, with difficulty tore his eyes away from the woman and looked at Morris. "If this lady has business with me, then what are you two doing here?"

"Two reasons," Morris said. "One is, you said you don't usually see people without an appointment, and there's a time factor involved with this assignment. Ashley needed to see you today."

"The other reason," Libby Chastain said, "is that the three of us are partners in this new enterprise. The partnership was our compensation for introducing our new friend here to the best – maybe the only – occult burglar in the world."

Sutorius pursed his lips and tried to keep his eyes focused on Chastain. Although she wasn't bad looking, next to the other woman, she was a hag. But if Sutorius tried to address the other woman, he found his concentration slipping in favor of the kind of erotic fantasies he hadn't entertained since his teens. So he said to Chastain, "Well, the scanner shows that none of you are carrying a weapon – I see you've even left your little knife behind today, Morris. And since magic is worthless in here... you may as well come in."

He stepped back and allowed them entrance. "You can leave your coats on that sofa there," he said. "We'll talk in my office."

Through the hobbit door they all went, and soon were seated around the elaborately carved coffee table.

Sutorius looked at Ashley and said, "So, Ms., er, Stone – how can I put my talents and experience to work for you?"

"Before we get to that, Mr. Sutorius, I need to explain something," Ashley said. "The fact is, I've come a very long way to see you."

"Oh? You don't live in New York?" Even though the blonde had not said anything remotely sexual, Sutorius found himself growing an erection of such engorgement that he hoped it would not show through his trousers and embarrass him.

"I do now," Ashley said. "But until recently, I lived far away from here, and I stayed there for a *very* long time. The place has different names, depending on what religious tradition you follow – Hades, Eblis, Gehenna, or just plain Hell – you know, the neighborhood *where the worn dieth not, and the fire is not quenched.* That last bit is from Mark, 9:48, by the way." She gave him a brilliant smile. "See? Shakespeare was right – we *can* quote Scripture to our own purposes."

Sutorius's befuddlement might have been comical, under other circumstances. He blinked five or six times, leaned forward, and said, "Excuse me? What on *earth* are you talking about?"

"I'm not talking about *anything* on Earth, silly man. That's my point. But perhaps it will be simpler just to show you what I *really* look like."

Morris and Chastain had unobtrusively turned their heads away, and now they closed their eyes. Both of them had seen Ashley in her natural, demonic state, and, to a certain extent, were hardened to the sight. But that did not mean they enjoyed it.

And the key feature of what was about to happen is that it *did not involve magic.* Although Ashley could work black magic with the best (or worst) of them, what she was doing now involved no spells, charms, or incantations. She was simply showing what she really was.

Ashley let Sutorius look upon her true form for exactly two seconds, a time period that was carefully calibrated. Too long an exposure – say, five seconds or more – could drive the average human incurably insane. Neither Morris nor Chastain would sanction that – and, besides, Sutorius could not tell them what they wanted to know if his mind were gone.

The similarity of real demons to the Elder Gods of Lovecraft's Cthulhu mythos were not lost on Ashley. She had once told Libby, "I never ran into Lovecraft in Hell.

From what I've read about him, he's certainly there – but it's a huge place, and not terribly well organized. I've always wanted to ask him if he got a glimpse of one of us before he started writing about Azathoth, Cthulhu, and all those guys – not to mention the effect they usually have, in his stories, on the humans who get a look at them."

In the case of Robert Sutorius, a two-second sight of Ashur Badaktu in all her glory (if that's what it was) was enough to send him to the floor on his knees, hands pressed tightly over his eyes, sobbing uncontrollably. Soon thereafter he vomited, although he apparently hadn't eaten a big breakfast, for which Morris and Chastain were thankful.

After a while, the sobbing abated, but Sutorius remained on his knees, eyes still covered tightly, rocking back and forth and whimpering. Morris stood up, went over to the stricken man, and felt under his coat for the pistol that Sutorius had displayed the other day. He found it, slipped the gun into his jacket pocket, then said to Libby, "Give me a hand, would you?"

Libby approached Sutorius from the other side. She and Morris each grabbed an arm and, at Morris's signal, lifted the man back into his chair. Libby sat down again, while Morris, as they'd agreed, prepared to play the heavy. He reminded himself of the stakes that could be riding on the recovery of the *Corpus Hermeticum*. Then he took a deep breath, yanked Sutorius's hands away and slapped him across the face, hard. Then he slapped him again, equally as hard, with the other hand.

"I want your attention," Morris told him. He leaned forward until his face was a few inches from Sutorius's own. "*Do I have your complete attention*?"

"Yes, yes, all right!" Sutorius cried. "What do you *want*?"

"What I want," Morris said, "is for you to understand the situation you find yourself in. That lady over there–" He pointed at Ashley, who was watching the proceedings with great interest "–isn't a lady at all. She's not even human. She's a demon, the real deal. I don't really need to explain to you what that means, do I – a guy who does the kind of work you do?"

"No, of course not," Sutorius croaked. "I've just never seen one before. And I didn't know they could... take human form like that."

"There's probably lots of things you don't know about demons," Morris said. "But here's something you'd better understand, if you haven't already – demons have no conscience, no scruple, no pity. None. And here's something else to keep in mind, too – they enjoy human suffering. Do you understand?"

"Yes, I know, all the books say the same thing. I understand. Why are you *doing* this?"

"Because I want you to understand your options, and you've only got two of 'em, podner. We've got a few very specific questions for you, about a job you did recently. Option one–" Morris held a single finger in front of Sutorius's face. "You answer our questions, truthfully, fully, and accurately. Then we'll leave, and you'll never see any of us again. You can take a nap, call a priest, get drunk, do whatever you want. It'll be over."

Morris held up a second finger. "Option two: we'll tie you securely to that chair, then Libby and I will go for a long walk – leaving you here, alone and helpless, with a demon. We'll be gone about an hour, but it'll seem like a lifetime to you. Then, when we get back, I'll ask my questions again, and you can decide whether you feel like answering. Hell, you'll probably *beg* me to let you answer."

Morris straightened up and turned to Ashley. "You remember what you promised, if we leave him with you?"

"Certainly," Ashley said. "There has to be enough of him left to answer questions. That means I can't take his tongue, or inflict too much brain damage. And I have to leave most of his teeth intact." She might have been at a garden club meeting, discussing the best way to transplant begonias.

Morris turned back to Sutorius. "You understand? That means *everything* else – every other part of your body – is fair game. She can do whatever she wants."

Sutorius tried to speak. "Listen, I–"

"I'm not quite finished," Morris told him. "Let's say you're a *real* tough guy, and even after everything Ashley's gonna do to you, you *still* won't talk. Well, then we'll just have to give up on you. But before we leave, we'll give you another nice, long look at this demon in her true form."

"They sometimes try to close their eyes," Ashley said. "But slicing off the eyelids takes care of that nicely. I'm sure we can find a razorblade, or a nice sharp paring knife, around here someplace."

"Please..." Sutorius had started to cry again. "Please, *don't let her touch me*. I'll tell you anything you want to know – *anything*. Just keep her the hell away from me!"

Twenty-Seven

IT TAKES A long time, even for a skilled practitioner, to conjure lightning. It was especially onerous for a wizard to arrange for lightning to strike somewhere far away, a destination visible only through a scrying spell. But it *can* be done, and Ware knew how to do it.

It was good – for their sakes, as well as his – that Ware's young associates were gone for the evening. If one of them had interrupted him once he was deep in the spell to cast lightning on the interfering Morris and Chastain, Ware would probably have killed him – or her.

Actually, Morris and Chastain hadn't interfered with any of his plans – yet. But if they'd been set on his trail by the FBI, it was only a matter of time before they became a nuisance. After all, he knew their reputation. One black magic practitioner whom he'd recently asked about the pair had said that together they seemed to constitute a "magical monkey wrench." They seemed to have a knack for getting in the middle of one's painstaking plans and somehow disrupting them. Well, they weren't going to interfere with Ware's plan – the stakes were too high, and he had already sacrificed too much.

He kept track of his targets this evening as they traveled by taxi from Chastain's condo in Manhattan to a large, square house in Brooklyn, a place whose exterior and surroundings were well lit by the nearby streetlights. Ware could see everything clearly.

A third person had joined Morris and Chastain on the sidewalk in front of the house – a rather striking blonde woman. She had accompanied the meddlers inside the house, which meant she was about to become what the military likes to call "collateral damage." The armed forces of several nations used that term, or one like it, because phrases like "a bunch of women and children blown to pieces by a bomb that missed its target" tended to upset the civilians back home.

The trio was still inside the house when Ware finally had his lightning prepared. All well and good – he would strike the roof with a bolt, almost certainly setting the whole place on fire. If Morris and Chastain tried to escape the blazing building, he had ready a second blast of lightning. He would burn them to cinders once they were outside.

Meteorologists throughout the New York City metro area were amazed to see a single storm cloud appear from nowhere to show up on their weather radar screens in the middle of a cold, clear night. Not only did such clouds rarely appear in winter, but they were almost always seen as part of a larger system, not a solitary soldier like the one hovering over the city. And such storm systems usually came together over bodies of water and worked their way inland, which meant their progress could be tracked via radar. An intense bundle of moisture didn't just form spontaneously. Except, like magic, one had just done exactly that.

The weather watchers were further amazed when the renegade storm cloud let loose two bolts of lightning right into the middle of Brooklyn.

In his basement workroom far away, Ware took a deep breath, pointed at the scrying pool where the image of the house could be clearly seen, and screamed out a word of power. His efforts were immediately rewarded, as a bolt of lightning struck the Brooklyn house containing his enemies and did – nothing.

Ware stared at the scrying pool. He had *seen* the bolt of electricity, probably containing a billion or more volts of energy, hit the roof of the house – with no result whatsoever. By all rights, the place should be ablaze by now.

Well, whatever anomaly had caused the lightning to misfire, it could not possibly happen twice. Ware focused his concentration like an argon laser. Pointing again at the house's image, he repeated the word of power, screeching it even louder this time.

Once again, his magic was successful. He saw the long, crackling to volt hit the house squarely. *And nothing happened*. It was as if the place was somehow immune to magic – and Ware knew that was impossible. He stared at the image of the undamaged dwelling for a few more seconds. Then, with a scream very different from the one he'd used to activate the lightning, he swept his arm across the table, sending the bowl crashing to the basement floor, where it smashed into a zillion little pieces, splashing water everywhere. What had just happened violated everything Ware knew about magic – and yet it *had* happened.

He stood there for ten minutes, spewing foul obscenities without once repeating himself. Then he stopped, went to the nearby sink, and splashed cold water on his face. He grabbed a towel, dried off, and went upstairs. He needed a drink, probably several. And he also needed to decide how best to deal with the extremely lucky Quincey Morris and Libby Chastain.

Nobody's luck lasts forever, he thought, *and theirs is about to run out.*

Jeremy Bliss was up relatively early the next morning, since he hadn't had a hangover to sleep off. He came into the living room to find Ware staring into the fire he had built in the small fireplace. Jeremy came in quietly, wanting to gauge Ware's mood before saying anything – the black magician, to whom he'd given his allegiance, was sometimes grouchy first thing.

But this was apparently not such a morning. Catching movement from the corner of his eye, Ware looked up, saw who it was, and went back to staring into the fire.

"Good Morning, Jeremy," he said absently. "Did you all have a nice debauch last night?"

"Yeah, I guess." True to her word, Elektra had bought him a lap dance at one of the strip bars they'd cruised last night. But the bleach blonde with sagging fake tits, who called herself Destiny, apparently was not in the habit of showering between shows. Her body odor had squashed Jeremy's libido like a bug. Instead of hoping to get off from the way she was rubbing her ample ass against his crotch, he had been relieved when the two-song set was finished. The tip Jeremy had given the dancer had reflected the amount of fun he'd had – in other words, not much.

"What'd *you* do last night?" Jeremy asked. "Anything interesting?"

"Yes, as a matter of fact. I tried to solve a problem that's been bothering me, but I couldn't get my solution to work satisfactorily."

Jeremy didn't know what to say to that, so he settled for "Oh. Sorry."

"It was quite an educational experience, actually," Ware said. "And one of the things I learned was that this problem may not be solvable at a distance." He rubbed his chin, still watching the fire. "I think my best course may be to hire a subcontractor."

"Yeah, that might be best." Jeremy had no idea what his master was talking about, and Ware knew it. "Go get some breakfast," he said to Jeremy.

Over the next twenty minutes, Ware's gaze remained on the fire, but his mind was elsewhere. Finally he nodded to himself, stood up, and went off to make some phone calls.

Twenty-Eight

QUINCEY MORRIS AND Libby Chastain sat in the back of a cab, both lost in thought. They'd left Robert Sutorius in his magic-proof house, still distraught but otherwise unharmed. Libby had offered to take him outside, where her magic worked, and cast a quick spell that would help him recover faster from the psychic damage he'd suffered. But Sutorius had said, "Haven't you done enough, already? Just go. If you're done with me, then just *go*."

On the sidewalk in front of his house, Libby and Morris had thanked Ashley for her invaluable help in getting past Sutorius's defenses. Each of them acknowledged, again, that they owed her a favor. It was understood that they would pay off the debt with anything that did not violate their own moral precepts, a stipulation that Ashley had found mildly amusing.

"It was fun, kids – let's do it again sometime," she'd said, and walked off to God knows where – although God might not have been the best person to ask.

At her condo, Libby made tea for both of them, adding to it a couple of herbs that, she said, "May be just what we need right now." Morris wondered if witches ever dispensed Prozac, but kept the thought to himself.

Libby sipped some tea and said, "Another middleman. That's rather... disappointing."

"But there's no question that Sutorius was telling the truth," he said.

She made a sour face. "No – no question at all."

"Still, it would be good to know if this antiquarian book dealer has a web presence." Morris knelt and retrieved his laptop from under Libby's couch. He sat down, opened it, and began to search the web.

A few minutes later he said, "Here we go. Adelson's Rare Books and Antiquities, Harvard Square, Cambridge Mass."

"Does it show the store?" Libby asked.

"Yep."

"Let me take a look, will you?"

Morris turned the computer so that Libby could see the screen. "Ground floor, facing the street," she said, nodding. "That's good."

"Why 'good?'" Morris asked her.

"Maybe I'm just being paranoid, but I was remembering the last time we visited Cambridge, a couple of years ago."

"Sidney Prendergast," Morris said flatly. "The Kingsbury Building."

"Exactly. We were investigating a black magician then, too. Remember? She burned the building out from under us – or tried to."

"I'm not likely to forget that occasion," Morris said. "If you hadn't whipped up something that let us defy gravity for a few seconds..." He shook his head.

"What's that got to do with this job, Libby? Christine Abernathy's dead, damn her soul."

She put a gentle hand on his arm. "Don't. Please."

"Don't what – talk about Christine Abernathy?"

"No, I mean, don't say what you did about her soul. Maybe it's because my training taught me to abhor curses – not foul language, you understand, I mean *real* curses – but that kind of talk makes me uncomfortable."

"Okay, I'll be more careful in future. But why are we talking about her, anyway?"

"I'm just glad we won't have to go high up in any office buildings in Cambridge this time out. Call it a feeling."

Morris looked at her closely. "You're not getting paranoid in your old age, are you Libby?"

"Old age? I'm four years younger than you are, Quincey Morris."

"You know what I mean. We don't even know for sure that we're going up against a black magician."

"Maybe, but from what we know about the *Corpus Hermeticum*, can you think of anyone else who'd want it? I don't imagine Mister Adelson is looking to sell the thing to some rich Harvard kid."

"No, if he sent an occult burglar after it specifically, he must've had a buyer lined up. He wouldn't have paid Sutorius so much money otherwise. Did you hear what that guy *charges*?"

Libby nodded somberly. "Yes, I heard every word he said. Every single one that we wrung out of him."

Morris slowly closed the lid of his computer, put it on Libby's coffee table, and leaned back on the couch. He seemed to find his cuticles to be of great interest.

"You're feeling shitty because of what we did to Sutorius."

"Yes, I am. How are *you* feeling about it?" she snapped.

Morris was silent for a bit. "Not happy, that's for sure. I sure as shit didn't enjoy it, like Ashley did."

"If you had, you wouldn't be sitting here now," she said. "I wouldn't associate with someone like that."

"Not even Ashley?"

It was Libby's turn for silence. "Ashley's different," she said at last. "She can't help what she is – but we can, you and I. We made the free choice to terrify that man within an inch of his life, with Ashley's help."

"Yeah, I know," Morris said. "We did it for the same reason that millions of people do bad things every day – not that it's an excuse. We told ourselves that the end justified the means."

"And did it? Justify the means?"

"We won't know that until we find out who wants that fucking book, and why. It probably *is* a black magician – which is a good reason to find and stop him – or her. Whether that justifies – let alone excuses – what we did to Sutorius is something we'll only know when it's over. If then."

They drank tea for a while. Then Libby said, "I'm pretty sure that black magic's involved, and not just because it seems logical."

Morris frowned at her. "What do you mean?"

"Something weird was going on while we were in that house – and I'm not talking about his anti-magic protection. This was something darker, more sinister. At one point, I *felt* something evil – not in the room with us, exactly, but close by, searching, trying to get at us. At the time, I thought it was just my conscience punishing me, but now I know better."

"What changed your mind?"

"I was in such a blue funk on the way home, I didn't even feel like telling you. But when we walked out of Sutorius's house, Quincey, the air *reeked* of black magic. And I didn't smell anything like it when we were going in."

Morris thought about that. "You figure somebody made a move on us in Brooklyn, and the house stopped it?"

"That's as good an explanation as any," Libby said. "And I think we should prepare accordingly."

"By doing what?"

"I think you should bring that knife of yours with you whenever you go out, and I'll give you a couple of protective charms to carry."

"Fine – thank you."

"As for me, instead of my original plan for tonight, which involved consuming a large quantity of vodka, I'm going to spend some time putting together a few defensive spells that I can invoke very quickly, if I have to."

"Sounds like a lot of trouble to go to."

"It is, but worth the effort," she said. "We had some good luck in Cambridge last time Quincey – that's why we're still alive. I'm not going to depend on luck anymore."

Twenty-Nine

In warmer weather, Harvard Square was a bustling place, full of strolling students, food vendors, street musicians, petition tables, and the best-educated panhandlers in North America. But in March, with the wind blowing off the Charles River at twenty miles an hour with gusts up to thirty-five, there were still plenty of people about, but they were all bundled up and walking rapidly, hoping to get home, get to class, get to work, get laid, get anywhere that's out of the damn wind.

Adelson's Rare Books and Antiquities was located a few doors down from the intersection of Mt. Auburn and Kennedy streets. As a building it was long, rather than wide, with a storefront that measured twenty-two feet across. Adelson's looked out on the Square through two small display windows, each of which featured a carefully lit display of books that, together, cost more than most mid-size cars.

The taxi dropped Morris and Chastain off in front of the store at about four thirty p.m., and they had to step carefully over a snow-covered curb to reach the red brick sidewalk. They did not linger over the window displays and instead walked rapidly to the heavy, wooden front door and slipped inside.

Neither of them had paid any attention to the coffee shop across the street, or to the man sitting at a window table who had gone through two sandwiches and six coffee refills waiting for their arrival. He was a large man with wide shoulders, a big jaw, and eyebrows so long and thick that they seemed to meet in the middle of his forehead. As Morris and Chastain went into Adelson's, the big man stood up, his knees cracking. Dropping a couple of twenties on the table, he headed for the door. He did not walk particularly fast, but everyone in his path moved aside to let him pass. A few moments later, the man was standing at the curb, waiting for a break in the traffic that would let him cross the street without mortal injury.

Inside Adelson's, the quiet was an almost palpable thing, in sharp contrast with the noisy street outside. But then, the rare book business tends not to attract a rowdy crowd. At this hour on a Thursday, it apparently had attracted no one at all; Morris and Chastain appeared to be the only customers.

Thirty feet or so from the front door there was a large antique desk. Behind it sat a small antique man with thick glasses and thin hair. Morris and Libby stood before the desk, with Morris feeling a bit like a tardy kid who has been sent to the principal's office.

"Mr. Adelson?" Libby asked. She did not quite whisper.

"No, I'm afraid not," the old man said. "My name is Schwartz, and I am the chief clerk. May I assist you?"

"We would really like to speak with Mister Adelson," Morris said. "It's a very important matter." He handed the man a business card that read "Morris and Chastain Investigations" with contact information for both New York City and Austin, Texas.

If Mr. Schwartz was impressed, he concealed it very well. "Mister Adelson normally sees people only by appointment," he said.

"He *is* in, then," Libby said. "Excellent. May I?"

She took the card back, wrote on the blank side "*Corpus Hermeticum*?" and returned it to Mr. Schwartz.

"If you'll show that to Mister Adelson, I think he'll give us a few moments of his time," she said, adding just a tiny bit of magical "push" to the words.

"Yes, of course," Mr. Schwartz said. "Excuse me a moment."

He was back within a minute. Seeming slightly surprised, he said, "Mr. Adelson will see you. If you would both follow me."

He led them to a door that opened onto a corridor. There was a door labeled "Utilities," another with a sign that said "Receiving," and a third door that had nothing on it at all. That was the door Mr. Schwartz knocked on. Hearing a voice from within bellow, "Come in!" he opened the door and motioned the visitors through. To the man behind the desk he said, "These are the people I spoke about, Mr. Adelson."

"Fine, Stanley, thank you."

Schwartz left, and the man seated behind the large, cluttered desk rose to greet them. In a voice that was too loud for the size of the room, he said, "Hello, I'm David Adelson – but then you've probably determined that already."

"I'm Quincey Morris, Mr. Adelson." Morris leaned over to shake hands. "And this is Libby Chastain."

"Yes," Adelson said with a smile. "*I* had determined *that* already. Do sit down."

The man from the coffee shop came into Adelson's about then. Closing the big door, he rested his back against it for a moment, looking around the shop with questing eyes. He raised his head slightly, almost as he were sniffing the air.

As he approached Mr. Schwartz's desk, the old man stared and asked "Can... can I help you sir?"

"Just looking," the man growled, and kept on walking.

Quincey Morris, meanwhile, had just concluded that David Adelson didn't look much like a man whose passion was rare books. He belonged on a safari in Africa or someplace, looking strong and manly as he shot something good and true and real. Adelson stood about 6'5", with a barrel chest that was clearly the source for the booming voice. His styled hair was white, as was the closely-trimmed full beard. He wore an ivory rollneck sweater and a pair of old Levis. The eyeglasses that hung around his neck by a cord were the only concession to the book business that Morris could see.

They hung their coats on a nearby rack, but Libby hung on to her leather purse, which now rested in her lap.

Adelson studied their business card, or pretended to. "So you two are partners. Why kind of things do you investigate, exactly?

"Whatever our clients ask us to, Mr. Adelson," Libby said.

"They come from all walks of life," Morris said, "and some of them have problems that are... unusual, if not outright bizarre."

"I see," Adelson said, although he clearly didn't. He turned the card over and looked at what Libby had written on the back. "*Corpus Hermeticum*," he read aloud, pronouncing each syllable distinctly. "I assume this is the name of a book."

"A very old one," Morris said. "1471, or thereabouts. It's the Latin translation of a book of occult knowledge. The original was written in Egyptian-Greek, but no copies of that are known to exist."

As Morris was speaking, Libby Chastain had slipped a hand inside her purse, to grasp a small vial she had put there earlier.

"Occult knowledge," Adelson said, tapping one corner of the card on his desk. "And you're interested in having us locate this book for you?"

Morris nodded. "We've heard that a copy – or rather, a set, since it's five volumes – has come onto the market recently."

Adelson raised his bushy white eyebrows. "Indeed? I confess I've never heard of the work, and I like to think I'm pretty well plugged into all the rumors and gossip that are rampant in the profession."

"This particular set was stolen recently," Morris said, "from a supposedly secure repository in Montana. An expert, fella name of Robert Sutorius, was hired to break in and get it. He pulled it off, too."

Adelson kept his face blank, but a pulsing vein suddenly appeared below his left ear.

After trying to stare Morris down without success, Adelson slammed one huge paw down on the desk with a sound like a gunshot. "If you're implying that I would have anything to do with stolen property," he said loudly, "you are sadly mistaken, sir. I'm afraid I must ask you both to–"

"Excuse me," Libby said. She stood up, leaned over Adelson's immense desk, and blew a small quantity of blue powder into his face.

"What the hell are you doing, woman? Is this–"

Libby sat down again and said the same three words

of power that she had uttered in Robert Sutorius's home. But the effect was very different this time.

Adelson immediately became calm. He sat there, blinking blue powder off his eyelashes, his face expressionless.

Libby had explained earlier that since she had cast the spell, she must be the one to ask the questions, although Morris could prompt her if needed.

"I'm going to ask you some things, Mr. Adelson, and your answers will be complete and utterly truthful. You will *want* to tell me the truth.

"Yes, of course." Adelson seemed to slowly come out of his trance. He swiveled his chair to face Libby, crossed his legs, and folded his hands over his midsection. "Ask away."

"Did you hire Robert Sutorius to steal the *Corpus Hermeticum*?"

"Yes, I did. I thought he did a marvelous job."

"Why did you hire him?"

"I had a client who wanted the book. Actually, he was only interested in volume five."

"Then why did Sutorius steal all of it?"

"He doesn't read Latin, and thought the volume might possibly have been shelved out of order. So, to be sure he had the right one, he took the whole thing."

"So he brought you all five volumes?"

"Yes. I increased his fee, since he had gone beyond the call of duty, as it were." Adelson chuckled at his little joke.

"Could you tell which one was volume five?"

"Oh, certainly. I'm quite proficient at Latin – in this business, you have to be. It only took me a minute to identify the volume that my client wanted."

"What did you do with the other four volumes?"

"I kept them. Even an incomplete set of a work that old is bound to fetch a good price, one of these days."

"Where are they now?"

"In the basement – locked up in the vault we keep for ultra-valuable books."

"What was your client's name?"

"He called himself Theron Ware. I assumed that was an alias. As long as he wasn't planning to pay by check, I didn't give a damn." Adelson chuckled again. He seemed to be having a great time.

I should try some of that powder myself one of these days, Morris thought. *On the other hand, maybe not. I've got far too many secrets that need keeping.*

"Describe Mister Ware for me, please," Libby said.

"Tall – not as tall as me, maybe around 6'2". Very thin. Skinny, even. Thirty-five to forty, I'd say. Had a thin beard like some of the younger men sport now. I think it looks stupid, frankly. He wore sunglasses and a hat when we talked, as if I gave a damn what he looked like."

"How many times did you two meet?"

"Just twice. The first time was when we made the deal. I told him I wanted half my fee in advance, and he didn't argue. The second time, he brought the balance of the payment due and picked up the book. I tried to interest him in the other four volumes, for a higher price of course, but he didn't want them. Said the fifth was the one he needed."

"Did he use the word 'needed?'"

"Yes, he did."

"What did your total fee come to?"

"A hundred and fifty thousand. Fifty of that went to Sutorius, of course."

Morris glanced at his watch. Libby had said that the

spell was good for fifteen to thirty minutes, depending on the individual. They were getting close to fifteen minutes already, so Adelson might lose his desire to cooperate any time now.

He said softly to Libby, "We should get those four books, if we can."

"Mr. Adelson," Libby said, "you know that those four volumes in your vault are stolen property."

"Of course they are – I'm the one who had them stolen."

"If you're caught with them, you'd probably go to prison. You know that, don't you?"

"Yes, I know. I worry about that, sometimes."

"But if you gave the books to us for safekeeping, there'd be nothing for you to worry about, would there?"

This time, Adelson hesitated for a second before responding. "No, there wouldn't."

"Would you like to do that? Let us take those books away before you get into trouble?"

A longer pause this time. "Yes, I suppose so."

"Let's go down to the vault now and get them. Would that be all right with you?"

"Well, I don't know if–"

"You *really* want to give us those books, so you can sleep better at night. Isn't that true?"

This time, Adelson waited so long before replying that Morris was contemplating telling Libby that the game was up, and they should get the hell of there.

"Yes, you're right," Adelson said slowly. "I suppose I *would* feel better, if I did that."

"Why don't we go right now, then?"

"Okay."

Adelson stood, as did Morris and Chastain. When Libby turned his way, Morris gave her a look that said, *I'm getting pretty nervous about this.*

Libby replied with a shrug and a facial expression that told him, as clearly as if she had spoken, *We might as well go all in.*

Morris thought about the implications of "all in." It means you either win big – or you lose everything.

Thirty

WALKING SLOWLY, AS if in a dream – or just coming out of one – Adelson led them from his office to an unmarked door in the store proper, Morris and Libby in tow. It seemed no new customers had come in since Morris and Libby had been shown to Adelson's office – with the exception of a large, hairy man near the back of the store who appeared to be absorbed in a large book with gilt binding.

From his post near the opposite wall, Mr. Schwartz observed the procession and asked, "Is everything all right, Mister Adelson?"

Adelson turned and looked at the man as if he had never seen him before. After a hesitation that went on far too long, in Morris's opinion, he said, "Everything's fine."

Unlocking the door, Adelson said, "We, uh, keep a lot of our stock down there, along with our most valuable books. Visitors are only allowed by invitation."

"Then how lucky we are that you invited us," Libby said.

"Yes," Adelson said absently. "Yes, quite."

He flicked on a switch and began to descend a set

of uncarpeted wooden steps. Libby followed him. Morris, who was last in line, pulled the door closed behind him. It had a key-operated deadbolt, so he couldn't relock it, even if he'd wanted to.

It was instantly clear that most of the interior decoration budget had been lavished on the showroom upstairs. Morris reached the bottom of the steps to find a concrete floor, a series of bare light bulbs, and two rows of large bookcases that spanned the length of the large room. The bookcases had seen better days, although the volumes they held all appeared to be free of dust.

Upstairs, the big man who had come in after Morris and Chastain replaced the book he had been pretending to look at. He walked rapidly over to Mr. Schwartz's desk, his shoes making no noise on the hardwood floor.

In the animal kingdom, a creature that combines size with stealth is to be greatly feared, for those are the components of doom.

The old man, absorbed in an issue of *The Bookman*, only became aware of the other's presence when his shadow fell across the page. Mr. Schwartz, whose hearing was acute for one his age, started in surprise. Looking up, he actually cringed a little.

The big man looked down and rumbled, "Restroom?"

"B-behind you," Mr. Schwartz said, pointing with a hand that was even more unsteady than usual. "Second door on the left."

That lavatory was supposed to be reserved for the staff, its use extended to the occasional wealthy client only with Mr. Adelson's permission. But Mr. Schwartz would have no more said "No" to that man than he would have stuck his hand down a whirling garbage disposal. He hoped the stranger would do his business in there and then leave. Someone like him didn't belong in Adelson's. He simply wasn't their kind of person.

Downstairs, Adelson led Morris and Libby down a long row between bookcases. At its end was a vault that had been built into the wall. It looked as if it might be large enough inside for a man Morris's height to stand upright, but just barely. The vault must have been installed before the invention of keypad lock controls – it still had a combination wheel that had to be turned to the correct sequence of numbers for the lock to disengage.

Instead of bending to the task of getting the immense door open, Adelson turned and looked at them, a deep frown on his face. "I'm not sure this is a good idea," he said slowly. "Those four volumes could be worth a lot of money someday."

Libby spoke to him as if to a not-very-bright child. "But, David, money will do you no good if you're in prison. Receiving stolen property is a serious crime, and if the police find out about that, they'll probably start looking into *all* your business dealings, going back for years. Who *knows* what they might find, David."

"Oh, well, yes. I try not to think about that," Adelson said. But he still did not turn back to the vault. Libby rested her hand on the back of Adelson's neck and put her mouth close to his ear. In a voice so low that Morris could barely hear it, she said, "Think of it, David. *Prison.* No more good food or fine wine. No more beautiful rare books. No more women. And there are some big, mean men in there who would probably want to use *you* like a woman, David. Do you understand?"

"Dear God," Adelson said, blinking rapidly. Then he nodded. "Yes, you should take those books out of here, right away."

"Of *course* we will," Libby said. "All you have to do is let us in."

Adelson turned and put three fingers around the large metal dial set into the vault's door. He began slowly to turn it.

MR. SCHWARTZ HAD become so engrossed in an article about bookbinding during the American Revolution that he actually forgot for a few minutes about the man who was using the staff bathroom. Then he heard the door open, looked up, and beheld something out of a nightmare.

The immense creature, which, under its thick fur, bore a resemblance to the man Mr. Schwartz had seen enter the lavatory, crossed the distance between them in three bounds. Mr. Schwartz was able to get to his feet – he managed that much. But his plan to scream for help was never realized. It is, after all, difficult to scream when a set of claws, that a grizzly might envy, have just torn your throat out. Mr. Schwartz collapsed to the floor, and a few seconds later, found the mercy of death.

A few minutes later, the thing that had killed him moved to the basement door, which he had seen Morris and Chastain go through a few minutes earlier. Nothing in his instructions covered the white-haired man who had gone with them, but he would die, too, of course. The rule was: never leave eyewitnesses. Besides, the creature was hungry. Very hungry.

Turning the doorknob with those claws was a

challenge, but after several attempts the door was open, swinging silently on oiled hinges. The creature began to make its quiet way down the stairs.

Adelson was having trouble getting the vault open. The spell that Libby had used to make him compliant had affected either his concentration, his manual dexterity, or both. He had made three attempts so far and was fumbling his way through number four when Libby Chastain said, "Let me help you, David. Why don't you step back and tell *me* the combination. I'll get the door open for us."

"But the combination's a *secret*."

"I know it is, David – but you were going to let us in, anyway, right? And I promise, after today, I will never, ever go near this vault again."

Adelson stared at her and said, reluctantly, "All right, just this once."

"Thank you, David. Now let's trade places."

Adelson took a step back, allowing Libby to kneel before the vault's locking mechanism. "Go ahead," she said.

"Right, to thirty-four."

"Got it."

"Left, to nineteen."

"Okay."

Right, to forty."

"Um-hmm."

"Left, to three."

"Yep."

"And then right, to twenty-one."

"That's it?"

"Yes," Adelson said, "now just turn the – what the fuck is *that*?"

Thirty-One

Quincey Morris whirled, gaped, and found he had just enough air in his lungs to say softly, "Mother*fucker!*"

The biggest werewolf he had ever seen was already halfway down the long aisle, its claws scratching on the concrete. The creature's shoulders were so wide that they were actually brushing against the bookcases on either side. That had slowed it down a bit – otherwise Morris would be dead already.

Being part man, part wolf, a werewolf combines the best (or worst, depending on your point of view) qualities of each: the man's intelligence and ability to walk upright, and the wolf's acute senses and animal cunning, combined with teeth, claws and musculature that are native to neither.

Morris was fumbling in his pocket for the switchblade. Against this thing, it might be as useful as a slingshot against a battleship, but the blade *was* coated with silver, deadly to werewolves. It was also the only weapon that Morris had.

Then an arm was pushing him aside desperately while Libby Chastain cried, "Move!"

Morris scuttled aside as Libby extended the first two fingers of her right hand in the direction of the werewolf, and pointed high over its head. Then, fingers spread wide, she lowered her hand until it was pointing at the floor, chanting, over and over, "Atqarab b'loa!"

Morris had heard her use that one before, and knew the words were ancient Aramaic for "Do not pass!"

The werewolf was only twenty feet away when it slammed into an invisible wall, bouncing off with a howl of pain and frustration to land on its back.

"Barrier spell?" Morris asked.

"Yes, but it's only in the space between these bookcases, and it won't hold for long," she said tightly. "Give me my bag!"

Morris scuttled back to the vault, where Libby had left her big leather purse. As he grabbed it, he saw that Adelson was standing with his back pressed against the wall, eyes huge and mouth hanging open. He was making a sound that sounded like "Wha-wha-wha?"

Morris didn't take time to explain. Even with Libby's spell in place, none of them *had* a lot of time.

"Come on!" he called to Adelson, then turned away.

He could have tossed the bag to Libby, but the way their luck had been running lately, she'd probably catch it upsidedown, spilling the contents all over the place. So Morris took an extra few seconds to reach Libby, who was still facing the invisible barrier she had created, pointing the same two straightened fingers to maintain the spell.

Coming up behind her, Morris snapped "Here!" Without turning away from the shield, Libby reached behind her and he slapped the bag into her hand. She immediately dropped to one knee, spilled the bag's contents on the floor, and began sorting through them with her free hand. Morris had the switchblade out now, the silvered blade glinting in the harsh light from the ceiling bulbs.

The werewolf had been stunned by its impact with the invisible shield, but it didn't stay that way for long. It came to its feet smoothly, growling in rage and frustration. Then Morris realized, with a sinking feeling, that they had a smart werewolf on their hands. Instead of clawing at the barrier in futility, the creature did something more appropriate for an ape than a species of *lycanthropus sapiens* – it began to climb the bookshelves, and within a few seconds was out of sight.

"Can he get around us?" he asked Libby.

Without looking up from her systematic rummaging, Libby said, "Damn straight. The barrier's high, but narrow. I can make something that'll surround us, but I can't do it quickly."

Morris turned until his back was just touching Libby's. With one of them facing in each direction, they couldn't be taken unaware. It was suddenly quiet in the basement – except for the continuing sound of "Wha-wha" coming from near the vault. Morris had forgotten about Adelson. He hadn't followed Morris, but had remained where he was. Adelson's brain must be befuddled by the remnants of Libby's spell, combined with the sight of something that his forebrain told him couldn't possibly exist. But his reptile brain, a far more primitive structure, had seen, and believed, and was terrified.

Morris knew he should run out there and drag the man back to relative safety, but he was torn between reluctance to leave Libby's back unprotected and the sure knowledge that Adelson was an innocent bystander in this struggle. Whatever a werewolf was doing down here in the bookstore's basement, it almost certainly hadn't come after Adelson. And Morris also knew that an innocent bystander is always one short step away from becoming collateral damage.

"Adelson!" Morris called softly, in a pathetic attempt at a stage whisper. "Come over here! You'll be safe with us!"

That last was an outright lie, but what was Morris going to tell him – the truth that joining him and Libby might increase Adelson's safety marginally, at most? As a motivator, the truth left something to be desired, as it often does.

Morris's internal struggle was abruptly cut short when it started raining books. The bookcases down here were so crammed full that someone had been stacking books on the top of the cases, and it was a number of those that were being dumped on them from above. Whether the werewolf intended this as a distraction, or a mere venting of its fury, Morris didn't know. He was looking up, one arm raised to protect his face from further literary incoming, when a three-pound First American Edition of *War and Peace* came sailing out of nowhere and fell on Libby Chastain's head.

Thirty-Two

Libby dropped like a puppet with its strings cut. The three vials she'd been holding rolled out of her limp hands and spilled across the floor.

Morris spared her a quick glance, then turned his face back up to where the enemy was. He was worried about Libby, but he had been in this business too long to start acting like a dumb hero. He could go to Libby and kneel over her unconscious form, calling her name and keening, just like on TV. Then the werewolf could jump on his unprotected back and tear his stupid head off, before devouring the two of them. But it looked like Libby's magic was lost to him for the time being – he was going to have to deal with this thing on his own.

But perhaps not entirely. Glancing down at his foot, Morris saw that one of the vials Libby had been holding had rolled in his direction, and its cap remained intact. Another quick look showed him that the container held a clear liquid, and Morris was pretty sure of what it was. Denatured alcohol is used in a number of white magic spells, and he knew that Libby carried some as part of what she sometimes called her "traveling hocus-pocus kit."

The shower of books from above had stopped. Morris scanned the top of the bookshelves for any sign of the werewolf, listened hard for any sign of its growls or breathing. Satisfied that he was probably going to be jumped in the next three seconds, he performed a deep-knee bend that allowed him to scoop up the vial quickly and return to a standing position.

Morris held the bottle where the light could fall on Libby's hand-written label: "Denatured Alcohol." He'd been right.

He gave a small nod. Morris was no magician, but alcohol has properties that even the layman can make use of, sometimes. He loosened the vial's cap, so that it would come off with a flick of his thumb. Now all he needed was an opportunity.

Fire was out of the question. Morris, wasn't a smoker, and didn't carry a lighter. He was pretty sure that Libby had a box of handmade wooden matches somewhere in her bag, but trying to hold a match, the vial, and the switchblade, with all three ready for instant use, required one more hand than he possessed. Besides, the vial held four fluid ounces, at most – he wasn't going to incinerate any werewolves with that. But the alcohol still gave him a small edge that he hadn't had a minute ago.

A few more books fell from above, then something much bigger either jumped or fell from up there, to land with a grunt about twelve feet from where Morris was standing.

Up close, the werewolf was no less terrifying than when Morris caught his first glimpse of it. He'd encountered a few werewolves before, and even killed one, once. But this specimen was *huge*. The size a werewolf assumes upon transformation is directly related to how big it is in human form, and Morris remembered that the man he'd seen upstairs had been built like a linebacker. He saw the creature look to where Libby lay on the floor behind Morris, still unmoving, and its lips pulled back from those immense fangs in what Morris assumed was the werewolf version of a smile.

Morris backed up slowly until he felt the heels of his shoes touch Libby's recumbent form. He didn't figure a few more feet of distance was going to make any difference when the thing came for him, but he was hoping that the werewolf, in human form, watched a lot of TV melodrama. In the fantasy land that is television, when the hero and his girlfriend face the big, bad monster the guy always puts himself between the girl and his adversary, in a "You'll have to go through me first" attitude. Sometimes, the idiot even says it out loud.

In real life, limiting your freedom of movement like that is a quick way to become Purina Monster Chow, with the girl to follow for dessert. But Morris hoped the werewolf would figure he was copying some TV hero, and was going to stand fast when the creature charged. In fact, Morris planned to hop backwards at the last instant, clearing Libby's body with the jump and landing behind her. He wasn't giving Libby to the werewolf – but if the creature found itself clawing empty air where Morris had just been standing, he might just have a chance to do something, with either the alcohol or the knife, or both.

Morris was no fool. Even with his little stratagem, he still put his and Libby's chances of survival at about one in ten. But a second ago he'd seen no chance at all, so you could say that things were improving for him. A little.

The problem is, werewolves are really, *really* fast, and there was a good chance that its claws would catch Morris in mid-jump, disemboweling him and leaving Libby unprotected, as well. A small part of Morris's mind concluded that he was going to die in the next few seconds, but he closed that operation down ruthlessly. The trouble with last thoughts is that they slow your reaction time.

The werewolf growled and began to move forward, taking its time with what it probably saw as easy prey. It may not have noticed that Morris's knife blade was silver-coated – or maybe it figured he'd never get the chance to use it.

Morris dropped into a semi-crouch. That made it appear that he was ready to do battle, but it would also give spring to his legs when he made the jump back. He was getting ready to play his last card in a really crappy hand – then Adelson appeared, and stabbed the werewolf in the back.

Morris hadn't seen the man's approach, since the immense werewolf was blocking his view. The werewolf, on the other hand, may have been so focused on Morris that its normally sharp ears had failed to detect the sounds Adelson made as he ran up from the vault, where he'd been cowering and babbling incoherently. The white-haired man held what looked like a pen knife with a four-inch blade – the sort of thing that a man like Adelson would use to cut twine-bound bundles of books – and he plunged it into the werewolf, screaming, "Get out of my store, you ugly fuck!"

The werewolf howled in pain, although any wound inflicted on it without silver would heal very quickly. It turned on Adelson, who had just raised the knife to stab the werewolf again – a blow that never landed, since it moved in and tore Adelson's knife arm clean off with its terrible jaws. The man's scream of pain and horror didn't last long, as the werewolf slashed one of its paws fiercely across Adelson's throat, nearly decapitating him.

The werewolf dropped Adelson's arm from its jaws and gave a howl of triumph. Then it seemed to remember Morris, who had made a quick adjustment to his strategy, in response to the changed circumstances. As the creature turned back around Morris jumped, all right – but *forward*. This brought him within three feet of an enraged werewolf, which should have brought his near-instantaneous death. Instead, Morris dashed the contents of Libby's vial into the creature's face, which meant that the better part of four ounces of pure alcohol went right into its eyes.

The werewolf howled again, this time in agony. It blindly swiped a paw in Morris's direction, but he was prepared and ducked, letting the bloody claws pass a few inches over his head. Then he moved in with the knife.

Quincey Morris had once spent a couple of hours with a man named Nick Reynolds, who had served six years for armed robbery in San Quentin, one of California's most notorious maximum security prisons. In the Q, as in most such places, the weapon of choice among prisoners is a handmade knife known as a shank. And that means some of the best knife men in the world can be found among the lifers at a maximum security penitentiary.

Reynolds claimed he had never shanked anyone himself, but had seen it done, more than once.

"Thing is, with a shank you've gotta be quick, but thorough. Can't take more than a few seconds, or you

might get caught by one of the hacks. But you don't want the son of a bitch recovering in the hospital and coming after you later, or maybe sending a few of his friends. So you gotta make sure. You don't just hit him once with the blade. Whether it's his front or back, you gotta get him three, four times, real quick – bam, bam, bam. Then you drop the shank, which, unless you're an idiot, has got the handle wrapped in tape, so there's no prints, and you walk away. That's how you use a knife, if you're serious about it."

Quincey Morris had never used a knife more seriously in his life. His arm moved like a piston – *one, two, three* stabs to the belly. He stepped back, to avoid the inevitable blind slash with the lethal claws. Then he moved in again, fast. The werewolf's paws were over his bleeding belly now, in an automatic protective gesture. That meant the chest area was exposed. Again the piston – *one, two three* – all in the area of the heart.

The werewolf gave one last, agonized howl and dropped to its knees, which allowed Morris to bring the sharp edge of the switchblade quick and hard across the exposed throat. Then he stepped back and watched the creature die.

The werewolf writhed in agony for a few seconds, and then it was still. Wary of deception, Morris waited – and watched the immense, furry monster transform into a large, hairy, naked man. A dead naked man.

Morris flicked blood off his blade, folded the knife, and put it away. A glance at Adelson showed that the man was beyond help – his head was attached to his body only by a partially torn spinal cord. Then Morris heard a soft moan from behind him followed by Libby Chastain's voice saying, "What… the fuck… hit me?"

Thirty-Three

"HOW MANY FINGERS?"

"Three."

"Close your eyes. Now open. How many fingers this time?"

"Still three."

"Keeping your head still, follow my fingers with your eyes."

"Yes, Quincey."

"Good. What's today's date?"

"Um – March 3rd."

"Who's Carnacki?

"A fictional ghostbuster, created by… William Hope Hodgson. It's also the name of your hamster. How's the little guy doing, by the way?"

"He's fine."

Morris leaned back and looked at Libby, who was seated on the bottom step of the staircase that connected the bookstore's basement with the sales floor.

"Well, I don't think you're concussed," he said. "Although we should get you to the ER and let professionals make that judgment."

She shook her head – slowly. "I'll be fine. But you know, it's funny."

"What is?"

"I never read *War and Peace* in college. I've always figured I'd get around to it someday – but this wasn't quite what I had in mind."

Morris gave her a quick grin. "Bad jokes means you're probably okay. But stay here for a few minutes, will you? I want to check the upstairs."

"Me and my throbbing head will be right here."

Several minutes later, she heard footsteps descending the stairs.

"Scoot over," Morris said. When she did, he sat down beside her.

"The old guy upstairs, Mister Schwartz – he's dead. Throat torn out. And it looks like our werewolf friend took a few precautions – whether before or after he transformed, I don't know."

"What kind of precautions?"

"He put the 'Closed' sign on the door, and locked it. He also turned off about half the lights up there."

"No wonder there haven't been any customers barging in – and good thing, too. That... thing killed enough people, as it is."

"And did you notice the surveillance cameras upstairs when we came in?"

"No, I didn't – but I'm not surprised. It seems like everybody's got them now."

"The system feeds into a digital recorder that was behind Mister Schwartz's desk. Somebody pulled out the hard drive, and smashed it."

"Clever little werewolf – well, not so little. So, there's no video of anything that happened upstairs. Are there any cameras down here?"

"No, I checked."

Libby sat there rubbing her head for a little while

before she said, "Poor Adelson. What must have possessed him, to take on a werewolf with a fucking penknife? Mind you, I'm glad he did, from what you've said."

"Maybe fear made him crazy," Morris said. "I know he was terrified by the thing. So was I, but at least I understood what it was. Adelson must've had trouble believing his own eyes. Maybe that led to some kind of psychotic break."

"And what you're being too nice to say is that my spell might have contributed to that, somehow."

"No way to be sure, is there?" Morris said. "I don't imagine the spell textbook, or whatever it is you learned magic from, has much to say about the effects of combining a rapidly fading compliance spell with sheer terror."

"No," Libby said soberly, "I don't suppose it does. So I'll never know whether I played a role in the poor man's death."

"No, I don't reckon you will," Morris said. "But you might keep in mind that what Adelson did, whatever his motivation, saved our lives – and also represented some payback for what happened to Mister Schwartz."

"My head hurts too much to consider complex theological issues right now," Libby said. After a moment she added, "I suppose calling 911 is out of the question."

"Not unless you fancy explaining to the Cambridge P.D. that of the three dead guys in here, two were killed by a werewolf. And the third fella – well, he was killed by me, but it's okay, officer, because he *was* a werewolf."

"Well, when you put it that way..."

"The cops would probably figure it was the most original insanity defense they'd ever heard."

"Then we'd better get out of here, before somebody from Adelson's family, or maybe Mister Schwartz's, comes down here looking for him."

Morris stood up. "Sounds like a good idea. But there's something I want to pick up before we leave."

"What's that?"

"Those first four volumes of the *Corpus Hermeticum*."

Thirty-Four

THE METROPOLITAN AREA (such as it was) of Sheridan, Wyoming, boasts about thirty thousand souls. Quite a few of them must belong to the Church of Jesus Christ of Latter-day Saints, since there are three Mormon centers of worship within the metropolitan area.

The night was clear and cold, so they had the heat going in the stolen Ford Explorer. The street where they were parked was in an affluent, well-lit neighborhood. But Ware had still found a patch of shadow for them to wait in.

"I thought all the Mormons was in, like, Utah," Mark said, from the back seat.

"Utah is their home ground," Ware said. "But they've spread out quite a bit since things got started in the 19th Century – not surprising, since their 'faith' encourages big families."

"They breed like fuckin' bunnies, is what you mean," Elektra said from the front seat.

"Inelegantly but accurately put, my dear," Ware said. "They're all over the world now – but the closer you get to Utah, of course, the greater the concentration."

Jeremy squinted at the big white house with green trim that was halfway down the block from where they sat. "Doesn't look like much, if a fuckin' bishop lives there."

"Your mind is still stuck in the Catholic model, Jeremy." Ware told him. "No palaces or fancy hats for the Mormons – at least, not at this level. Although their hierarchy in Salt Lake City is as grandiose as anything you'll find in the Vatican."

"Jeremy used to be an altar boy," Elektra said. "Until some priest started fucking his little bunghole. Although I kinda think he liked it, at least a little bit."

Jeremy muttered something in the back seat, but Elektra had sharp ears. "Did you just call me a *cunt*, Jeremy? Did you? Last night, you seemed to think my cunt was the finest–"

"I think it's about time for your counseling appointment, my dear," Ware said firmly. "You wouldn't want to keep Bishop Hayes waiting."

The young woman was silent at once.

"Go on, now," Ware said. "You know the signal once you've got him unconscious."

"Blink the porch light twice."

"Exactly."

As Elektra crossed the street, Jeremy said, "I thought you said that bitch was no good for this part of the work." His voice was petulant.

"Ordinarily she isn't – but I've given her a cover story that suits her persona very well," Ware said. "The fallen woman, a former prostitute, seeking redemption through the True Faith. It's a story as old as Mary Magdalene – although that lady's tawdry reputation is undeserved."

Mark took a few moments to parse Ware's last sentence. "You mean she wasn't a whore? That's what I always heard."

"No, Mary never traded sex for money. She was more of what today we'd call a star fucker, enamored of the so-called Messiah."

"How come you know stuff like this, Theron?" Mark asked.

"I read a lot."

Mark and Jeremy silently pondered the notion that someone would actually read a great deal – voluntarily. After a while, Jeremy asked, "What about those people who you said was looking for us – that Texan guy and the witch? You said you were gonna take care of them."

"Oh, I have," Ware said. "I hired the services of a most reliable subcontractor. He said the problem would be taken care of very soon. Sort of a 'final solution,' if you will."

He chuckled at that, and the other two joined him, although they had no idea what Ware had said that was so funny. Then it was silent inside the vehicle until Ware said, "The porch light – see it?"

"Blinked twice," Jeremy said. "Guess she's got him."

"Then it's time for us to go get him," Ware said, and put the vehicle into gear. "The Bishop has a date with my knife."

Thirty-Five

PETERS AND ASHLEY lay among the tangle of sheets, the sweat slowly drying on their bodies. Peters closed his eyes and entertained the two contradictory thoughts that usually occurred to him after sex with Ashley: *My God, that was fantastic*, and *One of these days, she's gonna kill me.*

Even though Ashley had been given human form before being sent over from Hell, Peters thought that the creature he sometimes thought of as his "pet demon" had managed to retain sexual appetites and capacities that few mortal women could match – or might want to.

Peters had no way of knowing that Ashley sometimes thought of him as her "pet human."

They lay quietly, Ashley apparently feeling no need for conversation and Peters lacking the ability, at least until he got his breath back. He had just decided he was capable of speech again when he heard a two-tone "ping," the sound clearly audible in the silence of the bedroom. Peters listened more carefully, and when the sound came again he said, "That sounds like it's coming from your purse. Is that your phone?"

"No, mine doesn't sound like that," she said. "I thought it was yours."

"Uh-uh."

The sound came again, and Ashley got up, frowning. Just as she reached the chair where she'd left her purse, the "ping" came once more.

Ashley rummaged in her voluminous Dior bag and pulled out a new-looking iPhone in a pink travel case.

"Cute," Peters said. "When did you get it?"

Ashley looked up, her heart-shaped face a study in puzzlement. "That's just it – I didn't. I've never seen this thing in my life." She looked again at the phone. "But it looks like someone's trying to text me."

"Who'd do that? You don't exactly know a lot of people, this side of Perdition."

"Let's find out," she said, and pressed an icon.

Whatever came up on the screen, Ashley stared at it far longer than it should have taken to read a brief message. When she looked at Peters again, she didn't appear puzzled – she looked scared.

"It's Astaroth. He wants me to text him back."

Astaroth was the demon, very high in the councils of Hell, who had sent Ashley and Peters to the human plane a year ago. Since he had the power to recall them to the Place of Eternal Torment at any time, they had both hoped never to hear from him again.

Peters got very quiet, but after a few seconds he shook himself, like someone trying to pull his mind out of a bad dream. "Wait a second," he said. "A text – from *Hell*?"

"I know," she said. "It transcends the physical laws of nature – but then, so do we, babe. So do we."

Peters nodded slowly. "All right, okay. But that doesn't mean it's all over for us. Can you imagine Astaroth being polite enough to send a text: 'Please return to Hell immediately?' That's not his style, and you know it. He'd just yank us back there. One second we'd be here in bed making the springs creak, and the next we'd be among the flames again, listening to the screams of the damned. He'd do it that way just to see the expressions on our faces."

Ashley gently tapped the phone she was holding. "Maybe you're right. But why would he go through the trouble to get in touch at all, then?"

Peters took in a long breath and let it out slowly. "There's only one way to find out, babe. Do what the man said. Text him back."

"Yes, I suppose you're right."

"Better do it now. Last thing we want to do with a guy – demon lord, I mean – like Astaroth is keep him waiting."

"Good point."

Ashley studied the phone for a few seconds, pressed a few more icons, and began to type with her thumbs. Then she pushed another icon and put the phone down.

"What'd you say?" Peters asked.

"Just that I was responding, as directed, and would humbly wait to receive his commands."

Peters snorted gently. "Humbly – *you*? Why do I have trouble getting my mind around that?"

She looked at him and said, with utmost seriousness, "With one like Lord Astaroth, humility is the only attitude that will not result in a great deal of pain. You, of all humans, should know that."

He rubbed a big hand slowly across his face. "Yeah, I do. Sorry."

"Not as sorry as you'll be once I get back in that bed with–"

The pink phone pinged again. Ashley picked it up and said, "Well, here goes nothing – or, rather, everything."

Ashley stared at the screen, her gray eyes narrowed. Then she grabbed the nearest piece of paper, which turned out to be an envelope containing the condo's electric bill, and began to look around frantically.

"A pen, I need a pen," she said tightly.

"If it's a text, you can save it–"

"*Get me a fucking pen.*"

"Right." Peters rolled out of bed and walked rapidly into the next room. In seconds, he was back with what she needed. "Here."

Ashley wrote on the back of the envelope, frequently consulting the phone's screen. Then she put the pen down, studied the phone for a few moments, and pressed an icon. Satisfied, she put the phone on the nightstand.

"I know you can save a text message, and I just did," she told Peters, "but I also know that if you press the wrong button, it's gone forever. I'm not familiar with this phone, and couldn't afford a mistake. This message gets lost, and I'm royally fucked. Or, rather, we are."

"Are you gonna show me, or what?"

"Of course," she said, handing him the phone. "There should be another message coming any second, though. This one is incomplete."

Peters stared at the little screen and read:

"*There is 1 like U, sent 2 open Gates of Tartarus. Spell in Corpus Hermeticum. Ritual calls 4 burning churches & shamans + big sacrifice center. U must sto*"

He handed the phone back to Ashley and said, "We better *hope* there's another one on the way, because this message is clear as mud."

"It's not quite that bad," she told him. "But, like you said, I sure hope there's more. There's a lot that I still need to know."

"I assume the last word here is intended to be 'stop.' Why didn't he at least finish the word, you figure?"

She picked up the phone and looked at the text message again. "He hit one hundred and sixty characters," she said.

He stared at her. "You mean Hell has to follow the rules of some stupid *phone company*? That's fucking ridiculous!"

"The whole idea of a text from Hell is absurd – but here it is, nonetheless. Why would someone in Hell use Earth technology?" She spread her hands wide. "No idea. Why didn't he just show up here and give us orders personally? He did when you were first sent here, right?"

"Yeah," Peters said. "He took on the aspect of a kindly old Catholic priest. Astaroth likes his little jokes."

"Whatever's going on, this doesn't look like a joke."

"You know what the Gates of Tartarus is? And the *Corpus Hermeticum*?"

"Yes to the first, and I learned of the second quite recently," she said. "But before I start with the explanations, let's wait for the next text. With any luck, it'll explain some things."

But there was no second text from the demon Astaroth. They waited for almost ten minutes in silence before Ashley said, "Well, fuck me, anyway."

"Gladly," Peters said. "But first I want you to tell me about the stuff that's in that text."

"I guess that's all we have to go on – for now, at least. If he can send *one* fucking text, why can't he send *another* one? *Damn*, that pisses me off!"

"I'd say you're beautiful when you're angry, but the truth is you're scarier than shit. Calm down a little, will you, babe?"

Her expression made him wonder if she was about to eviscerate him with the pen she was holding. Then she grinned and said, "Shit is scary? That doesn't mean we're giving up anal sex, does it?"

"Not on my account," he said. "But let's stay out of the gutter for ten minutes while you tell me about the Gates of whatever it was."

"The Gates of Tartarus." She went over to the bed and sat down next to him. "There is a legend in Hell–"

"Wait – Hell has legends?"

"Any society has its legends," she said, "and the society of the damned is like any other. Well, okay, not like any other – but, yes, legends. Now stop interrupting."

"Yes, dear."

She delivered a slap to his bare thigh that was more painful than playful.

"So, the legend of the Gates of Tartarus says that there is a way out of Hell – not to Heaven, which is forever closed to us, but to Earth, world of the hated humans, who were responsible for our Great Rebellion in the first place."

"Responsible? What the fuck did *we* do?"

Another stinging slap. "I told you not to interrupt. Humans are believed responsible because it is your very existence that offended certain angels, especially Lucifer, who was high among the angelic hierarchy. The idea that the Father, against Lucifer's advice, would create a race of... apes with souls was unbearably offensive to some of us who had existed as pure spirits since time began."

"Apes with souls, huh?"

She didn't hit him this time. "My view of humanity – well, certain parts of it, anyway – has undergone some revision since the time of the Great Rebellion. But many of the Fallen have not changed, and would love nothing better than to lay waste to humanity and everything it has created."

She picked up the envelope on which she had written Astaroth's text message. "If you want to talk about things that are scary, there are a couple of things in this message which should scare you down to the insides of your bones. The first fact is that the Gates of Tartarus are apparently not just legend – they really exist."

She turned and looked at Peters, and the expression on her face frightened him more than anything that had already transpired this evening. "The second fact – if I'm reading this right – is that someone from Hell has been sent to this side and given flesh, as I was. And this individual is apparently charged with throwing those gates wide open. The result, if he succeeds, will be, quite literally, Hell on Earth."

"Great," he said. "Just great. If I won't go to Hell, then they'll bring Hell to me. But what about this other thing–" he consulted the envelope "–the *Corpus Hermeticum*?"

"That," she said, "represents the only piece of good news to come out of this mess, so far."

Thirty-Six

THEIR SUITE AT the Charles Hotel had a view of the river, and Libby Chastain stood at the window looking moodily down at the water as she wondered whether there was any way the call she'd made to the police could be traced back to her.

Public phones are fast disappearing in the cellular age, but there are some left – including the one in Harvard Square they'd found a block from Adelson's.

With Morris standing nearby to keep anyone from getting close enough to overhear, Libby had used a minor bit of magic, to change her voice, and called 911.

"Emergency operator. How may I assist you?"

"Yeah, uh, listen – I just went into Adelson's bookstore in Harvard Square," she said in a soprano voice that was nothing like her usual alto. She gave herself a Boston accent, as well. "There's a guy in there, dead."

"Can I get your name please, ma'am?"

"There's a lot of blood," Libby said, and hung up.

She and Morris had decided that it was better for the police to find the carnage at Adelson's, instead of some family member, so they'd left the front door unlocked when they left. The sight of Mister Schwartz's body would lead the cops to search the place, and to discover the two corpses downstairs.

The 911 system would do an automatic trace, but Morris and Chastain would be long gone before anyone got around to looking. Libby had worn gloves, so fingerprints were not an issue, and they had checked that no surveillance cameras were trained on that area of the Square. Libby decided there was no way the call could come back to bite her, and she was glad she'd made it.

From the couch behind her, Morris said, "Unless Adelson was more heavily involved in occult stuff than he let on, that werewolf was sent after *us*. So, what I'm hung up on are the usual two questions that arise when somebody comes after us."

Without turning from the window, Libby said, "You mean 'who' and 'why?'"

"Them's the ones. A hit attempt usually means that we're getting too close for somebody's comfort. But I can't figure how what we've got now would bother *anybody*."

Libby turned and looked at him. "We've got the *Corpus Hermeticum* – four-fifths of it, anyway."

"And if the buyer wanted those other four volumes, he could have got them from Adelson. But all he wanted was volume five, and that's what he's got."

"He's got the book he wanted, and we've got shit," Libby said. "But maybe he *believes* we have more?"

"Where would he get an idea like that? Hell, how would the sumbitch even know we're looking? We didn't exactly call a press conference."

"All right, let's list the people who know we're investigating the book theft. Father Bowen, who's so embarrassed by it all, he's not likely to tell anybody."

"Agreed. Then there's the occult burglar, Sutorius. He knows we're after the book, because he told us he stole it, and who he stole it for."

"But Sutorius only knows Adelson, who was his client," Libby said. "And Adelson was surprised when we confronted him, Quincey. He didn't know who we were, or what we were after – I'll stake my reputation on it."

Libby saw that Morris was scratching his chin, his eyes distant. "What?" she asked.

"Sutorius only knew Adelson as his client," Morris said, "but I bet he knows a lot of people in the occult world. Shit, he'd have to. Could be he's looking for payback."

"So he did what – put the word out that we're after the book?"

"He might've. And maybe the word reached the ears of Mister Theron Ware."

"Theron Ware... there's something about that," Libby said, frowning. "When Adelson used it in his office, I remember a small bell going off in my head. I've come across the name before, but I couldn't for the life of me tell you where."

"Well, we can do what everybody else does when they want to know something." Morris opened his laptop and turned it on.

"You're Googling 'Theron Ware?'" Libby sounded amused.

"Why not?" Morris said, watching the boot-up sequence on his screen. "Can't do any harm. But first, I want to check out a couple of people who are near and dear to my heart. See if anybody's been talking about 'em recently."

"You and me, in other words."

"The very same. Okay, let's see here."

A few seconds later, he said, "Well there's a whole bunch of stuff about me, stemming from that mess at the Republican Convention last year."

"Not surprising."

"Not fun, either. I thought it might help business, at first – and I *have* gotten a lot of calls at the business number. Trouble is, most of 'em are either reporters or nuts who want me to find out if Aunt Edna is really in Heaven."

"I've been spared those – mostly," she said.

"That's because you were smart enough to keep your name out of the papers. Okay, let's try 'Morris' and 'Chastain' together."

He scrolled through a list of results, then stopped. "Uh-oh."

"Good news or bad?"

"Hard to tell. Listen to this, from the Branch Report, about a week ago:

"Sources inside the Justice Department have revealed that 'occult investigator' Quincey Morris, who was mysteriously freed from prison after facing a slew of federal charges stemming from the last RNC convention, has been hired by the FBI to investigate the series of fire bombings of churches and synagogues that have occurred over the last six weeks. Morris's 'partner,' one Elizabeth Chastain, calls herself a 'white witch.' Maybe she can use some magic to keep Morris out of jail this time."

"My Goddess, what a snarky bastard!" Libby said. "And it's not even true!"

"From what I hear, truth and this fella are just passing acquaintances," Morris said. "And as for snarky – that's what makes him fun to read, according to some people."

"But the FBI *hasn't* hired us. We told O'Donnell and Fenton that we couldn't take on the church burnings until after we had finished tracking down the *Corpus Hermeticum*."

"Yeah, I know. And I can't see either O'Donnell or Fenton telling this Frank Branch fella otherwise."

"Neither can I. Even if they were the type to do something like that, they'd have nothing to gain by it."

"Agreed. But the story's out in cyberspace, regardless of how it got there. Before we get too excited about it, let's see if anything else about us has shown up recently."

Morris spent twenty more minutes online, looking for anything that might connect him and Libby with the search for the purloined *Corpus Hermeticum*.

"*Nada*," he said, finally. "Not a goddamn thing."

Libby paced slowly around the room. "I suppose if Sutorius did rat us out, he didn't have to do it online. He could have made a few phone calls to the right people."

"Yeah, I know. I'm almost tempted to have Ashley pay another call on him, but–"

"*Quincey*." She was glaring at him.

Morris held up a pacifying hand. "Don't get upset, Libby. I was about to say, 'but I just don't have the heart for it.'"

"Me, neither," Libby said, mollified. "Besides, even if we got some names from him, there'd be no way to know if *those* people hadn't called others. It would be a waste of time."

"Speaking of names," Morris said, "you wanted to check out Theron Ware."

"Might as well – although it might turn out to be just some guy I went to high school with."

"Let's see." Morris typed some more, and waited.

"Okay, here you go," he said. "According to our

friends at *Wikipedia*, Theron Ware, in addition to being the name of an art gallery in Hudson, New York, is the title character in *The Damnation of Theron Ware*. It's a novel, written in 1896 by a fella named Harold Frederic. Says here it's considered a classic of American literature – but I don't remember coming across it at Princeton."

"They weren't teaching it at NYU either," Libby said. "At least, not in the English classes I took."

"Anyway, Theron Ware is some kind of Methodist preacher who ends up in upstate New York, where he loses his faith but gains... I'm not sure what. It's not really clear."

"Hmm. Not much joy there. Maybe I'm thinking of the art gallery, although I've never been – *wait*!"

After a few seconds, his eyes on the screen, Morris said, "Theron Ware is also another fictional character, it seems. In a book by James Blish called *Black Easter*. Came out in 1968."

"James Blish sounds familiar," Libby said. "Science fiction writer, right? Maybe that's where I heard it." She did not sound reassured.

"In the novel, Theron Ware is the name of a black magician who is hired by some rich guy – to open the gates of Hell, for twenty-four hours."

"Is that right?" Libby's voice held no affect whatsoever.

"There's a cross-reference here to *Black Easter*," Morris said. "Give me a second."

Morris read the new entry, then said, "Yeah, that's about it. Theron Ware is a wizard hired by some rich asshole who thinks it would be amusing to turn all the demons of Hell loose on Earth for one night. Problem is, when the time comes to send the demons back, they don't wanna go, and Ware can't make them. I gather this isn't one of those stories with a happy ending."

"No," Libby said in that same flat voice. "I imagine not."

Thirty-Seven

"So THIS OCCULT burglar type–" Peters began.

"Sutorius," Ashley said.

"Right, Sutorius. He admitted, under duress, that he'd stolen the *Corpus Hermeticum* for some book dealer in Boston."

"Cambridge. Yes, and he spoke truthfully. I'd have known if he lied."

"So, I guess we need to talk to Morris and Chastain."

"Indeed. But knowledge is power – before I get in touch with the delectable Libby, let's find out what we can about these church burnings. I saw a story about one on the news, but apart from giving a brief cheer for the arsonist, I didn't pay it a lot of attention. We don't even know how many have been burned so far."

"That should be easy enough to find out," Peters said. He turned toward the computer but then looked back. "Ashley."

"Forget it. I'm horny, too – but we just haven't got time right now."

"That's not what I was about to ask. When you mentioned cheering one of the church burnings, it kind of reminded me which side you're really on. What does it matter to you whether somebody opens the Gates of Tartarus? I mean, if they succeed, I suppose you could look at what happened next as one big family reunion."

She sat back and looked at him, her normally mobile face hard to read.

"Peters, you've been in Hell – not nearly as long as I have, but you've spent time there. Which do you prefer: there, or here?"

"Here, of course. But then, I'm human. This side of the Great Divide is where I belong. It's home. And here, nobody tortures me – apart from those times when you get a little frisky with the riding crop."

"You're right about one thing: Hell *is* my home – or, at least it had been for so long that human time can't even measure it. But that doesn't mean I enjoyed being there. It's supposed to be a place of punishment, remember? And it is, believe me."

"All right, I didn't mean–"

"I *like* it here, Peters. I like being able to see a sky that isn't burning. I like the change of seasons. I like being the most powerful creature in my immediate environment. I like the sex. Sometimes, I even like you. I have no interest whatsoever in returning to Hell, nor do I wish Hell to join me here. Is that answer enough?"

Peters nodded slowly. "Absolutely. Now let's see about those church burnings."

Half an hour later, they had compiled a list containing the pertinent information.

Feb. 2 – Duluth, MN. Catholic Church burned, with a priest inside. The body not completely consumed. Rumors about occult elements surrounding the priest's death, but authorities aren't talking.

Feb. 12 – ten day interval. Synagogue, Albuquerque,

NM. Rabbi's body found inside, too badly burned to tell if he was ritually murdered.

Feb. 22 – ten day interval. Baptist Church in Decatur, AL. Pastor's body found inside, again too badly burned to learn anything about mode of death.

Mar. 4 – ten day interval. Mormon Church in Sheridan, WY. Church's Bishop found inside, burned beyond recognition.

In each instance, at least one report described the fire as "very hot" or "very fast," suggesting the use of incendiaries.

"Sheridan was last night," Peters said, "which gives us nine days before the next one. Or is he done already?

"I doubt it," Ashley said. "Four isn't a number of power in black magic. But five is – definitely. That's why the pentagram, a five-pointed star, is used so often in spells and incantations."

"So the next one is the charm, so to speak."

"Probably – unless he's going for a multiple of five, like ten, fifteen, twenty, or whatever. That would add more power to the spell, but the stuff he's been doing provides immense power, already."

"And besides," Peters said, "his luck is bound to run out, sooner or later. A cruising police car is going to drive by the church just as he's coming out, or something else is going to get fucked up. It's only a matter of time."

"All of which strengthens the conclusion that the next burning will complete the ritual."

"So, what are we gonna do to stop it?"

Ashley reached for her phone. "I think," she said, "it's time to call in a favor."

Thirty-Eight

Morris and Libby watched the late local news, and learned that three men had been found dead in the shop of a prominent Harvard Square rare book dealer. Police considered each of the deaths to be homicides, but were releasing no other information at this time, pending notification of the next of kin.

The next story dealt with the national scene, reporting the fire that destroyed a Mormon Church in Wyoming and claimed the life of its pastor, Bishop Andrew Hayes. Arson was suspected, and the investigation was continuing.

"Another one," Libby said, clicking off the TV. That makes how many now – five?"

"Four, I think," Morris said.

"If it weren't for the black magic that Colleen sniffed out at the first one, I'd be inclined to label these as straightforward hate crimes."

"Even for hate crimes, they're pretty damn strange," Morris said. "The buildings and victims were all of different denominations – Catholic, Jewish, Baptist, and now Mormon. One of those isn't even Christian. From what I've read, haters tend to be pretty focused, especially if they're pissed off enough to resort to arson and murder."

"The only common factor is houses of worship and clergymen. What kind of psychotic fantasy would prompt someone to pick targets based on such broad criteria? Not 'I hate Catholics,' or 'I hate Jews,' or Mormons, or whatever. Instead, 'I hate everybody?'"

"And the wide geographical separation doesn't make any sense, either," Morris said. "Is it to avoid getting caught, or to carry out some ritualistic purpose, or what?"

"Beats the shit out of me, cowboy," Libby said.

Then the theme from "Bewitched" started playing.

Thirty-Nine

Libby picked up her phone, glanced at it, and said, "Well, now." She looked at Morris. "It's Ashley."

Morris's eyebrows rose as Libby pressed "Answer" and said, "Hi, Ashley."

"Hmm," Ashley's voice said. "Caller ID – or magic?"

"Who says Caller ID *isn't* magic? 'Any sufficiently advanced technology is indistinguishable from magic.'"

"Arthur C. Clarke, right?" Ashley said. "Very interesting man. But it's *real* magic I want to talk to you about."

"Fair enough. Quincey's here – I'll put you on speaker."

"But if you do, I won't be able to whisper sweet nothings in your ear."

"Guess we'll have to save that for another time," Libby said, and pressed some icons. "Okay, you're on speaker."

"I might as well do the same," Ashley said, "since Peters is with me. He hates feeling left out of things."

"So, what's on your mind?" Libby asked.

"Apart from the usual, you mean? How about the *Corpus Hermeticum*?"

"Okay – what about it?"

"Have you tracked it down yet?"

Libby hesitated. "Mostly. We've got four volumes out of five."

"Nice going, kiddo. Where's the fifth one?"

"We're still working on that," Libby said.

"*Crap*. Any leads?"

"Not much. A name, which is almost certainly an alias. Oh, and we're pretty sure that the guy behind the name tried to kill us today."

"Do tell. Well, I'm glad he failed – for any number of reasons. What'd he use – a spell?"

"No, a werewolf. The kind that don't need moonlight to transform, apparently."

"Gracious me," Ashley said. "I assume said lycanthrope isn't feeling too well, right about now."

"I think it's fair to say that he isn't feeling anything at all."

"You go, girl!"

"What's your interest in all this Ashley? I mean, I'm grateful for your help in tracking down the book, and all, but..."

"I didn't call to gossip, Libby, if that's what you're getting at. It appears that, once again, we have a common interest."

"Indeed? What's that?"

"I should start by telling you about a *very* unusual text message I got this evening..."

After Ashley had finished speaking, there was silence on the line.

"Libby? You still there?"

"Yes, I'm just trying to integrate this new information with what I already know, and come up with something that makes sense. It's making my head hurt. But before we get into that, there's a couple of things we learned from Adelson that you don't know yet."

"Hit me," Ashley said.

"One is the alias that the mysterious buyer of the *Corpus Hermeticum* was using – Theron Ware."

"*Black Easter*," Ashley said, almost at once.

"You know the book?"

"Know it? It's one of my faves. Interesting sense of humor this guy has – and it would seem to confirm that he really is interested in opening the Gates of Tartarus."

"Yes it would, wouldn't it? The other noteworthy item is that Mr. Ware was only interested in volume five of the *Corpus Hermeticum*. Adelson offered to sell him the whole thing, but all the guy cared about was the last volume."

"So, the crucial spell's in book five," Ashley said. "Must be. It would be nice to get a look at one of those."

"Good luck with *that*," Libby said. "Father Bowen said the only other two copies he knows about are locked up: one in the Vatican and the other in the Kremlin."

"Shit. I used to have some contacts in the Kremlin, but they joined us in Hell decades ago – although it seems like only yesterday. I still know a couple of guys in the Vatican, but neither of them is high up enough in the pecking order to have access to the secure room of the Vatican Library."

"Hell has people in the Vatican?" Libby said.

"Not demons, of course – more what the Soviets used to call agents of influence."

"I guess I shouldn't be surprised – but I confess I am, a little."

"It's like the man said in that James Bond movie, honey: 'We have people everywhere.'"

"We'll talk to Father Bowen," Libby said. "Maybe he knows somebody in Rome who can get a quick peek at volume five for us."

"It would be a big help," Ashley said. "Although I'm not gonna hold my breath waiting."

"I've been taking notes while you two have been talking," Morris said. "Trying to organize the information we have, versus what we still need to know. See if this makes sense to all of you.

"Here's what we know:

1. A demon made flesh, calling himself Theron Ware, is abroad in the world – specifically the United States.

2. Ware's mission is to conduct a black magic ritual that will open the gates of Hell, allowing its denizens to enter our world, with catastrophic results.

3. The ritual, Ware is using, can be found in volume five of the *Corpus Hermeticum*.

4. The spell apparently involves the ritual murder of clergymen, then burning their houses of worship down around them. Each sacrifice so far has involved a different religious denomination.

5. Four such sacrifices have taken place. They seem to be occurring at ten-day intervals, which, if that's the pattern, means the next one will be nine days from now.

6. Ware appears to know that Libby and I are on his trail, and has tried to have us killed once already.

"Now here's what we don't know, but need to find out, pronto:

A. How many more sacrifices does Ware need to perform to complete the ritual? Although, I agree with

Ashley that five makes sense, given that number has a powerful role in black magic.

B. What does Astaroth mean in his text when he refers to a 'big sacrifice center?'

C. Where will the next (and presumably last) sacrifice take place?

D. Assuming we can find the answer to 'C,' how do we stop the bastard?

"That's what I've got, kids," Morris said. "Did I leave anything out?"

"Only this," Peters said. "If we fuck this up, will Ashley put in a good word for us when Satan takes over?"

"I've always loved your sense of humor, Peters," Ashley said. "Now shut up."

Forty

"I DON'T THINK you understand what you're asking, Mister Morris," Father Bowen said. "Access to the room in the Vatican Library where that book is kept is strictly limited. To get in requires written permission, and only three Cardinals are authorized to give it. Or His Holiness himself, of course."

"Can you get permission?"

"If I could, the application process would take months – the Vatican's bureaucracy is notorious for inefficiency. And, frankly, my application would prompt some very hard questions."

"Like what?" Morris asked.

"Like, why I am seeking permission to examine a book that I supposedly have a copy of, right here at the monastery."

"Could be it's time for you to come clean about the theft, Father."

"If I thought it might do any good, I would confess my sin of negligence, believe me. But such an admission would only be regarded as proof that I am not to be trusted with such dangerous material. I would never be allowed within a mile of that library."

In Cambridge, Quincey Morris massaged his temples,

as if he felt his head was going to explode – which is exactly how he *did* feel.

"Maybe if you explained to someone in authority what stakes are involved," Morris said. "You know, the opening of the gates of Hell, the end of the world as we know it, stuff like that, he might be willing to make an exception – just this one time."

"Your sarcasm isn't helpful, Mister Morris. If I were to relate a story like that to anyone in the Vatican, I would be promptly branded a lunatic and denied access to *any* sensitive materials. And I'm not entirely sure that the whole thing isn't, in fact lunacy. I know you and your... colleagues believe it – but it's really too melodramatic, in my opinion. There must be some more plausible explanation."

"Uh-huh. Well, if my *colleagues* and I don't figure out a way to stop this, I'll look for you at the fire pits, Father."

Libby Chastain was sitting cross-legged on the bed, her laptop open to a map of the United States while she tried to make sense of the locations chosen for the church burnings. Morris ended the call and said to her, "One of the downsides of using a cell phone is that you can't slam the thing down when you've just finished talking to an idiot."

"Well, you could," Libby said. "But it would be rather hard on the phone. I gather Father Bowen wasn't being helpful."

"Not in the slightest. In order to avoid looking foolish, he's rationalized away the evidence that's staring him in the face. Maybe if I sent him a cake with a pentagram drawn on top, he'd be more interested–"

"*What did you say?*"

Morris looked at her quizzically. "I said that I should send Bowen a big cake with a–"

"Pentagram. That's what I *thought* you said."

Libby searched quickly through her bag and came up with a pen. Consulting her notes, she began drawing right on the screen of her computer.

"There's probably some program that would allow me to do this digitally," she said. Her voice held an undercurrent of excitement. "But I haven't got time to fuck around with it. Here – look at this."

Morris sat on the bed next to her and looked at the computer screen. "First church burning – Duluth." She drew a big dot over that city on her map.

"Next one – Albuquerque." She drew a second dot.

"Then Decatur, Alabama." Another dot.

"And a couple of nights ago, Sheridan Wyoming." A fourth dot joined the others.

"We already knew all that, Libby," Morris said reasonably. "I don't see what we're gaining by looking at it on a map."

"No? Then watch this."

"Duluth to Albuquerque." She drew a line connecting the two points.

"Albuquerque to Decatur." Another line on the screen.

"Decatur to Sheridan." She added the line.

"Now," she said, "what've you got – or, rather, almost got?"

Morris stared at the computer screen for several seconds. "Motherfucking son of a bitch," he said, with feeling. "He's drawing a pentagram, right over the United States."

"Exactly," Libby said. "And, although my lines aren't perfectly straight here, look where the final point has *got* to be."

"Austin," Morris said. His voice was almost steady. "Austin, Texas."

"Yep," Libby said. "Your very own hometown."

Forty-One

EIGHT DAYS LATER, the group that Morris privately thought of as his "War Council" met for the last time. The venue, as it had been all week, was a conference room at the Austin DoubleTree Hilton.

Had minutes been kept, they would have shown that those attending were:

- *Quincey Morris, whose privately-owned company, QM Reclamations, Inc., had booked the facility.*
- *Libby Chastain, Mr. Morris's business partner.*
- *Special Agents Dale Fenton and Colleen O'Donnell from the FBI's Behavioral Science section.*
- *Eleanor Robb, representing an organization informally known as the Sisterhood, of which Ms. Chastain and Agent O'Donnell were both longtime members.*
- *Malcolm Peters, formerly of the Central Intelligence Agency and now a private consultant.*
- *Ashley (aka Ashur Badaktu, former resident of Hell), partner of Mr. Peters in every sense of the term.*

Morris opened the meeting a little after nine a.m. by looking around the oval conference table and saying,

"Not to be unduly dramatic, but this is it."

Ashley whispered to Peters, "If that's his idea of undramatic, I'd just love to see what he thinks drama *is*."

"If our understanding of the way these people operate is correct, they will hit a house of worship someplace in Austin tonight. Their M.O. – if you'll pardon me sounding like Jack Webb – is to abduct a clergyman, take him to his church, ritually murder him, and then burn the building down, using state-of-the-art incendiary devices. They have been known to leave traces of black magic behind, but not in all cases. To stop them from succeeding tonight, we have taken what measures we can. On that issue, maybe we should hear from the FBI next."

Everyone looked toward Fenton and O'Donnell, who sat side-by-side. "We're here because our boss is persistent," O'Donnell said. "She persuaded an Assistant Director that the church burnings represent serial homicide, rather than a civil rights matter. Then we received a tip from a usually reliable informant–" she gestured toward Morris "–that the church burners/murderers would strike in Austin next."

"We've got the Austin Police Department on the alert," Fenton said, "along with the Travis County Sheriff's office. *But*–" He looked toward his partner.

"*But*," she said, "there are an estimated five hundred to five hundred and fifty houses of worship in the metropolitan area, depending on how you define a 'church.' There isn't enough manpower in the P.D. and Sheriff's departments combined to put a cop at each one of them – even assuming that they had nothing else to do tonight."

"And, since this is a town of close to a million people," Fenton said, "there's usually plenty of work for the local law on any given night. They're not gonna treat this like the President's coming to town – not based on an anonymous tip, even one that comes by way of the Bureau."

Morris nodded and turned to the woman seated across from Fenton. "Ellie?"

"There's also the problem that even if the police *did* turn up in the right place and at the right time, they're not prepared to defend themselves against the demonic power that the being calling himself Theron Ware can wield," Ellie Robb said. "These black magicians have avoided confrontations with the law up to this point, but there's no reason to believe they would be anything but ruthless in dealing with interference. So I've been working with Libby and Colleen in an effort to offset their power."

"We've been able to prevail upon twenty-four members of the Sisterhood to put their lives on hold for a week and join us in Austin," Libby said. "They are all experienced practitioners of white magic. We've rented twelve cars, since they're going to work in teams of two."

"Assuming we all survive the night, Ellie," Morris said, "send me the bill for those rental cars, as well as the hotel. I'll take care of it."

"No, I don't think so, Quincey," Ellie said. "The Sisterhood has a contingency fund for emergencies, and this situation certainly qualifies. Anyway–" She gave him a tight smile "–I expect we all have an equal stake in making sure that the gates of Hell remain closed."

Libby went on, "Our twenty-four sisters have spent the last several days becoming familiar with the city, and will be mobile at six tonight. In the event that the specific location of the next atrocity is identified, a blanket text will send the address to each car, and the sisters will get there as quickly as they can."

"Speaking of moving quickly," Fenton said, "Colleen and I have a car on loan from the local field office. It's got a siren and flashers, which should get us through traffic faster than otherwise. We'll get the text if it's sent, and we're also gonna monitor the local police radio band."

"Peters and I will stay here," Ashley said. "It's a central location, and I should be able to reach any place in town without too much trouble." She grinned. "Besides, that means we can fuck while we're waiting."

Among those few humans who knew her, Ashley's name was rarely used in the same sentence as words like "appropriate."

"Libby and I will remain here, too" Morris said. "As Ashley said, it's a central location – unlike my house, which is on the west side of town. I've got a few friends on the Austin P.D., and one of them will let me know if anything likely shows up on their radar."

He stood up. "Thanks, everybody. If we pull this off, I'll buy all of you breakfast tomorrow morning. If we don't..." Morris's face, already serious, became somber. "... then hunger's likely to be the least of our problems."

As the others drifted out, Morris went over to a nearby window and looked out at his city. Fenton joined him. After a few moments he said, "Nice day."

"It usually is, around these parts," Morris said. "But I hear it might storm later."

Forty-Two

SEVERAL HUNDRED AUSTIN police officers and sheriff's deputies, along with administrative staff, knew that the church burners might strike in their town that night. A secret like that is difficult to keep when so many are privy to it.

At about the time that Morris's meeting was breaking up, the following item appeared online in "The Branch Report":

Word has it that ghostbuster Quincey Morris (who managed to evade numerous federal felony charges following antics at last year's RNC convention) is telling authorities in Austin, TX that the infamous "church burners" will strike there next. Is it any coincidence that Austin is where the occult cowboy calls home? Maybe his witch girlfriend Libby Chastain did his horoscope and says it's a bad time to travel.

It's easy to set up a Google Alert for any term or phrase that interests you. At least two people had established a Google Alert using the phrase "Quincey Morris." One was Morris himself, although today he was too preoccupied to read any email that didn't appear urgent.

The other was someone who called himself Theron Ware. Although, like Morris, he had plans for the evening, he monitored his email regularly throughout the day. The Branch Report item on Quincey Morris had been live for only twenty-four minutes when Ware read it.

He called to his acolytes and showed them what was on his laptop's monitor. "That motherfucker," Elektra growled. "I figured he'd be dead by now – and the bitch, too."

Mark had to read the item twice to make sense of it. "Geez, boss, I guess that means we hafta cancel tonight, huh?"

But Jeremy had seen what his master had seen, although not as clearly, of course. "We can use this, right Theron?

"Indeed we can," Theron Ware told them. "But I need to do some research, first."

"Whatcha gonna look up, boss?" Mark asked.

"I want to see if we have any kindred spirits in the Austin area. In a city that size, I'm sure we must."

"You gonna have them take out Morris for us? And his bitch?" Elektra wanted to know.

"No," Ware said, "I have something more... subtle in mind. Now leave me be, for a while."

Forty-Three

THE SUN WAS setting over the city as Ashley started unbuttoning her blouse. She knew Peters was watching, so she took her time before finally removing it.

"You can take this guy, right?" Peters asked. "I mean if push comes to shove."

"Which guy is that, sweetie?" Ashley said, unhooking her bra. She didn't really need one, but liked the effect that taking it off had on Peters.

"You know which guy – Theron Ware, or whoever he really is."

"Oh, him." She unbuttoned her black too-tight-for-business-wear pants and pulled the zipper down. Slowly. "If we're talking about magic, it depends on how powerful he is. I am of the fourth rank among the Fallen. If his position is higher, he's stronger. If lower, he's weaker. If he's fourth rank too, it's a tie."

"So, the outcome's already determined, even before you mix it up?"

"I said if we're talking about magic." She slid the pants, a little at a time, past her slim hips. "There's more to it than that."

"You *are* planning to explain it to me, right? I mean, *before* we fuck."

"You know what I think is adorable about you? After what you probably consider a significant amount of time, you still get hard whenever you see me naked."

"Half the time, I get hard when I see you dressed. Don't change the subject."

"I thought getting you hard *was* the subject, honey." She kicked the pants aside and now wore only a thong.

"Ashley. Come on."

She signed theatrically. "I explained to you once before, when you asked if I could be killed. What did I tell you?" She snapped the thong's elastic waistband, but did not lower it.

"You're making it hard to concentrate."

"That's the whole idea, dummy." She slid one hand down the front of the thong and began rubbing herself slowly. "Come on. Answer the question and you get a treat, just like a good doggie."

"You said that although your spirit was immortal, the body you inhabit could be killed, just like anybody else."

"See – you *were* listening. Such a *good* boy." Her hand began moving faster.

"So if I shoot him in the head, he dies like everybody else?"

"It's an express ticket back to Hell – unless he uses magic to block it, or turns you into guacamole first." She finally let the thong fall to the floor. "You weren't planning on shooting me, were you Peters?"

"Not with any gun but this one, baby."

"That's my boy!"

Forty-Four

SGT. NATHAN EISINGER was holding down the desk at the Sixth Precinct when the phone rang at nine twenty-two.

"Sixth Precinct. Sergeant Eisinger speaking."

"Sergeant, this is Harry Crenshaw at HomeGard Security."

"Yeah, hi. What's up?"

"One of our clients, the Sikh Temple on East Twelfth Street, just had the silent alarm go off."

"Somebody broke into this Sick Temple?"

"I think it's pronounced *Seek*."

"Whatever – you got a break-in, or not?"

"Yeah, somebody broke in, or tried to. I just double-checked the alarm, and it's not malfunctioning. I already sent one of our cars over there, but procedure says to notify A.P.D. as well – so, that's what I'm doin'."

"You got an address?"

"It's 134 East Twelfth, out near where it intersects with Springdale."

"Okay, we'll check it out, thanks."

Eisinger broke the connection, then switched to a dispatcher. He told her to send a car to check out a possible 412 in progress at the Sikh temple. Then he remembered something else he was supposed to do. He looked up a number and called it.

"Whalen."

"Lieutenant, it's Sergeant Nate Eisinger, at the Sixth."

"Yeah, hi."

"Hi, uh, sir. Sorry to bother you at home, but I got a note here says I'm supposed to call you if we get something hinky goin' on at any church tonight."

"That's right. What've you got?"

"A 412 in progress at the Sikh temple on East Twelfth. I don't know if that counts as a church, but I figured I better let you know."

"You did right, Sergeant. Somebody's broken into this Sikh place?"

"That's what the alarm company says. I got a car on the way over. So do they."

"What's the full address?"

"It's 134 East Twelfth, out near Springdale."

"Okay, thanks."

Forty-Five

QUINCEY MORRIS WAS on his third Diet Pepsi. Tension made him thirsty, and he was not fool enough to consume any alcohol tonight. He was trying to focus on the Local Politics page of the *American Statesman* when the phone in his shirt pocket began playing the "X-Files" theme.

Morris grabbed the phone, almost dropping it, and answered. He listened closely, grabbed a pen, and wrote something on a nearby pad. Then he said, "Thanks, Marty, I appreciate it."

He turned his head toward the connecting door and called, "Libby!"

Libby Chastain was there within moments. "What is it?"

"We might have something. A break-in at a Sikh temple. Who've we got near East Twelfth and Springdale?"

Libby went to the heavily annotated Austin street map that was tacked to a nearby wall. She peered at it for several seconds before saying, "That's Abigail and Eloise. They're closest."

"Right." Morris checked his list of phone numbers and made a call.

"This is Morris. We've got a possible at 134 East

Twelfth. It's a Sikh temple, should be pretty hard to miss. Check it out, quick as you can and call in, okay? Right, thanks."

Libby sat on the edge of the bed, hands clasped together tightly. "Sikhs, huh? I was wondering if our pal would get around to them. What is it about this spell that requires a different religion every time?"

"Maybe the idea is to piss God off every which way you can," he said.

"And then He opens the gates of Hell because He's mad? Or She?"

Morris made a face. "Nobody ever said magic had to–"

The phone at his elbow began making music.

"Morris."

He listened for a few moments.

"Okay, looks like this is the one. There are cops on the way – you know what to do. I'll alert the others. Wait for them to get there – or at least some of them. Do *not*, I repeat *not* go in there by yourselves. Right, bye."

He looked at Libby. "Eloise says there's definitely black magic coming from that temple – and it's recent."

Libby stood up. "Okay, then. Battle stations."

Morris handed her a sheet of paper. "Here's your list. Maybe you should call from your room, so we're not talking over each other."

"Good idea." Libby turned and walked, very fast, toward the connecting door.

Morris glanced again at his list, brought up his phone's directory, and touched an icon.

Two floors below, Ashley had just enjoyed her third orgasm when the phone near her head began playing Gregorian chant..

"Yes," she said into it, a little breathlessly.

"It's Morris. Looks like we're on."

"Excellent. Address?"

"A Sikh temple at 134 East Twelfth. That's over near–"

"I've got the map memorized – I know where it is."

"See you downstairs in three minutes."

"Gotcha."

"Ashley, one thing."

"What now?"

"When we get there, try not to kill anybody, unless absolutely necessary."

"Oh, it'll be necessary, believe me."

Forty-Six

THE LOW, TAN brick building on East Thirty-Fourth Street might have been mistaken for a school, apart from the triangular orange flag that flapped in the breeze above it and the large sign near the front door that read "Sikh Temple of Austin."

When Morris's blue Mustang skidded to a halt at the curb, he saw that a number of the others had arrived already and were standing on the sidewalk in front of the dimly-lit building or across the street, in the shadow of a closed Rexall drugstore. In between, on both sides of the street, a number of cars were parked haphazardly – their drivers had apparently been in as big a hurry as Morris was.

He spoke to Ellie Robb first. "How many of the Sisters are here?"

"Fourteen. They've all been alerted, of course, but some were probably a good distance away when the word went out."

"We can't wait. Spread them out around the building, will you, and tell each one to start her spell whenever she's ready."

"Right." Ellie turned on her heel and moved away swiftly. The members of the Sisterhood would each be putting down the same anti-black magic spell, which would be strengthened by every additional white witch who joined in.

Morris saw Fenton and O'Donnell and waved them over. Each wore an amulet around their neck designed to protect against black magic, and Colleen carried a wand. "Have you done a recon?" Morris asked.

"Simple construction," Fenton said. "Two stories. Small windows. Front, back, and sides – one door apiece."

"The locks look easy," Colleen said. "A simple disengagement spell should do the trick."

"Good," Morris said. He looked at the police car parked directly across from the entrance. "Cops okay?"

"Both asleep," Colleen said, "along with two rent-a-cops who arrived right after them. They'll remember nothing when they're awakened."

"Excellent," Morris said.

Ellie Robb came back and said, "Everyone's in position, except for one Sister who I asked to stay in front and direct the new ones as they arrive."

"All right, then," Morris said, and blew out a breath. "Time to go in. Libby and me in front, Fenton and O'Donnell left side, Peters and Ashley right side, and Ellie, you've got the back door. Assignments clear?"

Nodding all around.

Morris looked at his watch. "We go in exactly sixty seconds from... *now*."

The small group dissolved like a football huddle breaking up. Libby had her wand ready in one hand. Morris was carrying a long-barreled Desert Eagle automatic. Its load of .50 caliber silver-tipped cartridges had been blessed, just like Morris's switchblade, by the Bishop of El Paso.

Libby glanced at the immense pistol. "Where was that when the werewolf dropped by Adelson's the other day?" she murmured.

"Home. Didn't think I'd see any werewolves in Boston. Live and learn."

At the elegantly carved wooden front door, Morris said, "Okay, get it open, please."

Libby lightly touched the tip of her wand to the lock, said a few words in Latin, listened for the "click," then looked at Morris. "Done."

Morris looked at his watch. "Fifteen seconds. Ten. Five. Time to go."

Morris grasped the knob, which turned without resistance. He and Libby walked in quietly.

Only a few of the ceiling lights had been turned on. There was enough illumination to see that it was a surprisingly plain room, with none of the statues, candles, or elaborate architecture that Morris knew from other religions. There was also plenty of light to see the small group of people who were kneeling in a circle near the front of the temple.

They looked up, startled, as Morris and Libby walked in. Bare seconds later, the side doors burst open, almost as one, to admit four of Morris's colleagues. A moment later, he saw Ellie Robb enter from the back door.

One of the Satanists – if that's what they were – stood up, holding what looked like a wand. He pointed it at Morris and Libby and said a couple of words that Morris couldn't hear. Then a ball of flame the size of a grapefruit headed their way, very fast. Libby waved her wand once, said a single word, and the fireball disappeared. "Is that the best you got?" she said softly.

Then Ashley let go a burst of some kind of energy that was too fast for the eye to follow – and a moment later the arm that had held the fireball-shooting wand was smoldering on the floor. Its former owner, who appeared to be a man in his mid-twenties, stared at the severed appendage for several seconds. Then he remembered to scream.

All of Morris's team had kept moving toward the group. Fenton and O'Donnell were displaying their IDs now, yelling, "FBI, freeze! Don't move, or we'll shoot!"

The other four Satanists, three men and a woman, had gained their feet and stood in shocked surprise. The one who'd fired a wand at Libby was back on his knees, though, screaming in pain and clutching the place where his shoulder had been. Blood poured between his fingers.

"I don't think that was strictly necessary, Ashley," Morris said.

"It's done now," Ashley replied, not sounding remotely contrite. "Oh, all right, here."

She bent over the injured man, yanked his remaining hand away from the bleeding stump, and pressed her own hand firmly against it. She said two words in a language Morris didn't recognize, and at once wisps of smoke began to rise from the wound.

The screaming redoubled, which Morris would not have thought possible. Then it stopped, as the man mercifully fainted.

"See?" Ashley said to Morris. "Cauterized. He won't even bleed to death now."

Morris directed his attention to the wounded man's three associates, who were now clearly terrified. Two of them held wands. "Drop them," Morris said. "Now!"

Their hands opened immediately, letting the slim, foot-long magic instruments fall to the carpeted floor.

Morris looked at the would-be Satanists more closely.

Barely out of their teens, all dressed in the black, creepy-looking clothing that is usually associated with the goth subculture.

Libby picked one of the wands and examined it. "It's precharged," she said. "Nothing more than an occult storage battery. I've seen them before One of these, and a few words of power, and you can work magic – once, maybe."

Some of the limited light came from the five squat black candles that burned in a circle on the rug. In the middle of them lay a cat, dead. It had been sloppily disemboweled.

"Who *are* you people?" Ellie Robb demanded. "And what in the Goddess's name are you doing here?"

"It was this guy showed up, today around noon," one of the men said. "He was a magician – he showed us the cool shit he could do. He said we could get power just like him, if we did like he told us."

Morris felt his stomach sink like an elephant in quicksand. "This man," he said, "came to you, gave you the wands and a ritual and said to come here and... butcher some innocent animal."

They nodded, although the phrase "innocent animal" seemed to confuse them.

"He told you to come here tonight, didn't he?" Morris said. "It had to be tonight."

More nodding from the goths. "Dude even did a spell over us," the woman said. "He said it would make us strong, and, like, scary."

"*Scary,*" Ashley said. The contempt in her voice could have curdled milk.

"I think–" Morris said, but then stopped. In the distance he could hear sirens. He listened for a few moments. There were several sirens wailing at different pitches, but they didn't seem to get closer. They weren't headed for the Sikh temple at all.

"Sounds like fire trucks," Morris said. He looked at his companions bleakly. "Guess there's a big fire someplace – someplace *else.*"

Forty-Seven

"This is Bill Stuart. I'm coming to you live from a raging fire that has destroyed the Eighth Street Mosque, one of only two Moslem worship centers in the city. Fire officials said that the first alarm came in around ten thirty, and they responded very quickly. However, Fire Chief Roger Upton told me that the building was fully ablaze when the first trucks arrived.

"We've learned that the mosque was administered by Dr. Muhammad Faisil, a Saudi-born American citizen who also served as the prayer center's Imam, or holy man. He led the Friday night services here for many years, and he is held in high regard by the local Islamic community. We have been trying to reach Dr. Faisil for comment, but have been unable to locate him in the chaos that you see all around me. As soon as he becomes available, or there are new developments in the story of this tragic blaze, we'll be back live to bring you up to date. For now, this is Bill Stuart, Channel 3 news, reporting from South Austin."

Forty-Eight

Two hours later, Quincey Morris and Libby Chastain sat in Morris's living room, half-drunk and waiting for the apocalypse.

Libby dropped a few more ice cubes in her glass, then topped it with Grey Goose vodka, grateful that Morris always kept some on hand. Her hands were not quite steady.

"He suckered us," she said, not for the first time. "Bastard knew we were waiting for him and he sent those... idiots to the Sikh place."

Morris took a sip of Jack Daniel's, by no means his first of the evening, and carefully put the glass aside. His hands were not steady, either. "First he laid a bunch of black magic hoodoo over them, so that our sensitives would smell it from outside, along with those stupid wands. Then we'd figure it was the real deal. Which is just what we did. Yup. Just what we did."

After a while, Libby said, "Quincey?"

"Um?"

"Why hasn't it happened yet? It's been hours since that mosque burned. I mean, how long does it take to open the fucking gates of Hell?"

"Dunno. Guess they'll get it done, sooner or later. Later's okay with me."

"We'd know, wouldn't we – even in here?"

"Yeah, I'm pretty sure that if the world was ending, we'd have noticed something."

He looked at big Desert Eagle, which he'd left on the coffee table. "Once it starts, once we're sure... I don't know if I'd be inclined to wait around for the demons to come for me. Think I might take my chances with God's judgment, although I'm not sure how He feels about me, lately."

Libby Chastain stared at the gun for a while. "Quincey?"

"What?"

"If you decide to... do it that way, would you... will you...?" Libby swallowed. "Will you kill me, first? I'm not sure if I'd have the nerve to do it myself. But if you're not going to be here anymore, then I don't want to be, either." Libby began to cry softly.

Morris's throat was so tight, he was having trouble making words come out, but he finally managed to say, "'Course I will, if that's what you want. I won't leave you for them. How could I leave you behind, when I love you so much?"

Libby was crying harder, now. "I – I love you, too, Quincey. I guess I always have."

Twenty minutes later, there was a bright flash at the windows, followed, an instant later by a loud boom. Then there were sounds on the roof, like a million tiny footsteps.

Libby looked towards a window, eyes wide. "Is it...?"

Morris looked, listened, and tried to make his bourbon-addled brain focus on something that seemed very familiar. Then he gave Libby a lopsided grin and said, "No, just a thunderstorm. The weather guy on TV said we might get one late tonight."

So they sat, and drank, and waited for the end of the world. In time, they fell asleep.

Hours later, they awoke to find sunshine, chirping birds, and a gentle breeze blowing. The world was still there.

Forty-Nine

QUINCEY MORRIS AND Libby Chastain stood on Morris's front porch, drinking coffee and watching the traffic pass by in the street, just as it always did. First, though, they'd turned on the television, to find that the most interesting thing to happen in the world overnight had apparently involved a young British prince cavorting naked in a Las Vegas fountain.

Libby sipped from the mug Morris had given her and said, "I have the worst hangover of my entire life – but, right now, I wouldn't trade it for anything."

"I know just what you mean," Morris said, "as well as exactly how your head feels."

They watched the world go by for a few more minutes before Libby said, "Do you suppose they could be just... playing with us? The demons, I mean."

Morris shook his head, instantly regretting the movement. "I doubt it," he said. "You take a bunch of kids who've been looking through the front window of a candy store and drooling for – well, forever. Then, one night, the door to that place swings wide open. I don't see them hanging around on the sidewalk for a while longer, just to tease the people inside."

"You make a nice analogy," Libby said. "Okay, then – what happened? Why didn't the world end last night? Not that I'm complaining, mind you."

"I was about to say, 'Beats the hell out of me,' but that might be an unfortunate turn of phrase. I haven't got the faintest idea, Libby. But once my head stops pounding, I thought I'd make a few calls to folks who were with us last night, see what they think. You might want to do the same."

"Sounds like a good idea." Libby studied her coffee mug with great interest, or appeared to. "You know, last night, while we were sitting inside, waiting to die – or worse – we probably said some stuff..." She let her voice trail off.

"Did we? My memory of it all is pretty vague," Morris said. "I know we talked, from time to time. Probably got pretty maudlin, what with the booze, and all. But I can't recall anything specific. Can you?"

"I had some weird dreams, once I drifted off," Libby said, "and it's hard to separate what really happened from what didn't. But, no – I don't remember anything in particular."

"Just as well, I'm guessing. We were pretty drunk."

"Yes," Libby said. "It's probably just as well."

Fifty

Over the next several days, there were a number of conversations between and among those who had been involved in the desperate effort to keep the gates to Hell firmly closed. The good news was that they had apparently succeeded. The bad news was that none of them could understand how success had been wrested from the jaws of a defeat that seemed poised to devour them all.

That the Eighth Street Mosque had been the target of Theron Ware's crew there was little doubt. In the wreckage, fire investigators found the remnants of incendiary devices that were identical to those used in the four other recent arsons involving houses of worship. Also found among the ruins was the charred body of a man whom dental records identified as the mosque's *Imam*, Dr. Muhammad Faisil.

There was no shortage of theories among the group members to explain what had happened – or rather, what had *not* happened.

Malcolm Peters: "Ashley and I had figured that the 'magic number' of church burnings was five, or a multiple of five – since that's a very important number in black magic. I thought that Ware would go with five, because every new sacrifice put him and his crew at risk of being caught. But maybe he's an arrogant bastard, and he's gonna keep going until he hits ten, or fifteen, or whatever fucking number he has in mind. Maybe he's making more than one pentagram – who knows? I think we'd all better keep an eye on the news – if there's another church burning with the same M.O., it shows that Ware is still in business – which means we're still in business, too."

Ashur Badaktu, aka Ashley: "I think the stupid bastard's fucked it up. The fifth sacrifice must not have been enough to open the Gates of Tartarus. There was some additional sacrifice, or ritual, or spell necessary before the Big Barbeque, as I like to call it, could happen. Ware attempted it, and failed. And there are no do-overs in black magic. If he blew it, the chance is lost – unless he wants to start all over again, with five more sacrifices. Personally, I think he's dead and gone. When Ware screwed up, whatever major demon gave him flesh and sent him over here probably got disgusted and yanked him back home. My guess is, we'll never hear from him again."

Special Agent Dale Fenton: "I'm no longer convinced that any of the people behind this are demons, or even magic practitioners. Maybe the black magic that Colleen sniffed out the first time has another source. This could be simply a group of vicious lunatics traveling around the country, randomly killing clergymen and burning their churches. Serial killers, in other words. I grant you, the Bureau has never seen serial murder carried out quite like this, but there's a first time for everything. Or maybe the killers have read too many comic books, and they really *believed* that creating a pentagram with the locations of their crimes would open the gates of Hell.

If so, then they were clearly mistaken – thank Heaven."

Eleanor "Ellie" Robb: "What we may have here is an example of divine intervention. I think it entirely possible that Theron Ware and his cohort did everything right – from their own evil perspective, I mean. They carried out a bloody, depraved ritual that would really have opened the gates to Hell. I understand that there are some among the Infernal, such as Astaroth, who feared that such a catastrophe would bring on Armageddon, the final battle between Heaven and Hell. But what if God, or the Goddess, or however you wish to call our Creator, decided that it was not yet time for Armageddon, and simply forestalled the spell by saying, 'No – this will *not* be permitted.' I think it's as good an explanation as any, and better than some I've heard."

Fifty-One

And so everyone went home – except for Quincey Morris, who was already there. He offered to drive Libby Chastain to the airport, and she accepted, but on the way neither of them had much to say to the other. Silence between them was usually comfortable, a simple acknowledgment that there was nothing interesting to talk about at the moment. But this time the quiet had an uneasy quality – although, if asked, neither of them could have told you why.

As the Mustang slowed to a halt outside the door to the United Airlines terminal, Morris reached down and popped the trunk so that Libby could retrieve her bag.

Often at such moments or parting, Libby would lean over and kiss him on the cheek – but not this time. "Pleasure saving the world with you again, cowboy – if that's what we did," she said. "Let me know if you get a lead on book five of the *Corpus Hermeticum*."

"Will do," Morris said crisply.

She got out, slammed the door, and turned toward the rear of the car. Through the half-open window Morris called, "Libby!"

She turned back and looked at him.

They held the look for half a second before Morris said, "You take care now, hear?"

Libby gave him a half-smile and said, "Sure will. You too."

Then she was gone.

Fifty-Two

NOTHING IN OAKLEY, Kansas, could ever be called "booming," including the motel business. So Roy Hastings, owner, manager, and desk clerk of the E-Z Rest Motor Hotel was delighted to rent three rooms – and for a whole week, no less! – to the rather odd crew who had rolled in a couple of days ago. Even better, the guy who seemed to be in charge, Mister Ware, had said he didn't believe in credit cards – so he'd given Roy a non-refundable cash deposit big enough to cover the rooms, as well as any conceivable damage that the four of them could have done to the place. Hell, for that amount of cash, they could cart off the entire contents of each room, plumbing included, and Roy would still be ahead financially – with a bunch of catch that the IRS didn't have to know about.

They were a strange bunch, though. Mister Ware – a good looking fella in his mid-thirties – seemed all right, but the three who he referred to as his "charges" had made Roy a little uneasy. If they'd tried to register alone – without Mister Ware and all his cash, that is – Roy might reluctantly have told them he had no vacancies.

The one they called Jeremy had a boyish face but crazy eyes and the other man, Mark, had a big, muscular body but the kind of vacant look on his face that said not too much was going on upstairs. Then there was the woman, Elektra. She had a slutty way of dressing that Roy kind of liked, but her face reminded him of that movie he'd seen on HBO a couple of years back, about this crazy hooker in Florida who had killed a bunch of guys before being caught and electrocuted.

But appearances could be deceiving, as Roy would be the first to admit. They were religious folks, and if they were right with the Lord, then they were okay with Roy Hastings, too.

They must be Godly – Mister Ware had spent quite a bit of time talking with Roy about the different churches in town. He said that his little group were looking to settle in Oakley, and wanted to find the kind of church that would make them feel most welcome. He'd been very interested in the size of the congregations, and the number of people who usually attended Sunday services.

Roy, a Methodist, had answered as many of the questions as he could, and had even called a couple of friends who attended other churches to get more information. He hoped that Mister Ware and his group would find the kind of church they were looking for soon – Sunday was only three days away.

Fifty-Three

It took a while for Morris's nerves to recover completely, but after a week had passed from "The Night the World Was Supposed to End, But didn't," he no longer jumped at loud noises. There was, it seemed, no second shoe about to drop. The Apocalypse had been averted, although Morris would have been easier in his mind if only he could have understood *why*.

He would have welcomed the distraction of a new assignment, but none had been forthcoming. Things appeared to be slow in the ghostbusting business. Morris spent a lot of time searching online news sources for information about any new church burnings, but America's houses of worship had apparently been left inviolate following the destruction of Austin's only mosque.

Then he began to consider the possibility that the spell might not require the bloody pentagram to be drawn over a map of the U.S., and started to wondering if the one calling himself Theron Ware had set up shop in another country, there to begin his campaign of fire and murder afresh. But nothing showed up in the international news reports to confirm his fear.

Eight days after that chaotic, fearful night in Austin, Morris's shoulder muscles had finally unclenched fully, and he actually felt like eating a full meal, for a change. He was mentally running down the list of friends who might like to join him for dinner at one of the city's nicer restaurants when he got the call that made his body tighten up all over again.

"Mister Morris, this is Father Bowen. I'm relieved to hear your voice – I've been trying to reach you since yesterday."

"My phone's been on, far as I know, Father. And if this is about the *Corpus Hermeticum*, I already told you–"

"I'm not in Montana, Mister Morris – I'm in Rome. I have no doubt you would have answered my call if you'd received it, but the local phone companies are on strike. Their computers are still processing local calls, but international calls aren't going through – or haven't been, until now. Something about the satellite uplink. Same for email. I'm just glad I've finally reached you."

"What are you doing in Rome, Father? Trying to keep your job?"

"No, quite the contrary. I shall probably lose my job, at the very least, once the cover story I gave them falls apart, as it will, eventually."

"Now you've lost me. What cover story? To who?"

"To Cardinal Abruzzi, who is in charge of the restricted room of the Vatican Library. I told him there was some doubt as to the authenticity of volume five of the *Corpus Hermeticum* that we had in Montana, and I wanted to compare his version against ours, which I'd brought to Rome with me."

"But the one you had in Montana is missing."

"Cardinal Abruzzi doesn't know that – yet. But he allowed me access to the Vatican's copy on the condition that, when I'm done, I show him in person what disparities exist – by comparing the Montana copy, side-by-side, with the Vatican's. At which point my deception will be revealed, and I'll be forced to suffer the consequences."

"That seems like a big step you've made there, Father. I had the impression that you had no interest in taking any chances, the last time we spoke."

"My refusal has weighted heavily on me ever since then. I could not stop thinking of the consequences for the world if you were right, and I, in my arrogance and pride, were wrong. And I thank God for those sleepless nights now, for surely it was He who sent them."

"Why do you say that?"

"Because you *were* right. The ritual described in book five of the *Corpus Hermeticum* really *is* designed to open the Gates of Tartarus, allowing all the denizens of Hell to invade our world."

"Uh, Father, there's something you should know about that. Last week–"

"Last week, there was a mosque burned in Austin, where you live. Is that right?

"Yes, it is. And afterwards–"

"And afterwards, the world did not end, so you assumed you'd been wrong the whole time."

"Something like that, yeah."

"You *were* wrong, Mister Morris, but because only because you lacked all the relevant information."

"Father if there's a chase here, I'd suggest you cut to it."

"The Gates of Tartarus don't open after the fifth sacrifice, Mister Morris – but after the *sixth*."

"Sixth? But a pentagram's only *got* five points."

"True, but it also has a *center*. And according to the ritual, which I finished translating just yesterday, the sixth sacrifice must take place in the center of the pentagram that has been created by the points of the first five."

"In the center of the pentagram."

"Yes, and unlike the initial sacrifices, which called for the murder of a member of the clergy, this one calls for wiping out the entire congregation – by fire – while they are engaged in worship services."

"And the interval between five and six is still ten days?"

"Yes, which means the final sacrifice will take place the day after tomorrow."

"Where, exactly, do you know?"

"As I said, the phone and internet services have been unavailable here since I finished the translation. It is almost as if the Devil himself wanted to stop me from reaching you. I'm glad he has been thwarted."

"Father, your point is–"

"I couldn't remember the location of all five of the sacrifices, and have been unable to look them up on the internet that I had no access to. But I assume you have that information handy."

"Yes, I do. Hold on."

Morris was back on the line in four minutes.

"Looks like the center point is someplace in Kansas," he said. "It's not near any of the larger population centers, so I'm gonna need a more detailed map to figure out where, exactly. Unless you have any more information for me, I've gotta go now, Father."

"Go, then, Mister Morris. And may God go with you."

Fifty-Four

Twenty minutes after speaking with Father Bowen, Morris was on the phone again, calling the people who had joined him in Austin just over a week earlier.

And no one answered.

Morris hoped it was simply a question of Libby, Elly, Peters, Ashley, Fenton, and O'Donnell all being away from their phones, and that he wasn't an undeserving victim of the "Boy Who Cried Wolf" syndrome. But all he could do, in each case, was leave a message – which is what he did.

"*This is Morris. We were wrong – the gate to Hell didn't open the last time because there's one more sacrifice to go, in the center of the pentagram. This isn't speculation – I just heard from a priest who translated book five. And it's all going down Sunday, the day after tomorrow. Near as I can figure, the exact center is someplace called Oakley Kansas, a little burg in the northwest corner of the state. There's no air service, so I'm flying to Denver and driving the rest of the way. I need your help. I'm not sure I can take this guy by myself. I sure as hell can't sniff out black magic, and there's a dozen churches in Oakley to choose from. I need you to meet me, as soon as you can get there, at the Buffalo Bill Motel, a couple of miles outside Oakley. Please do this. We fought the good fight – or tried to – in Austin. We need to do it again, one last time. Otherwise it* will *be the last time – for all of us."*

Fifty-Five

THE FIRST PRESBYTERIAN Church of Oakley was located in a quiet block of Maple Street, and as the blue SUV drove slowly past Theron Ware said, "This should serve very well. According to Pastor Lewis, whom I phoned an hour ago, Sunday services start at ten thirty and attract between one hundred and fifty and two hundred self-righteous prigs who worship the Sheep-Savior."

Sitting behind Ware, Mark furrowed his brow. "He said that about his own church?"

Ware stifled the impatience he usually felt at Mark's stupidity. He could afford to be patient – success was very nearly at hand, and afterward he would never have to hear Mark's idiotic questions, ever again.

"No, that's my own interpretation of his remarks," Ware said. "The important thing is two hundred people, more or less, will be inside that building on Sunday. That's a manageable number, don't you think?"

Elektra was seated next to Ware. She peered through the side window at the building. "You think it'll be enough for… you know?"

"I'm quite sure it will be," Ware said. "Our master will be very pleased. And you will, *each of you*, receive your reward soon thereafter."

Fifty-Six

A GENTLE SNOW was falling as Morris pulled into the courtyard of the Buffalo Bill Motel at about four fifteen on Saturday afternoon. He slid the rental car into an open slot near the motel office and went inside.

"I've got a reservation," he told the clerk, a blonde, painfully-thin woman in her early fifties. "Name of Quincey Morris."

She consulted her computer. "That's right, Mister Morris. Got it right here. You'll be staying with us for two nights?"

"Yeah," Morris said. "After tomorrow, it won't... sorry – that's right, two nights."

"Would you fill this out for me, please?"

As Morris handed back the completed registration form, he asked, "Have you had any folks from back East check in today? New York, maybe, or Baltimore?"

She hesitated. "I'm not supposed to give out that kind of information... but, no – you're the only one's checked in all day, and I've been on the desk since six."

"Great," Morris said, although it was clear he felt

otherwise. "Tell me, have you got a list of the local churches? Tomorrow being Sunday, and all."

"You'll find that in your hospitality book, Mister Morris. Every room's got one – should be right on top of the little desk in there."

"Okay, fine. How about a town map – got any of those?"

"Yes, sir, got some right here. Have to charge you two dollars, though."

"No problem – I'm sure it's worth every penny."

The motel lady had told him true. In his room – which was larger and cleaner than he expected in West Podunk, Kansas – there was indeed a small desk, and on it a binder marked "Guest Hospitality." Mostly it contained ads for local stores and restaurants, but the last page was headed "Places of Worship." Listed underneath were the names and addresses of thirteen local churches. Morris wasn't superstitious, but he hoped the number didn't mean bad luck – either for him, or for the world.

He spent the next hour with the city map, marking on it the location of each church on the list. He wasn't surprised to find that all of them were of some Christian persuasion or other. Oakley had Catholics, Episcopalians, Baptists, Lutherans, Presbyterians, and a few that Morris wasn't sure about, like the Gateway Fellowship Church. Pity, in a way. A nice Buddhist temple would have been a likely target for Ware and made his job easier. But right now, it looked to him like *Mission "fucking" Impossible*. "Where the hell's Tom Cruise when you need him?" Morris muttered.

He tried to figure out something useful he could do by himself tomorrow morning. Just driving around town until he saw smoke billowing in the air seemed stupid and futile. Besides, by the time he saw smoke, it would already be too late.

Morris had brought the Desert Eagle, disassembled in his checked luggage. He'd halfway expected a hassle from TSA anyway, but they'd let the bag go through. Morris would have welcomed the chance to blow Theron Ware's brains out, but he didn't figure the demon was going to make himself a passive target, any more than Ashley would have.

He was contemplating the wisdom of calling in a bomb threat to every church in town tomorrow morning when there came a knock on his door.

He picked up the Desert Eagle, cocked it, and held it alongside his leg – just in case Theron Ware or any of his crew had decided to be proactive about their security. Morris placed himself against the wall next to the doorway, grasped the knob left-handed, and flung the door open, ready to deal with whoever, or whatever, stepped through it.

Nobody came through the door, but after a moment he heard a woman say, "Take it easy, cowboy. Nobody here but us good guys."

Morris carefully lowered the hammer of his weapon. He'd have known that voice anywhere. "Come on in, Libby."

Fifty-Seven

THOSE WHO WISHED to bring the world to an end were up early Sunday morning – although, in truth, only the one calling himself Theron Ware knew that was the real objective.

They made certain preparations to their motel rooms and left before dawn, without bothering to check out. It was still dark when they entered the First Presbyterian Church, bringing with them six large, brightly-wrapped, beribboned boxes. Each box, which would not have looked out of place under a Christmas tree, bore a card reading, "Do not open until after today's service."

The boxes were distributed at strategic points around the church. The locations were chosen to facilitate the spread of the fire that would break out during the morning's worship service. If some impatient soul tore off the wrapping early, he would find a container of hard plastic, sealed by magic and impossible to open.

The incendiaries in place, Ware and his group then broke into Wilson Tire Company, a low, wide building directly across the street from First Presbyterian. They did not turn on the lights, but there would soon be sufficient daylight coming through the windows for their purpose.

Ware opened a large, leather satchel and began to lay out the magical implements and ingredients for the final spell. He talked to the others as he worked.

"The church service starts at ten thirty. That is also the time when I will activate the spell that will ignite the devices we left behind at the motel. The resulting conflagration should draw every fire truck, ambulance, and police car in this town, and probably more. That will put them all several miles outside the city, and well out of our way."

"What time's the Big Barbecue start across the street?" Jeremy asked, with a tight grin.

"I want to allow for any late-comers," Ware said, "so we will start the ritual at ten forty-five. Or, rather, you will, my loyal and trusted friends. While you read aloud the text of the spell, I will use my magic to set off the incendiaries in the church, and then to keep the doors sealed, lest any of the *faithful* manage to escape their well-deserved fate."

"When's... *he* gonna show up?" Elektra asked.

"You mean My Lord Lucifer? Once the ritual is completed, and the good Presbyterians across the way have been reduced to charred bones and ash, things should start to happen."

"He oughta be pretty happy, with all the shit we done for him, the last few weeks," Mark said, his bravado as transparent as the store's large front window.

"I'm not sure happy is a word I would use in connection with My Lord Lucifer, but he should certainly be pleased with us – pleased enough to give us reward beyond measure."

"Anything we want, right?" Mark asked. "Money, pussy..."

"Power, like yours," Jeremy added.

So softly that only Ware could hear her, Elektra breathed, "Beauty."

"Everything you have ever dreamed of shall be yours," Ware said with a silken smile. "You have my word."

"What about you, Theron," Jeremy asked him. "What do *you* want?"

"I'll let that come as a surprise," Ware said. "But I guarantee you this – you will be in awe of what I will achieve. Literally."

"Sounds really cool," Mark said. "I can hardly wait."

"Nor can I," Ware said. "Nor can I."

Fifty-Eight

MORRIS AND CHASTAIN were up early, too – although, in truth, they had barely slept at all. Libby Chastain was up most of the night preparing contingency spells, and Morris was too tense to manage more than an hour's doze in his room's easy chair.

Through a combination of phone calls and checking several churches' websites, they had learned that the earliest religious service in Oakley this morning would be the eight o'clock mass at St. Joseph's Roman Catholic Church. The last, as far as they could tell, was the worship service at Kroner Baptist that began at noon.

Their strategy for preventing the end of the world had been articulated by Morris just after four in the morning. "We'll take separate cars and cruise the churches, beginning about seven thirty. If you get a whiff of black magic at any of them, you'll pull over and find a place to put the anti-combustion spell into operation. I'll keep moving, in case what you smell is a fake-out, like last time. If I find any church on fire, I'll call you on my cell, and you'll hightail it over there, while I try to disrupt their spell any way I can."

"And if the church where I am turns out to be the real deal, then I'll call you," Libby had said.

"And I'll get back there, quick as I can. I don't imagine Ware and his bunch will take kindly to having their plans disrupted, and you may attract some hostile attention, once they figure out that you're in the field."

"*Hostile attention.*" Libby had mustered a thin smile. "A fancy way of saying that they'll probably try to kill me."

"Yep – but I don't plan to let 'em," Morris said.

"Good."

Fifty-Nine

MORRIS HAD MAPPED out a route that would take them past all thirteen of Oakley's houses of worship. They began at seven thirty, with a slow drive past Saint Joseph's, where the first mass was due to begin in half an hour. Libby went first in her rental Buick, with Morris a few hundred feet behind in a Camry.

The first time they drove the circuit, it took twenty-two minutes. But then, they had to slow down to look for street signs. The second time, they made it in eighteen minutes. Traffic was light, that early on a Sunday, but they knew it would pick up as Oakley's God-fearing citizens started making their way to the religious services of their choice.

Midway through the third circuit, Morris picked up his phone and speed-dialed Libby.

"Hey, cowboy."

"How're you doing for gas, Libby?"

"Just over half a tank. You?"

"Closer to a quarter. Better pull into the next open gas station, so we can fill up. Be a shame to have the world end because one of us ran out of gas on the way to save it."

"Amen to that."

They stopped at a Shell station, bought gas and took a quick bathroom break. Then it was on the road again.

When nothing had happened by ten o'clock, Morris began to second-guess himself.

What if there's a church that wasn't on the motel list? Should've checked the list against the phone book, dammit. What if Theron fucking Ware drew his pentagram different from mine, and he's outside some church eighty miles away getting ready to tell every demon in Hell, "Y'all come on over!"

He kept these thoughts to himself. There was no point in messing with Libby's head, and besides, there was nothing else they could do right now, except keep on keepin' on.

Then at ten thirty-nine he saw Libby's brake lights come on. A moment later, his phone rang.

"Yeah?"

"I think I've got something," Libby said tightly. "I'm pulling over."

Morris did the same, and noticed that they were on Maple Street a few hundred feet down from the First Presbyterian Church. He sat with the motor running and waited.

Libby's voice came out of his phone speaker. "Definitely black magic. It's fresh, and it's close. I'm going to get out and look for someplace to set up for my anti-fire spell."

"Okay, I'll keep cruising," Morris said. "Call me when you're sure this is the big enchilada – if it really is."

"Will do."

Morris pulled into traffic, passed Libby's parked car, and kept going. He did not look back, no matter how much he wanted to.

Sixty

LIBBY CHASTAIN DROVE into the parking lot at First Presbyterian, found a parking spot, and popped the trunk. What she always thought of as her "magic kit" was in there, all primed and ready to go.

Libby opened the large briefcase and took out a small bowl. Into it she quickly poured a mixture of ingredients she had prepared the night before. Then she picked up a wooden match she had made with her own hands, sparked it alight with a thumbnail, and set the contents of the bowl burning. Thin white smoke rose from the bowl, gradually filled the trunk, and spilled out of the sides. Libby opened a small book to a page she had earmarked and began to read aloud in ancient Greek. Every few minutes, she stopped, picked up a small bottle of clear liquid, and added three drops to the bowl, whose contents continued to burn, producing more smoke than should have issued from the small amount of materials involved.

Across the street, Theron Ware stood behind the counter at Wilson Tires and said, "Got our little friend, Elektra?"

She passed him the small metal cage they had purchased at a pet store the day before. Inside it, a black and white rat sniffed the air curiously.

Ware grasped the rat's tail and lifted it out of the cage. "Begin!" he told the others.

As Elektra, Mark and Jeremy began to read the words they had practiced so often, Ware put the rat down on the counter. He grasped the rodent around the middle, picked up the sacrificial knife he was so used to employing on humans, and cut its throat. As the rat began thrashing in its death throes, Ware slit it open and, in one smooth motion, disemboweled it. The rat spasmed once more and lay still.

Ware would have preferred to sacrifice a clergyman again, but that wasn't practical this time. The rat would have to do. But soon every clergyman in the world would be at his mercy – his and that of the Master he served.

He set up two slim black candles and lit them by simply touching each with the tip of his index finger. Then came a small silver bell, said to be made from some of the same coins paid to Judas Iscariot so long ago. Ware rang the bell five times.

Finally, he produced a slim black wand, forked at the tip like a snake's tongue. As his minions continued the words of the ancient ritual, Ware stepped to the large window of Wilson Tires, which gave a clear view of First Presbyterian across the street. He pointed the wand at the building and said a word of power five times. That would set off the incendiaries inside the church. Soon he would be able to hear the screams. Remembering the fancy wrapping that hid the fire bombs, Ware stifled a giggle, along with the urge to sing a verse of "Happy Birthday."

Now it was time to magically bar the doors. He waved the wand in a broad "X" pattern five times, said another word of power, and pointed the wand at the church again. All three doors were now sealed – and if any of the panicking fools inside thought to get out by breaking windows, they would find that a very daunting task, thanks to Ware's spell.

Smoke should now be leaking out through the roof as the fire took hold inside. Ware looked upward – and saw nothing.

He stood watching for perhaps ten seconds then turned to his acolytes and shouted, "Stop!"

They looked toward him, shock on their faces, but did as they were told. In the quiet he should be able to hear the screams of people burning alive, and those about to be. Ware listened – and heard nothing.

His eyes bulged as he fought the fury that threatened to turn him into a raging lunatic. Now was not the time to give in to base impulses. He said to the others, "Something's wrong," and walked closer to the window. He scanned the street for the source of the interference, then looked over at the church building itself, finding nothing. His gaze continued moving right, to the parking lot adjoining the church – and in a moment, he saw it: a thin stream of white smoke coming from someplace out of his line of sight.

Ware was torn. He would have loved nothing more than to go over there and turn the interloper into a puddle of steaming goo, but he had to keep the spell going. The fire may not have started yet, but those doors had to remain closed. The last thing Ware wanted to see was those happy cretins cross the street leaving after the service concluded, oblivious of the doom that they had somehow escaped. He had to keep the containment spell in place – and as soon as the white magician was dealt with, the incendiaries would ignite and the barbeque – prelude to a much greater fire – would begin.

Ware turned to his minions, whose faces constituted three distinct studies in dismay and confusion. Pointing through the window he said, "Someone in the parking lot is blocking my magic, I don't know who or how."

Jeremy started to say something, but Ware's hand slashing through the air silenced him. "Whoever it is, he can't fight me and you at the same time. So go over and kill the motherfucker, then return here at once. Go on!"

"Where is he?" Elektra asked, ever practical.

"There's a plume of white smoke in the parking lot – he'll be under it."

"But boss," Mark said, "we ain't got no weapons."

"Then use your stupid fists!" Ware snarled. "Or pick up a rock and bash his fucking head in. Now go!"

As they started for the door, Ware said, "Elektra – take the sacrificial knife. If those two fools can't get the job done, then cut the bastard's throat with it."

"Absolutely!" Elektra dashed to the counter, grabbed the knife, then followed the others out to kill the interfering magician.

Sixty-One

Libby Chastain was focused intently on keeping her own spell going. She assumed that Theron Ware had already cast the spell to ignite the incendiaries she was certain were inside the church. If she relaxed her concentration for a second, Ware's spell would get through and the conflagration would begin. Libby had another spell that was designed to put out fires, but it would take a minute or two to cast – and a lot can burn in a few minutes.

The part of her mind still attuned to her environment heard running footsteps approaching and closing fast. She had a protection spell ready, but to use it she would have to relax her protection of the building. She assumed that was exactly what Ware had in mind. On the other hand, if Ware's creatures reached her, the spell she'd cast would stop with her heart.

Libby should have planned for this, but hadn't, and it was hard to think while using so much of her mind and will to maintain the spell holding back the fire.

The footsteps were close now, and she could hear labored breathing as well. She had just decided to let the spell go and protect herself, hoping to quickly extinguish the blaze once it started, when she heard a wet sound of impact.

A man's voice made a sound like "Uh!" and there was the sound of a body hitting the ground only a few yards away. The other footsteps slowed, and a moment later the "thud" was repeated and a second voice, also male, gave a loud grunt. There came again the sound of something heavy collapsing to the pavement.

Silence for a second or two. Then more footsteps, moving fast and very close now and a female voice screeching, "Fucking kill you!" and the wet sound came again and Libby's back and head were spattered with something that could only have been blood. Something heavy fell behind Libby, practically at her heels, and there was a clanging noise as a metallic object bounced off the pavement and was still.

Libby tried never to exult in the deaths of fellow human beings – for death was surely what she had just heard occur, several times – but she was relieved that the spell was still in place and would not have to be lifted, even for a few seconds. She would mourn the dead later – her job now was to prevent more people from dying.

Sixty-Two

INSIDE THE TIRE store, Ware had watched incredulously as the three dupes who had served him so well were gunned down by an unseen sniper. He'd heard no shots, which meant the shooter was either a considerable distance away or had used a silencer. From the angle the bodies had fallen, it was clear that the gunman was stationed behind the store and somewhere up high, probably on a rooftop. Ware had no intention of putting himself into the line of fire – but then, he didn't have to. He would go outside and, using the building for protection, lob fireballs toward the white smoke until its creator was destroyed. Then he could continue with the final sacrifice. Once that was completed, the sniper, along with all humanity, would have bigger things to worry about.

Ware stepped out onto the sidewalk. He breathed in, gathering his power, and prepared to send the first ball of fire hurtling toward his enemy. Then a voice to his right said, "I wouldn't do that, if I were you."

Ware immediately pivoted toward the voice and saw that its source was a woman – a beautiful blonde in a long, expensive-looking overcoat, unbuttoned down the front, standing fifty feet away. She carried no weapon that he could see and yet seemed utterly without fear, or even tension. This was puzzling, but Ware had no time for distractions. He would incinerate this bitch and get back to his main task.

The fireball he'd been about to fling across the street went flying toward the interloper instead, who calmly lifted one hand, palm outward. She said a word of power that Ware recognized and the fireball was suddenly flying right back at him. He pointed a finger at it, said two words, and the fireball disappeared.

Ware made a slashing motion with one hand, and said a different word of power. At once a hundred knives, each razor-sharp, were hurtling toward the blonde with blinding speed.

The woman extended a fist, said something that Ware couldn't hear, and the knives dropped harmlessly to the pavement. Then she pointed two fingers at his feet, said another word, louder this time, and the ground began to open right where he was standing. Ware pointed downward, clenched his hand into a fist, and said a word that caused the fissure to disappear.

Ware shunted aside the surprise and panic that threatened to grip him. He extended his left palm toward the woman, uttered a phrase in ancient Chaldean, and a bright bolt of energy, that would turn the woman to dust, shot forth from his hand. She lifted her own hand, palm outward, and another bolt of energy met his halfway. The two forces stopped, pushing against each other like evenly-matched football linemen, neither advancing.

Without dropping his hand, Ware focused his concentration for maximum power as he asked the interfering bitch, "What *are* you?"

Continuing to push against his attack with equal force, she said, her voice showing some strain now,

"Ashur Badaktu, one of the fallen, demon of the fourth rank."

Ware had a thousand questions about how one of his own kind had arrived here, and why she was opposing him, but all he said was, "Belial Frandola, demon of the fourth rank, at your service. Well, not really."

"So..." she said musingly. "We appear to be equals."

"That's right, you fool, so stop this stupid game of yours. You can't *possibly* harm me."

"No, but I can," said a voice behind him, and Ware had only begun to turn toward this new threat when Quincey Morris squeezed the Desert Eagle's trigger, blowing the top of Theron Ware's head into a hundred tiny pieces and sending his enraged spirit straight back to Hell.

The one hundred and seventy-nine people inside the First Presbyterian Church did not hear the shot, for the church organ was pumping and they were all busy singing, with gusto, "O God Our Help in Ages Past."

They would never know the unlikely forms that such help could sometimes take.

Sixty-Three

"Libby, can you do anything about the bodies?" Morris asked. "I'm not sure the local law would find our explanation convincing, even if it would be true, and I've had enough jail to last a lifetime."

Libby scratched her chin. "Discorporation would take a while, and there's no way of knowing when the church service is going to let out. I can do a transportation spell, though – move the bodies someplace else."

"Got any ideas where?"

"How about inside this place?" Ashley said, jerking a thumb at Wilson Tires. "Looks like Ware was using it as a base, anyway. Since I'm sure the good citizens of Oakley observe the Sabbath–" Ashley kept most of the sneer out of her voice "–the bodies won't be found until tomorrow morning."

Morris looked at Libby. "Gives us time to get out of Dodge," he said. "Or Oakley, as the case may be."

"All right, I'll go get started." Libby nodded toward what was left of Theron Ware. "Maybe you two could carry this one inside? It's only a few feet, and quicker than magic."

"I think we can manage," Morris said.

"No carrying necessary," Ashley said as she watched Libby head back to the parking lot. "Just open the door for me, and I'll float him in. Keep the blood off our clothes."

"Good idea," Morris said.

A few minutes later, all four members of the Theron Ware cabal had found a temporary resting place behind several stacks of all-weather radials.

Morris looked at Ashley. "I assume the rifle work was Peters?"

She nodded. "He's on the roof of an apartment building three blocks from here. Or he was. He'll probably be waiting at the curb when we get there."

Libby was scanning the street. "No surveillance cameras. I guess a town this small can't afford them."

"One less thing to worry about," Morris said. "Let's pick up Peters and get out of here."

"I'll ride with Libby," Ashley said.

As Libby pulled the Buick away from the curb, Ashley looked at her and said, "So, Libby, when am I going to show you my secret to multiple orgasms?"

Libby smiled without turning her head. "I'm pretty sure I know that particular secret already."

"Not the way I do it, you don't."

At the next red light, Libby looked at Ashley for a couple of seconds. "We both live in New York. I expect to be home in a couple of days – how about you?"

"Yeah, most likely."

"Then why don't you give me a call, later in the week?"

"All right," Ashley said, and smiled. "I believe I will."

Sixty-Four

PETERS SLID THE rifle case into the trunk of the rental Toyota before joining Morris in the front.

"Nice shooting," Morris said, and pulled back into traffic.

"Thanks. I wasn't sure how best to help out, but when I saw those three heading right for Libby, with one of them carrying this big pig-sticker, I figured I ought to discourage them."

"I'd say you did that, all right."

A few minutes later, Peters pointed off to the west. "Wonder what that is."

Morris looked and saw a large plume of gray smoke rising from someplace a few miles distant. "I wonder if that's Ware's diversion," he said. "Bastard. Hope nobody else died – there's been enough of that today."

"It explains one thing though – no cops."

"I hadn't thought about them, but you're right," Morris said. "And speaking of things I didn't think about – why didn't you call?"

"When?"

"When you got my message."

"You didn't say to call – you said to haul ass way the hell out to Kansas, so that's what we did."

"I didn't see you at the motel. Were they out of rooms?"

"Hell, we just got into town two hours ago," Peters said. "Our flight out of New York sat on the tarmac at LaGuardia for over an hour and a half, and that made us miss our connection in Chicago. Ashley wanted to turn everybody in the control tower into toads, but I convinced her that it would only delay things even more."

"Be kind of fun to watch, though."

"I understood the impulse, that's for sure. Anyway, when we found you'd already left the Buffalo Bill, we figured the action would all be in town, where the churches are. Guess we were right."

"And just in time, too. Thanks."

"*Da nada*. Stopping the end of the world was in our best interest too, you know."

"You two are a good team," Morris said. "And I meant to ask you – what have you and Ashley been doing since you got out of jail?"

"Living off the money and credit cards that Astaroth gave me when he sent me back to this side," Peters said. "But Ashley's starting to get restless."

"Not a good thing."

"She was saying that we ought to set ourselves up as occult investigators, kind of like you and Libby. I mean, who better to deal with the supernatural than a demon and a former damned soul, right?"

"Sounds like a perfect fit," Morris said.

"You won't mind the competition?"

"The way things have been going," Morris said, "I'm pretty sure that there's plenty of work for all of us, podner."

Sixty-Five

FENTON TOOK ANOTHER sip of Libby's excellent coffee and put the cup down, careful to use a coaster.

"So that's why we didn't respond to your message, Morris. No cellular service where we were. No bars at all."

"Alaska, huh?" Morris said.

"About eighty miles north of Nome," Fenton said.

"Sue sent us up there as soon as we got back from Texas," Colleen O'Donnell said. "I barely had time to do my laundry. But she had a good reason to be in a hurry."

"Some Eskimo shaman was fooling around with an old totemic ritual, and managed to raise up half a dozen dead folks," Fenton said. "Then the stupid bastard realized he didn't know how to control 'em."

"Zombies in Alaska," Libby said. "Who'd have thunk it?"

"Zombies in *northern* Alaska," O'Donnell said. "If I had any itch for Arctic exploration, that pretty much scratched it – for life."

"But you got it sorted out, I take it?" Morris said. "The zombies, I mean."

"Yeah, but it took us a whole week," Fenton said.

"Didn't even hear your voicemail until we got back to the lower forty-eight. Since the world hadn't ended while we were gone, I figured you'd managed okay without us."

"Just barely," Morris said. "Just barely."

"But you didn't ask Quincey to fly up here from Texas just to tell us about the zombies, did you?" Libby asked.

"No," Colleen said. "We're authorized to offer you guys some more 'consulting' work, if you want it."

Morris looked at Libby for a moment before asking, "What kind of consulting did you all have in mind?"

"Well, it's kind of complicated," Fenton said, toying with his coffee cup. "For starters – do either of you know what an *afreet* is?"

The End

MIDNIGHT AT THE OASIS

This is for
Kingston Ignatius Bleau

Welcome to the world, little man.

"No beast is more savage than man,
when possessed with power
answerable to his rage."

– Plutarch

"The purpose of terrorism is to terrorize."

– V.I. Lenin

"You can't put the genie back in the bottle."

– Larry Webster

One

May 1, 2011
0138 hours

THE TWO HELICOPTERS knifed through the still, warm air like vengeful ghosts, flying as close to the ground of Eastern Afghanistan as was safely possible. They were Sikorsky Black Hawks that had been extensively modified for missions exactly like this one. The alterations (all classified Top Secret) made the ships relatively quiet, hard to see from the ground, and virtually invisible to radar.

In addition to the helicopter crews, the mission personnel included twenty-four SEALs assigned to the Navy's Special Development Group (known to the media as SEAL Team Six), a dog named Cairo (for sniffing out explosives and tracking, if necessary), a Navy midshipman who was the dog's handler, a civilian translator fluent in both English and Arabic, and one other.

Thomas Powell was also a SEAL, his MOS listed as "Demolitions Expert." This was a lie, but a necessary one. Powell's real military occupational specialty did not appear anywhere in the Navy's official nomenclature.

Powell was a combat magician, and the object he held

across his lap was not an assault rifle. It was a carefully-designed, titanium magic wand.

Once intelligence reports had named a certain house in Abbottabad as Geronimo's likely hiding place, a Pakistani doctor on the CIA payroll had been sent in, on the pretext of vaccinating the house's residents. The visit had two purposes. One was to get miniscule tissue samples from each person vaccinated. Even though nobody thought the doctor would be allowed anywhere near Geronimo, the other people in the house were believed to be family members. If so, some of them would carry Geronimo's DNA, which the CIA had on file for comparison.

The other reason for getting the doctor on the property was to see if he brought back traces of black magic. There were whispers that Geronimo was protected by more than human power – which would explain why the old bastard had survived so long – and there were a very few people high up in the U.S. government who knew enough to treat such rumors seriously. To that end, the doctor wore under his clothing a very special amulet that had been programmed (the military's term for "ensorcelled") to be sensitive to the presence of black magic.

The "vaccinations" completed, the doctor had made his way to a nearby CIA safe house. There he had dropped off the tissue samples and taken off the amulet, worn on a silver chain around his neck. These materials were smuggled out of Pakistan in a diplomatic pouch, and were at Langley within forty-eight hours. There, a doctor with a Top Secret security clearance compared the harvested DNA with the known sample from Geronimo. Conclusion: suspicion confirmed.

In another part of the CIA's sprawling complex, an expert with a very different set of credentials examined the amulet, employing tools and procedures not to be found in any the Agency's manuals. Her conclusion was the same as the DNA expert's: suspicion confirmed.

As a result, Thomas Powell, the U.S. Navy's only SEAL-qualified combat magician, was quietly added to the mission's Table of Organization and Equipment.

Following completion of BUD/S, the immensely difficult SEAL training program (Powell's class had started with a hundred and thirty men and graduated fourteen), he had volunteered to spent six months in the United Kingdom, under the tutelage of a former SAS sergeant major who was said to be the greatest combat magician living. Powell never found reason to doubt that assessment. Once his magical training was completed, he had been assigned to one of the SEAL teams, with the understanding that he would be available for "special missions," as needed.

Lieutenant Brad Marcellus, the team leader in Powell's chopper, was checking the magazine of his H&K MP7A1 submachine gun for the fourth time when a voice spoke into his left ear. "We've just crossed into Pakistani airspace, sir," the pilot said calmly. "Estimated time to the LZ, sixteen minutes."

"Roger that," Marcellus said into his throat mike.

The risk factor of the mission had just ratcheted up tenfold. Since everybody from the Commander in Chief on down knew that notifying the Pakis about this mission in advance would have been tantamount to taking out a full-page ad in the *Islamabad Tribune*, America's nominal ally had been kept in the dark about the planned operation. That meant, technically, that the U.S. Navy had just invaded Pakistan.

In the unlikely event that the choppers were noticed by the Pakistan Air Force, the mission team had both fighter jets and helicopter gunships on call. Two heavily-armed Chinook helicopters containing twenty-four more SEALs were waiting in a deserted stretch of desert three miles away. They would be called in if Pakistani ground forces tried to intervene.

With this mission, the U.S. government was risking, at worst, war with Pakistan. But no one who knew about the mission had the slightest doubt that the objective was worth taking the chance.

In no time at all, the pilot's voice came through Marcellus's headset again. "Estimate one minute to the objective, sir."

"Roger." Marcellus turned to face the rest of the team. Raising his voice a little, he said, "Sixty seconds out and counting, people. If anybody wants to change his mind and go home, better speak up now."

That raised several grins, and a little nervous laughter. Every man in that chopper had volunteered for the mission. Even the dog would probably have signed up willingly, if you'd asked him. They had trained hard, assaulting specially-built replica buildings over and over again.

Operation Neptune Spear had been in the works for five weeks. Now it was showtime.

"We have visual ID of the objective," the pilot's voice said. "Beginning descent now."

"Doors open!" Marcellus yelled.

The SEALs seated closest to the large sliding doors on either side of the aircraft pulled them back, giving those inside a clear view of the rapidly approaching ground, and allowing them to lay down fire if a threat emerged from the compound while they were still in the air.

The plan was for the Black Hawk to land briefly in the compound's northeast corner and disgorge Powell and four other SEALs, along with the dog and his handler. The chopper would then rise again and hover over the house while the remaining SEALs inside fast-roped down onto the roof.

When Helmuth von Moltke said, "No battle plan ever survives contact with the enemy," he knew what he was talking about – even if nobody ever told him about magic.

Powell was staring out the portside door, scanning the compound for the kind of threat he had been brought to deal with, but it was one of the other SEALs, stationed at the starboard door, who spotted the first sign of trouble.

"Dude just came out of the house," said the SEAL, a Boatswain's Mate named McDonald. "Waste him, Lieutenant?"

"Is he armed?"

"Negative, far as I can tell."

"Then leave him until we're on the ground," Marcellus said.

"Roger that."

Something in the air made Powell uneasy. He turned in his seat and said to McDonald, "The guy you spotted – where is he?"

McDonald pointed. "There – about fifty feet from the front door." The chopper was about three hundred feet over the ground now.

"Got him." The man on the ground stood with his hands spread wide, as if in supplication or surrender. Powell recognized the posture; it represented neither.

"I think we better take this guy out, Lieutenant," he said urgently.

Before Marcellus could reply, there came the sound of a human voice, but amplified a hundred times, saying the same phrase, over and over: "*Harif men sama! Harif men sama!*"

All at once, the Black Hawk lost all power. Blades, rotors, electrical systems – all dead as a doornail. In the sudden silence, Powell could hear the pilot's voice clearly, even though the closed cabin door. "Brace for impact!"

Powell had an all-purpose counter-spell ready, and he said the words of power quickly, hoping to reverse the bad mojo that the wizard below had just laid on the helicopter. It worked – the blades began turning again – but the helicopter had already been in freefall for six seconds, which, that close to the ground, was four seconds too long. Their rate of descent slowed, but Powell could feel the tail dragging along the compound's concrete wall, and that meant they were screwed. A few seconds later, the ground came up and slammed the chopper to a halt, the noise bouncing off the high walls of the compound. Something snapped in the superstructure, and they abruptly listed to the left.

Marcellus was the first to find his voice. "Anybody hurt?" In SEAL terms, "hurt" meant broken bones or uncontrolled bleeding. No one on the team responded affirmatively.

Powell figured that things could have been worse. His counter-spell had turned a potentially fatal crash into something you might charitably call a hard landing – although it was clear that, if and when they extracted out of the compound, it wasn't going to be in this particular bird.

Marcellus started giving orders. "Out the starboard door, fast! Alpha Team first, then supplemental personnel, with Bravo Team last. Move out!"

"Supplemental personnel" meant the translator, the dog, his handler – and Powell.

A few seconds later, they were all on the packed dirt of the compound, the helicopter's tilted body between them and the house. The other chopper was hovering a couple of hundred feet above them, and the members of the other SEAL contingent were fast-roping to the ground.

Marcellus turned to Powell. "Was that what I think it was that brought the bird down? Some kind of magic?"

"I'm pretty sure that's what it was, sir."

"So they've got a fucking – whadoyacallit – wizard in here?"

"Yes, sir, I'm pretty sure that was the guy we spotted coming out of the house."

"Can you take him?"

The standard SEAL response to a question like that was supposed to be "Of course I can take him, sir! Hooyah!" But Powell figured that Marcellus would be better served by honesty than machismo. "There's no way to tell, sir."

Marcellus looked at him for a moment, then nodded. "Guess we'll find out." He turned to the rest of the group. "Chopper crew stays here. Braddock, Marshal, you stay with the bird, too. Prepare thermite charges to blow it, at my command. We can't fly it out, and we're sure not leaving it behind for the Pakis to sell to China."

He pointed to a smaller building within the compound. "Alpha Team, secure the guest house. Kill anyone who resists or shows a weapon." He indicated the translator and the dog's handler. "You two stay with Bravo – but be ready to come quick if I call. Powell, you're going in the big house with us. Let's move out."

Keeping to the shadows, they jogged in single file toward the three-story house and whatever awaited them inside.

Two

They used small charges of Semtex to blow the front door off its hinges, and went in fast, weapons at the ready. What they found inside was not what they expected.

The CIA had cut electrical power to the house a few minutes before the raid team had arrived. Each man had a powerful flashlight attached to the barrel of his weapon. A dozen bright beams crisscrossed the room, to reveal... nothing.

The ground floor appeared to be one huge room with plain white walls, a dirt floor, and a whole lot of emptiness. There was not even a staircase leading to the second floor, which was ridiculous, since there obviously *was* a second floor.

"What the fuck, Lieutenant?" one of the SEALS said.

"Wait one," Powell said, and reached into one of the canvas pouches riding on his web belt. The other members of the team used these containers to carry extra ammunition, but Powell's contained materials far more unusual – and just as dangerous.

From the pouch Powell brought out a glass vial whose contents seemed to glitter like flakes of silver. He poured most of the powder into his open palm and flung it into the air in a wide arc. While the powder was still airborne he said, loudly, "*Vascate*!"

At once the large empty room disappeared, replaced by a smaller one that looked like a living room. It contained traditional Arab furniture, cheap art on the walls – and a set of stairs leading up.

"An illusion," Powell told the team.

Several of the SEALs stared at Powell, but Marcellus broke their bewilderment. "Check the other rooms first. This floor's gotta be secure before we go upstairs. Come on, let's go!"

They cleared each of the ground floor rooms the way they had been taught – overlapping fields of fire, watching each other's back, being wary of booby traps.

"Floor's clear, Lieutenant," one of them told Marcellus ten minutes later. "Not a creature stirring."

"The fuckers are upstairs, then," Marcellus said. "Let's go find 'em. Fire Team One goes first." He pointed at Powell. "I want you with them, third in line. Just in case."

"Aye, aye, sir," Powell said. He looked toward the stairway grimly. The magician defending this place was good – there had to be more tricks up his sleeve than a simple illusion spell. *Well, I've got a few tricks up my sleeve, too, motherfucker.*

They made their cautious way up the stairs without drawing fire of any kind. The second floor presented them with three closed doors and a corner where the hall bent to the right. "Team Two checks the rooms. Team One, keep that corner covered," Marcellus said softly. "Anybody comes around it who doesn't have his hands up, zap him."

Powell was getting a lot of bad vibes from around that corner. He didn't believe in intuition, but his witch sense was well developed. Something bad was close by – he could *feel* it.

The three rooms were checked and found empty. Marcellus was about to give the order to continue when Powell said softly, "I've got a bad feeling about what's around that corner, Lieutenant."

Marcellus looked at him. "That's it? Nothing more specific?"

"No, sir, but I've learned to trust my feelings when it comes to stuff like this."

"Well, we can't fucking stay here all night." Marcellus thought for a few seconds, then motioned for one of the team members to join him.

"Martinez, you're carrying the telescopic mirror?"

"That's affirmative, sir."

"Unlimber it. I want to know what's around that corner."

"Aye, aye, sir."

Martinez slipped off his pack and removed from it several sections of aluminum tubing and a mirror about the size and shape of a dinner plate. The tubes were threaded so that they screwed together, like a custom-made pool cue. Within a minute Martinez had six feet of tube assembled, the mirror securely attached at the end. He walked to the corner, put his back flat against the wall, and slowly extended the mirror until it could reflect what was in the corridor, if anything was.

Martinez watched his mirror, and Powell watched him. He saw Martinez squint, apparently unsure of what he was looking at – then his eyes grew wide, as if he realized he was seeing something that had no business being in that house, or any house, ever. Powell was about to sidle over next to him and ask what was going on when a great tongue of flame shot down the corridor from the direction Martinez was looking.

The flare of light and heat lasted only a second or

two. The carpet was smoldering a little, sparks winking in it here and there like fireflies, and Powell could see that the wall was scorched in places – but nothing was burning. Yet.

Martinez had quick reflexes, and he had yanked back the pole holding the mirror as soon as the flames had appeared. But all he held now was about four feet of aluminum tubing. The rest of the pole, along with the mirror it had carried, was a small pool of molten metal, gently steaming on the corridor's carpet.

Martinez turned toward Powell, and the expression on his face was one that Powell never expected to see on a Navy SEAL. It combined shock, confusion, and – most improbably – fear.

All the other team members had their weapons trained on the bend in the hallway, ready to repel the assault that was sure to follow the gout of flame. But no attack came.

Marcellus looked at Martinez and made a summoning motion. Although not invited, Powell decided he'd best join the upcoming conversation.

Marcellus led them into one of the rooms that had already been cleared, but kept the door open; if anything happened in the hallway, he wanted to know it instantly.

"How many of them did you see?" Marcellus asked softly. "Besides the guy with the flame thrower, I mean."

Martinez seemed to have his feelings of shock and awe under control now, but he still looked uneasy as he said, "Weren't no flame thrower, Lieutenant – not the way you mean it. Weren't no guys, either."

Marcellus looked at Powell. Then he turned back to Martinez and said, "Just tell us what you saw, or think you saw. I don't care how fuckin' wacko it sounds – just tell it."

Martinez cleared his throat. "It looked –" He stopped, then tried again. "It looked like... a fucking *dragon*, Lieutenant!"

Marcellus kept his face impassive. "A dragon," he said flatly.

"I know it sounds psycho, sir, but –"

"Just do what the Lieutenant said." Powell kept his voice calm, even though his mind wanted him to start screaming. "Tell us what you saw."

Martinez swallowed, his prominent Adam's apple bobbing up and down. "Okay, like I said, it looked like some kind of dragon, right out of the movies – green, scales, fangs, the whole nine yards. And the fire that zapped the mirror – that came from its mouth, I swear."

"Anything else you noticed?" Powell asked him.

"Well, I only got a couple seconds' look," Martinez said, "but I'm pretty sure the fuckin' thing had, like, wings."

Marcellus took in a breath and let it out slowly. He looked at Powell. "You figure they got another illusion going on, here?"

"No, sir," Powell told him. "I'm pretty sure what they've got is a fuckin' dragon."

Three

MARCELLUS RUBBED HIS right temple, as if hoping to pull a solution out of his mind by main force. SEALs, especially officers, are trained to make quick decisions, but even BUD/S doesn't address the tactical problem of how to overcome mythological reptiles.

"So, what do I tell those guys out there?" he asked Powell. "That we're gonna launch an assault on a fuckin' *dragon*?"

"You could, sir, but I wouldn't advise it."

"You wouldn't advise *telling* them?"

"No, I meant that I wouldn't advise launching an assault."

"Explain that."

"I'm no expert on these things, sir – they don't appear very often. I'm not even sure if our weapons could harm it. Maybe, but maybe not. Anyway, you saw what happened to the mirror. Anybody who turns that corner is gonna be instantly incinerated."

"So, how would you suggest we carry out our mission? And we *will* carry out that mission. For SEALs, failure is not an option – and that's *especially* true this time."

"I know that, sir," Powell said. "And I think I've got an idea."

"Tell me."

"The dragon was summoned – or created, I don't know how these things are done – by the same guy who brought down our chopper and set up that illusion downstairs."

"Their magician."

"Affirmative. He's the key. Destroy him, and the fruits of all his magic disappear – including that thing around the corner."

"Fine, we'll destroy the bastard. How do we find him?"

"I figure he's pretty close to the dragon – probably behind it. Something like that beast, you can't control it from a distance."

"That's not real helpful, Powell. If he's behind the dragon, and we can't take down the dragon, that means we can't get to him."

"*We* can't, sir – but maybe I can."

"How?"

"From behind."

"How the fuck are you gonna do that? There's no way to approach that hallway from the other side. You've seen the builder's plans, same as I have. There's no stairs on that side."

"I wasn't planning to use stairs, sir."

Walking through walls is not impossible, for a trained magician – but it is dangerous. Aside from casting the spell properly, the practitioner must give his passage through the foreign matter every iota of his concentration. Otherwise, he might materialize too soon and join his atoms with those of whatever substance he was trying to pass through. The result would mean his death, or something far worse – his consciousness could become part of the wall itself, in effect burying him alive until the day, perhaps decades from now, when someone knocked the wall down and set him free. Unless, of course, there was a fire in the meantime.

The other problem, assuming you got through, involved where you ended up. If you were dumb enough to pass through a fifth-story wall, you were setting yourself up for a five-story plunge to the ground. Go through the wall of a furnace room, and you just might find yourself inside the furnace.

Powell was reasonable certain that the wall he was looking at was the one where the hallway terminated on the other side – the hallway containing the dragon, and presumably the wizard controlling it. Go through the wall, and come out behind the wizard and his fire-breathing pet. In theory.

The element of surprise should give Powell the advantage in the confrontation to follow. The Arab wizard might well have defensive spells ready to go, but he wouldn't be expecting attack to come from his rear. Probably.

Powell took off his pack and set it down. The more weight he was carrying, the harder it would be to pull this off. He stepped to the wall, stopping when his nose was just a few inches from the plaster. In one hand he held his wand; the other hand gripped a SIG Sauer P226 automatic, the SEALs' favorite all-purpose handgun.

Powell took a deep breath, closed his eyes, and began softly to recite the words of the spell.

Two minutes later, Powell sensed that his feet were on solid ground and opened his eyes. It seemed that luck was with him, since 1) he had apparently picked the right wall, 2) he had made it through said wall with all his parts and implements intact, and 3) neither the dragon nor the wizard who controlled it seemed to be aware of his presence – yet.

Martinez had not been exaggerating what he'd seen. *Yep, that's sure as shit a dragon, all right.* Imagine Godzilla's little brother, except in green. Now give him wings, big pointy ears and the ability to spout fire from his mouth. What Powell was looking at was like that, except ten times worse. Then there was the odor – at close range, the dragon smelled like a fishing boat full of mackerel that had been left in the sun for three days.

The wizard, who was crouched next to his noxious pet, appeared to be one of Geronimo's Saudi countrymen – at least, he was wearing the long white cotton *thawb* that is the standard in that country. He wore a red and white check head cloth, held in place by a double circle of black cord.

Powell must have made some kind of sound, or maybe the wizard simply felt his presence – some of them can do things like that. The man, who looked to be in his sixties, rose from his crouch, turning toward Powell as he did so. A fierce battle of magicians, East versus West, might have ensued, and Powell seriously considered taking part. Then he reconsidered.

Take too long. Besides, I might lose.

Powell quickly brought up the SIG Sauer, and shot the old man in the chest. Twice.

At the sound of the shots, the dragon's head turned toward Powell. It gave a roar that shook the walls, and Powell figured that the fire breath would be next. He realized that he had neglected to prepare a spell for this eventuality, and was about to pay for his stupidity by dying in the most painful way possible.

Then the wizard, who was sprawled on the floor bleeding, kicked his legs a couple of times and was still – and the dragon, whose image would haunt Powell's dreams for years to come, disappeared into thin air.

Powell stared at the place where, a moment earlier, his death had been standing. Then he looked at the wizard, dead in a pool of his own blood. With a deliberate effort, he pulled himself together and prepared to continue with his mission.

"All clear!" he yelled, or tried to; his voice just now would barely have carried across a small room. Powell drew more breath into his lungs. "*All clear, Lieutenant. I got the bastard!*"

Martinez appeared cautiously from around the corner of the hallway, surveyed the scene for several seconds, then withdrew.

A few seconds later, Marcellus appeared. He began walking rapidly toward Powell, then paused to call over his shoulder. "Come on, let's go!"

When Marcellus reached him, the first thing he said to Powell was, "Are you okay?" Receiving an affirmative response, he then asked, "What's that you've got all over you?"

Powell realized he was covered with a fine white powder. "Must be plaster dust," he said. "Picked it up on my way through."

"You actually did it, didn't you? Walked right through a fuckin' wall."

"Yes, sir."

"Outstanding work." Marcellus turned to look at the still form on the floor. "And that's the wizard, huh?"

"Yes, sir, although we were never formally introduced."

"I'd say you gave him all the introduction he needed. And the dragon – there really was one?"

"Affirmative, sir. If my buddy over there had taken another two seconds to die, I figure I'd have been guest of honor at my own personal barbeque."

"Glad he didn't linger, then." Marcellus looked at the nearby flight of stairs. "That the only way up?"

"Far as I know, yes, sir."

"That means Geronimo is up there someplace, and it's time for us to complete our mission."

Marcellus turned away from Powell then, and began to deploy his troops for the final assault.

Four

43 hours later

Excerpt of President Robert Leffingwell's
Address to the Nation
Delivered live, via television

My fellow Americans:

Tonight, I can report to the American people and to the world that the United States has conducted an operation leading to the death of a terrorist who has been responsible for the murder of thousands of innocent men, women and children, both in the United States and abroad. It was more than ten years ago that a bright September day was darkened by the worst attack on the American people in our history. The images of that day are now part of our collective national memory: the hijacked planes; the twin towers burning like funeral pyres; black smoke billowing up from the Pentagon.

The men who carried out these brutal attacks did not represent the Arab people or the religion of Islam.

Rather, they reflected the terrible, twisted vision of a single man – a man who has finally faced the justice that was promised by my predecessor on the day those attacks occurred.

Two days ago, elements of our special operations forces conducted a raid on a house in Pakistan, a building that was located after more than a year of intense work by our intelligence agencies. After a brief firefight, our troops killed the man who was the mastermind behind the attacks that ended the lives of so many Americans, and scarred the souls of so many more...

Five

April 9, 2012

AT A LITTLE after 4:00 p.m., the avenger was sitting at an outdoor café in Paris's eighteenth *arrondissement*, reading one of the city's many Arabic-language newspapers. A man in his mid-fifties, Dr. Abdul Nasiri had coal-black hair and a full beard, both lightly sprinkled with the gray of middle age. His blue pinstripe suit was of excellent quality, and his Rolex watch had an alarm that reminded him five times daily of the time for prayer.

In the unlikely event that someone was keeping track of such matters, at that moment in time Abdul Nasiri could be considered the third most dangerous man in the world. The dubious honor of first and second place would have been awarded to North Korean President Kim Jong-un and Ayatollah Khomenei, Supreme Leader of Iran, respectively. If Dr. Nasiri (Ph.D. in Anthropology earned at the Sorbonne, no less) was aware of his distinction, he bore the knowledge lightly.

Nasiri had taken a vow on the day he learned of the death of the man whom he revered above all others. He had seen on Al Jazeera the video of the American president; the dog had been barely able to contain his joy as he reported the Sheik's death to the world.

They believe that the struggle died with the Sheik, in that house in Pakistan. They think they are safe now. They will soon learn otherwise.

Six

AT 4:15 PRECISELY, another man approached Nasiri's table. Nasiri saw him, stood, and extended a hand.

"Peace be upon you, brother," he said in Arabic.

"And upon you also," the other man replied. He carried a small suitcase, which he set down in order to shake with Nasiri. He could have carried the suitcase in his left hand, but he came from people for whom the left hand has only one purpose, and old habits die hard.

Nasiri invited his guest to sit, and signaled a waiter to bring more tea. They would not speak of important matters until the waiter was again out of earshot.

The tea was delivered, and the guest added milk and sugar and took a long, appreciative sip. Jawad Tamwar's hair and beard were darker than Nasiri's – this was unsurprising, since he was only forty-two years old. His suit, however, was clearly of inferior quality. Tamwar cared little for what westerners would call the finer things in life. He was a man in love, and committed deeply to that love. His demanding lover was jihad.

Jawad Tamwar had what some might have considered a checkered past. Born in Pakistan to a wealthy family, he had spent three years at the National University of Sciences and Technology before dropping out to study instead at a Saudi-funded *madrassa* that had taught him to embrace Wahhabism. This stern, radical branch of Islam holds that it is the will of Allah for the devout to destroy infidels. In the mid-1990s, Tamwar had been a star pupil at the al-Qaeda training camps in his native country, then spent several years as a bomb specialist for Hamas in Lebanon's Beqaa Valley. Later, he helped fight against the American occupation of Iraq, under the notorious Abu Musab al-Zarqawi, from 2003 until the latter's death in 2006.

In 2007, Tamwar made his way to Paris, in the hope of joining a jihadist organization there. Finding no such entity in the French capital, he had tried to start one among the city's more radical Arab students. This effort brought him to the attention of the French security forces, and consequently he spent two years in Clairvaux Prison on sedition charges.

When Nasiri found him in 2010, Tamwar had been living in a Paris slum, broke and near-starving. Since that time, Jawad Tamwar's fortunes had improved considerably.

When he was certain that the waiter was out of earshot, Nasiri said, "So, my brother, what news do you bring me concerning our mutual... project?"

Tamwar put down his half-empty cup and said "I can report success in some aspects – but, I regret, only in some."

Nasiri's eyes narrowed. "Explain."

"First, I can tell you that the account we had from our source in Kabul was true, despite the doubts that both of us had."

"I had assumed that was the case," Nasiri said archly. "Otherwise, nothing else you had to tell me could have been considered a 'success.'"

Tamwar bobbed his head. "Yes, yes, of course."

"So, the old man actually did it – he managed to capture an *afreet.*"

"This I can say with certainty," Tamwar said, "for I have seen it with my very eyes."

"There are many clever so-called 'magicians' in that part of the world," Nasiri said. "Are you quite certain you were not taken in by some clever conjuring trick?"

"Absolutely certain, my brother. Not only did the *djinn* come forth from the lamp when Hosni summoned him, but –"

"Wait!" Nasiri said, slapping the table lightly. "Are you saying that this creature actually resides in a *lamp*? As was related in the *Thousand and One Nights*?" He gave Tamwar a very direct look. "I will not insult you, my brother, by asking if you are making sport with me."

Nasiri was asking *precisely* that – and if he did not like the answer, the consequences were likely to be severe.

"I am aware of how ridiculous it sounds," Tamwar said. "And I asked the old man a question very similar to the one you just asked – or rather, did not ask – me."

"Yes – and?" Nasiri's look of impending doom was still very much in place.

"The choice of vessel was Hosni's idea of a joke. He thought it would be amusing to confine the creature in an old oil lamp, like the one described in the story of Aladdin. He said he wished to show respect for what he called 'literary tradition.'"

Nasiri made a derisive sound. "He is a fool."

"In some respects, yes," Tamwar said. "But the fool has nonetheless captured an afreet, and I swear to you that it is genuine."

"And how did you establish that?"

"First, as I began to relate, I saw the thing issue forth

from the lamp as smoke or fog, and then assume an aspect quite marvelous to behold."

"Describe this aspect."

"It had the shape of a man," Tamwar said, "but taller – by at least three meters."

"So, about five meters in all?"

"So I would estimate, my brother."

"What else?"

"He had great horns issuing from his head. They curved back upon themselves, like those of a ram."

"Indeed," Nasiri said. "And were there any other features of note?"

"Just one more – the afreet was *made completely of fire.*"

That caused Nasiri's eyebrows to rise. "Fire? Truly?"

"Indeed. It was difficult to look upon without sunglasses. Fortunately, I had a pair with me."

Nasiri nodded slowly. "It makes a certain amount of sense. The Holy Qur'an tells us that the djinn were made of smokeless fire."

"A fair description, brother. Although the thing was made of flames, no smoke issued forth from it."

Nasiri stroked his beard. "I suppose there is no possibility that the old man somehow hypnotized you into *believing* you saw a horned creature made of fire?"

"I had prepared for that possibility," Tamwar said. He reached for the suitcase that sat next to his chair and pulled it into his lap. He clicked the latches, reached in, and removed an oddly-shaped object, which he put on the table between himself and Nasiri.

It was an irregularly-shaped lump of metal, about the size of a large apple. Nasiri took it from the table and examined it closely for nearly a minute before looking up. "And what is this you have brought me, brother?"

"It may be more useful," Tamwar said, "to tell you what it once *was* – a steel bar, about half a meter in length."

Nasiri peered again at the object in his hands. "It looks as if it has been put through a blast furnace."

"In a sense, it has," Tamwar told him. "I told Hosni that I wished the afreet to melt it for me, and he bid the creature to do so." He gestured toward the hard, shapeless blob. "That took, perhaps, five seconds."

"Five seconds," Nasiri said. "Allah be praised."

"I thought that, given our ultimate purpose, it would be useful to see how the afreet's power could affect steel. I grant this is a much smaller quantity than we have in mind to subject to the creature's power, but I found it an impressive demonstration, even so."

"Even so," Nasiri agreed. "We must have this power at our disposal. I assume you have taken the appropriate steps to obtain it."

Tamwar shifted in his chair. "That is where matters become... complicated," he said. He did not meet the other man's gaze.

Slowly and with great deliberation, Nasiri placed the chunk of melted steel back on the table. "Explain."

"I offered Hosni a great deal of money for the vessel containing the afreet," Tamwar said. "Money that, under certain circumstances, I might even have been willing to pay. But he would have none of it."

"What is this man," Nasiri asked, "an ascetic? He has no interest in money?"

"On the contrary, he likes money very much – likes it to the point of greed."

"He wanted you to pay more?"

"No, he did not wish to sell it at all. He said he would be happy to direct the creature to do our bidding – for the right price. But he insisted on retaining ownership."

"This is unacceptable," Nahiri said. "You know as much."

"I do, yes. That is why I returned the next night, and brought Mujab Rahim with me."

"Ah, Mujab, excellent. He has a way of... cutting through difficulties."

"It was my intent to have him cut through the difficulty posed by the old man's throat, as soon as I had secured two items. One of these, the lamp containing the afreet, was obtained without difficulty – it was in the same place the old man had showed me the night before."

"You *had* the lamp, yes? What else did you want of Hosni?"

"The means to command the lamp's inhabitant."

Nasiri frowned. "I thought whoever held the lamp was in control of the afreet."

Tamwar shook his head. "I regret to say that what was written in the *Thousand and One Nights* does not always apply in this world where we live. But Hosni had already showed me what he used to control the afreet – a small piece of the Seal of Suleiman."

Suleiman is the Arab name for Solomon the Great, king of ancient Israel.

"It is said that Suleiman was able to command many djinn to obey him," Nasiri said musingly. "There is even an account of an afreet who strove to win Suleiman's favor by fetching for him the throne of the Queen of Sheba, which he did in the twinkling of an eye."

"Hosni told me that the great Suleiman once imprisoned an evil djinn in a bottle whose seal was stamped with the image on his ring," Tamwar said. "I do not know whether this is true, but I saw Hosni command the afreet by holding a small fragment of what he assured me was the King's Seal."

"It must be very old," Nasiri said. "Three thousand years, or more. I am surprised that there are any still extant."

"The old man said that he knew of several more, in the hands of private collectors or museums."

"How large was this fragment?" Nasiri asked him.

"About the size of a man's thumbnail. But he said one must be a wizard in order to compel the afreet with it."

"We *have* a wizard," Nasiri said. "Sharaf Uthman is well accomplished in the black arts. What we do *not* have, as I understand it, is that piece of Suleiman's Seal, and I want to know *why* we do not have it!"

Tamwar spread his hands apologetically. "It was my intent to obtain both the lamp and the Seal when Mujab and I returned to Hosni's dwelling place. We overpowered the old man easily enough, and the lamp was exactly where it had been on my prior visit. But of the fragment of the Seal there was no sign."

"The old man must have hidden it. Did it occur to you to *ask* him?" Nasiri's scorn could have curdled milk.

"Of course we asked him, brother. And when he refused to tell us the location of the fragment, we stripped him and tied him splayed out on the top of his dining table. Then Mujab went to work with his knife."

"Mujab can be very persuasive," Nasiri said. "Do you mean to say that he failed to break this old man?"

"He never had the chance," Tamwar said. "After perhaps five minutes of Mujab's ministrations, Hosni expired."

"He *died*?" The scorn in Nasiri's voice was replaced with disgust. "What happened – did that fool Mujab let his knife slip?"

"No, brother. He was not even working near a vital organ when Hosni stopped breathing." Tamwar shrugged. "Unless one considers the penis a vital organ. In my opinion, the old man suffered a heart attack. We attempted to revive him, but..." He made a helpless gesture.

Nasiri seemed to be controlling himself with an effort. "You searched his dwelling?"

"With great thoroughness. We found neither the fragment nor any sign of where it might be hidden."

"You said this fragment was quite small. He might have swallowed it, or stuck it up his ass. Did you check?"

"Yes, brother, we did." Tamwar made a face, as if certain unwelcome images were coming back to him. "Nothing."

Nasiri nodded. He spent perhaps half a minute staring into his empty cup before declaring, "We need more tea."

When the waiter had come and gone once again, Nasiri said, "You have done well, brother. I do not mean to suggest otherwise. You have delivered into our hands a weapon that will make the crusaders' women weep."

Nasiri drank some tea then said, "The trigger of this grand weapon is a fragment of Suleiman's Seal. The one that Hosni possessed is apparently lost to us."

Tamwar started to apologize, but Nasiri stopped him with a raised hand. "This simply means that it is up to us to find another."

Seven

The present day

THE FBI'S BEHAVIORAL Science Unit is located in the basement of the FBI Academy in Quantico, Virginia. Perhaps unconsciously reflecting the problems with which the unit deals, the halls of Behavioral Science constitute a maze of corridors and passageways that seemingly follow neither rhyme nor reason. One of the more innocuous jokes about the building goes, "Whenever the rats in the Psych Department at UVA get too smart for the mazes, they send 'em over here."

Some of the office doors down in Behavioral Science have signs; others have name plates. But the majority of the offices, conference rooms and labs are identified only by a number. One such room is 0138, the office shared by Special Agents Colleen O'Donnell and Dale Fenton. The anonymous door looks no different from any of the others, except someone has applied to it a sticker about the size of a silver dollar that reads, "What would Mulder and Scully do?"

Neither Fenton or O'Donnell had put the sticker there – but they hadn't removed it, either.

Fenton arrived for work a little after 9:00 to find his

partner already in their office, absorbed in something displayed on the screen of her laptop. He said, "Hey, Colleen," and received a distracted-sounding "Hey" in return.

Fenton hung up his coat, sat down behind his cluttered desk, and looked again at his partner. "What's so interesting?" he asked. "Something to do with work, or are you looking at lesbian porn movies again?"

"I never watch that stuff at work anymore – I told you that," she said absently. It was one of several running jokes they had between them.

Colleen sat back in her chair, closed her eyes, and rubbed them gently. "Somebody hit the Oriental Institute a couple of nights ago."

"Oriental Institute? Sounds like someplace where they study kabuki theatre and karate," Fenton said.

"In this case, 'oriental' refers to the Middle East," she said. "I guess it's the original usage of the term. The Oriental Institute is a museum and research center attached to the University of Chicago."

"Okay, so person or persons unknown broke into some museum in Chicago. Why should we care?"

"Because of what they stole and the way they stole it," she told him.

"I'm sure you're gonna elucidate that for me, but before you do, tell me one thing – how do you even know about this? It doesn't sound like something the Chicago field office would be investigating."

"They're not, far as I know," she said. "But the Chicago police are, and a member of the Sisterhood is fairly high up in the city government out there. She heard a few things about the break-in, got a copy of the Chicago P.D.'s file on the case, and sent it to me."

Colleen O'Donnell was a white witch.

"If the Sisterhood's interested, must be something spooky about this break-in," Fenton said.

"It's no third-rate burglary," she said. "*Pace* Richard Nixon."

Fenton grinned. "Sounds like our kind of case," he said. "Maybe you'd better tell me about it."

Colleen glanced at her laptop's screen. "One interesting feature was the way the thief or thieves gained access to the building."

"What's interesting about that?"

"Nobody can figure out how they did it," she said. "No windows or doors smashed, no locks jimmied, no breach of the roof or basement."

Fenton nodded slowly. "You're thinking it was magic."

"That's one explanation," she said. "Or it could just be a master thief who's so good, he can get in and out without a trace. If that was the only interesting feature, I doubt that Greta would have bothered to contact me."

"Greta's the Sister in Chicago."

"Uh-huh."

"So, what else about the case is bothering her?"

"The thief or thieves ignored some very valuable artifacts, including a bunch of diamond-encrusted jewelry dating back to the Caliphate period. They headed straight for the" – she checked her computer monitor again – "Archaeological Iron Storage Research Project, which is located in the basement. Once again, they got past a couple of good locks and an expensive alarm system, without leaving any sign of how they did it."

Fenton frowned at her. "This Archaeological Storage Project –"

"Archaeological Iron Storage Research Project," she said.

"Whatever. It doesn't sound all that sexy, you know?

Not like the kind of place somebody would go to a lot of trouble to rip off."

"I'd tend to agree with you," Colleen said, "if I didn't know that the thieves took just one item, and what that item was."

"Stop milking it for suspense, Colleen. What'd they get?"

"The only thing missing was a single piece of metal," she said. "Very, very old. Greta says there's been some disagreement among the experts at the Institute as to what it is, but the majority opinion seems to be that it's a fragment of the Seal of Solomon."

Fenton stood up slowly and walked the few paces to where Colleen was sitting. He went behind her chair and bent over so that he could read the screen of her laptop along with her. For his benefit, she went back to the top of the report and slowly scrolled down. Then she showed him the long e-mail she'd received from her sister witch in Chicago.

Fenton straightened up, his back creaking a little, and went over to lean against the door, next to the shelf containing Colleen's collection of Buffy action figures.

"That business about the Seal of Solomon kinda fits in with the security briefing we got a couple of weeks ago, doesn't it?" he said.

"Yeah." She gave him a fleeting smile. "Kinda."

Fenton studied the tops of his highly-polished black wingtips for a few moments. "You didn't say anything about those two security guards," he said mildly.

"I was getting to them," Colleen said.

"Throats cut, ear-to-ear. They probably bled out in less than a minute." He shook his head slowly. "Seems to me that somebody who's good enough with magic to get past all those security precautions should have been able to deal with a couple of guards without killing them."

"You'd think so, wouldn't you? Sounds like somebody enjoys using a knife a little too much. And there's this."

She scrolled through the report some more, then stopped. "The blood spatter analysis. Their tech, some guy named Morgan, is pretty good. He figured out from the blood smears that both bodies had been moved slightly after death, as if they were being repositioned."

"Repositioned how? You mean he posed them?"

"No, the only thing it accomplished, apparently, was to change the way they were lying on the floor. Morgan doesn't know if it means anything, but when the perp was done, both bodies were facing east."

"East?" Fenton pulled at his right ear a couple of times. "You mean, toward the sunrise?"

"That's one possibility," Colleen said. "But it reminded me of something I vaguely remembered reading, so I did a little digging around on the 'Net."

"Digging around? How long have you *been* here, anyway?"

"Since about 6:30."

Fenton looked at her for a few seconds in silence. "Bad dreams again?" he asked softly.

Without meeting his eyes she said, "Yeah, whatever," and gave a tired shrug.

Colleen was an survivor of child abuse, and often suffered from nightmares in which her father played a starring role. He thought, not for the first time, that if the old bastard wasn't already dead, Fenton might feel obligated to pay a visit to Pittsburgh and kill him.

The last thing Colleen wanted from him was sympathy, so in a businesslike tone he asked, "And what did your excavation of the Internet turn up?"

"I bookmarked the page. Just a second." After some

pointing and clicking, she said, "It took me a while, but I finally got to the *halal*."

"Congratulations. You gonna tell me what that is?"

"The Moslem dietary code. Analogous to the kosher rules that Orthodox Jews are supposed to follow. In fact, very similar. Moslems and Jews have more in common than either like to admit, sometimes."

"So these are rules Moslems use in preparing food?" Felton was starting to wonder where this was going.

"Exactly. And I was especially interested when I came to the *dhabihah*. Before you ask, that's the procedure to follow when you're slaughtering animals for meat, like cows and goats."

"Oh." Fenton thought he could perceive her destination now, and he didn't much like it.

Colleen squinted at the computer screen and said, "Listen to this: you're supposed to use a very sharp knife and make a quick, deep cut that severs the windpipe, jugular vein, and carotid artery. The idea is to make death as quick and painless as possible, but also get all the blood out of the animal before it dies. Blood in meat is considered unclean."

"Okay, I can see the connection with the murder of the two guards," Fenton said. "But come on, Colleen. There are only so many ways to cut a guy's throat. Doesn't mean the perp was imitating Moslem ritual butchery."

"Maybe not," she said. "But remember how the bodies were found? They'd been turned to face toward the east."

Fenton felt a chill traverse his spine. "Yeah, so?"

"So, according to the *dhabihah*, the devout butcher says 'In the name of Allah' as he swipes the knife – and he's supposed to be sure that the slaughtered animal is facing toward Mecca."

Fenton studied his wingtips a bit more. Then he sighed and said, "Feel like a trip to New York, drop in on some friends?"

"I thought you'd never ask."

Eight

AND THAT IS how Fenton and O'Donnell found themselves in the Big Apple a few days later, having mid-afternoon coffee with Quincey Morris and Libby Chastain in the living room of Libby's condo.

After some friendly shop talk about their recent cases (Morris and Chastain had been coping with murderous witchcraft in Kansas, while O'Donnell and Fenton had recently fought brain-hungry zombies in Alaska – which shows that not all occult detection takes place in New York or L.A.), Colleen O'Donnell leaned forward in her chair and said, "We're authorized to offer you guys some more 'consulting' work, if you want it."

Morris looked at Libby for a moment before asking, "What kind of consulting did you all have in mind?"

"Well, it's kind of complicated," Fenton said, toying with his coffee cup. "For starters – do either of you know what an *afreet* is?"

Morris scratched his cheek. "I've heard the word somewhere, but..." He turned to Libby. "Some kind of djinn, isn't it?"

Libby was frowning. "Yes, one of the nastier varieties, if I remember right. Some kind of affinity with fire, I think." She said to Colleen, "I didn't get an awful lot about them in my training – did you?" As white witches, Colleen and Libby had each received considerable instruction in arcane lore en route to mastering the Craft.

"Not very much, no," Colleen said. "But I've done some research recently, and I think the reason so little is known about them – in Western magical tradition, anyway – is that the djinn tend to avoid humans."

"I've never had to mess around with them myself," Morris said, "so I'd guess you're probably right." To Libby he said, "Something I've never been real clear about – is 'djinn' just another name for 'demon'?"

"No, not really," she said. "I believe they're considered a separate species – wouldn't you say so, Colleen?"

Colleen made a face. "As usual, the various sources don't agree. Some of the traditions lump djinns in with demons, but you're right, Libby. Most of them don't."

"I've been reading the same stuff that Colleen has," Fenton said. "At least, I do when I can make sense of it. Way I figure it, the smart money holds that djinns are supernatural creatures, very powerful, but they don't live forever, the way demons do. Some of the sources say their lifespan is double that of a human's, others say that it's closer to five hundred years. But they *are* mortal."

"If it bleeds, we can kill it," Morris muttered.

Libby turned to him. "Sorry?"

Morris shook his head slightly. "Just quoting an old movie."

"Well," Libby said to Fenton, "now you know how much we know about afreets – which amounts to not a whole heck of a lot. Does that end the conversation, or do you want to tell us why you asked, anyway?"

"Oh, we'll tell you," Fenton said. "Partly because it would be good for us to get your thoughts on the case, and partly because we hope you'll *take* the case."

"What you and Quincey know about afreets is still more than most people," Colleen said. "And you two are more qualified to take on an investigation like this than anyone else we know."

"Slow down, the both of you," Morris said. "Investigation of *what*? Has somebody seen an afreet shopping in the kitchenware department at Macy's, or something?"

"Wish it was that simple," Fenton said. "What we're trying to do is put together a puzzle. We only have a few pieces so far, so we don't know what it's gonna look like. But what we can see right now looks... troubling."

"Then maybe you'd better show us the pieces you *do* have," Libby said.

"Be delighted to," Fenton said. He emptied his coffee cup, and sat back. "One of the pieces comes to us courtesy of U.S. counterintelligence," Fenton said. "The information I'm about to give you comes care of the CIA, our very own FBI, and, the NSA."

"NSA?" Libby said. "I'm not familiar with that one."

"NSA is the National Security Agency," Colleen said. "Not very cloak-and-dagger, those guys. They sit down there at Fort Meade, Maryland, with about a zillion computers, monitoring communications traffic from all over the world."

"Didn't they cause something of a ruckus during the Bush Administration?" asked Morris. "The second one, I mean. For listening to people's conversations without warrants?"

"They only need a warrant if either half of a communication exchange – the sender or receiver – is in the U.S.," Fenton said. "But, yeah, for a while there I guess they didn't bother, even though the special FISA court that grants warrant applications has never, ever said 'No.'"

"But everything's above-board and legal these days," Colleen said, managing to keep a perfectly straight face as she did so.

"Absolutely," Fenton said. He didn't crack a smile, either. "But the point is, one of NSA's missions is to monitor what's called 'terrorist chatter' – phone, text, and internet messages among people who are on somebody's list of bad guys."

"Considering how many bad guys there are out there, that must amount to a hell of a lot of data," Morris said.

"It sure does," Colleen said. "But the computers are pretty good at separating the wheat from the chaff. Usually."

"And most of the wheat goes to the CIA for translation and analysis," Fenton said. "And lately, they've been finding some interesting patterns."

"Interesting in what way?" Libby asked.

"You have to understand," Fenton said, "that these guys – meaning jihadists – talk in code, even on networks they believe to be secure." He grinned. "Just as well for them, of course, since nothing is all that secure, any more. Anyway, for the last six months or so, a phrase has begun cropping up in some of their most 'secure' communications: 'midnight at the oasis.'"

Morris and Libby looked at each other in puzzlement. After a moment Morris, who was older, said, "Wasn't that a pop song over here, back in the 'eighties? Sung by Maria somebody."

"You don't quite win the trivia context," Colleen said, "but you're pretty close. There was a song popular on the charts here in 1974 called 'Midnight at the Oasis' by a woman called Maria Muldaur. It was her only hit song."

"So what are you telling us?" Morris said. "That the jihadists are listening to golden oldies now?"

"Possible, but unlikely," Fenton told him. "Most of the guys giving us trouble in the Middle East these days weren't even born in 1974. We've researched the song, the writer, and the artist, and haven't turned up a damn thing that would link any of them to some dude, or woman, whose last words are likely to be '*Allahu akbar*.'"

"The phrasing could be coincidental," Colleen said. "I mean, considering the part of the world we're talking about. But in any case, it's clearly code. We can be fairly certain that if somebody's planning something nasty, it won't take place at midnight, and the location won't be a watering hole in the fucking desert somewhere."

"A reasonable conclusion," Libby said. "But what's this got to do with afreets?"

Fenton leaned forward. "Well, here's the thing: the translators have identified another word that has been showing up in the chatter, usually in the same sentence with 'midnight at the oasis,' and that one is 'dromedary.'"

"A dromedary's a type of camel, isn't it?" Libby said. "It seems of a piece with the 'oasis' reference."

"Yeah, sure," Fenton said. "Entirely consistent. But this is where we had some luck. You remember that raid a team of Navy SEALs conducted in Pakistan a while back – when they took out –"

"– the most wanted man in the world," Morris said. "'Course I remember – it was a huge news story. So?"

"So, the SEALs," Fenton said, "being highly-trained, intelligent guys, took back with them everything in that house that wasn't nailed down – and probably a few things that were. The CIA people have been going through it with fine-toothed combs ever since."

"And here's where the luck part comes in," Colleen said. "One of the computer disks the SEALs brought back was apparently some kind of codebook. The file had been corrupted, so they weren't able to get all of it, but they did retrieve some interesting bits and pieces. And one of those was the information that 'dromedary' was their code for 'afreet.'"

Morris nodded slowly. "Okay, so you now have a link in terrorist chatter between 'midnight at the oasis,' whatever that is, and a powerful kind of djinn." He spread his hands a little. "But I'm still not sure what all the fuss is about, guys. Talk is cheap, and I reckon that's true whether the dialogue is in English or Arabic. It's probably just some jihadist's fantasy."

"I might be inclined to agree with you, Quincey," Fenton said. "But there's one piece of this puzzle that you haven't seen yet, and I think it makes all the difference."

"Four nights ago," Colleen said, "one or more thieves broke into the museum of the Oriental Institute in Chicago. Despite the name, this place specializes in the Middle East, not the Far East. Part of the museum's research center is something called the Archaeological Iron Storage Research Project. My understanding is that's where they store the really old metal objects, under ideal conditions of temperature and humidity. If you've got an artifact that's five thousand years old, you don't want it deteriorating any more than it already has."

"Do they actually have some?" Morris asked. "Five thousand-year-old relics, I mean."

"I believe they do," Colleen said. "And some that may be even older still – although now they've got one fewer than they used to."

"Somebody got in there and ripped one off," Libby said.

"You got it," Colleen said. "Somebody who was able to get past a lot of fairly sophisticated alarms without leaving any trace at all."

Libby tilted her head a little. "Magic?"

"It seems likely," Colleen said. "But there's more."

"The magician, or maybe one of his buddies, likes to use a knife," Fenton said. "He cut the throats of two guards from behind. And once they'd bled out, he arranged the bodies so that they were facing toward Mecca."

Morris and Chastain exchanged looks, but said nothing.

"And here's the kicker," Colleen said. "Only one thing was taken from that room. Although not all the experts who've examined it agree, most of them are of the opinion that it was a fragment of the actual Seal of Solomon."

"Well, shit," Morris said.

"I take it you understand the significance, Quincey," Colleen said.

"They used to say Solomon could command demons, didn't they?" Morris said somberly.

"Them – and djinn as well," Fenton said. "According to the Qur'an, anyway – which I'm inclined to regard as a reliable source in this instance."

"I begin to see your concern, guys," Libby said. "Some of the connections are a bit tenuous, but it's a reasonable assumption that some would-be terrorists have got themselves an afreet, and now also possess the means to control it."

"Especially since one of them apparently has some skill at magic," Colleen said.

"Even worse than that," Morris said, "is the fact that you're no longer dealing with a bunch of guys in Saudi Arabia or Yemen or someplace, whose phone calls the government's listening to from seven thousand miles away."

"You got that right," Fenton said with a grim nod. "These bastards are right fucking *here*."

"But why do you need Quincey and me?" Libby asked. "This sounds like the kind of thing you guys investigate all the time."

"Normally we would," Fenton said. "But the Counter-Terrorism Division is all over this one. If they find us on the trail as well, our boss is going to have a hell of a problem explaining what Behavioral Science is doing there."

"And Goddess help them if they do manage to find these people," Colleen said. "I mean, what're they going to do against an afreet, which they don't even believe exists? It'll be a massacre."

"The afreet is kind of the ultimate weapon of mass destruction," Fenton said. "So, will you guys take this on? I hate to use tired clichés like 'Your country needs you...'"

"But your country needs you," Colleen said.

Morris asked Fenton, "Does it need us badly enough to pay five hundred a day, plus expenses?"

"Sure," Fenton said. "We burn up more than that just turning the lights on for an hour."

Libby turned to Morris with a slight smile. "What do you say, cowboy? Time to saddle up and get back on the trail?"

"I reckon it is," Morris said. He was not smiling at all. "I reckon it is."

Nine

Morris helped carry cups, saucers and plates (Libby had served some of her famous cheesecake) into the condo's kitchen. As they loaded the dishwasher, Libby said, "So a group of terrorists have got themselves a pet afreet. Putting aside the question of what we'll do about that when we find them –"

"You don't know?" Morris asked. "I was hoping you'd have that part all worked out by now."

"*Me*? I thought figuring out how to destroy the creatures of the night was *your* department," she said, smiling.

"I'll have to get back to you on that." Morris rinsed off a plate and handed it to her. "Anyway, you were saying..."

"I was saying that I don't even know how the heck we're going to *find* them. I've got a feeling that looking up 'afreets' in the *Yellow Pages* isn't likely to be too helpful."

"You don't think so?" He gave her the last coffee cup and turned off the water. "Well, so much for *my* plan."

Libby briefly assessed the half-full dishwasher, and closed the door. "But seriously, folks ..."

"But, seriously, I think our FBI friends sometimes have a tad too much faith in our ability to pull the solutions to nasty problems out of... thin air."

She gave Morris another smile. "I thought for a second you were about to say 'out of our ass.'"

"I thought about it," Morris said. "But I'm trying to be a little less vulgar when I talk."

"Good fucking luck with that," she said.

"With you as an inspiration, Libby, how can I fail?" Morris shook his head in mock despair. "But I still think Colleen and Dale might be expecting too much from us."

"Maybe that's because we've always managed to overcome the forces of evil so far," she said.

"A streak of luck only lasts until it's broken."

She looked at him. "What's got you all morbid, all of a sudden?"

Morris gave a shrug, but didn't say anything. He appeared to be finding Libby's garbage disposal to be of intense interest. Libby decided to wait him out.

After a little while, Morris said, "I was going through my wallet last night – you know, throwing away some of the accumulated junk – and I came across an old business card." He looked at Libby. "It was John Wesley Hester's."

Hester had been a British occult detective, and a friend of Morris's. He'd died while investigating a case of demonic influence in England, as Morris had learned only a few weeks earlier.

Libby was silent herself for a bit, then she said, "I kind of liked John Wesley. He was a good guy, for the most part."

Morris gave her a look. "For the most part?"

"Well, there was that time in London when he had one Scotch too many and grabbed me on the ass."

"You mean a couple of years ago, when we went over there on that Castor thing? You didn't say anything at the time."

She tossed her head, slightly. "Didn't seem worth mentioning, at the time."

"Did you slap him? You should have."

"No, but I did threaten to turn him into a toad if he ever did it again. That seemed to do the trick."

"You never turned anybody into anything in your life, Libby," Morris said with a frown.

"True," she said. "But John Wesley didn't know that."

Morris chuckled. The chuckle quickly turned into a laugh, and that got Libby started. The two of them stood in her kitchen, mourning the dead by laughing their asses off.

As Morris fetched out a handkerchief to dry his eyes, he said, "Oh, John Wesley. He could be an asshole, sometimes."

"A good man, nonetheless," she said.

"Yeah, I know," he said.

"He died doing the work he was born to do, Quincey. The same work your family's been doing for – what – five generations?"

"Yeah, five, if you count the guy who died outside Castle Dracula."

"You once called it 'the family business,' and you were right. It's what you do. It's what *we* do."

He gave her a lopsided smile. "Yeah, it is, isn't it?"

"And the reason we've survived this long has nothing to do with luck – it's because we're good at what we do. You and me, Quincey Jonathan Morris, we kick ass."

It was a full-on grin he gave her this time. "Yeah, you're right, Elizabeth Catherine Chastain. Kicking ass is what we do."

She took in a big breath and let it out. "Then let's find this fucking afreet, so we can kick its ass, too."

"Sounds like a plan – or it would, if we actually *had* a plan."

"I've got one – well, not a plan, but at least a starting point."

"That's more than I've got, so let's hear it."

She leaned against the range. "We travel so much, it's hard to tap into any informal sources of information."

"There's the Internet. We could just Google 'afreet.'"

"Yes, and I plan to. But that only gives us access to the public stuff. We both know that there's some kinds of information that nobody's going to post online. Ever. Fortunately, we have a friend who's plugged into a *lot* of the private stuff. Or 'the weird shit,' as he likes to call it."

"Barry Love, everybody's favorite occult private eye."

"None other. Barry might well have heard something useful – or if not, he probably knows somebody who does."

"It's worth asking him, that's for sure." Morris reached for his phone, thought a moment, and put it back in his pocket. "No point in calling him. He doesn't like talking on the phone unless he initiates the call. And he doesn't have voice mail – I think he's afraid someone will leave a curse along with his messages, or something." He checked his watch. "He's usually in his office late at night. Want to head over there with me, about ten?"

Libby bit her lip for a second then said, "I can't tonight, Quincey. I – I have a date."

Morris looked at her. In a flat voice he said, "Do you now."

Libby crossed her arms over her chest. "I have the right to a private life, Quincey."

"I know you do."

She made an attempt at a smile. "It's just that I'm

getting kind of tired getting myself off with the Hitachi all the time."

"That's too much information, but I understand, Libby."

"Do you?"

He shrugged. "I'm doing the best I can."

"It's not like I'm getting in over my head. I know how to take care of myself."

"I'm sure you do. And I hope you will."

"Count on it."

"Okay, then." Morris began to walk toward the kitchen door. "I'll see if I can catch up with Barry tonight. Give me a call at the hotel tomorrow, and I'll let you know what I find out, if anything. Okay?"

"Of course. Let me –"

"It's all right," Morris said. "I know my way out."

So she stayed where she was, arms crossed, leaning against her four-burner range. A few moments later, she heard the condo's door open and close.

She stayed that way for several minutes, looking at nothing. Then she sighed, and went off to take a shower, her second of the day. Her lover didn't care about body odor, but Libby had always been fastidious about such things – even when she was dating human beings.

Ten

MAO TSE-TUNG HAS famously written that "The guerrilla must move among the people as the fish swims in the sea." Dr. Abdul Nasiri had read Mao, as well as Che Guevara, Frantz Fanon, and other masters of guerrilla warfare. Although he held neither the intention nor the hope of fomenting a revolt against the crusader government of the United States, Nasiri understood the value of protective coloration. That was why he had chosen Dearborn, Michigan as his base of operations.

The ninety-eight thousand or so people who live in this Detroit suburb include at least forty thousand Arabs and persons of Arab descent. Many of them are Lebanese, whose forebears came to America in the first half of the twentieth century, drawn by the hope of employment in the auto industry. But the last fifty or so years have seen an influx of immigrants from all over the Arab world. Dearborn today constitutes the largest Arab community in the United States.

Nasiri had dispersed his small group of jihadists around the city as they all waited for the day of vengeance. He had provided each man with money to live on, although he had encouraged them to blend in by finding jobs in the community. A man with a job does not face questions about where his money comes from.

He had himself found employment as an adjunct faculty member at Detroit's Wayne State University, teaching Middle Eastern history and culture to young idiots who were utterly oblivious to the fact that their privileged lives were built on the misery of a people most of them had never even heard of, let alone met. Nasiri could have cheerfully slit each of their throats – especially the females, immodest trollops who labored under the absurd delusion that they were the equal of men. He kept his rage in check by imagining the shock and sorrow that would be stamped on their faces on the day they learned of the revenge that Nasiri's cohort had wrought upon their infidel dog country – in memory of the man known to jihadists as the Sheik, but more important, in the glorious name of Allah.

The job at Wayne State was such perfect cover that Nasiri had violated one of the core principles of operational security, bringing his group onto enemy ground so far in advance of the strike. Proper procedure would have called for all of them to remain outside of America until the summer, to minimize the chance of discovery by the authorities – but the teaching position had been available for the spring semester, which meant it started in January. Had he waited, Nasiri might have been forced to accept employment in some menial position that would be an affront to his dignity.

Although he kept them separated for security reasons, Nasiri liked to bring his men together from time to time, to remind them that they were united by a shared purpose and that their labors in the land of the Great Satan would soon bear glorious, bloody fruit.

They met in a different location each time, always a

public place, summoned by Nasiri's text message on two hours' notice. On this day the venue was Omar's Al Shabash Restaurant, a small place on Warren Avenue, just a few blocks down from the Islamic Center of America, North America's biggest mosque. Omar's was rarely crowded at three o'clock on a Saturday afternoon, and a small gratuity to the owner guaranteed Nasiri and his friends a table far enough from the other customers to allow conversation in privacy.

Nasiri arrived half an hour earlier than the others. This allowed him to stake out the table he wanted and to determine if anyone appeared to be taking undue interest either in him or the restaurant. If he found any reason to expect surveillance, a simple coded text to the others would instruct them to abort the meeting and expect further instructions later.

But Nasiri saw nothing to cause him concern. The meeting would take place as planned.

Jawad Tamwar was the next to arrive, as had been planned. He spotted Nasiri at once, but did not approach his table. Instead, receiving Nasiri's nod, Tamwar went to the counter and purchased a kabob-to-go. He would eat it at a bench outside, watching the others arrive to see if either of them had attracted undue attention – or a tail.

Mujab Rahim walked in five minutes later, exactly on time. He exchanged polite greetings with Nasiri and sat down, ordering a Coca-Cola from a waiter. Although Coke was available worldwide under various names, Rahim had discovered the cold, sweet beverage only recently, and had apparently developed a fondness for it. It was rare to have the opportunity to discern Rahim's feelings about anything. The man's thin face, with its improbably blue eyes, was always impassive, and would doubtless have remained so whether he was eating a meal, having a woman, or cutting an infidel's throat – although Nasiri suspected, quite correctly, that Rahim would have enjoyed the latter activity far more than the others.

Ten minutes later, Sharaf Uthman joined them. He was the oldest of the group, and he had been a practitioner of black magic for the last twenty-six of his sixty-four years. It was his magic that had circumvented the locks and alarms at the Chicago institute, allowing them to retrieve the fragment of metal said to be part of Suleiman's Seal.

Uthman could have magically overcome the guards that night, leaving them harmlessly unconscious for hours – but Rahim had insisted on solving the problem with his knife, and Uthman had decided not to gainsay him. Even with his abilities, the magician thought it wise to walk carefully near the empty-eyed Rahim.

Uthman ordered a cup of black tea and sat fidgeting until it arrived. The tea was followed moments later by Jawad Tamwar, who had left his post outside now that the last of the group had arrived.

"All is well, brother?" Nasiri asked him.

"All is well," Tanwar assured him, which meant neither of the other two had been followed. Tanwar ordered green tea and had just begun to sip it when Nasiri turned to Uthman, looked at him quizzically and said, "You seem ill at ease today, brother."

The wizard nodded glumly and said, "There is a... problem that has arisen with Rashid."

Rashid was the name of the afreet, as it had informed them on one of the few occasions that it had been allowed out of its lamp-prison. Since Uthman possessed magical skills – and was the only one among them who spoke the ancient Arabic dialect that was the afreet's sole language – he had been entrusted with the creature's care and security. In an effort to make sure the afreet would obey his commands on the day of vengeance, Uthman periodically allowed the creature to leave the lamp – after first surrounding it with a circle of salt beyond which no djinn might venture. Uthman also had the piece of Suleiman's Seal that he had helped purloin from the museum in Chicago. That kept the afreet under his control.

The first time Uthman had called the creature forth from the lamp, he had taken a grave risk, as he had been fully aware. If the artifact was a fake, or if for some reason the salt circle did not contain the afreet within it, Uthman could have suffered an instant, fiery death. But such was his commitment to jihad that he had taken the chance – and Allah had given him success. But that success, as he had recently learned, was not absolute.

Nasiri was staring at him now, and the expression on that face would have frightened a lesser man. Truth be told, it made Uthman a bit uneasy, too. "You will speak to us of this 'problem.'"

Uthman nodded hastily. "Of course, my brother. Last night at midnight I allowed the –"

"Rashid." Nasiri's voice cut in like a scimitar. "You call him Rashid."

"Forgive me, my brother," Uthman said. "I allowed Rashid to venture forth from... his dwelling. As usual, he tried to bargain for his freedom..."

Eleven

Fifteen hours earlier

"I WOULD GRANT thee all that thy heart desirest, o great wizard," thundered the double-bass voice of Rashid the afreet. **"All thou needst do is free me from this prison, that I may return to my own place, and my own kind. But before departing, it would please me to bring thee all good things that thou might wish."**

They were in the garage of the small house that Nasiri had rented for Uthman in one of Dearborn's quieter neighborhoods. Each time before summoning forth Rashid, Uthman invoked a cloaking spell to cover the inside of the garage, lest the afreet's mighty voice should awaken the entire block.

"I have told thee before, mighty Rashid," Uthman said, "that I may not free thee before the task that I will set thee is complete. Elsewise, my life would be forfeit at the hands of my master, a man of fearful disposition. And I know thou art indeed powerful, but only in the matter of fire. It may be that some of thy brethren could deliver to me wealth, power, and a *hareem* of comely maidens. But thine own talent is to burn, and nought else. Let us not feign otherwise between us, for deceit is an offense against Allah, before whom all creatures, man and djinn alike, must be obedient and humble."

"Then mayest thou at least speak to me of this great task thou wouldst have me perform as the price of my freedom? Thou hast said little of it to this time, and I would know its nature."

"Since thy gift is for fire, then it is fire that I would have of thee. There is a great building – in this land, but far removed from here. At a day and time that has been chosen by my master, I would have thee unleash flame mighty enough to destroy this great structure, and all who may be found within it. Then thou wilt be set free, to return to thine own folk, far from the affairs of men."

The afreet studied him. "A great building, as thou sayest. And how many cubits doth it measure, from the ground to the sky?"

"I cannot answer thy question in numbers of cubits. Indeed, I know not the exact length and width and height of this structure. But I have images of it that thou mayest study – behold."

Uthman reached into a nearby cardboard carton and removed several sheets of paper. Each was an image of the same building, but seen from different angles. Uthman had simply found them online and printed them. Many photos and artists' renderings were freely available to anyone with an internet connection.

There was no point in handing the papers to the afreet. For one thing, Uthman knew how unwise it would be to pass any part of his body over the ring of salt. For another, he was quite certain the paper would burst into flame the instant that the afreet touched it. So he contented himself with displaying the photos for the creature's perusal, slowly, one after another.

"A great structure, indeed," Rashid rumbled. "Grander

even than the Caliph's palace in days of old. And doth each of those tiny squares thou hast shown me represent a chamber where a man might dwell?"

Uthman realized that Rashid was referring to the building's many windows, which could be seen in the photos. The structure was going to be used for commerce, not apartments or condos, but Uthman saw no reason to confuse the issue.

"Aye, great Rashid. Each of those shows a single chamber. The building is perhaps one of the largest to be found in this land of infidels."

"Then I must tell thee that what thou askest is not within Rashid's power. I will be unable to do thy bidding and make of this building a tower of flame."

"*What!* Do not defy me, disobedient one. Thou wilt serve my will on the appointed day, lest I smite thee unbearably!"

As long as the afreet remained under his control, Uthman could use his magical ability to cause the creature great pain, as he had demonstrated the first time he had summoned it forth from the lamp – just to make clear who was in charge.

"Smite me as thou wilt. It changes nought. I do not defy thee, o mighty wizard. Rather, I am unable to carry out the task which thou hast set me."

"But thou art Rashid the Mighty, before whom the whole earth once trembled!"

"Aye, 'twas once true – all who looked upon Rashid feared him, and with reason. But I have been confined within the lamp for many centuries, without nourishment. It shames Rashid to say that he has grown weak with the passage of so much time."

Uthman's mind raced. If he reported to Nasiri that the afreet would not carry out vengeance on the crusaders as had been planned for so long, Uthman's life would almost certainly be forfeit. Nasiri would either disbelieve him, and kill Uthman for incompetence – or he *would* believe Uthman, and realize that the wizard was of no further use to him. Either assessment would mean Uthman's death, and that end might be neither quick nor painless. Nasiri had been known to be vindictive when his plans were thwarted.

But then, as Uthman contemplated what Rashid had just told him, he realized the full implications of the afreet's words.

"Thou hast said that thy power has diminished for want of nourishment, o mighty Rashid. Would thy strength be restored to its full glory if such nourishment were provided to thee?"

The afreet considered the question, or pretended to. "**Aye, such a thing might well be. If Rashid is fed, Rashid may grow strong again, and hence be able to fully perform thy will on the fateful day.**"

Uthman had the sinking feeling that whatever food the afreet needed would not be available at his neighborhood Kroger, but there was only one way to find out.

"Then say unto me, o great djinn – what food must thou have to regain thy power, which once made the very earth quake in fear?"

So Rashid told him. Uthman had been right; none of the local establishments, not even the mighty Wal-Mart, was going to stock what he needed to make this creature happy.

Twelve

NASIRI STARED, AS if Uthman had just grown a second head. "The heart of a *lion*? Have you lost your *mind*?

Uthman spread his hands. "I only report what the – what *Rashid* told me. He is apparently quite serious."

Nasiri looked at the other two men, as for support, but they appeared to be as baffled and dismayed as him. To Uthman he said, "How would one such as Rashid have developed a taste for the hearts of lions? There are no such creatures native to the Land of the Prophet, unless you count Africa – and even there, the Muslim countries are all north of the Sahara. Whatever jungle cats remain on the continent are surely to be found south of the great desert."

"That is true now, brother," Uthman said, "but it was not always the case. I did some research on the Internet late last night, and learned that lions could be found throughout the lands of Arabia until about seven hundred years ago. The fossil evidence is very clear, I understand."

"Your diligence does you credit, brother," Nasiri said. It did not sound like a compliment. He began drumming the fingers of his right hand softly on the table.

Jawad Tamwar spoke up for the first time since

joining the group. "I have an idea, but I do not know if carrying it out is possible."

Nasiri waved a hand toward him. "Pray proceed, my brother."

Tamwar looked at Uthman. "You can do magic, brother. You have the ability to make things happen that are not of the physical world."

Uthman nodded cautiously. "That is true – sometimes."

"Then can you not... conjure up the heart of a lion to give to our hungry friend?"

The wizard thought briefly, then shook his head. "It is not possible, I fear. Magic cannot create something from where nothing exists – at least, magic as *I* understand it has no such power."

After a few moments, Nasiri leaned forward. "All right, then. You say that you cannot conjure something from nothing. What about conjuring something from something else?"

Uthman wiped one hand across his face. "I regret that I am unable to follow your reasoning, my brother."

"What if you had the heart of, say – a cow? That should be easy to obtain. Could you transform the heart of a cow into the heart of a lion?"

Uthman considered the idea for at least a quarter of a minute. "I cannot say with certainty, my brother, but I think not. Changing the essential nature of a thing..." He shook his head slowly. "It would be very difficult to do, and I have never heard or read of such a spell succeeding. I will, of course, make the attempt, if that is what you wish."

Nasiri gave a disgusted snort. "No, brother, I would not want you to overtax yourself."

The insult stung, but Uthman kept his mouth shut.

Rebuking Nasiri was a risky business at the best of times – and this was far from the best of times.

The men sat silently for a time, until Rahim spoke up, mildly startling all of them. He made a slight gesture toward Uthman. "With our brother's magical ability, not long ago we were able to get into a museum, despite its locks, alarms, and... guards." That last word brought a quick smile to Rahim's face; Uthman managed to conceal his revulsion, with effort. "Other locations also have locks, and alarms, even guards," Rahim said.

Eyes narrowing, Nasiri said, "I do not grasp your meaning, brother." His words contained little of the irritation he had shown toward Uthman. Even Nasiri was careful not to anger Rahim unnecessarily.

Rahim shrugged, as if what he meant was obvious. "There are these places the infidels have, for their amusement. They are called, I believe... zoos."

Thirteen

QUINCEY MORRIS HAD been pleasantly surprised to find Barry Love behind his desk in the run-down old building on Forty-First Street. The private detective kept office hours that could be described as erratic, at best. Morris once asked Love why he didn't book appointments in advance, like other detectives. Love had looked at him with a crooked grin. "If I don't know when I'm gonna be in here, they won't know either."

"They?"

"You know – *them*."

"Oh, right." Morris had pretended to understand. "Gotta watch out for *them*."

"Exactly."

Barry Love had been knee-deep in what he called "the weird shit" for a number of years. If there was something not-quite-natural going on in New York City, he always seemed to find himself dragged into it – exorcisms, séances, killer ghosts, Barry had seen it all. He had very few friends – but fortunately for him, among that small number were Quincey Morris and Libby Chastain.

Morris sat down in one of Love's creaky visitor's chairs and said, "I was wondering if you knew anything about afreets."

Love absently scratched his three-day beard stubble. "You mean the species of djinn?"

"Uh-huh."

"There was a rumor that one of them was driving a cab here in the city, for a while." Love lit a cigarette with hands made unsteady by too much caffeine. "But that was probably bullshit, and, anyway, it was years ago."

"The kind of afreet I'm interested in probably wouldn't be pushing a hack," Morris said. "If he did, it would most likely explode on him."

"Oh, that's right," Love said. "They're supposed to be something like fire elementals, aren't they?"

"That's what I hear."

"What's your interest?"

Morris briefly outlined the problem that the FBI's unofficial "spook squad" had asked him and Libby to look into.

"I'm glad to hear that you guys are still working together," Love said. "You and Libby make a good team, but when you came here alone tonight, I kinda wondered."

"Oh, we still work together," Morris said. "But Libby couldn't make it tonight. She has a date."

Love looked at him for the space of three heartbeats. "And?"

"And nothing. Libby's busy this evening, that's all. She has the right to a social life."

"That last part sounds like a quote," Love said.

Morris sighed. "I guess it is, at that."

Love peered at him some more. "You jealous?"

"Libby's not my girlfriend, podner. You oughta know that. I'm not jealous of anybody."

Love flicked ashes onto his carpet – not for the first time, judging by the carpet.

"Okay, if you say so. What's bugging you, then?"
Morris gave him a look.
"You're about to point out that it's none of my damn business," Love told him. "And you're right, too." He took a long drag, exhaled and said, "Talk about it or not, my friend. It's up to you."
Morris studied the ash-stained carpet for a few seconds before saying, "She's off having lesbian sex with a demon."
Love blinked. "Well, that's something you don't hear every day. Even *I* don't. What's the part that bothers you – the lesbian sex, or the demon?"
"The demon, of course. Libby' s sex life is none of my business."
"Okay." Another drag, another long exhale. "Libby's gay?"
"No, she's bisexual," Morris said. "As if it's any of *your* damn business, either."
"You're right – it isn't." Love flicked more ashes. "This demon thing kinda bothers me, though."
"She's not like the kind of demon you usually deal with, Barry."
"That right?"
"Ashley was given flesh and sent over to this side in order to thwart one of Hell's nastier plots."
Love's eyebrows went up a little. "Hell was thwarting itself?"
"It's complicated. There are factions, apparently. One of them didn't want the plot to succeed, because they figured it would bring on Armageddon, and they might lose."
"'Complicated' is right," Love said. "Did this have anything to do with the mess you were involved in at the Republican convention last summer?"
"Yeah. Electing Stark was the big plot."

Barry Love stubbed out his cigarette in an overflowing ashtray and lit another one. "Last I heard, Stark didn't get to be President. But Ashley's still here?"

"Yeah," Morris said. "Apparently the big-deal demon who sent her over has forgotten about her. For now, anyway. It seems there's a civil war going on in Hell, or something."

"Couldn't happen in a nicer place. So, okay – Ashley's not a predator like most demons, you're not jealous, and I assume you're not down on gays –"

"Oh, hell, no."

"So what do you care if Ashley gets it on with Libby?"

Morris studied the carpet a bit more. "Look, I've met Ashley several times. She's done Libby and me a couple of big favors. I even kind of like her."

Love looked at him closely. "But?"

"But that's like saying I like my pet cobra. I can never let myself forget what it really is."

"Is Libby in this relationship consensually?"

"I don't know if you can even call it a relationship, but yeah, sure."

"Libby's a big girl. I guess she can take care of herself."

"You know, that sounds like a quote."

Barry Love laughed a little, but then the cigarette smoke got him coughing. When that was over he said, "I haven't heard anything about an afreet in a very long time. But maybe some people – and I use the term loosely – I know can be of help. To save time, maybe you should ask them yourself."

"I would, if I knew who they were," Morris said.

"Tell you what – there's a bar a couple of blocks from here, on Forty-Third Street. Place called Strangefellows."

"*Strangefellows?* Seriously?"

"Yeah – why? You've heard of it?"

"Actually, no. But there's bar in the U.K. with the same name. It's in a part of London where not many people go – and some who do go later wish they hadn't."

"I know that place, too," Love said. "It's in the dark part of town – I mean *really* dark."

"Yeah, that's it."

"I know a guy who hangs out there – he's kind of in the same business as you and me."

"Messing around with the weird shit?"

"Yeah, that's John, all right. So, look – meet me in our local Strangefellows, tonight around midnight. Maybe I can put you together with somebody who knows about this afreet.

"I appreciate it, Barry, I really do." Morris stood up, and the two men shook hands. "See you later tonight, then."

He was opening the door when Love said, "Quincey."

Morris turned back. "What?"

"Try not to worry about Libby. She'll be okay."

"I hope so, Barry. I really do."

Fourteen

Libby Chastain, body damp with sweat, lay back on her queen-size bed and waited for her heartbeat to return to something like normal. When she could speak again, she said, "That was even better than last time, and last time was about the best I'd ever had."

"See? Told you." Ashley settled her blonde hair on the pillow next to Libby.

"Where on earth did you learn to do that thing with the flat part of your tongue?"

"It wasn't anywhere on *earth* that I learned it, Libby."

"Oh, right. Sorry – I forgot."

"No need for apologies. In fact, I regard your forgetting as a positive step."

"A step toward what?"

"Toward normalizing our relationship," Ashley said.

"I'm not sure that this relationship – if that's what it is – could *ever* be considered 'normal.'"

Ashley turned her face toward Libby and grinned. "Paranormal, maybe?"

"That sounds a little closer to the mark," Libby said. "What does Mal Peters think of this paranormal relationship?"

Peters, a former CIA hit man, had been a damned soul

in Hell when he'd been given flesh and sent across with Ashley to assassinate demon-possessed Senator Howard Stark. Having apparently been forgotten by the demon who'd sent them, Ashley and Peters now lived together and were, for lack of a better term, lovers.

"Peters doesn't tell me who I can fuck, Libby. I don't tell him, either – although I really can't imagine him wanting another woman, when he's got me to warm his bed."

"Not only is she a great fuck, but she's modest about it, too," Libby said. "You're quite the package, Ashley."

"I know. But if you're concerned about Peters's feelings, then I'll bring him along next time. Your bed looks big enough for three, and Peters is really a pretty good lay for a human. A male human, I mean."

"I don't do that kind of stuff," Libby said, a bit stiffly.

"What kind of stuff, sweetie?"

"Threesomes, foursomes, moresomes." Libby turned on her side, facing away from Ashley. "People have tried to interest me in that stuff before, but it's just not my scene."

"Because that's not the kind of thing your mother would think a good girl does?" Ashley said quietly.

No response.

"Libby?"

"Yeah, something like that, I guess."

"Hmmm." Ashley reached over and gently rested a hand on Libby's ass, which was still moist from her recent exertions. "Most people would probably say," she continued, "that a good girl doesn't eat pussy, either – and certainly not as well as you do, my dear."

No response again, although Ashley felt Libby's muscles tense under her hand.

"And according to most definitions of the term,"

Ashley said, in that same quiet tone, "I'm fairly sure that a good girl doesn't fuck demons, either."

Libby remained silent. Ashley's hand stayed where it was for a while, and then it went exploring.

"You know the thing about good girls?" Ashley said, her voice a caress to match her hand. "They never get to have any *fun*."

After perhaps two minutes, Libby gave vent to a long, low groan. She turned back toward Ashley, who removed her newly-slick hand.

Libby slowly brought her face down toward Ashley's, until their noses were almost touching. She stared into Ashley's eyes – not as easy as it sounds, for there was something in those eyes that was not quite human. "Maybe –" The word stuck in Libby's throat, so she tried again. "Maybe I'm not as good a girl as I thought I was."

The human form of the demon known as Ashur Badaktu brought her hand around until it rested lightly on the back of Libby's neck. "No," she said, in a voice that was almost a growl. "You're better."

She pulled Libby's head down until their lips were first just touching, and soon grinding against each other. Matters proceeded along fairly predictable lines from there.

An hour later, Ashley came out of Libby's bathroom, still wet from the shower. She walked into the bedroom, drying her hair with a fluffy towel, and saw Libby still lying in bed. "I halfway expected you to join me in there," she said teasingly.

"I don't really care for shower sex," Libby said. "Too cramped. I keep banging my elbow against the wall and stuff."

"Pity," Ashley said, and smiled at her. "But if you

keep lying there like that, I've got a feeling I'm going to be needing another shower before I go."

Libby pulled a sheet up to cover herself. "Better?"

"Not better," Ashley said, "but a bit less distracting." She turned to the mirror and picked up a comb. Looking at Libby's reflection, she said, "I take it that means you're not interested in going again. I wouldn't really *mind* taking another shower, you know."

"I'm sure," Libby said. "But I am, for the moment, sated, thank you very much." Libby smiled. "Seriously – thank you very much."

Ashley touched an index finger to her pursed lips. "Sated," she said, as if repeating a word she'd never heard before. "Whatever must that be like?"

"Maybe you'll find out, someday," Libby said. "In the meantime, I wanted to ask you something."

"Ask away. I am, after all, a font of knowledge."

"That's what I was hoping," Libby said. "So, do you perchance know anything about afreets?"

Ashley frowned at her reflection. "You mean those genie things?"

"Exactly. Quincey and I may have to go up against one – assuming we can find it."

"Really? Be sure to wear an asbestos overcoat. Those boys do like to burn things up."

"So I've heard," Libby said. "Know anything else about them?"

"Well, David once killed an afreet with his sling, I believe."

Libby frowned at her. "I thought that was Goliath, the Philistine – or are we talking about a different David?"

"Same David, different occasion. His battle with the afreet didn't make it into the Bible, for some reason – but then, so many inconvenient things didn't."

"But this was the same deal as the Goliath story? David flung a stone into its forehead?"

"Similar, but not the same," Ashley said. She put the comb down and picked up her tube of lipstick. "Instead of a stone, Dave used his sling to fire off the pit of a date. Those things are oval-shaped, you know. Not very aerodynamic. But he carved it down with his knife, to make it fly better. It would seem he did it right." She shook her head. "That afreet never knew what hit him."

"*Dave?* People called him *Dave?*"

"No – just his family and close friends got to do that." Ashley smiled into the mirror. "Or the Hebrew equivalent, anyway."

Libby shook her head in wonderment. "So that's what I have to do, if confronted with an afreet? Zap it in the forehead with a rounded-off date pit? Seriously?"

"Actually, any kind of pit would probably do the job. The ancient text says, 'Thou shalt smite the afreet with a fruit stone, thrown with great force and power. Thus shall its life be ended.' That's a rough translation, anyway."

"Translation from what?"

"Ancient Assyrian."

"I mean from what text?" Libby asked.

Ashley shook her head. "You wouldn't recognize the name, honey. The last copy was destroyed when Julius Caesar burned the Great Library at Alexandria."

"If you say so." Libby rubbed the bridge of her nose. "I've seen pictures of the kind of sling that David supposedly used. A small pouch with two long leather thongs attached to it, right?"

"That's the one. You whirl it over your head to build up momentum, then let go of one of the thongs while making a throwing motion toward your enemy. The Apache Indians were still using something very similar as late as the nineteenth century. In the right hands, one of those things can be quite lethal."

"I'm pretty sure I don't have the right hands, at the moment," Libby said. "And developing a set would probably take more time than I've got, right now."

"Three to six months of practice ought to do it," Ashley said with a smile.

"Exactly what I just said – more time than I've got. Whatever these jihadists have in mind – assuming they even exist – my guess is they probably won't wait three to six months to get around to it."

"Speaking of thongs," Ashley said, picking up her underwear and pulling it on, "do you think I look good in this one?"

"You'd probably look good in a burlap sack," Libby said. "But, yeah, you look fantastic."

"Flattery – I love it." Ashley reached for her white silk blouse. "You know, honey, I don't think you'd need to use a sling to take down this afreet. David used one, because that was what was available in his low-tech era. But you've got quite a few other options. Hell, for that matter, why not just use magic to fling a peach pit at the thing? Or a hundred peach pits?"

"Not allowed," Libby said. "We can't use white magic to hurt people, remember?"

"Um, I'm not sure that afreets qualify as *people*, sweetie."

"If it's humanoid and has achieved reflectivity," Libby said, "then I'm pretty sure the rule still applies."

Ashley was pulling on her tight black pants as she said, "You whities put so many limits on yourselves, I'm surprised there are any of you left." She buttoned up, looking at Libby. "Pleased, in this case, but still surprised."

"It is what it is," Libby said. "You said something about other ways of firing off a fruit pit?"

"What does it matter, if you can't *use* any of them?"

"Who says I can't? I can use a fucking *Uzi* if I want to, Ashley. The moral consequences of that are between me and the Goddess. But as long as magic's not involved, the Sisterhood doesn't care."

"Oh, well, then. Let's see ..." Ashley slipped on her tan Manolo Blahniks. "There are slingshots that are used for hunting. I assume those have enough velocity to ruin any afreet's day. You point them like a gun, and squeeze a trigger – this is not your father's slingshot, honey."

"Sounds promising," Libby said.

"Then there are those paintball guns."

"What? *Paintball?*"

"It's a game played by alleged adults who think war is actually fun. After two hours in a real war, most of them would be crying for their mothers. They run around specially built courses in camo fatigues, shooting at each other with these gas-propelled guns that fire little balls filled with paint, to prove when somebody's been shot. There's quite an industry that's grown up around it, I understand."

"That's worth looking into, then," Libby said. "Thank you."

Ashley headed toward the door of the bedroom. "Don't get up, honey – I know the way out." She stopped suddenly and looked at Libby. "What's wrong?"

"Nothing. You're just the second person to say that to me today, that's all."

Ashley tilted her head a little. "You and Quincey have a lover's spat?"

"We aren't lovers, Ashley – you know that. If we were, you wouldn't be here."

"In that case, I'm glad that you're not. Where *is* Quincey tonight, anyway?"

"Trying to track down a guy we know, who might have a line on this afreet. I'll find out tomorrow whether he succeeded."

"So, you two might be on the road again, soon – busting ghosts and saving the world from the forces of evil."

"Could be," Libby said.

"Well, call me when you get back – or not, if you want to go back to being a good girl."

"I'll have to give that some thought."

"You do that."

"Goodnight, Ashley."

"Goodbye, Libby."

Fifteen

EVER PUNCTUAL, QUINCEY Morris arrived at Strangefellows Bar and Grille at midnight precisely. He'd been mildly amused at Barry Love's choice of meeting time. Of course, there was the widespread notion of midnight as the "witching hour," when magic practitioners supposedly held their revels, although Barry Love probably knew better. Morris's experience was that, when it came time to party down, most witches (of the "black" variety or otherwise) were more interested in the phase of the moon than a particular hour, as long as darkness had fallen – dancing naked in broad daylight can get you into trouble.

According to legend, witches and wizards had chosen midnight to gather because it was the hour when the dark powers (whatever they were supposed to be) were at their strongest – that myth went back to Shakespeare, if not earlier. Trouble was, the existence of time zones meant that it was always midnight somewhere. Morris had sometimes wondered if the dark powers kept moving west every hour, in order to keep their evil at maximum potency.

There was also the notion popular in some circles that 3:00 a.m. was the "devil's hour," being the exact opposite side of the clock from 3:00 p.m., the supposed time of Christ's death. The problem with declaring three in the morning as the moment when demons came out to play (apart from the time zone issue again) was that nobody on Golgotha that fateful day was wearing a watch. The hour had been arbitrarily selected by the Catholic Church centuries later, as had the date of Christmas. Curious about the "devil's hour," Morris had dome some research, only to find that the designation had been invented out of whole cloth by a Hollywood scriptwriter, for some dumb movie about an exorcism gone wrong. Thus do legends begin, sometimes.

In Morris's not inconsiderable experience, *every* hour was potentially the devil's hour. Anyone who felt protected from the powers of Hell at some particular time of day was deluding himself.

In contrast to the dark cavern that Morris had been expecting, Strangefellows was well-lit and noisy, with most of the booths and tables occupied. Going by the haze of smoke that hovered over the big room, this was one of the many bars in the city ignoring the no-smoking ordinance. Morris scanned the room; the place seemed to be some kind of supernatural watering hole – neutral ground where different creatures could drink without fear of being eaten, sometimes literally – not unlike the establishment of the same name in the dark side of London.

He could discern the auras of four different witches scattered around the room – three white, and one black. A couple of guys sitting at the bar looked like ghouls, and Morris could not help but wonder what their preferred bar snack might be. Several diminutive figures sat around a circular table at the far side of the room, but Morris couldn't tell if they were dwarves or trolls. You have to get close to tell the difference, and Morris had no interest in doing so.

Then he saw Barry Love, sitting in a corner booth and talking to a man in a black leather jacket. Not wanting to interrupt, Morris was about to look for a seat at the bar (away from the ghouls, whose bad breath is infamous) when Love looked up and waved him over.

As he drew closer, Morris saw that Love's friend had droopy eyes that made him look like a basset hound. He had heavy eyebrows and thick brown hair to match, a fair amount of which was also sprouting from his ears. Morris stood near the edge of the booth, unsure what side Barry Love wanted him to sit on. Love looked at his drinking companion and said, "Larry, this is Quincey Morris, the guy I was telling you about." He looked up at Morris. "Quincey, meet Larry Talbot."

Talbot eased out of the booth and stood up to shake Morris's hand. He was bigger than he'd looked sitting down, and Morris noticed that the palm of Talbot's big hand was covered with a tuft of coarse hair.

"Pleased to meet you, Mister Morris," Talbot said. "Barry's told me a lot about you, although I'm pretty sure I heard your name a few times before tonight."

"Don't believe everything you hear," Morris told him. "Just the good stuff. And call me Quincey, okay?"

"Sure, Quincey, thanks." Talbot turned to Love. "I gotta get going – I'll catch up with you later in the week, okay?"

Love said, "Sure – take care." Talbot gave Morris a friendly nod, and lumbered off.

At a gesture from Barry Love, Morris sat in the place opposite him that the big man had vacated. Morris looked at Talbot's departing back and said to Love, "Werewolf, isn't he?"

Love gave him a crooked smile. "Guess you noticed the hairy palm. My Aunt Rita would have said that means he jerks off a lot – but then she also used to tell me that a girl could get pregnant from French kissing. Yeah, you're right – he's a lycanthrope."

A waitress came to the table, and Morris ordered bourbon and water, which appeared before him with commendable dispatch.

"I had a bad experience with a werewolf near Boston, not long ago," Morris said. "I'm pretty sure he'd been hired to kill me – and Libby."

"Yeah, I've heard that some lycos've been hiring out as hit men – or hit wolves, I guess. But that's not their normal behavior – don't judge the whole pack by the actions of a few rogues."

"I wasn't planning to," Morris said. "So, did your furry friend have any info about my little problem?"

"No, he didn't know anything about either afreets or the Seal of Solomon. But I guy I talked to earlier tonight did have one interesting fact – or he said it was a fact, anyway – about afreets."

"I'm all ears."

"He said he had it on good authority that they like lion hearts."

Morris closed his eyes for a second. "Wait – you mean they were brave, like Richard the Lionheart? That's not real helpful, podner."

"No, pay attention," Love said. "I didn't tell you they're *like* lionhearts. What I said was *they like lion hearts*. As *food*, man."

"Afreets eat the hearts of lions? Shit, no wonder lions are almost extinct."

"What my guy told me was that they don't *need* food, since they're spiritual beings, so my guess is they leave the lions alone, most of the time. But if they're going to eat, seems like lion hearts are their snack of choice."

"Not exactly something you can pick up at your local Stop & Shop, is it?" Morris said. "So afreets don't have to eat lion hearts – they just like to. Weird."

Love shrugged. "Humans don't need chocolate – despite what a lady of my acquaintance tells me. But lots of us eat it, anyway."

"Sure, but supernaturals are different from us. They're more... primal."

"I know what you mean," Love said, "and I tend to agree. But there are exceptions. I once ran into a vampire called Jerry –"

"That sounds like the start of a limerick," Morris said. "*There once was a vampire named Jerry, whose meals were frequently scary.*" That drew a laugh from Barry Love.

"Jerry..." Morris said, shaking his head. "What is the supernatural world coming to?"

"They aren't all named 'Vlad' or 'Anton,' Quincey. You know that, same as I do. Anyway my point was, Jerry was a vamp, with the typical vamp liquid dietary needs. But he also liked apples, as a snack. Go figure."

"You learn something new every day," Morris said. "You said this Jerry *liked* apples. Past tense?"

"Yeah, I heard he went out to California, and got himself killed by some high school kid. Jerry always was a –" Love stopped speaking and looked at the entrance. "Somebody just came in who might be worth talking to," he said. He waited a couple of seconds, then waved his arm in the direction of the door. "Here he comes. Scoot over, will you?"

Morris moved over far enough to leave room for somebody to sit next to him. The man who approached the table stood about 5'5", with a head that looked too large for his body and thin black hair that was plastered over his skull with too much dressing. He looked out at the world with brown eyes so hooded as to be only half-visible.

"Hi, Kaspar," Barry Love said. "How're you doing tonight?"

"I find that I am very well, thank you." His voice was soft and velvety, like a cat's purr. The shaded eyes glanced toward Morris, and the little man continued, "I do not believe, however, that I have the acquaintance of your friend here."

"Kaspar, meet Quincey," Love said. "Quincey, this is my old buddy Kaspar. With a 'K.'" No last names this time, Morris noticed.

Kaspar turned toward him and sketched a slight bow. "A great pleasure to make your acquaintance, sir." Wondering where the little man had picked up his archaic speech, Morris extended a hand. "Likewise, I'm sure."

Kaspar's arms remained at his sides. "I assure you that I mean you no offense, Mister... Quincey, but I never shake hands. The very idea is abhorrent to me."

Morris withdrew his hand and settled for a friendly nod. "No problem," he said. He'd met a few germaphobes before – assuming that was Kaspar's quirk, and not something weirder. It was probably just as well – shake with a guy like Kaspar, and your first instinct would be to wipe your hand on your pants leg.

"Why don't you join us for a few minutes?" Love said. After a moment's hesitation, Kaspar replied, "It would be my pleasure." He slid in next to Morris, who unconsciously moved as far to the right as he could, until his leg was touching the wall.

"What're you drinking?" Love asked.

"I believe I will have an absinthe."

Well, that figured. Absinthe has only been legal for sale in the U.S. since 2007, although the supposed hallucinogenic properties that once had it banned worldwide were largely mythical. The real reason it had been outlawed here was that the drink had been a favorite product of amateur distillers in the South, who often left in impurities that could kill you. Nowadays, consuming absinthe properly is a fussy, pretentious process; it fitted a guy like Kaspar like a custom-made suit.

Once the drink order was placed, Barry Love said to Kaspar, "I wanted a few minutes of your time. I was wondering whether you knew anything about afreets."

Kaspar frowned, which seemed to involve most of the muscles of his face. "The fire djinn, you mean?" He shook his big head slowly. "Apart from what one may read in the *Thousand and One Nights*, I regret to say that I know nothing."

"So," Morris said, "I reckon that would mean you haven't heard of anybody smuggling one into the country."

Kaspar looked at him. "Alas, no. Although it should be acknowledged that such smuggling would be laughably easy. If one had an afreet confined inside a vessel, a jar or lamp or some such, one could without risk hand it over to a customs inspector for perusal. Unless the official knew the proper incantation, and had the courage – or the stupidity – to use it, the vessel would appear quite empty."

Then the absinthe arrived, and Kaspar had to go through the whole ritual – the slotted spoon, the sugar cube, the ice water – all to make the emerald-green drink palatable.

Neither Morris nor Love interrupted this procedure, but once Kaspar had finished, and taken his first sip,

Love said, "How about the Seal of Solomon? Heard anything about that?"

Kaspar moved his thin shoulders in an elaborate shrug. "If one refers to legend, the Great Seal was said to be of immense power over the spirit world, having been given to the King by the Creator Himself. It supposedly gave Solomon dominion over demons and djinn alike."

After another swallow of the green liquor, Kaspar went on, "However, if one wishes to speak in contemporary terms, much is speculated, but little known for certain. It is widely believed that the Great Seal was broken into pieces millennia ago, the fragments scattered to the four winds."

"What about something a little more recent?" Love said.

"Today?" Kaspar gave the most elegant snort that Morris had ever heard. "As one might imagine, there have been many 'sightings' throughout the Middle East, most proven bogus. A true fragment was said to be held by a Chicago museum – until recently, that is. There have also been persistent rumors that the Knights Templar possess one, but –"

"Wait a second," Morris said. "The *Knights Templar*?"

The big head turned toward Morris again, its facial expression looking mildly offended. "That is what I said, yes."

"The order of warrior-priests, started in the Middle Ages."

"Yes, the very same." Kaspar's voice had taken on a supercilious tone.

"The ones that were destroyed by..." Morris tried to remember.

"Philip IV of France," Love said, looking as perturbed as Morris felt. "Early thirteen hundreds, I think."

"Right, that's him," Morris said. "He owed the

Knights a pile of money, right? Rather than pay off, he had them framed for heresy and burned at the stake – damn near all of them. Wiped out the whole Order."

The little man's smile was so smug, Morris felt the urge to wipe it off – with his fist. "Perhaps one should say '*supposedly* wiped out,'" Kaspar said.

Morris and Love looked at each other. "So, what're you saying, dude?" Love asked skeptically. "That the Templars are still around, and they've got a piece of Solomon's Seal?"

They were treated to another of Kaspar's frowns. "You know I dislike being called 'dude,' Barry." Seeing the near-homicidal expression on Love's face, he continued hastily, "But the answer to the first part of that question is 'almost certainly,' and the answer to the second is 'that remains speculation.'"

"Why '*almost* certainly'?" Morris asked him. "Either you know for sure, or you don't."

"As you may have noticed," Kaspar said, "I strive to express myself precisely. Since I have never – to my knowledge – personally met a member of the Knights Templar, I cannot attest to their existence with absolute certainty."

"Then how can –" Barry Love began.

Kaspar stopped him with an upraised palm. "Several individuals whom I trust have attested to the very contemporary existence of the gentlemen you mention. Therefore, I am reasonably certain that the Knights Templar represent a very real presence in the world."

"So, these fellas are still around, and they just might have gotten their hands on a piece of Solomon's Seal," Morris said. "That right?"

"Succinctly, albeit inelegantly put, Mister... Quincey." Kaspar favored Morris with a ponderous nod. "That is exactly the meaning I have been attempting to convey."

"Where can we find them?" Love asked him.

"Alas, that is information that I do not possess."

Barry Love gave Kaspar a very direct look. "You wouldn't be holding out on me, would you, old buddy?"

"I assure you, the thought would never occur to me."

"That's good," Barry Love said, "because if I thought you were... Hey, did I tell you that I ran into Van Herder last week?"

Kaspar's face had gone completely still. "No," he said in a flat voice. Morris would have bet that the little man was incapable of a monosyllabic response to anything.

"Yeah, he's still got that bar over in Jersey, as a front for his... other operations," Love went on. "We had a couple of drinks, shot the shit for a while, just like old times. He asked me if I'd seen you lately. Said there's something he wants to discuss with you, pretty badly."

Kaspar's eyes did not leave Barry Love's face. In the same emotionless tone he asked "And?"

"I told him that I thought you'd moved out west – you know, for your health. I said the last I heard, you'd set up shop in Denver, or maybe it was Santa Fe."

Kaspar produced another slow nod. "Thank you."

Love waved one hand dismissively. "No problem. I'm always willing to tell a few white lies – for my friends. We're still friends, aren't we, Kaspar?"

"Of course we are, Barry," replied the little man, and Morris thought he detected a thin sheen of sweat on the oversize face. "Why ever would you think otherwise?"

"Well, sometimes I wonder –"

"I assure you, I spoke the truth when I said that have no idea how to get in touch with the Knights Templar – but I can refer you to a man who very probably *does* know."

"Who's that?"

"His name is David Kabov," Kaspar said. "At least, that is the name he goes by these days. He is retired now, but I know for a fact that he did business with the Templars in years past. More than once."

"David Kabov." Barry Love said the name as if he were tasting it. "Where can we find him?"

"As I said, he is retired," Kaspar said. He pulled a cocktail napkin toward him. "Do you have a pen?"

"I do," Morris said, glad to be contributing to the conversation once again. He took a silver pen from his pocket and put it in front of the little man. He had once put out the eye of a vampire with that pen, but figured that information was more than Kaspar would wish to have, especially in his current agitated state.

Kaspar printed slowly on the napkin for a minute or so, pushed it across the table to Love, and handed back Morris's pen, all without speaking.

Love picked up the napkin and squinted at it. "David Kabov," he read aloud. "Sweetwater Village, #114, 3945 West Oakland Park, Fort Lauderdale, Florida, 33311."

He looked up. "An old folk's home?"

Kaspar gave him half a smile. "I believe the preferred term is 'retirement community.'"

"Yeah, sure. How old is this guy Kabov, anyway?"

"He would be in his mid-seventies now, I believe."

Morris put his pen away and asked, "What exactly did he retire *from*?"

"I am quite certain he would prefer to answer that question personally," Kaspar said. "Assuming, of course, that he will speak with you at all."

"How about a phone number?" Love said. "Or maybe an email address."

Kaspar shook his head like a banker turning down a

mortgage application. "This man does not talk on the telephone – ever. And if he even *has* an email address, he guards it quite closely."

"What is this fella," Morris said, "paranoid?"

The half-smile reappeared on Kaspar's face. "You may call it that, if you wish. Although I believe someone once observed, 'It's not paranoia if they're really out to get you.'"

"Somebody's out to get this Kabov?" Love asked. "Who?"

"I believe that question is also one best answered by the man himself, assuming –"

"Yeah, yeah," Love said. "So, what're we supposed to do, fly all the way down to Lauderdale and just knock on his door?"

"No," Kaspar said. "I think that could be unwise, and quite possibly dangerous."

Morris looked at him. "Dangerous?"

"Indeed, yes. This was once a *very* dangerous man – professionally dangerous, one might say. It would, I think, be a mistake to assume that age has transformed the Lion of Judah into a pussycat."

"*Lion?*" Morris clamped a hand onto Kaspar's forearm. "What do you know about lions?"

Kaspar stared at him. "*Unhand* me, sir!"

Once Morris had let go, Kaspar pulled the arm in close to his body and said, "I do not know what prompted such *extreme* rudeness on your part, but I assure you, I know nothing more about lions than anyone else who owns a television. The term 'Lion of Judah' is a very old one, and uniquely applicable to David Kabov, as you may learn, should you ever meet him."

"Let's get back to that," Love said. "How *do* we meet this guy, if we can't call, email, or visit him?"

"What you do is write him a letter," Kaspar said. "To that address. Use my name, if you wish. Indeed, you probably should."

"And this letter should say what, exactly?" Love asked him.

"Write that you wish to call on him, at a specified date and time. You should allow at least three days' lead time from when you post the letter, the mail being what it is these days."

"Should we say what we want to talk to him about?" Morris asked.

Kaspar gave him a sideways look, but addressed the answer to Barry Love. "That will not be necessary, but you should indicate in your letter how many of you there will be – I strongly advise no more than two – and a brief description of each person. And if you do visit him, be punctual."

"So what if we do all this," Love said, "and show up at his door – punctually, I mean – and the guy isn't even home? That'd be a pretty good example of what they call a fool's errand, wouldn't it? And I don't know about Quincey here, but I *hate* feeling foolish."

"You need have no concern on that score," Kaspar told him. "I understand that he rarely goes out. The only questions are whether he will admit you – and what kind of reception you will receive." He tossed off the last of his absinthe and stood up abruptly. "I wish you good fortune – whatever your ultimate object may be. Now if you" – he gave Morris another sideways look – "*gentlemen* will excuse me, I have business elsewhere that has already been delayed long enough."

As he watched Kaspar head toward the door, Morris said, "You know, I don't think he likes me."

"If you wanted to be buddies, then you shouldn't

have grabbed him," Love said. "He's weird about stuff like that."

"I just thought it was a pretty odd coincidence that he's sitting here and talking about the Lion of Judah, when fifteen minutes earlier you were telling me that afreets like to snack on lion hearts."

"Maybe, but stuff like that does happen – otherwise, *coincidence* wouldn't be a word." Love leaned forward a little. "I kept saying *we* in front of Kaspar, so as not to confuse the issue," he said. "But you know I'm not going to Florida with you, right? I can't leave the city right now, Quincey – there's too much weird shit going on."

"Anything I can help with, before I leave town?"

"Probably not. You ever hear of a guy called Pinhead?"

Morris shook his head. "Sounds like some old Dick Tracy villain."

"This guy's a villain, all right, but the kind that would give Dick Tracy screaming nightmares." Love signaled their waitress. "You want a refill?"

"No, I better get going. But thanks for all your help, amigo. At least I've got a lead now." Morris slid out of the booth and stood up.

"Say hi to Libby for me," Love said. "Is she gonna be heading down to Florida with you?"

"I hope so," Morris said. "I really do."

Sixteen

THE DETROIT ZOO is not actually *in* Detroit. It occupies a hundred and twenty-five acres of ground in Royal Oak, two miles north of the Motor City. It is a well-designed modern facility, and a great deal of money has gone into building and displaying the animal collection over the years. The Detroit Zoo has it all (almost), from aardvarks to zebras. They've got bears (black, grizzly, polar, and panda), giraffes (reticulated), and pythons (also reticulated), as well as rhinos, kangaroos, gorillas, and penguins.

And lions. Six of them.

The newly redesigned Lion Habitat was only a few years old. It consisted of seven and a half thousand square feet of faux-savanna surrounded by a seventeen-foot wall full of glass panels, for easy viewing from outside. An interior wall further divided the enclosure into two sections, each occupied by its own three-member "pride" of lions. Keeping the two groups separate was essential; during mating season male lions have been known to try getting frisky with the females of another pride. In the lion world, this is a good way to get a set of three-inch claws raked across your importunate leonine face.

Of course, the division also made things a bit easier for anyone contemplating breaking into the enclosure to kill one of the lions.

Three men who had that precise goal in mind were now sitting in a stolen Ford Econoline van. The vehicle was parked about a hundred and fifty feet from the zoo's exterior fence, in sight of one of the secondary gates used for deliveries. Abdul Nasiri was far too valuable to risk apprehension (according to Nasiri, anyway), so the raid had been entrusted to Jawad Tamwar, Mujab Rahim, and Sharaf Uthman.

The zoo had closed to visitors at 5:00 p.m. It was now 10:22. Nasiri had obtained a very detailed map of the zoo, and by now the three men had it virtually memorized. Once Uthman used an unlocking spell to get the delivery gate open, they knew exactly how close they could take the car to the lion enclosure – about eight hundred feet from the exterior wall. The rear of the van contained two lightweight aluminum ladders that would extend to a length of twenty feet. One of these would get Uthman to top of the lion enclosure, where he would cast a spell that would send the three lions inside into a sleep so profound that it would verge on coma. Then Tamwar would join Uthman atop the wall, and Rahim would pass up the second ladder, which they would wrestle over the wall, setting one end firmly onto the ground of the lion enclosure. The two ladders would then be leaning against the wall from each side, their top rungs only a few feet from one another. Rahim would then climb the ladder himself, bringing with him a small plastic cooler half full of dry ice.

The three of them would climb down into the enclosure and get their bloody work done. Afterward, they would reverse the process to get back out – only this time the cooler would be heavier – by about two pounds.

In theory, Uthman could have used magic to levitate all three of them over the wall, both coming and going. But levitation magic is very stressful, and Uthman was no longer a young man. It simply would not do for the levitation spell to fail them when it was time to leave – especially since the surviving two lions would eventually awaken. Hence the ladders.

A disagreement had arisen over which of them would remain outside the enclosure to deal with any prowling security guards; Nasiri's research had revealed that the zoo had four such men working the night shift. Rahim had volunteered (nay, almost insisted) to be the outside man, but his probable method of dealing with an errant guard was precisely what Nasiri wished to avoid.

"The crusader police will devote far more time and resources to investigating the death of a guard than they will of an animal." Nasiri had pointed to an image on his computer monitor. "Even one so majestic as this." Nasiri had looked at each of them at this point, but had stared at Rahim a bit longer than the other two. "You will kill someone only if the alternative is being identified or captured. Our brother Sharaf assures us" – and here Uthman had come in for his own long, intense look – "that his magic is sufficient to disable anyone who might discover you, so let it be done that way. Keep your righteous thirst for the crusaders' blood in check a bit longer, my brothers. It shall be slaked, *more* than slaked, very soon now."

It had therefore seemed logical that Uthman, the wizard, should remain outside the lion enclosure while the others went in to do the bloody work of the evening – but the other two had raised firm, if respectful, objections.

"I do not doubt our brother's power to work miracles," Tamwar had said. "Have I not seen him do so more than once already? But if perchance one of these lions should prove less... susceptible to his power than even our wise brother might expect, it would be essential to our mission for him to be on hand to deal with the creature at once, lest disaster befall us all."

The thug Rahim had typically been more blunt. A product of the Cairo slums, he had never seen a zoo before – had not even been aware that they can be found in the Middle East. But Rahim knew enough to realize that even his skill with a knife would be no match for an awake, angry lion. He was also motivated by his own crude notion of fairness. "Our brother assures us that his magic will render the great beasts harmless," Rahim had said. "He should be therefore be with us to suffer the consequences, just in case he should be proved wrong."

It had finally decided that Uthman would cast an aversion spell on the ladder, as well as on the parked van. A variation on what infidel magicians called the Tarnhelm Effect, the spell would not render either the ladder or van invisible, but rather would cause the eye of anyone passing to unconsciously avoid looking at them. Unless a strolling guard should actually walk into the side of the van, for instance, he would pass by without even registering its presence. That arrangement would have to do.

Thus it was that the three fighters for jihad had found themselves on the hard-packed earth inside the Detroit Zoo's lion enclosure. Each carried a backpack containing essential materials. Uthman's, of course, contained magical implements and materials he might need. Rahim bore the small plastic cooler and dry ice.

And Tamwar carried a pack containing several medical instruments, including several veterinary scalpels and a device that is known among surgeons as a rib-spreader.

The moonlight, combined with the park's ambient lighting, provided enough illumination for the men to see where they were walking, and to observe the three still forms that lay a few hundred feet away. They had discussed the operation a hundred times in planning, so there was no wasted conversation now. The three men set off stolidly on their mission. They had a djinn to feed.

Seventeen

FROM THE *DETROIT Free Press*:

LION MUTILATION PUZZLES, ANGERS OFFICIALS

By Frances Dooley, Free Press Staff Writer

(Royal Oak, March 19) Officials and employees of the Detroit Zoo are outraged over a daring break-in last night that has left one of the facility's prize lions dead and mutilated.

The invasion, which occurred sometime between 10:00 p.m. and 6:00 a.m., involved one or more persons, who entered the lion enclosure and killed Samuel, one of only two male lions in the zoo's collection.

A zoo employee, speaking anonymously, said that Samuel's corpse was mutilated, apparently resulting in the removal of the animal's heart.

Louise and Mimi, the two female lions also living in that section of the enclosure, were not harmed, according to zoo officials. How the intruders were able to kill the male lion without harming, or being attacked by, the two females, is one of many questions facing zoo officials and Royal Oak police.

Roger Wigton, the zoo's Director of Animal Health and Safety, said blood samples would be taken from the two female lions, as well as the corpse of Samuel, to determine if the animals had been drugged.

Police said that the intruders apparently entered the zoo grounds through a service gate, although the gate has an alarm that was neither set off, nor apparently disabled.

The zoo has a system of security cameras that cover the entire park, both outdoors and indoors. However, the system apparently went down last night, since nothing was recorded after approximately 10:00 p.m., zoo officials say.

Police theorize that the zoo's central computer was somehow hacked, disabling both the video system and the alarms, thus allowing the intruders to enter, do their bloody work, and leave undetected.

Authorities are not ruling out the possibility that some kind of occult ritual may be at the root of the crime. "I've seen reports over the years of animals being used by these devil-worshippers as sacrifices," said Royal Oak Police Chief Frasier Boone, "but that's always involved small animals, like dogs, cats or chickens. If some of those sickos are in our community, we will identify and prosecute them, to the fullest extent of the law. This kind of cruelty will not be tolerated."

Police said that arrests are expected in the near future.

Eighteen

Libby Chastain came in to her living room from the kitchen, holding a half-full pot of coffee. "I thought I'd have a second cup," she said to Quincey Morris. "How about you?"

"I'd love one, thanks," he told her. Morris never declined Libby's coffee. She mixed her own, from freshly ground beans. The ingredients of what she called "Libby's Brew" were no mystery: Jamaican Blue Mountain, Hawaiian Kona, Free Trade Columbian Dark, and something called Kicking Horse Coffee, which is roasted in Canada (although, of course, they don't grow the beans there). The proportions, however, were a closely held secret, having been learned – Libby sometimes claimed – from a hundred-and-forty-two-year-old witch in St. Louis who credited her age and general spryness to the fact that she drank a pot of the stuff every day.

Knowing what went into the stuff, Morris had tried to recreate it in his own kitchen a couple of times. The results, although very tasty, were never quite as good as Libby's Brew. He'd said as much once, and she had replied, "Oh, you probably forgot to add the eye of newt. Crucial ingredient."

They had already exchanged the relevant parts of what they had learned the night before. Libby had told Morris that it might be a good idea for them to find a device that would fire a fruit pit through the air with reasonable speed and accuracy. Morris had related what he'd found out in Strangefellows, in the company of Barry Love.

"So, although djinns are associated with the Middle East, the fruit pit doesn't have to come from there?" Morris asked.

"No, it doesn't," Libby said. "Not according to Ashley, anyway. Good thing, too – the only fruits native to the Middle East with pits in the center are dates. And their pits are oblong."

"Good enough for David, apparently."

"Yes, but he used a sling, and even then had to trim the date pit down to something more circular, so it would fly better."

"Well, as long as it doesn't matter..." Morris scratched his chin. "What are you thinking about using?"

"To an extent, the choice depends on what we use to fire it – a slingshot, one of those paintball guns, or something else."

"Um. I assume you've been doing research," Morris said. "Which fruit has the biggest pit?"

"Looks like the papaya," Libby said. "But those things can have pits that weigh a half pound, or more."

"Too big for our purposes, then – unless we get Roberto Clemente or somebody to throw it at the fucking afreet. And I think we might have trouble getting Roberto interested in the gig."

"Quincey." Libby's voice reflected the smile on her face. "Roberto Clemente was a right fielder, not a pitcher."

"Oh."

"And he'd be operating under the additional disadvantage of being dead."

"Well, you know what I mean."

"Yes," Libby said. "No papaya pits for us."

"Guess we'll have to try some of the others, like avocados and peaches, and see which works best in our chosen mechanism of propulsion."

"'Mechanism of propulsion.'" Libby smiled again. "You've got such a way with words, Quincey – it almost makes up for the fact that you don't know shit about baseball."

"There's lots of things that I don't know shit about," Morris said. "And one of them is the Knights Templar – the current incarnation, anyway. That's why I was thinking about dropping a line to this David Kabov fella, then paying him a visit in a few days. Care to come along?"

"I might as well. Some warm sun would feel good, right about now, although I don't imagine we'll be staying all that long."

"Not unless Kabov tells us that the Knights Templar are based in Miami Beach, or someplace."

"Guess we'll have to find out," Libby said. "While your letter's in transit, maybe we can check out some 'propulsive mechanisms.'"

Morris tossed down the last of his coffee. "You know, I remember hearing about a stripper who was famous for shooting ping pong balls out of her, um, neither regions. Wonder if she'd be of any use to us."

Libby thought for a minute, then nodded solemnly. "You might be on to something there, Tex. Could be just what we need to kill this afreet."

"Um, it was a joke, Libby. I was just foolin' around."

"No, think about it. If we send Bambi – or whatever her name is – after the afreet, firing peach pits at him out of her twat – heck, there's a good chance the darn thing will just die laughing."

Nineteen

Sweetwater Village Retirement Community consisted of a number of near-identical small houses that the property management insisted on calling "bungalows." Each sat on a small lot full of grass, kept green, even in the current drought, by a sprinkler system that never seemed to stop running. Most of the houses had discreet signs that said "quiet, please" or some variation. So seriously did the management take the residents' wish for peace and quiet that no motorized vehicles were allowed anywhere on the facility, although Quincey Morris assumed that exceptions must be made for delivery trucks – not to mention ambulances. But everyone else traveled by electric golf cart, which visitors could rent from the management office for a nominal fee. As he and Libby Chastain made their near-silent way through the winding streets, Morris noticed some golf carts parked in driveways that appeared to have been heavily customized – sort of like low-power hot rods. He supposed the old folks had to express their individuality somehow, but he thought the red one with "Pussywagon" painted on the sides in yellow script was both tawdry and over-optimistic.

There was a golf cart parked in the driveway of #114, but it was as plain and unadorned as the day it had come out of the box. Morris parked their borrowed vehicle behind it and checked his watch: 2:59. Good. Morris had written to David Kabov that he and a female companion would call on Mister Kabov at 3:00 o'clock, and he had been told that Kabov insisted on punctuality.

The hour had struck – silently, of course – by the time he and Libby reached the pastel-blue front door, so Morris rang the bell. While waiting for a response from within, he looked around, noting that a security camera was mounted ten feet above the door, aimed at the exact place where he and Libby were standing. Morris looked at the little house next door, then at the one across the street. Neither had a similar camera in place. Apparently David Kabov wanted to know for certain who was standing on his front step.

After half a minute or so, there was a loud *click*, and the door swung open a few inches under its own weight. Morris waited for someone inside to open it the rest of the way, but when nobody did, he pushed the door slowly open himself and stepped inside, Libby close behind him. She'd told Morris that she had a couple of defensive spells prepared, in case their reception should be hostile.

A short hallway behind the door led into a larger room that was so gloomy Morris couldn't tell whether anybody was in there or not.

"Mister Kabov? I'm Quincey Morris. I sent you a letter a few days back."

A voice came from the dimness within. "Close the door." It was strong and sure, not the quivery voice of an old man.

Libby complied, and the voice said, "Please come in. Be so good as to move slowly, and to keep your hands in plain sight." The voice had an accent that Morris couldn't place, although Kabov's last name suggested Eastern Europe. The man named Kaspar had referred to him as the Lion of Judah, and that meant Israel. The two were not incompatible – many of Europe's surviving Jews had settled in Israel after the war.

Morris's eyes were adjusting now, and he could see that ahead of them was a living room, with the lights out and curtains drawn. He thought he could make out a man-sized figure seated in a chair.

As Morris reached the entrance to the living room, the man said, "To your right you will find a fairly comfortable sofa. I would be obliged if you were to sit down, side by side, Mister Morris to my left."

They did as instructed. Morris's eyes were almost fully used to the gloom now: the man was seated in what appeared to be a wheelchair, facing his guests from about twelve feet away over a low coffee table. There was some kind of blanket across his legs, and both his hands were tucked underneath it. There was a vague shape detectable under the blanket that Morris was fairly sure was not a kitten.

"I am David Kabov," the man said. Some amusement entered his voice as he went on: "But then you knew that already."

"I'm Quincey Morris, as I said at the door. And let me introduce my colleague, Libby Chastain."

Libby nodded toward the man and said politely, "Mister Kabov."

"Good afternoon, Miss Chastain. Welcome to my home."

Kabov looked at Libby for a few moments, then turned back to Morris. "You look like your photos, Mister Morris," he said. "There are quite a few of them in the Internet, as you may know. It would seem that you got into some trouble at the Republican Party's convention last year, and were arrested for it."

"All a misunderstanding," Morris said. "It took a while to clear it up, but all the charges have been dropped."

"A misunderstanding," Kabov said. "Yes, I'm sure that's all it was." If any sarcasm was intended, he kept it out of his voice. "Several of the articles I read described you as some sort of 'occult investigator' – or, less respectfully, a 'ghostbuster.' Is that what you do, Mister Morris – investigate matters involving the occult?"

"All the possible answers I could give to that question boil down to the same thing," Morris said. "Yes – that's what I do."

Kabov nodded, and looked at Libby. "And Miss Chastain. As I understand it, you have a long association with Mister Morris, although you did not join him last year in durance vile. Several stories I read online described you as a 'witch' – normally a most disrespectful way to refer to a lady, but I gather in your case the term was meant literally. Are you, Miss Chastain? A witch?"

"Yes, Mister Kabov, I am. More precisely, I am a practitioner of white witchcraft, which means –"

"I know what it means," he said, "but thank you for your willingness to explain. So, then." Kabov shifted a little in his wheelchair, but his hands remained underneath the blanket. "What do an occult investigator and a witch want with me?"

"A man in New York told me that you might know how to get in touch with the Knights Templar," Morris said.

"A man? What man?"

"He was introduced to me as Kaspar, with a 'K.' I never learned his last name, or even if Kaspar was his real first name. But that's what he answered to."

"Large fellow, is he? Built like one of your football players? Scar just below his left ear?"

"No," Morris said. "The fella I met was pretty small, barely five foot tall, although he did have a big head – too big for his body, really. And I don't remember any scar."

Kabov nodded slowly. "And where in New York did you meet this Kaspar?"

"In a bar called Strangefellows. We were introduced by a friend of mine, a private detective named Barry Love."

Kabov regarded them in silence for ten or fifteen seconds. Then he said, "Mister Morris, a few feet from you there is a floor lamp. Would you be so good as to switch it on? I could pull the curtains, of course, but I prefer not to be visible to the outside world."

Morris felt for the switch, found it, and clicked on the lamp. The hundred-watt CFL bulb threw a bright light that had them all squinting for a few seconds until their eyes adjusted, although Morris would have bet that Kabov's eyes were already narrowed against the glare before the lamp was turned on.

Morris saw that their host appeared to be, as advertised, in his mid-seventies. His hair was iron-gray, although he still had most of it. David Kabov's eyes were a cold, pale blue that looked at the world without the aid of glasses, although it was possible that he wore contacts. He wore jeans, New Balance running shoes, and a loose-fitting Hawaiian-print shirt.

The muscles visible in his forearms, combined with the breadth of his shoulders and those pitiless eyes, suggested to Morris that at one time it would have been a particularly bad idea to get on this man's wrong side. Maybe it still was.

Kabov's big, knuckly hands were in sight now, and he pulled the blanket aside to reveal one of the smaller models of the Uzi submachine gun, once the favored weapon of the Israeli Defense Forces. Morris peered at the weapon, and it looked to him like the safety was off, and the selector switch was set to "Full Auto."

"Please excuse the armament," Kabov said. "There are still some people abroad in the world who regard my continued existence as a mistake requiring urgent correction – or would, if they knew I was still alive. It is possible that one or more of them will come through that door, someday."

"Or try to," Morris muttered, still looking at the gun.

Kabov grinned at him. "Or try to," he repeated. "That is why I keep my little friend handy, but I think perhaps I should put him away now. May I offer you both some ice tea? I just brewed a pitcher this morning, and it came out rather well, if I say so myself."

They both accepted his offer; Libby asked for a little lemon in hers.

"I will be just a few minutes," Kabov said – then, in one fluid motion, he stood up from the wheelchair. He walked to what Morris assumed was the kitchen, carrying the Uzi, his steps neither unsteady nor hesitant.

Twenty

KABOV RETURNED CARRYING a tray laden with three tall plastic tumblers, which he placed on the coffee table. Morris noticed a slight bulge at the man's right hip, underneath the garish shirt, which seemed a size or two larger than it should be. Kabov might have left his automatic weapon in the kitchen, but that didn't necessarily mean he was unarmed.

Handing one of the tumblers to Libby, he said, "This one has a little lemon juice, as requested, Miss Chastain." He gave another tumbler to Morris and took the third for himself. Then he stepped back to the wheelchair and sat down.

With a slight smile, Kabov said, "I apologize for my little deception. But everyone around here believes me to be confined to this chair, as the result of an old, unspecified injury. I find it useful to be thought of as a semi-invalid."

Libby sipped some ice tea and said, "Wonderful." She took another swallow then said, "We had heard that you were... cautious."

Kabov grinned for a second, revealing a good set of teeth that did not appear to have come from a factory.

"I would wager that whoever spoke to you about

me," he said, "did not use a word like 'cautious,' but something closer to 'paranoid,' yes?"

Libby gave him a tiny smile. "Perhaps."

"I do not find it offensive," Kabov told her. "I would refer you to that great American philosopher, Mister Woody Allen, who said: 'Being paranoid doesn't necessarily mean they're not out to get you.'"

"Who do you believe is out to get you?" Morris said. "If you don't mind my asking."

"Broadly speaking, there are two groups from which potential assassins might be drawn," Kabov said. "One is my old enemies in what these days is called radical Islam. I gather the term 'Arab terrorists' is considered politically incorrect these days."

"You mean al-Qaeda?" Libby asked. "Those guys?"

"That name would figure on what is probably a long list, yes. Although my battles against those people go back before Osama bin Laden – or rather, the late Osama bin Laden, God rot him – ever dreamed of financing a terror network."

He shifted in his chair. "My name is not David Kabov," he said, "although that is close enough to the one I was born with. For a number of years, I held a series of responsible positions in the *HaMossad leModi'in uleTafkidim Meyuhadim*, although you probably know it simply as the Mossad."

"Israeli intelligence," Morris said.

"Quite," Kabov said.

"So, you're a native Israeli?" Libby said.

"There are very few of my generation who can call themselves 'native Israelis,' Miss Chastain. Most of us came to the newly-born state of Israel from other places. My parents were Russian Jews, who emigrated to Poland before I was born, on the mistaken assumption that it would be a safer place for people of our faith to live. Their lack of foresight ultimately cost them their lives, as well as those of my brother and two sisters – and very nearly my own."

Now that he knew what to look for, Morris was not surprised to see the small, faded tattoo on the inside of Kabov's left forearm. It was almost certainly a serial number – the kind put on men, women, and children as they were processed by the Nazi guards into places like Dachau and Auschwitz.

"But, yes," Kabov went on, "I lived most of my life in Israel, and for many years I fought her enemies – from Black September to black magicians."

Morris had a tendency to slouch when sitting, but Kabov's last phrase made his spine straighten, seemingly of its own volition. "Black magicians, you say?"

Kabov nodded. "Yes, Mr. Morris. Some of Israel's enemies will use any weapon in an attempt to destroy her. On several occasions, they have resorted to the black arts." He glanced toward Libby. "As I'm sure Miss Chastain knows, the only effective defense against magic is magic itself."

"Are you saying that you're a magic practitioner?" Morris asked.

"No, Mister Morris. I lack the talent. But I often worked closely with practitioners – the Mossad has several on staff. And, as I'm sure you know, there are sometimes spells that a layman such as myself can manage, given the proper training and equipment."

"Like a charged wand, you mean," Libby said.

"Yes, exactly. I employed such devices more than once. My success on those occasions was probably due as much to good luck as it was to good magic. But I was able to accomplish my goals."

"Is that how you came into contact with the Knights Templar?" Morris asked him.

"Ah, the warrior-priests." Kabov flashed the grin again, and leaned forward a bit. "Do you know there was a day, during their first incarnation in the Middle Ages, that the Knights Templar slaughtered Jews as readily as they did Saracens? Both were 'unbelievers,' you see." He sat back. "I am glad to note that the Catholic Church's attitudes on such matters have changed over the centuries – at least somewhat."

"We were amazed to learn that the Knights still existed, after all this time," Libby said.

Morris nodded. "The other surprise is that we'd never heard a whisper about these fellas before. Between us, Libby and I pretty much know everybody who's anybody in... paranormal circles. Or so we thought."

"The Knights Templar are very secretive," Kabov said. "They are used only for very special missions. The rest of their time they spend in meditation, prayer – and training."

"They probably keep their heads down partially because they remember what happened the last time around," Morris said.

"Few heads of state possess the power to do something similar these days," Kabov said. "But that memory may nonetheless play a role in the Knights'... discretion."

"Do they operate out of some kind of headquarters?" Libby asked him. "Is there a 'Knights Templar Central?'"

"No, they are dispersed throughout the world," Kabov said. "Perhaps in an effort to forestall a repetition of the calamity that befell them in the fourteenth century. Their North American training facility is located in rural Ohio, not far from the city of Toledo."

Morris and Libby looked at each other for a second. "Seems like kind of a strange place for a secret military operation," Morris said. "I assume it *is* secret?"

"Oh, yes, very much so," Kabov said. "As for it being an unlikely location" – Kabov spread his hands slightly – "perhaps that is the very reason they have chosen it."

"Could be." Morris paused for a couple of seconds, then said, "I had to do some business in that area a few years ago – fella out there was having a werewolf problem. As I recollect, there's a fair amount of open country around Toledo. Lots of places the Knights could have set up shop. Would you be willing to give us specific directions?"

"I might," Kabov said, "if I knew the reason you want to make contact with them."

Morris and Libby took turns summarizing what they knew about the afreet and its potential uses. It didn't take long, since they knew so little.

When they had finished, Kabov sat silently for a little while, his nose resting on the tip of his steepled fingers. At last he said, "You may be on to something with that fruit stone idea, Miss Chastain. Have you determined how you are going to fling your peach pit at the creature, assuming you have the opportunity?"

"A friend of ours named Peters is working on that for us," Libby said. "He's ex-CIA, and he knows quite a bit about weapons – although he's never had to deal with one like this before."

"I used to know a CIA man who called himself Peters, back in the old days," Kabov said musingly. "It's a common American name, of course. In any case, that man is almost certainly dead now."

"Yes," Libby said, her face and voice carefully neutral. "Almost certainly."

Kabov gave her a sharp look, but it faded after a moment. "However," he said, "the myth concerning the effect of a thrown fruit stone on the various species of djinn is just that – a myth – and as such is unreliable. You are wise, I think, to prepare what you Americans call a 'back-up plan.'"

"And that's why we want to talk to the Knights Templar," Morris said. "In the hope that we can talk them into parting with their fragment of the Seal of Solomon."

"The Seal, yes," Kabov said. "Solomon was, of course, a great king of my people. That, along with my experience in matters of the occult, may make me more familiar with the stories concerning the Great Seal than some others might be."

"Any insights you'd care to share with us?" Morris asked.

"Less an insight than a question," Kabov said. "The fragment of the Great Seal that was stolen from that museum – what were its dimensions, do you know?"

Morris and Libby both shook their heads. "We never thought to inquire," Libby said. "Does it matter?"

"Quite possibly," Kabov said. He gave a bark of laughter. "This may be one of those few instances, Miss Chastain, when size really *does* matter."

Libby's expression suggested she thought she might be the butt of a joke. "Excuse me?"

"Forgive my vulgarity," Kabov said. "But it is true, nonetheless – assuming anything so shrouded in legend and superstition can be considered 'true.'"

"I don't know if Libby is still following you, Mister Kabov," Morris said. "But I know you just lost *me*."

"My point, Mister Morris, is that bigger *is* better – at least when it comes to bits of the Great Seal."

"Better – how?" Libby asked.

"According to several ancient sources – ancient, but still written centuries after Solomon – there seems to be a direct relationship between the size of the fragment and the amount of power it invokes."

"The bigger the piece... the more powerful it is?" Libby said. "Seriously?"

"So the legends say," Kabov told her. "That is why I asked you if you knew the size of the fragment that was stolen – which is, presumably, in the hands of your would-be terrorists."

"I expect that's something we can find out," Morris said. "But how about the piece the Knights own – do you know how big *that* is?"

"I had no idea that they even possessed one," Kabov said. "My ignorance is unsurprising, mind you. I'm sure the Knights regard such information as being on a strict 'Need to Know' basis – and I have not had the need to know such things for quite some time."

"Then I reckon we'll have to go and ask," Morris said. "Will you tell us how to find them?

Kabov nodded slowly. "Yes, I believe I will – and more than that. I am going to provide you with a letter of introduction to their Father-General."

"And that should get us in?" Libby asked.

"Yes, Miss Chastain, I believe so – and, more important, it will also allow you to get *out*."

Twenty-One

HEAD SOUTHEAST OUT of Toledo, Ohio along Route 25, perhaps on your way to the college town of Bowling Green, and you pass through an agricultural area, stretching for miles on either side of the two-lane road. Exactly twenty-one-point-three miles from where Route 25 begins, there is an access road, marked by a small wooden sign. In the middle of the sign is a symbol in red, consisting of four triangles arranged to form what some might assume to be a cross. Above the symbol is painted, in black letters, "Private Road." Below the red triangles, the same black paint has been used to write "No Trespassing."

The road was narrow, and Quincey Morris was cautious as he turned the maroon Ford Focus they'd rented from the Avis counter at Toledo Express Airport. No sense messing up the paint job by getting too well acquainted with one of the poplars lining the road as far down as he could see. Driving no more than twenty-five miles an hour, Morris followed the road for the better part of a mile until it led him to a sharp bend. He made the turn and almost immediately stopped.

Before them was a chain link fence, at least ten feet tall and topped with barbed wire. In the middle of the fence, straddling the road, was a closed gate – tall, made of metal bars and topped with a security camera. Above the gate was a sign that read:

TEMPLE SECURITY
TRAINING CENTER
NO ADMITTANCE WITHOUT PASS

In front of the gate stood two men. They wore black military fatigues, with baseball caps and shaved heads. Web belts laden with pouches and equipment encircled their waists. Each man sported a pair of those wraparound sunglasses that are all the rage among Southern prison guards, if the movies are to be believed. Morris figured the color of those outfits must make the guards damned uncomfortable in the height of summer. Then his attention was drawn abruptly from their clothing to their armament.

They each carried a short-barreled automatic weapon with a long, curved magazine. Morris was no gun expert, but the guns looked to him like the Heckler & Koch MP5s favored by the Dallas SWAT team. The weapons were attached to slings over each man's left shoulder, allowing him to let go of the gun – if, say, he wanted to beat somebody to death instead of just shooting him.

The guards walked up to either side of the car. They seemed to have all the time in the world.

Morris's window had already been partly open; now he rolled it all the way down, but slowly – it never pays to startle people carrying submachine guns.

The man on Morris's side said, "You folks are trespassing on private property. You need to back that thing up, turn it around, and get back down the road you drove in on. *Right now.*"

His voice was louder than it needed to be, considering how close he was standing to the car. The man probably figured it was more intimidating that way – as if somebody carrying an MP5 *needed* to be any more intimidating.

"That doesn't seem real friendly," Morris said. "I'd heard the Knights Templar were more hospitable." That was bullshit Morris had made up on the spot, but he wanted to get the conversation headed in the right direction.

"The *what*? Knights *who*?" The guard's face and voice combined incredulity and aggression with the kind of skill that Morris thought belonged on a Broadway stage – unless, of course, it was genuine.

The man took a step closer. In the same loud tone he said, "Mister, I think you are fucking with me. And if that's what you have in mind, you oughta know that the last smart-ass who fucked with me is buried under *that* tree right fucking *there*." He jabbed an index finger toward a giant oak a hundred or so feet off to his right.

Nice way for a priest to talk, Morris thought. Then he realized that acting un-priestly was probably part of the gate guards' job description.

Libby kept her attention focused on the man standing outside her window, especially on his hands. She had a couple of spells prepared in case things got ugly – but she and Morris had agreed the night before that if she had to use one, it would mean their mission to the Knights Templar had failed.

Morris said, "If it's all right, I'd like to reach under my coat and very slowly take out an envelope, which I will then very slowly hand to you."

"What's in the envelope?" the guard asked with a half-sneer. "Your will?"

"It contains a letter of introduction to your boss, Father-General Reinhart," Morris told him. "It's written by somebody whose name the Father-General will recognize."

The guard stared at Morris, his eyes unreadable behind the opaque lenses of the sunglasses. The silence went on just long enough for Morris to start wondering if he and Libby had made a very bad mistake in coming here, and then the guard extended his open left hand, keeping his right close to the trigger of the MP5.

"Do it slow." The guard's tone was almost conversational now. "Just like you said."

Moving as if he was underwater, Morris removed from his jacket pocket what the man calling himself David Kabov had given them – a long white envelope with "Father-General Thomas Reinhart, K.T." on the front in Kabov's crabbed handwriting.

The guard took the envelope and stepped back. He looked at the name written on it, held it up to the sunlight for a moment, then squeezed the envelope between his big fingers.

Checking to see if it's thick enough to be a letter bomb, Morris thought. The envelope contained just a single sheet of paper; after a moment, the guard looked back at Morris and said, "Turn your engine off, please."

It was the first instance of courtesy the man had shown. It probably meant that Morris and Libby weren't about to be riddled with 9mm bullets.

The guard said to his partner, "Watch 'em, Charlie," and turned away. He walked about fifty feet and pulled from his belt a military-style radio. Whatever he said into it was too faint for Morris to hear, and he spent most of the conversation listening anyway. Finally he said, more clearly, "Yes, sir," and replaced the radio on his belt.

The guard turned toward the gate, which allowed him to look inside the compound – although the only things visible from here were trees, rocks, and a narrow macadam road. He stood, hands on hips, as if waiting for something.

He did not have to wait long. Within two minutes, a black Chevy Suburban, the kind favored by the U.S. Secret Service, could be seen approaching the gate from inside the compound.

The vehicle came to a halt a few yards from the gate. Another man, dressed like the gate guards, got out from the passenger side and walked to the gate. The guard holding Kabov's letter handed it through the bars to the new man, who gave a nod of acknowledgment and got back into the Suburban. The vehicle immediately began to turn around and was soon heading back the way it had come.

They would have to wait now. Morris said to the guard who'd taken the envelope from him, "Figure this is going to take long?"

"Don't talk," the man said stolidly.

A little later, Morris started to say something to Libby, and the guard gave him as "I said '*Don't talk*.'" This time, his voice had some snap in it.

Morris had glanced at his watch when the Suburban left with Kabov's letter; forty-six minutes had elapsed before the guard's radio gave a hiss of static, followed by a man's voice. "*Wender to O'Malley. Come in.*"

The guard, whose name was apparently O'Malley, immediately began walking away from the car as he pulled the radio from his belt. Morris heard nothing of the ensuing conversation, but it wasn't long before O'Malley was back.

"I'm gonna need you folks to exit your vehicle,

please," he said to Morris. "Leave the keys – we'll park it somewhere safe until you're ready to leave."

Morris opened his door and got out, relieved to hear the use of "please" again, along with the implied assumption that he and Libby would be departing, eventually – and under their own power.

To Libby, O'Malley said, "Ma'am, I need you to come around to this side of the vehicle. And Charlie is gonna have to take a look inside your bag."

Libby handed her big leather purse to the guard named Charlie and went around the car until she stood a few feet from Morris.

"Just stand easy there for a second, folks," the first guard said. He did not quite point his MP5 at them, but the business end of the barrel wasn't aimed all that far away, either.

Charlie poked through Libby's bag, and he took his time about it. The only object he removed briefly was a six-inch metal tube that could be telescoped out, like a radio antenna, to a length of just over a foot. It was Libby's collapsible magic wand, already charged, and had served her well several times in the past.

Charlie examined it long enough to ensure that the tube wasn't a weapon, returned it to the purse, and nodded at his partner, who said, "We'll have to frisk you folks now, and it's gonna be a little more thorough than the pat-down you get at the airport."

He looked at Libby. "I apologize for the indignity, Ma'am, but we haven't got a woman available to carry out the search on you – and nobody goes through that gate who hasn't been checked over first. 'Course, you could always elect to wait out here while your friend goes inside and conducts his business. Up to you."

Libby shrugged. Her face and voice carefully neutral,

she said, "It's all right. Do what you have to do."

"All right, then. I'm gonna need you folks to separate a little more, and put your hands on the roof of the vehicle, at least two feet apart. Good. Now I want you to spread your feet apart. More. Okay, now walk 'em back towards me. More. A little more. All right, then. Maintain that position until I tell you it's okay to move. Go ahead, Charlie."

Morris withstood the search stoically. He had been frisked many times in jail, and was used to it. He felt bad for Libby, though, even as he was grateful that she had elected to accompany him inside the compound. At least the guards weren't being assholes about it. Morris reminded himself that these guys were probably priests. Then he thought about some of the recent scandals involving Catholic clergymen, and was somewhat less reassured. But it had to be done, anyway.

Five minutes later, the search was over, the gate was open, Morris was following Libby into the back seat of the now-returned Suburban.

They were, it seemed, off to see the wizard.

Twenty-Two

In his cramped office at Wayne State University, Nasiri had spent the better part of an hour grading papers written by young idiots whose command of the English language was considerably inferior to his own – and he had not begun learning the language until he was twenty-eight years old. He had just finished writing in the margins of one such pitiful effort, "No, Iranians are not Arabs – they are Persians, which is an entirely different ethnic group. And 'all right' is two words, not 'alright,'" when the phone on his desk began ringing.

"This is Doctor Nasiri."

"Peace be upon you, Doctor," an accented voice said. "This is Michael."

Michael was the code name for the wizard, Uthman. Nasiri had ordered him to use it in all electronic communication, just as he had forbidden the use of Arabic. He knew that the computers at NSA were programmed to home in on any U.S. telephone conversation in Arabic, or even one in English that used words like "Allah" and "jihad."

"Hello, Michael – how are you?" It was unusual for Uthman to contact him by phone – it meant something had gone wrong, somewhere.

"I ran into your friend Robert yesterday." "Robert" meant "I want to meet with you," while "yesterday" referred to "tomorrow."

"Did you? And how is Robert?" Nasiri's repetition of the name meant he agreed to meet Uthman tomorrow.

"He is very well, I think."

"I'm glad to hear that. Where did you encounter him?"

"At the cinema." "Cinema" meant the proposed meeting place would be the Arab American National Museum, on Michigan Avenue.

"The cinema, yes." Nasiri confirmed the meeting place. "What film did you see?"

"The new one about the secret agent, James Bond. It was very enjoyable."

"I have heard that was a good one. Did you attend the three o'clock show?"

"No, the one at eleven a.m."

The name of the film was irrelevant, since there was no way to predict what would be playing in the local theatres on a given day. But the time was important – especially once Nasiri added two hours, as per the procedure that he and his group were using.

"Yes, I see." The time for the rendezvous was agreed upon.

The two of them chatted about the nonexistent Robert for a few more minutes, but the important information had already been transmitted. They ended the call with mutual pleasantries.

After he had hung up, Nasiri stared at the phone without really seeing it. He was trying to enumerate all the things that might have happened, and what his response would be to each one. Then he gave a mental shrug. Speculation was a waste of mental energy. He would find out what had gone wrong soon enough.

Twenty-Three

ONE OF THE guards slammed the door of the Suburban shut, and a moment later Morris heard the double *click* as both rear doors were locked, presumably by the driver. He wore black fatigues, too – just like the man sitting in the shotgun seat, cradling another of the ubiquitous MP5s.

The windows in back had been treated with the film you find in some limousines – the stuff that makes it impossible to see into a car, while still allowing the occupants to see out. Except in this case the film was on the *inside*, preventing anyone sitting in back from seeing out through the rear and side windows. Of course, you couldn't put that stuff on the windshield; Morris was feeling mildly clever for noticing that, until the driver said, "I'm going to raise the divider now, folks, but I'll put the ceiling light on for you. Sit back and relax – it'll be a short trip."

A low-wattage bulb over their heads came on just as a plate of thick glass rose in front of them. It was covered with the same translucent film as the windows – when the divider slid into place, no light entered the back seat from outside the vehicle. The Suburban started moving, and Morris found that he was grateful for the overhead light, dim as it was. Complete darkness under these circumstances would have been pretty hard on the nerves.

He turned to Libby. "These guys think of everything," he said and tugged at his earlobe, sending her the message that the rear compartment might well be bugged. Libby nodded her understanding and said, "Seems like they do."

"Sorry you had to undergo that search back there," he said.

She gave him a half-smile. "It's all right, Quincey. I didn't just wander out of a convent, after all. Besides, it wasn't as bad as it could have been – the guard did what was necessary to make sure I wasn't concealing a weapon, but that's all. He didn't treat himself to a good time at my expense."

"Glad to hear it."

A few minutes later, Morris felt the vehicle slow, then come to a stop. There was another click as the driver unlocked the rear doors, and almost immediately both doors were pulled open by men in black fatigues. Morris and Libby got out without waiting to be told.

They were standing at the rear of a long, low building covered in white stucco. It sported several doors along its length, each with a number painted above it. Through the nearest door – number four – came another man wearing what seemed to be the standard uniform around these parts. He marched over to the Suburban and said, briskly, "Mister Morris, Miss Chastain? I am Father-Major Pearson. Will you follow me, please?"

Without waiting for a response, Pearson did an about-face and headed back the way he had come. Morris and Libby followed, and a few feet behind them came the two guards who had opened the doors of the Suburban.

The corridor they entered was painted institutional

green, its monotony relieved only by a couple of bulletin boards, a fire extinguisher – and a large crucifix. At the fourth door on the right, Pearson stopped, bringing the rest of the little procession to an abrupt halt. He knocked twice, and a man's voice on the other side of the door called, "Come in." Pearson opened the door wide, and gestured for Morris and Libby to precede him. He followed them into a windowless room whose walls were covered with maps, exploded diagrams of several weapons, and another large crucifix. Pearson said to the man behind the desk, "These are the two people you wanted to see, sir."

The man looked at Morris and Libby, put down the pen he'd been writing with, and said, "Thank you, Father-Major. Dismissed."

"Yes, sir." Pearson did another about face, marched out through the door, and closed it behind him.

The man who, according to David Kabov, was the commander of the Knights Templar in North America stood up from behind his plain metal desk, his shaved skull glistening in the fluorescent light. Father-General Thomas Reinhart looked to be in his early fifties. He wore the standard black fatigue pants, but above these was a gray t-shirt with RANGER printed on the front. The shirt was a little tight, displaying arm and chest muscles that appeared to have been set in concrete. Reinhart didn't have the physique of a bodybuilder – for one thing, he only stood about 5'9". His musculature was functional, rather than impressive. He looked like someone who could do five hundred pushups and then get up and punch your lights out, all without breaking a sweat.

"Mister Morris, Miss Chastain," he said. "I am Thomas Reinhart, but then I gather you knew that." He did not offer to shake hands, but did gesture courteously toward a pair of armchairs. "Please sit down."

Morris had expected that Reinhart would speak to them from behind his desk, using the furniture to reinforce his authority. Instead, the warrior-priest perched on the edge of his desk, facing them. "The man you know as David Kabov has earned the Order's trust," Reinhart said, "and he writes asking that we accord the same to you two. But I never trust strangers based on a single recommendation, so I had to keep you waiting while I made a couple of phone calls and did some research of my own."

"I assume the fact that we're sitting here means that you were able to confirm Kabov's recommendation," Morris said.

"You assume correctly. Some people whose opinions I value speak highly of you" – he turned his head and nodded at Libby – "and Miss Chastain here, who, I understand, is a practitioner of witchcraft."

"Only of the white variety," Libby said. "I have no truck with Satan, or his works. Quite the contrary, in fact."

"So I understand. I have heard some accounts of that business you two were involved in a couple of years ago, in Iowa."

"Idaho," Morris said. "People always get those two confused."

"Apologies." Reinhart looked at Libby again. "There was a time when Mother Church made no distinction between forms of witchcraft – any witch was seen as a servant of the devil, and hence deserving of death."

"I know," Libby said tightly.

Reinhart produced a smile that seemed genuine, and possessed no small amount of charm. "Fortunately, we are more enlightened about such matters these days – at least this Order is. So I agreed to have this conversation even though you, Miss Chastain, are a witch, and Mister Morris here appears to be a convicted felon."

Morris shook his head. "Arrested, but not convicted. In fact, all the charges were later dropped."

"I'm aware of that," Reinhart said. "Sometime, I would be interested to hear from you what that business at the Republican convention was all about. We heard some rumors that were really quite intriguing." He gave them an expressive shrug. "But I'm sure you've not come here to swap war stories. So tell me, what *do* you want with the Poor Fellow-Soldiers of Christ and the Temple of Solomon?"

"Strangely enough," Morris said, "or maybe not so strangely, our business has to do with King Solomon himself."

Reinhart raised his eyebrows. "Indeed? Please continue."

"We've been told that your Order possesses a portion of Solomon's Great Seal," Libby said.

Reinhart said nothing, but in the bright light Morris thought he saw the man's pupils dilate.

"If that's the case," Libby went on, "we... well, we'd like to borrow it."

Reinhart stared at her for perhaps five seconds. Then he scratched his jaw and said, "There are several ways I could respond to this. One option is simply to tell you that we do not possess, nor does anyone in the Order possess, anything to do with the Seal of Solomon."

"No disrespect, sir, but you've pretty much closed the door on that one," Morris said. "If you're considering multiple responses to our request, then it means you have the Seal. If you didn't, then only one response would be necessary – or possible."

Reinhart produced that hundred-watt smile again, and actually made it look genuine. *He's got no business having a smile like* that, Morris thought. *Not a guy who probably knows twelve different ways to kill me with his bare hands.*

"You make a good point, Mister Morris," Reinhart said. "Although there's the possibility that I am falsely implying that we do have the Seal, as a ruse to gain more information from you."

"I thought priests weren't supposed to lie," Libby said.

"Incorrect, Miss Chastain. We're not supposed to lie *without a good reason.*"

"True or not, you seem to have abandoned direct denial as a response," Morris said. "What else have you got?"

"Well, there's always indignation," Reinhart said. "That's the one where I say 'How dare you come in here and ask for one of the most sacred relics there is, over which generations of men have spilled their blood?'" Reinhart made a dismissive gesture. "And so forth."

"Sounds like you've decided not to go with that one, either," Morris said.

Reinhart nodded slowly. "Quite right – although it's the one I would normally use." He took in a long breath and let it out slowly. "You two appear to be serious people, and what I've heard and read about you in the last hour confirms that assessment."

He went around behind his desk, sat down, and pulled a pad of paper toward him. "I make no promises," he said. "But if you will tell me, in detail, why you want our fragment of the Great Seal, I will give your request serious consideration. Fair enough?"

Morris and Libby nodded. Then, as they had with David Kabov, they took turns relaying what they knew, suspected, and feared about a certain djinn and those who controlled it.

When they had finished, Reinhart sat staring at the page of closely-written notes he'd made. Looking up, he said, "So if our fragment of the Seal is bigger than the one being used by these alleged terrorists, that makes it more powerful – and will allow you to take control of the djinn away from them."

"That's what Kabov told us, yes," Morris said.

"You are said to be a witch of considerable ability, Miss Chastain. Why can't you use your magic against the creature?"

"For a couple of reasons," Libby told him. "One is, I can't use my magic to directly bring harm to anybody, and that includes djinn – at least, I think it does. It's not the sort of question that comes up very often."

"No, I imagine not," Reinhart said. "And the other reason?"

"Djinn are a unique species," Libby said. "Neither human, nor angel, nor demon. I have it on good authority that such a creature is probably immune to any magic that I might be able to employ, even if I wasn't using it for destructive purposes."

Reinhart's eyes narrowed. "What authority are you referring to?"

"I... I'd rather not say. It came from a confidential source, but one whose expertise I've relied on in the past." *Besides, if I tell you I've been fucking a demon, you'd probably throw my ass out – if not burn it at the stake.*

"As you wish," Reinhart said. "So, if you go into battle with this djinn, the only weapon in your arsenal right now is a mechanically-fired peach pit?"

"Avocado," Libby said. "They're bigger. Greater mass equals greater impact – I hope."

"How do you plan to find the people who control this creature, assuming they actually exist?"

"We're still working on that," Morris said. "No point in going after them until we have a reasonable chance of surviving the encounter."

Reinhart added something to the notes he'd been making. Then he put down his pen and said, "I need to give this some serious thought, and prayer. I also want to consult with a couple of my senior commanders, whose opinions I value."

"How long do you figure this will all take?" Morris asked.

"Probably several hours. During that time, I invite you to be my guests."

Morris looked at Libby, then turned back to Reinhart. "Well, having come this far..."

"Yes, quite." Reinhart stood, walked to the door, and opened it. "Father-Major Pearson!"

Within seconds, Pearson was standing in the doorway. "Yes, sir?"

"Escort our guests to the Officers' Day Room. Make sure they have whatever they need."

"Yes, sir."

"And let our brother officers know that the Day Room is off-limits to them for the next six hours."

"Yes, sir."

Pearson turned to Morris and Libby. "If you will follow me, please?"

And so they did. They even acted as if they had a choice.

Twenty-Four

AT ONE O'CLOCK, Nasiri was standing before an exhibit of medieval Arabic art when Uthman appeared at his elbow.

"Peace be upon you, my brother," the wizard said quietly.

"And upon you, too." Nasiri also kept his voice down, even speaking Arabic. In this building, in this city, Arabic was more likely to be used than English. There were perhaps a dozen other people in the large, open room, but none of them stood nearby. If someone did approach the art exhibit, Nasiri and Uthman would casually move on to another area, far enough away from other people to keep them safe from prying ears, regardless of the language they used.

"What did you wish to discuss with me so urgently, my brother?" Nasiri asked.

Uthman took a moment before answering. "It concerns... Rashid," he said.

"I surmised as much," Nasiri said, and waited.

"I allowed him egress from the lamp, last night – after first surrounding it with an unbreachable barrier of magic, of course."

"Again? Why must you continue to do such things?"

"For the same reason that a lion tamer works with his big cats on a regular basis, brother – to remind them who is dominant. Otherwise, he may face an unpleasant surprise on the day he performs before the crowd."

"I am not certain that I find such an analogy convincing," Nasiri said.

"I believe it is very appropriate," Uthman told him. "The fragment of Great Suleiman's Seal that we have is not very large. As I have explained to you, the size is directly related to its power."

"I hope you are not about to suggest that we secure a larger relic for you – even assuming that one could be located somewhere."

"No, brother – I am aware that that would be all but impossible. My own resources – which are considerable, I may say – have been unable to uncover any other verified fragment anywhere."

"Very well, then. So you let our friend out of his container, to re-establish your dominance over him. What is the problem that caused you to get in touch with me?"

Uthman hesitated again, and Nasiri felt a worm of unease begin crawling through his guts.

"The comparison of my work to that of a lion tamer was perhaps more apt than you realize, brother," Uthman said. "In both cases, a degree of caution, or restraint, is called for. The man in the cage has his whip and chair, perhaps even a revolver. However, the power these accord him is limited. One can push a lion or leopard only so far without risk of bloody rebellion. The same is true of our friend in the lamp, despite my possessing a piece of Great Suleiman's Seal."

Nasiri kept the irritation off his face, but allowed it to show in his voice. "Brother, if there is something you wish to tell me, I think it would be a very good thing for you to say it outright."

Uthman nodded nervously. "You recall, I am sure, that... expedition that three of us – led by myself, of course – undertook some six weeks ago, in order to provide what Rashid said was essential nourishment."

"I am hardly likely to forget it, and the risks involved in securing the... organ that Rashid required."

"Then we must prepare ourselves to endure more risks, brother," Uthman said. "Because he wants another one."

Twenty-Five

MORRIS WAS READING an article in the current issue of *Military Strategy* about how Napoleon could have won at Waterloo when Father-Major Pearson returned for them.

The Officers' Day Room at Knights Templar headquarters was the size of a living room in a large house, and was furnished with a number of couches and easy chairs – all a bit worn, but undeniably comfortable. The room also contained some low tables, a widescreen TV, a cooler containing soda and bottled water, and a coffee maker whose product was far better than Morris would have expected. Libby favored tea, and that was available, too. They had been brought surprisingly good food from the Officers' Mess, and allowed use of a nearby restroom – with an escort to and from, of course.

Then Pearson appeared in the doorway and said, "Mister Morris, Miss Chastain – if you'd come with me, please." They followed him back to Father-General Reinhart's office, although Pearson did not accompany them inside this time.

Reinhart was behind his desk, and after Morris and Libby were seated, he said, "I won't waste your time, or my own, with a lot of social pleasantries designed to lessen the sting of rejection. The fact is, I have decided not to allow you the use of, or access to, the fragment of the Seal of Solomon that the Order has in its care."

After a few seconds of silence, Libby said, "I see. May we know why?"

"No, you may not. The reasons are several, and they involve information that cannot be disclosed to those who are not members of the Order. In any case, the reasons don't matter – since I have no intention of debating the matter with you."

Morris stood up, and Libby followed suit. "Well, it is what it is, I reckon," he said, keeping what he felt mostly out of his voice. "I assume you'll have us driven back to wherever our car is parked."

"Of course," Reinhart said. "Unless you'd care to stay and discuss the possibility of a *quid pro quo*."

Morris and Libby just stared at him. After a moment, Reinhart said, "*Quid pro quo* means –"

"We *know* what it means," Morris said. "It means you want to play 'Let's make a deal.'"

"I never play, Mister Morris. My work is far too serious for games. But as to the deal aspect – you may have that right. I would suggest you both resume your seats."

They did.

"The Order – or, at least, the branch of it which I have the honor to command – has a problem," Reinhart said. "And it is one that you, Miss Chastain, may be uniquely equipped to help us address."

Libby nodded warily.

"It is my understanding," Reinhart went on, "that you are proficient in what is called 'psychic dowsing' – the ability to locate something, or someone, using only a map and pendulum."

"We call it 'remote location,'" Libby said. "But you're essentially correct. However, if I'm searching for a person, I need an object that is closely associated with him – or her. Something that has been touched, or worn, many times."

"I don't believe that would be a problem," Reinhart said. "Have you been successful with this technique in the past?"

"Yes, I have," Libby said.

"May I ask how many times?"

"I've employed it five times for real," Libby said. "As opposed to exercises while in training. I was successful four times out of five."

"What was responsible for the single failure? Do you know?"

She shook her head. "I was never able to determine that. It could have been that the person I searched for was not in the area covered by the map. Or maybe the object I was using to make a psychic connection wasn't personal enough. There's no way to tell for sure."

Reinhart nodded, then wiped a hand along the length of his rough-hewn face. He looked from Libby to Morris, and back to Libby.

"You may have noticed," he said, "that we are very careful about security here. We have to be – our very survival depends on it. That's why you were brought here in a closed car, and your movements have been restricted since your arrival."

Reinhart learned forward. "Miss Chastain, I am about to violate the essence of our security policy, and I do so only because we need your help. I won't ask Mister Morris to leave the room for this discussion, since I have no doubt that you would tell him about it later. I would expect no less – I understand that the two of you have worked together closely for quite some time."

"Yes, we have," Morris said. "Libby has saved my

life several times, and I may have done so once or twice for her, as well. We don't have secrets from each other – professional ones, anyway."

"I accept that," Reinhart said. "But what you are about to learn must go no further than this room. I *cannot* stress that strongly enough. If one of you were to reveal our secrets to anyone – *anyone* – we would hear of it, eventually. And then –" Reinhart sat back in his chair, suddenly looking very tired. "I would have the regretful necessity of ordering your deaths."

"I thought you were a priest, *Father*," Morris said. "Doesn't the Fifth Commandment say, 'Thou shalt not kill'?"

"In fact, it doesn't, Mister Morris. The commandment reads, 'Thou shalt not do murder.' And keep in mind that I am also a soldier. Centuries ago, the founders of our Order were told by His Holiness the Pope that taking a life in the service of Christ, regrettable though it may be, is not murder."

"Some Christian ethicists might well argue that point," Morris said.

"Let them. That interests me not at all. What does interest me is that you and Miss Chastain understand the inevitable consequences of breaching our security."

"You make yourself very clear," Libby said. "But something that isn't clear, not yet, anyway, is the terms of the deal you're offering us."

Reinhart studied his big, rough hands. "If you agree to help us find this... missing person, and your efforts prove successful, you may have our relic of Solomon's Seal, to use as you wish. We would prefer to have it returned to us, but we recognize that may not be possible. Your chances of surviving an encounter with this afreet, even with the piece of Solomon's Seal, are, frankly, unpromising."

Libby gave him a razor-thin smile. "Your confidence is inspiring."

"I am merely being realistic."

"What if I agree to help you, but the procedure doesn't work?"

"Then we will bid you and Mister Morris farewell, with our thanks for trying. Is that agreeable to you?"

Libby glanced toward Morris, who nodded his agreement with what he knew she was about to say. "Yes," she said, "it is."

Twenty-Six

"*Indiana?*" Jawad Tamwar's voice, although surprised, remained respectful. "Must we travel such a distance, brother? There must be closer places where we can find another captive lion to butcher."

"There are," Nasiri told him. "The state of Michigan contains several other zoos with lion exhibits. And that is the problem."

Mujab Rahim frowned in perplexity. "I am sorry, my brother, but I do not understand this riddle."

Nasiri forced his voice and manner to patience. Rahim might not be among the smartest of Allah's creations, but his courage, obedience, and knife skills made him invaluable to the group.

"If we choose a second zoo within Michigan," Nasiri said, "the authorities may notice a pattern. If we were committing murders, let us say, they would be lost among the many killings that occur in this misbegotten country every day. But removing the hearts of captive lions..."

"Unusual enough to stand out," said Uthman, the wizard. He and Nasiri had already discussed this between themselves. "It is quite possible."

"I mean no disrespect, brother," Tamwar said, "but what does it matter? If the stupid police notice that someone in Michigan is killing lions for their hearts, how could it be traced to us? And who among them would possibly understand the significance of what we are doing?"

"As to the first question," Nasiri said, "it is basic operational security. The knowledge that we who are killing lions – although I hope it is Allah's will that this one will be the last – can be found in Michigan is more information than I wish the police to possess. As their idiotic detective stories say, it would be 'a piece of the puzzle.' And this piece I would deny them. At present, they know nothing of us. For the sake of our holy mission, I would keep it that way."

"And when you say that none of them would understand the significance of our actions," Uthman said to Tamwar, "you are almost correct, my brother. Almost, but not quite. There are some individuals in the United States who may have enough knowledge to make the connection. Their FBI is said to have some agents with occult knowledge – not many, but a few. And even one is too many."

"There are also some people not directly connected with the authorities whose knowledge is a danger to us," Nasiri said. "There is a magician in Chicago named Dresden, I understand."

"And the woman Blake in St. Louis," Uthman said. "She also might recognize the signs."

"A *woman*," Rahim said. He did not bother to keep the disdain from his voice.

"She is dangerous, nonetheless," Uthman said. "I have no doubt that we could destroy her if she became a nuisance, but it would pose a distraction. We do not need distractions at this stage of the operation."

"And that is why we will venture outside Michigan

to find our afreet's next meal," Nasiri said. "That is my decision."

The others knew better than to raise further objections.

"Where must we go, then, brother?" Tamwar asked. "Has that been determined yet?"

"It has," Nasiri told him. "In Center Point, Indiana there is a place calling itself the 'Exotic Feline Rescue Center.' It seems perfect for us."

"They take in big cats from other zoos that have closed, circuses that go out of business, that sort of thing," Uthman said. "According to their website, they have a dozen male lions, and almost twice as many females. It is an embarrassment of riches, my brothers. And no high walls to climb."

"When do we leave?" Rahim asked glumly.

"Soon," Nasiri said. "There are some details to be worked out, but – soon." He glanced toward Uthman. "We must not let our afreet go hungry much longer."

Twenty-Seven

"THE MAN I want you to find is a member of our Order," Reinhart said. "Father-Captain Andrew Dalton."

"How did he end up among the missing?" Libby asked. "Do you know?"

"Indeed I do," Reinhart said grimly. "Father-Captain Dalton was almost certainly abducted."

Morris looked at him. "You mean he's being held for ransom?"

"I wish it were that simple," Reinhart said. "If someone was demanding ransom, we would pay it. We would do so grudgingly, of course, and with the expectation that one day we would have a settling of accounts with the kidnappers. But no ransom has been demanded."

"Do you know why he *was* taken, then?" Libby asked.

"We not only know why, Miss Chastain – we also know by whom."

Libby blinked a couple of times. "I assume you're going to explain all of this, using small words that even Quincey and I can understand."

Reinhart gave her a smile lacking in either charm or humor. "Of course," he said. "For starters, you should understand that Father-Captain Dalton is a Sensitive. Do you know what that means?"

Libby nodded slowly. "As I understand it, a Sensitive can sense human emotions, even if there's no outward sign of them. Some people say they can read minds, but I've never encountered that particular talent, and I'm not sure it's even possible. I have met a few Sensitives, though."

"That's essentially correct," Reinhart said. "Thanks to his ability, Father-Captain Dalton is expert in detecting deception – better than any machine ever invented by man. He is also adept at identifying demonic influence – a talent that was known in the old days as 'witch smelling,' I believe. No offense."

"None taken," Libby said. "As I said earlier, the Infernal has nothing to do with me, or the kind of magic I practice."

"Yes, quite," Reinhart said.

"Is that why your man was taken?" Morris asked him. "Somebody needs some witch-smelling done, or thinks he does?"

"No, I'm quite certain that Father-Captain Dalton's ability as a sort of human lie detector is the reason he was abducted."

"Abducted how?" Morris asked. "I'm pretty sure that somebody, or even several somebodies, didn't just walk in here and grab the good Father. Not with the kind of security you fellas have – not to mention the armament."

"No, that's not how it happened," Reinhart said. "Perhaps I should back up a bit. A couple of months ago, we – the Knights Templar – were approached through an intermediary by a member of a rogue CIA unit called the Clandestine Operations Group."

"Wait," Morris said. "The terms 'rogue' and 'CIA' don't really belong together. I mean, something is either part of the CIA, or it isn't."

Reinhart gave him the humorless smile again. "You'd think so, wouldn't you? But this group's activities are so secret, the CIA doesn't even acknowledge them officially. Most of the CIA doesn't even know they exist."

"I don't get it," Libby said. "I'm no expert on intelligence operations, but the CIA is already ultra-secret in practically everything it does. Are you saying there's a unit that's *ultra*-ultra-secret?"

"That's exactly what I'm saying, Miss Chastain. Nice turn of phrase."

"But" – Libby made a helpless gesture – "what's the *point*? Why would one group need to be more secret than everybody else?"

"Because they violate U.S. law on a regular basis," Reinhart said. "The CIA is forbidden to engage in assassinations, but these people do. The agency is, by charter, not allowed to operate within the United States – but this group does. No government agency is allowed to take U.S. citizens into custody and hold them indefinitely, without either charge or trial. But – guess what? And no organ of the U.S. government, either civilian or military, is permitted to engage in torture for interrogation purposes – not since the last Bush administration, anyway."

"Torture?" Morris said. "Are we talking about waterboarding here?"

"For these people, waterboarding is just a warm-up," Reinhart said. "Drugs, sleep deprivation, hooding – not to mention plain old agony. Fire, electricity, joint dislocation, rape – the whole Gestapo repertoire is theirs, and more."

"My Goddess," Libby said softly.

"If this group is supposed to be so ultra-secret," Morris said, "how come you know so much about them?"

"We have contacts among many of the world's intelligence, military, and law enforcement organizations," Reinhart said. "None of whom would ever acknowledge our existence, of course. We receive a good deal of information from them."

"So you think that this bunch of super-spooks has kidnapped your man?" Morris asked.

"I am certain of it. As I said, they made contact with us. They had heard about Father-Captain Dalton, and wished to 'borrow' him for an unspecified period of time."

"What for?" Libby asked him.

"They didn't say, but I expect they have come to the realization that all torturers do, eventually – the information they're getting is unreliable. Most people will say whatever they think the interrogator wants to hear, just to make the pain stop. Sometimes they speak the truth, sometimes they tell half-truths, and often they just lie."

"And they just wanted you to give Father Dalton to them," Libby said.

"Oh, they offered their usual incentive – *money*."

Morris did not think he had ever heard the word said with so much contempt before.

"The Order has no shortage of funds," Reinhart went on. "But even if we were destitute – to do business with those kinds of people? Unthinkable."

"So, you turned them down," Morris said. "Then what?"

"Then nothing – for about six weeks. At which time Father-Captain Dalton received word that his mother had suffered a massive stroke, and was dying. He asked permission to go to her, and was given leave. All routine."

"Did he travel with a security detail?" Libby asked.

"No, he went alone. The members of our Order do

not normally travel with bodyguards when on personal business. Their anonymity is their protection."

"But not this time," Morris said.

"Quite so," Reinhart said, sounding tired. "Not this time. Father-Captain Dalton was headed for Nashville, Tennessee, where his mother lived – and died. He never made it. Nor has he been seen, or heard from, since."

"Makes you wonder if his mother's stroke was due to natural causes, after all," Morris said.

"It does now, yes. But as the old Yiddish saying goes, 'It's easy to be smart, after.'"

"So you want me to use one of Father Dalton's personal items, a map, and a pendulum, to locate where he's being held by these CIA creeps," Libby said. "Then what?"

"Then we'll go and get him," Reinhart said.

"In a military operation," Libby said.

"Of course. I think it's extremely unlikely that if I showed up at their front door, hat in hand, and asked for Father-Captain Dalton back, that I would receive anything but a bullet for my trouble."

"You're probably right about that," Morris said.

"I'm well aware that what I'm asking poses potential conflicts of interest for you two. Before we proceed further, I need to know whether you'll be able to resolve them."

"What conflicts of interest are you referring to?" Libby asked.

"One has to do with the nature of white magic, Miss Chastain. My understanding is that, as a practitioner, you are not permitted to use magic to hurt anyone. Not to belabor the obvious, but if we carry out a raid on wherever the Clandestine Operations people are holding Father-Captain Dalton, a number of people are likely to be hurt, probably fatally."

"Yes," Libby said. "I had assumed as much."

"Does that pose a problem for you?'

"No, it doesn't. If I had to consider the possible long-term consequences of my magic, I'd never be able to cast anything. I can't lay a curse on anyone, okay? I can't call down lightning on somebody's head, no matter how much I might want to. But as for what you're asking – I don't see any impediment. Heck, from what you've told me, I'd be acting on the side of the angels, anyway."

Reinhart looked at her with narrowed eyes. "So, you're accepting my account of recent events, and those involved in them, at face value? I appreciate your trust, Miss Chastain, but some might call it naiveté."

Libby smiled at him. "I may not be a Sensitive like your Father Dalton," she said, "but I'm pretty good at deception detection myself. I know you haven't been lying to me."

"You said there was more than one conflict of interest," Morris said.

"The other one should be pretty obvious," Reinhart said. "If Miss Chastain is successful, we plan to attack people who are employed by the U.S. government. You would be, indirectly, taking up arms against the United States. Does that bother you?"

Morris thought for a moment. "It's been a long time since I saw the government of my country as a single, united entity. Far too often, the left hand and the right hand don't talk to each other. As far as I'm concerned, the people you've described don't represent the United States, either in spirit or in law. I don't consider myself a traitor for helping you."

"On that, Quincey's speaking for both of us," Libby said.

"Then I suppose we might as well get started," Reinhart said.

Twenty-Eight

Libby leaned over the map of the United States spread out on Reinhart's desk. "Since you think there's a good chance that Father Dalton is being held in this country, we'll start here. If I don't get anything, we'll check Canada and Mexico. And if those come up empty, I'll move on to any other country you think he might be in – as long as you have a map of it."

"That won't be a problem," Reinhart told her. "You can find a map of just about anyplace on the Internet these days."

Libby was holding about eight inches of fine silver chain, from the end of which hung a four-ounce piece of quartz. The stone had been carved into a triangle, and covered with several arcane symbols by Libby herself. Whenever possible, a witch makes her own tools.

She had spent almost half an hour casting the spell that would make the quartz into something more useful than a small piece of rock. Libby had cast a spell on the chain, as well.

"Okay, here goes," she said. The three other people in the room – Morris, Reinhart, and Father-Major Pearson – all came over to the table, but stood on the side opposite Libby, as if to give her room.

Libby held the chain in her right hand. In her left she clutched a rosary which, Reinhart had assured her, had been handled by the missing Father-Captain Dalton many times – and probably by no one else. Holding the tip of the pendulum about six inches from the map, Libby began to swing it in a slow, gentle arc, moving north to south and back again. She started with the west coast and slowly moved east. But it was not until she had reached the eastern seaboard that she gave a small start and said, "Oh."

"Something?" Morris asked her.

"Maybe."

Libby kept the pendulum swinging over the east coast now. Taking small steps to the left and right, she varied the angle at which the stone passed over the map. After a few minutes, she straightened up.

"I'm getting a definite hit over the area around North and South Carolina," she said. "Time to move on to maps of those states, and see what we get."

Rinehart had a Rand McNally Large Scale Road Atlas of the United States, and he opened it to the page for South Carolina. He laid the book on the table, weighting down the corners with a stapler, tape dispenser, paperweight and book.

Libby repeated the procedure, slowly traversing the map of South Carolina on a north-south axis, and then going west-east.

"Nothing," she said finally. "Let's try North Carolina."

Reinhart found the correct page and replaced the atlas on the table in front of Libby. She started again, moving left to right. When the pendulum was over the eastern part of the state, she said, softly, "That's more like it. Now, let's narrow this down." Without looking up she said, a little louder, "Quincey?"

Morris was ready with a ruler and a fine-point pen. Libby kept the pendulum moving and said, "Mark it."

Careful not to get in the way of the swinging stone, Morris placed the ruler on the map and carefully lined it up with the axis Libby's pendulum was following. He followed the ruler's edge with the pen, leaving a thin black line traversing the state.

Keeping the pendulum swinging, Libby changed position slightly, so that its arc was along a different angle. After a few moments, she repeated, "Mark it."

They did this four more times, then Libby stopped, and stepped back. She looked at Reinhart. "See if that gives you anything useful."

The three men pored over the map, although Morris hung back a little to stay out of the way.

"South of Hertford," Pearson said. "Almost in – what's this – Albermarle Sound."

"Looks closer to that peninsula there," Morris said. "See – where the land juts out like that?"

"You're quite right, Mister Morris," Reinhart said, still bent over the map. "The center point does seem to be on that peninsula, and I believe I know why."

Reinhart straightened up and looked at Libby. "Congratulations, Miss Chastain. I do believe you've given us what we needed – the start of it, anyway."

He turned to Morris. "What your colleague seems to be indicating is something called the Harvey Point Defense Testing Facility. The Navy once used it to test munitions, hence the name."

"'Once'?" Morris said. "Past tense?"

"Yes, indeed," Reinhart said. "For the last forty years or so, it has been one of the most secret training facilities used by the CIA."

"Again," Morris said, "how is it you know?"

"Well, what specifically goes on there is highly classified," Reinhart said. "But the base's purpose is pretty much an open secret in certain circles. I believe you can even look it up on Google."

"I'm glad I found you a promising location," Libby said. "Is that it, then?"

"Not quite, Miss Chastain," Reinhart said. "As I understand it, the facility at Harvey Point is sizeable. We can't expect to take over the whole place and search the buildings, one at a time, at our leisure. This is a raid we're planning – get in, get our man, and get out again, fast. So we need to know *exactly* where Father-Captain Dalton is being held."

"I don't mind continuing," Libby told him. "But if this place is highly classified, I doubt that Rand McNally has published a map of it – or that anybody else has, either."

"I wonder," Reinhart said musingly. He turned to Pearson. "Satellite photos?"

The Major nodded slowly. "Could be, sir. Stranger things have happened."

"Find out – ASAP."

"Yes, sir." Pearson turned and marched out of the room.

Morris looked at Reinhart. "You guys have your own satellites?"

"Unfortunately not. But it may be that we don't need to, in this instance. Services like Google Maps and Bing provide access to hundreds of thousands of satellite images taken over the last ten years or so."

"But the government wouldn't let classified stuff get into those databases, would they?" Morris asked.

"Not deliberately, no. But there are so many satellites in orbit, taking so many pictures every day, that a lot of stuff gets past the censors, just due to sheer volume. You'd be surprised at some of the things we've found online."

"Can you work with satellite images?" Reinhart asked Libby. "As opposed to maps, I mean."

"I never have," Libby said, "but I don't see why it shouldn't be possible. Any image I can swing the pendulum over would probably be okay."

"Good," Reinhart said. "I hope to have some satellite photos for you shortly. In the meantime, I'm afraid I must ask you to spend a little more time in our day room."

Libby shrugged. "We've spent time in worse places."

Twenty-Nine

It was nearly three hours later when Father-Major Pearson came to the day room and brought them back to Reinhart's office. On the short walk through the corridors, Libby asked him, "Success?"

"The Father-General will tell you about that." Clearly, "discretion" was listed near the top of Pearson's job description.

The news was good, it seemed – when they came in, Reinhart was bent over the table, studying a sheet of paper about three feet square.

Reinhart looked up and smiled. "It took a while, but we found an image of Harvey Point on Bing Maps that the CIA had neglected to classify. It's quite detailed."

Libby walked closer to the table. "Bing Maps gave you something this size?"

"No, we fed the image into our computer and had it enlarged," Reinhart said. "We sometimes have to make our own tactical maps, so we've got the necessary software and a very large printer."

Libby got out her pendulum and went to work. It did not take her long to cover the entire facility. Before long, Morris was next to her, working with the ruler and pen to mark on the sheet of paper the arc that Libby's pendulum was making.

"Mark it," Libby said. Then she moved a little, changing the angle. "Mark it."

Soon there were six lines drawn on the satellite image. They intersected on a rectangular building near the bottom of the page, set well away from the others.

"It figures that these people would want as much privacy as possible," Reinhart said. "They probably don't want the screaming of their prisoners to disturb the other people working there – most of whom probably have no idea about the monsters in their midst."

"So now you have to plan and carry out your rescue mission," Morris said. "And I hope all goes well – I really do. But as the Lone Ranger used to say, 'I think our work here is done.'"

Reinhart turned his attention away from the satellite photo. "Yes, Mister Morris, it is. I hope you and Miss Chastain here will accept the Order's gratitude."

"With pleasure," Libby said. "I'm also ready to accept the Order's fragment of the Seal of Solomon."

Reinhart stared at her. "Miss Chastain, I hope I did not create the wrong impression," he said slowly. "We will honor our part of the bargain, of course – once we have determined that you have fulfilled yours."

"I was under the *impression*," Libby said, "that I've just spent the last hour doing *exactly* that."

"I'm afraid not," Reinhart said. "Your work was certainly impressive, and the fact that you ended up with the Harvey Point Facility gives it a degree of verisimilitude. But we do not yet know for certain that Father-Captain Dalton is being held there."

"For the love of the Goddess, what more do you *want* from me?" Libby said sharply.

"From you? Nothing more," Reinhart said. "I agree that you've done everything you can. But we won't know if you were right about Father-Captain Dalton until we actually see him. And that won't happen until we go in there to get him."

Libby was clearly on the verge of losing her temper – something that Morris thought would benefit none of them right now, least of all Libby. He laid a gentle hand on her arm and said to Reinhart, "So you're saying that after your raid on this place in North Carolina, we can have your piece of the Seal."

"Assuming that Father-Captain Dalton is there, yes. The Order keeps its bargains, Mister Morris."

"Forgive me for being blunt," Morris said, "but what if you get there, and he's dead?"

"He won't be," Reinhart said. "He is no good to these people as a corpse. They'll keep him alive because they want him to work for them, although when he declines they may try methods of persuasion that are... unpleasant."

Morris was persistent. "And what if he decides to escape these 'unpleasant methods' by killing himself?"

"He won't do that, Mister Morris."

"And you're sure of that because...?"

"I'm sure of it because he is a Catholic priest, and our church teaches that suicide is a mortal sin. Dying with such a sin on your soul means that it is consigned to Hell."

Morris stared at Reinhart for the length of two breaths. He made sure that his voice was calm when he said, "So when is your raid on this place going to take place?"

"That's impossible to say, since I just learned of Father-Captain Dalton's presumptive location. And even if I knew, I couldn't tell you."

"Security," Morris said. He kept most of what he was feeling out of his face and voice.

"Exactly. But I can tell you this much: we won't waste any time. The sooner we get Father-Captain Dalton away from these CIA renegades, the better – and in the process, perhaps we can teach them the folly of interfering in the Order's affairs."

Libby had been studying Reinhart's face. Now she said, "You're going to kill them, aren't you? The people in that building – you're planning to kill them all."

"That information is classified, Miss Chastain."

"Of course it is." The bitterness in Libby's voice could have curdled milk.

"Aren't you afraid of retaliation?" Morris asked. "I don't figure you can kill a bunch of CIA guys without risking some pretty serious consequences."

"There will be no consequences, Mister Morris."

"You sound very certain," Libby said.

"That because I am certain – for two reasons. One is that the 'CIA guys' in question are, remember, renegades. They have been operating without the official sanction of the Director of Central Intelligence, and if he knew about them, he would disavow them instantly. The organization will not avenge them – they might even thank us, if they knew who we were, which they will not."

"I sure hope you've got that figured right," Morris said. "What's the other reason you feel safe?"

"Our obsession with security, which your associate seems to disdain so deeply. We are not here in Ohio with the permission of the United States government – we are here without their knowledge."

"A few people know," Morris said. "David Kabov, for one."

"Mister Kabov is an old comrade-in-arms, and is to be trusted. The very few people who know about this facility are all trustworthy. They also know that if they were to betray that trust, they would die."

Reinhart picked the satellite photograph up from the table.

"Now, if you'll both excuse me," he said, "I have a great deal to do. Leave your contact information with Father-Major Pearson here, and then he will have you returned to your car. You'll hear from us, assuming matters reach the conclusion we're all hoping for."

"And what if they don't?" Libby asked. "What if you pull off your commando raid, and he's not there?"

"I imagine you'll be hearing from us then, as well."

Thirty

AL'S SHOOTING RANGE on West Thirty-Fourth Street was usually closed until noon on weekdays. But Peters had slipped Al a few bucks and got him to open – just for Peters and his friends – today at 10:00 a.m. He wanted to be able to carry on a conversation about the ballistics of fruit pits without the competing noise from other shooters.

Peters was already there when Libby and Morris arrived, although they were punctual. And Peters wasn't alone.

"Hello, Libby," Ashley said. "Long time no see."

"Hi, Ashley." Libby was friendly, but reserved. Morris shook hands with Peters and gave Ashley a brief hug.

Libby had pretty much decided that she wasn't going to have sex with Ashley anymore. If, as Hemingway once said, "What is moral is what you feel good after, and what is immoral is what you feel bad after," then Libby's trysts with the demon-made-flesh who called herself Ashley didn't meet the criteria for morality. Sex with Ashley left Libby feeling sated, weak in the knees, and... vaguely soiled. It wasn't worth the 'dirty' feeling – not even for the best sex she'd ever had in her life. At least, Libby was pretty sure it wasn't.

Fortunately, Ashley didn't bring up their past love life, or even act especially flirtatious. Being Ashley, she couldn't help being at least a *little* flirtatious.

"I started with avocado pits, since they're the biggest, but I also tried out a few others, just for shits and giggles," Peters told her. "You said any fruit stone could take out an afreet, right?"

"That's what the expert told me," Libby said. She glanced toward Ashley, who merely smiled. That smile was enough to make Libby's undies a little damp, but she forced herself to concentrate on what Peters had to tell her.

Peters had been a CIA assassin in a prior existence. Killed in the line of duty and consigned to Hell almost thirty years ago, he had been sent back to earth, along with Ashley, to assassinate a demon-possessed presidential candidate whom one faction in Hell feared was about to bring on Armageddon – a battle that the demons in that faction feared their side would lose. Since then, the divisions in Hell had led to all-out civil war. Amidst the chaos, Peters and Ashley had apparently been forgotten about – although they both knew that could change at any time.

"Come on over to this target bay," Peters said. He was a big man, but he moved easily, the way some football players do.

Libby had expected to see some paintball guns ready for use, but instead Peters had left on the shooting bench a rifle that looked like a real firearm, and a couple of slingshots. One of the slingshots was the standard Y-shaped base with an elastic band attached, but the other was decidedly odd-looking. As if reading her mind, Peters said, "I tried working with paintball guns, but gave it up as a lost cause."

"Really? How come?"

"Problems with range, mostly. Of course, one of the problems here is that we have no idea how far you're going to be from this fucking afreet, assuming you ever go up against him. But I figure there's a good chance it'll be more than fifty feet."

"As you said, there's no way to know," Libby said. "But why are you using fifty feet as a benchmark?"

"Because that's the maximum effective range of even the most powerful paintball gun. Am I using terms you're not familiar with?"

Libby gave him a lopsided smile. "Well, maybe that 'maximum effective' thing."

"Okay, then – a quick lesson. Any propulsive weapon, whether a gun, bow and arrow, or slingshot, has two kinds of ranges we can talk about. 'Propulsive,' by the way, just means it shoots stuff through the air. Okay?"

"So far, so good."

"The two kinds are 'maximum range' and 'maximum effective range.' Maximum range refers to the farthest the weapon can shoot something. Take the M-16, the standard infantry rifle, back in the day. Maximum range is about three thousand, six hundred meters – that's how far you can expect the bullet to go before it drops to the ground. Okay?"

"Sure." Libby had learned in the past that when men talk to women about guns, they tend to act as if they're dealing with five-year-olds. But since she liked Peters, she didn't let his unconscious condescension bother her. Much. She glanced toward Morris, who combined a shrug with a wry expression to say, *The guy's doing us a big favor. Let him show off, if he wants to.*

"But since you're firing a weapon in order to hit something specific, maximum range is a useless concept.

Instead, you worry about maximum *effective* range – the furthest distance at which you can reasonably expect to hit what you're aiming at. The maximum effective range of the M-16, for instance, is about five hundred and fifty meters. Beyond that distance, the chances of you nailing your target will drop off big-time. Okay?"

"Gotcha. So you're saying that if I'm expecting to hit something more than fifty feet away with a paintball gun, then it's Tony Soprano time."

Peters frowned at her. "Sorry?"

"*Fuhgeddaboudit.*"

He laughed. "Yeah, that's about it."

"And that's why you've brought this rifle? I didn't think regular guns could fire fruit stones."

"They can't," Peters said. "This is an air rifle."

"Really? I remember a guy who lived across the street from me when I was growing up – he had an air rifle. But it looked nothing like *this*."

"His was a toy, really. This thing is a weapon."

She nodded toward the rifle. "May I?"

"Sure, go ahead."

As she picked it up, Peters said, "When it comes to air rifles, that's the *crème de la crème*. It's a Sam Yang Dragon Claw – .50 caliber, and about twice as powerful as anything else out there."

Morris gave a soft whistle, but made no other comment.

Libby estimated that the air gun was about three and a half feet long. It was lighter than she'd expected: less than ten pounds, she was sure. The stock and grip were of highly-polished walnut. "Does it have two barrels?" she asked Peters. "Like an over/under shotgun?"

"No, that thing underneath the barrel is where you charge it with compressed air."

"And where do you get that?"

"For something you can carry around with you, I'd recommend a scuba tank."

"*Seriously*?"

"Afraid so," Peters said. "The gun applies a lot of air pressure to the projectile. To get strong air pressure in the gun, you need a high-pressure source for the air."

"Does every air gun need its own scuba tank?"

"No, most of the others use gas cartridges that you attach right to the gun. But that gives you a lot less power."

Libby gently put the air rifle back on the firing bench. "And I need that much power, because...?"

"Because it gives you the greatest range. And that's why this situation is so frustrating – we don't know what range you'll have to shoot from, or how big your target will be. But this thing gives you the best possible chance."

"Speaking of target size..." Libby turned to Ashley. "You're the expert on afreets, Ashley. How big *are* these guys, anyway?"

"That question's not as simple as it sounds," Ashley said. "Afreets, like all djinn, lack physical bodies. So when they manifest to humans, they can take any form or size they want."

"Terrific," Libby muttered.

"But the good news is that they usually want to impress, if not terrify humans. So they tend to pick a size that's pretty damn big – which should mean an easy target."

"What kind of range does this thing have?" Morris asked.

"That's where things get kind of complicated," Peters said. "With a steel ball, or some of the special aerodynamic ammunition they make for this, you've got a MER of at least two hundred yards – which is twice what you can expect from any other air rifle, even the good ones."

"But we'll be shooting some kind of fruit stone, not steel balls," Libby said.

"I know. That's why it's complicated. Any kind of fruit stone has lighter weight than the standard ammo, and greatly reduced mass. That means less muzzle velocity, which translates into a shorter range."

"Hmmm." Libby frowned. "How much shorter?"

"Less than half," Peters said. "Let me show you."

He picked up the rifle. "We'll start with standard ammunition," he said.

There was a plastic toolbox on the bench. Peters opened it and removed a box full of ball bearings, each about the size of a pea, and began to load the rifle.

"How many rounds does it hold?" Morris asked him.

"Three. Then you have to recharge."

"*Three?*" Libby said. "That's all?"

"Keep in mind that the air in this thing is under incredible pressure – that's why it shoots so far. If you wanted to hold more pressure safely, you'd need a gun that weighs fifty pounds, or more. And nobody makes one like that."

"So, if we have to use this thing for real," Morris said, "we'd better get the job done with three shots, or not at all. Can't see an afreet agreeing to a time-out while we get the scuba tank and recharge the gun."

"Doesn't seem likely, does it?" Peters said. "Okay, we're in the 'large-bore rifle' section, which means it's just over a hundred yards down range."

There was a length of heavy-gauge wire running the length of the shooting alley. Using a detachable clip, Peters attached a man-size silhouette target to it and pressed a button. A pulley attached to the wire rapidly sent the target down range, to stop at the end.

"Normally, I'd be telling you to put on ear protection now," Peters said. "But you won't need it with this baby."

He worked a lever at the side of the rifle, raised the gun to his shoulder, took careful aim, and fired. The sound of the shot was no louder than a cap pistol.

"Let's take a look." Peters put the rifle down and pressed another button, bringing the target back to him. There was a hole the size of a dime in the "9" ring, just outside the bullseye. "Not bad, for firing without a rest," he said.

He pulled from the box a plastic baggie containing several small, round objects. Unlike the ball bearings, they were white and lacked the glitter of metal. "Cherry pits," Peters said. "I tried filing down some of the bigger pits, like peach and avocado, to fit the gun, but they didn't give any better ballistic results."

"But cherries aren't in season now," Libby said.

"I know. I had some shipped in from Australia."

"Must've cost you a small fortune," Morris said.

"It did. And since cherry pits aren't of uniform size, I had to go through quite a few to find some that would fit the gun. Fortunately, Ashley likes cherries."

Ashley smiled, and with a perfect Humphrey Bogart imitation said, "We was all cherry once, kid."

Peters opened the bolt and inserted the cherry pit. He sent the target downrange again, brought the gun to his shoulder, and fired.

When he brought the target back, there was still only one hole in it. "Clean miss," he said. "Just as I expected."

"You've tried this before," Libby said.

"Been working on it on and off for about a month," Peters said. "It gave me something to do."

"Besides fucking me, you mean?" Ashley tried for a hurt expression that none of them believed for a second.

"Even my legendary capabilities are limited, sweetie, even if yours aren't," Peters told her. To Morris and Libby he said, "I've only got one shot left without recharging, so I won't waste it. Watch what happens when I bring the range in to about seventy-five yards."

He sent the target out again, stopping it before the end of its tether. He reloaded the rifle with another cherry pit, aimed, and fired.

This time, the target had a second hole in it – through the "6" ring."

"Still not pinpoint accuracy," Peters said, "but not bad. Seventy-five yards is your limit if you're shooting at something the size of this target. Aim at something bigger, and you can add to the range a little – maybe up to eighty-five yards. But the gun isn't your only option."

He picked up the strange-looking object that had been sitting on the bench next to the rifle. It had a plastic pistol grip attached to a four-pronged stainless steel frame. Two of the prongs were joined by a leather strap, and a piece of rubber tubing (the kind doctors use to tie off your arm before they stick needles in you) with a small pouch in the middle was attached to the other two prongs. It looked like the bastard child of a ray gun and an Erector set.

Peters picked it up. "This here is a hunting slingshot."

Libby stared at the contraption. "People use this thing to hunt? Hunt *what*?"

"Birds and small game, mostly – rabbits, woodchucks, stuff like that. I talked to a guy at the sporting goods store a couple of weeks ago who said he'd once brought down a deer with one. Of course, he also claimed he'd nailed Madonna – so take it for what it's worth."

"*I've* nailed Madonna," Ashley said.

They all turned and looked at her. "Really?" Morris said.

Ashley shrugged, and produced a smile of pure lasciviousness. "Actually, no – but she's on my 'To Do' list."

"That's my girl," Peters said.

He reached back into the box and brought out a ball bearing the size of a marble. "This is the standard ammunition – proper shape, a lot of mass, and very hard."

He picked up the slingshot. Slipping his left hand between the lower pair of prongs, he wrapped his fingers around the plastic grip.

"I see what that does now," Morris said. "It's a brace for your wrist."

"Exactly," Peters said. "The people who use them take this stuff very seriously."

He pressed the button to send the target forward, but stopped it about halfway down the alley. "Fifty yards," he said. "That's about the maximum effective range for this kind of ammo."

He picked up a ball bearing, placed it in the pouch, and pointed his left hand toward the target. He then pulled the pouch toward him, stretching the elastic tubing that gave the slingshot its power. When the elastic was at its limit, he let go. There was a thin "snap," and an instant later, the target jerked as something big passed through it.

When Peters reeled the target in, a hole the size of a nickel was through the "8" ring. "I'm not real good with it yet," he said, "but I haven't put in a lot of practice."

He produced another plastic baggie, this one full of small brown spheres. "Avocado pits," he said. "A lot of these are perfect spheres, and those that aren't, sometimes you can improve them with a file."

He sent the target back out. "Same distance," he said. "Fifty yards."

Peters placed an avocado pit in the slingshot's pouch and said, "These are lighter than the ball bearings, so I'm going to raise my point of aim a bit."

He extended his arm again and let fly. The target,

when returned, had a new hole that barely touched the edge of the outside ring.

"The pits are lighter than the balls by quite a bit," he said. "So they don't fly as true. So, if you're planning to hit something about the size of an elephant, you'd be okay at fifty yards – maybe a little more."

He placed the slingshot on the bench. "And that, folks," he said, "is how you can kill an afreet. Maybe."

Libby looked at him. "Maybe?"

"Maybe, if the legends are true," he said. "Maybe, if the weather's not humid – that'll slow the passage of any object through the air and decrease your range. Maybe, if there's little or no wind. Wind can fuck even a rifle marksman up." He glanced toward the weapons resting on the bench. "I shudder to think what a good breeze will do to these things."

"Thanks for all your efforts, Mal," Libby said. "You've been a great help. Still, the limitations of our fruit pit slingers make me glad we've got a Plan B."

"What's that?" Peters asked.

"A fragment of the Seal of Solomon," Libby said.

"You got one?" Ashley seemed genuinely happy for them. "That's great! Where'd you find it?"

"We haven't quite got it yet," Morris said. "But we're expecting to have it soon."

Both Ashley and Peters look a little confused.

"It belongs to the Knights Templar," Libby said.

"Those guys?" Peters said. "I didn't even know they still existed."

"They're real careful about security," Morris said. "Maybe obsessively so."

"Can't really blame them," Ashley said, "considering what the King of France did to them the last time they were out in the open. So, they've got a piece of

Solly's Seal, and they're going to let you have it? Pretty generous of them."

"It's for services rendered," Libby said. "I can't say more than that."

"How come?" Peters asked her.

"One, because I promised," she said. "And two, because they threatened to kill us if we blabbed."

"They always were a nasty bunch," Ashley said. "But then I never had much use for priests of any kind."

"I'm not surprised," Morris said. "But we've got good reason to take these guys seriously. We have to wait a while, but I'm confident we'll have a piece of the Seal soon."

"What're you going to do in the meantime?" Peters asked.

"Practice with our new toys," Libby said. "And maybe have a chat with the FBI."

Thirty-One

Libby Chastain was in her kitchen making a sandwich when, in the living room, her phone began to play the theme from the old TV show, *Bewitched*. She got to the phone quickly, checked the caller ID, then answered.

"Hey, Colleen."

"Hey, Libby. Sorry I couldn't answer when you called – Fenton and I were out on the shooting range."

"Yeah, I know what that's like," Libby murmured.

"Excuse me?"

"Just talking to myself," Libby said. "Sorry."

"So what's up?"

"I was wondering if the Bureau has gotten a line yet on those terrorists – the ones who supposedly brought an afreet into the country."

"We haven't heard a thing from Anti-Terrorism," Colleen said. "I was kind of hoping you and Quincey might have turned up something."

"We've learned a few things about how to fight an afreet, but we haven't picked up a clue as to who might have one. Well, maybe one tiny clue."

"I'm all ears."

"Quincey recently talked to a guy who knows a lot about this stuff. Although afreets don't need to eat, apparently, they *do* have a preferred snack. Care to guess what it is?"

"I assume we're not talking about chips or pretzels here," Colleen said.

"Uh-uh. Lions' hearts."

"That's not the brand name of some weird food, is it? You're talking about *real lions*?"

"I most certainly am."

"Well, that's something you don't pick up at Costco – unless they've added to their product line since I was last in one."

"No, I'm pretty sure you'd have to do your shopping at a zoo," Libby said.

"What do you know that I don't, Libby?"

"Well, I know that if you Google something like 'attacks on lions,' you'll find that a couple of zoos have been broken into over the last few months. In both cases, only one animal was harmed – a male lion, who was killed and butchered on the spot. The only organ found missing, in each instance, was its heart."

Colleen was silent for a few moments, then said, "It can't be easy, getting close enough to a lion to do all that – even a captive lion."

"No, it can't. And it's probably harder to do it without leaving any useful trace, or being seen by patrolling security guards, or showing up on video surveillance cameras – cameras which suddenly went dead for no reason anybody can figure out."

"You're thinking magic," Colleen said. It wasn't a question.

"I certainly am, Sister mine. I most definitely am."

There was another silence on the line. "What we're talking about here wouldn't invite Bureau involvement, Libby. Animal cruelty, much though I despise it, comes under the local area's jurisdiction. And so does breaking and entering. Neither of those is a federal crime."

"How about crossing state lines to avoid prosecution for the aforementioned crimes?"

"You mean –"

"One of the zoos that got hit is in Michigan. The other one's in Indiana."

"Well, now..." Libby could almost hear Colleen thinking. "I don't know if I can talk Sue into assigning this to Dale and me. Chasing serial killers is one thing. Serial lion killers – that's something else."

"Maybe if you explained to her that it's connected to more of the 'weird shit.'"

Sue Whitlavitch, the Section Chief of Behavioral Science, was well aware that not all the evil in the world is caused by natural forces. And she knew that Colleen O'Donnell, being a white witch, was uniquely qualified to deal with the kind of crime that had a supernatural origin.

"It's sure worth a try."

"And if you turn up anything interesting..."

"You'll be the first to know," Colleen said. "Well, second – right after Sue."

"That's good enough for me."

Thirty-Two

More than a month passed before Libby got the call she had been waiting for.

"Miss Chastain, this is Thomas Reinhart."

It took Libby a second to make the connection, since the Father-General had not used his title. It was another second before she figured out that this was yet another security precaution on Reinhart's part.

"Oh, yes, hi, uh, Mister Reinhart. I've been hoping to hear from you."

"And now you have. I wonder if you could pay us a visit sometime soon? We still owe you payment for that excellent work you did for us last month."

"Yes, of course. I take it everything worked out all right?"

"If it had not, I would not be calling."

"Were you able to –"

"I would rather discuss that with you in person, Miss Chastain." Reinhart had a way of making Libby feel like a third-grader who had been sent to the principal's office.

"Of course, I understand. Have you been in touch with... my associate?" She didn't know if saying Quincey's name would violate Reinhart's notion of security.

"No, I have not. You performed the service, so it is you I have called. You're welcome to bring Mister Morris with you, of course, should you wish to."

Not a security problem after all, apparently.

"All right, fine. Is there any special time –"

"I will see you whenever you choose to arrive, Miss Chastain. Just give your name – and Mister Morris's, if he's with you – to the people at the front gate."

"Okay, sure. Terrific. I'll see you in a couple of days, then."

"Goodbye, Miss Chastain."

Thirty-Three

AND SO IT was that two days later Libby Chastain and Quincey Morris found themselves driving a rented car down Ohio's Route 25 in the middle of the afternoon.

As they drew close to the turnoff, Morris said, "I didn't want to make the waiting worse for you over the last month, so I kept my mouth shut, but it occurred to me more than once to wonder if the good Father-General hadn't just decided to blow us off. I mean, what were we gonna do – take him to court?"

Morris lowered his voice a little. "*Your honor, the plaintiffs in this case allege that the defendant, head of an organization that nobody acknowledges even exists, did enter into a legally-binding agreement with my clients to transfer to them ownership of a portion of the Great Seal of Solomon, so that they could employ it to prevent unnamed terrorists from using an ancient djinn to commit an unspecified terrible act against this great nation of ours.*"

"I thought about that a few times, too," Libby said. "But more often I found myself wondering if the raid hadn't gone so badly that Father-General Reinhart and his team were either all wiped out or taken prisoner. And then whoever was left in charge of the Knights would say he'd never head of us *or* our deal."

"You think the commanding general would take part in an operation like that himself?"

"You've met the man, Quincey. Can you imagine him doing anything *else*?"

"You may have a point there."

They were quiet for a few minutes, then Morris said, "Once we've got that piece of the Seal of Solomon, do you know what to do with it? Assuming we ever run into the afreet, that is. Do you just wave it at him, like a cross with a vampire, and yell, 'Begone'?"

"It's not quite that simple, I'm afraid," she said. "There's an invocation of sorts – a prayer, really – that I found in a very old book. It seems to apply, so I've memorized it. Easy to do – it's not very long, even if it *is* in ancient Chaldean."

"And this invocation is going to let you take control of the afreet, if you back it up with the Seal of Solomon?"

"No – what it does is to set the afreet free from bondage," Libby said. "In other words, it would take control of the thing away from our hypothetical terrorists."

Morris frowned. "So you set the thing free from the evil wizard, or whatever he is, without gaining control of it yourself. Is that an improvement, really? What if the thing decides to barbecue everybody in a ten-mile radius because he's pissed off?"

"He might, Quincey. He just might. But from what I've read, afreets don't like the world of humans and try to avoid it. They have their own dwelling places – some say whole cities – deep underground. I'm betting that if he's turned loose, the afreet will just want to go home."

"That's a hell of a bet, Libby. With damn high stakes."

"I know – but it may prove to be the only game in town, if this afreet turns out to really exist."

"Here's hoping you never have to play."

"You and me both, cowboy. You and me both."

Then they were at the gate of the Knights Templar complex, confronted by two guards – different men from last time, but similarly clothed and armed.

Morris rolled his window down all the way. "Quincey Morris and Elizabeth Chastain, to see Father-General Reinhart. We're expected."

"Yes, sir," one of the guards said. "Would you turn your engine off, please?"

The other guard moved to the side to give himself a clear field of fire through the windshield. Morris, who tended to be a little jumpy in the presence of automatic weapons handled by strangers, had a brief moment of paranoia. *What if the good Father-General has decided that security trumps everything else, including human decency? What if he's decided that Libby and I know too much about his operation?*

Then the other guard approached Morris's window and said, "Can I see some ID from both of you, please?"

After examining and returning their driver's licenses, the guard removed the radio from his belt. Without bothering to walk out of hearing range, he said into it, "Mister Morris and Miss Chastain are here, to see the Father-General."

After listening for a few seconds, he said, "Roger that," and put the radio away.

"Transportation will be here very shortly to take you folks into the compound," the guard said. "Just sit tight for a minute, okay?"

And it wasn't really much more than a minute before a Chevy Suburban pulled up to the gate from the other side. The guard saw it and said, "Would you folks exit the vehicle now, please? Leave the keys in it – we'll park it for you someplace safe."

It occurred to Morris that Libby would have to endure the indignity of another search, and he was about to protest the necessity when the guard said, "Just follow me, if you would, please," and led them through the just-opened gate to the rear door of the Suburban. He opened the door and motioned them inside.

The one-way film was still in the windows, and as the driver politely told them he was about to raise the divider, Morris thought, *So, we're pals now – just not really* close *pals.*

A few minutes later, he and Libby were standing outside the same long, low building, waiting for an escort to come out to greet them. He did so with commendable dispatch, but Morris was mildly startled to see that it was not Father-Major Pearson. *Well, everybody deserves a day off, once in a while.*

Morris had assumed they'd head right to the Father-General's office again, but instead they were brought to the Officer's Day Room, which was again empty of officers or anyone else. He thought that meant they'd have to cool their heels indefinitely, but he was wrong.

He and Libby had barely sat down when they heard the sound of approaching footsteps from the corridor, and a moment later Father-General Reinhart was striding through the door, another man in black fatigues close behind him.

They rose as Reinhart came over to shake hands. He appeared warmer toward them than during his last visit, but the man was still no contender for the Mister Congeniality trophy. Then again, in his job, a friendly disposition was probably a drawback.

"Miss Chastain, Mister Morris, good to see you again."

"Hello, Father-General," Morris said. Then, without really thinking about it he added, "I was a little surprised not to see Father-Major Pearson. I had the impression that he was your aide."

Reinhart sobered immediately. "Yes, you are correct. He was. I regret to say that Father-Major Pearson is no longer with us."

"He's left the Order?" Libby asked. "Not that it's any of our –"

"No, Miss Chastain," Reinhart said. "I mean that Father-Major Pearson has left this life and gone to the embrace of Our Savior. He did not survive the action at Harvey Point."

"Oh, I'm so sorry," Libby said.

"I appreciate your sympathy, Miss Chastain, but it is unnecessary. He is with God, now."

The calm certainty of that statement sent a small chill down Morris's spine. But then, he supposed that was the essence of the Knights Templar – give your life fighting for God, and you win an express ticket to Paradise. Morris wondered if the Father-General ever considered that the exact same spirit motivated every jihadist who ever strapped on a suicide vest.

"However," Reinhart said, lightening a little, "the man whom we went there to rescue is very much alive – thanks, in part, to your efforts."

He turned to the man who had come in with him, and placed a hand on his shoulder. "This is Father-Captain Andrew Dalton."

Dalton was of average height, with the typical muscular build of the Knights Templar. His face looked thin and haggard, as if the man had undergone some unpleasant experiences recently. Morris held no doubt that he had.

But Father-Captain Dalton's worn countenance bore a grin now as he was introduced to the visitors.

"This is Mister Quincey Morris," Reinhart said.

Dalton grabbed Morris's outstretched hand and shook it vigorously. "Thank you," he said. "Thank you so much."

"And Miss Elizabeth Chastain, who goes by 'Libby.' It was her ability that allowed us to locate you with such precision."

Libby held out her hand, too, but Dalton ignored it and put his arms around her in a tight hug. "Thank you so much," he said. "I wish you –"

Father-Captain Dalton suddenly stopped speaking, and a moment later pushed himself away from Libby, as if she had caught fire. He took another step back, staring at her. His maudlin expression had been replaced with one of shock, horror – and hatred.

"Anathema," he breathed, and then, more loudly, "Anathema!"

Libby's face was a study in confusion, but Morris remembered what Reinhart had said about Father-Captain Dalton's talents as a Sensitive. He could read people's emotions, tell when they were lying – and he was also a witch-smeller.

Dalton turned to Reinhart, who was looking pretty confused himself. "Father-General, this woman is cursed by God! She consorts with demons! She positively *reeks* of the Infernal!"

Reinhart's eyes narrowed. "Are you certain, Father-Captain? This woman has rendered us a singular service."

"Then she has done it for her own dark purposes! She is a wolf in sheep's clothing." He pointed an accusing finger like a gun at Libby's face. "*And this wolf stinks of Hellfire!*"

Reinhart turned to Libby, his face grim. "Well, Miss

Chastain?" he said somberly. "What is your response to these accusations?"

"They are not accusations, Father-General!" Dalton appeared nearly hysterical now. "They are *facts*!"

"Hush, now." Reinhart laid a calming hand on Dalton's arm. "Let her speak."

Libby's mouth opened and closed a couple of times. Finally, she managed to push words out. "F-Father-General, in my work, of course I have come across all manner of supernatural creatures. My job is to *protect* humanity from them, not – not to *consort* with them!"

"So, you admit to having had contact with the Devil?"

"No, of course not! But I have had some experience with the demonic, yes. You – you asked Quincey when we first met about what happened last summer at the Republican convention. Well, demons were involved! Senator Stark, who was the leading candidate, was demonically possessed! Quincey and I arranged for an exorcism!"

"Senator Stark?" Reinhart's voice was incredulous. "Isn't he the one who was shot three times by his own aide, and nearly died? Did you have something to do with *that*, too?"

"No, I wasn't there for that part. But the exorcism didn't work, I know that much!"

"So, you're telling us that a member of the United States Senate is possessed by a demon? I grant that it would explain a great deal about what goes on in Washington these days."

"No, no, it's gone now, it left when Stark almost died. It's – it's complicated."

"I have no doubt that it is," Reinhart said.

"She's *lying*!" Dalton cried. "*You've* had contact with the demonic, Father-General. So have I. We don't carry demon smell on us the way this woman does. She has been *wallowing* in it!"

"All right, Father-Captain Dalton. Your insight is valuable, as always. But I think you should go to your room now. I'll speak with you later."

"But Father-General –"

Reinhart motioned to one of the two guards standing at the door. "Father-Sergeant, be so good as to escort Father-Captain Dalton to his room, and see that he gets some rest. Stay with him until you're relieved."

"Yes, sir. The guard led the unprotesting Dalton out of the room. He was crying softly now.

Once they were gone, Morris said quietly, "He's been under a lot of strain, poor guy." He was hoping that Reinhart would put Dalton's accusations down as the ravings of a man who had been broken by torture. But he was not optimistic.

"Mister Morris," Reinhart said quietly, "do you support Miss Chastain's account of the last Republican convention? Was Senator Stark possessed by a demon?"

"Yes, sir, but there's a lot more to it than that," Morris said. "As she says – it's complicated."

"Yes, to be sure." Reinhart turned to Libby. "I don't know what game you two are playing. Father-Captain Dalton has had a rough time lately, yes. But he is the most consistently reliable Sensitive I have ever seen."

"Father-General," Libby said, "I can –"

Reinhart held up a hand. "Enough. You have performed a valuable service for us, even though it has proved your undoing. That, and that alone has earned you both the right to leave here with your lives. But do not come near this place, or the Order, again – you will not be so lucky a second time."

Morris could tell that Libby was at the edge of tears,

but she held them back as she said to Reinhart, "What about that piece of Solomon's Seal? We had a deal, remember?"

Reinhart looked at her speculatively. "Is *that* what it was all about? Did you have some plan for the Seal of Solomon? It had nothing to do with that afreet you were going on about?"

Libby tried again. "No, I –"

Reinhart held up his hand again. "I said *enough*. The real reason for your actions doesn't matter. The Knights Templar don't make deals with the Devil, Miss Chastain – *or* with his representatives. Now get out of here, before I change my mind."

He turned to the remaining guard. "Get them to their car. And make sure they leave the compound immediately. If they attempt to do anything else, you are authorized to shoot them."

He turned on his heel and stalked out of the room.

Thirty-Four

"So these fucking *priests* told you never to darken their door again, all because you had the odor of demon on you?" Ashley said. Her voice was a bit unsteady. "Then what are you doing *here*?"

Libby raised her head from between Ashley's thighs and said, "Might as well be hanged for a sheep as a lamb."

"But what about the afreet? Are you just going to rely on those pea-shooters Peters gave you?"

"You talk too much." Libby lowered her head again, and after a few moments Ashley forgot all about talking.

Later, as they lay intertwined in her big bed, Ashley said, "You're taking a big risk, going against an afreet with nothing but peach pits."

"Might not even have to do that," Libby said sleepily. "Can't even find the damn thing."

After a few minutes, Libby's breathing started to deepen as she slid into sleep. "This compound the Knights have," Ashley said softly, "that's the one in Missouri, right?"

"Hm? No... Ohio."

Ashley waited ten seconds, then said, very quietly, "Sure, that's right. It's just outside Columbus."

"Uh-um. Toledo."

"Of course. Goodnight, sweetie."

"'Night, Ashley."

Thirty-Five

TIME PASSED, AS it has a way of doing. Spring reached full bloom, then eased into summer. And still the terrorists and their afreet did not strike – if there *were* any terrorists. If there *was* an afreet.

Libby Chastain and Special Agent Colleen O'Donnell had phone conversations about the lack of progress.

"What do you think, Colleen?" Libby had said, during one such call. "Is this a case of terrorist chatter being nothing more than a big load of hot air?"

"The Goddess knows I hope it is, Libby. But the people at NSA who've been analyzing the stuff say it seems like something really is in the works."

"Are the jihadists still talking about midnight at some fucking oasis?"

"I asked a guy I know at NSA," Colleen said. "He said they picked it twice more in the past month, and once the month before that."

"You sure this isn't just some al-Qaeda guy's idea of a joke?"

"Could be, but if so, it's a pretty subtle one. And from what I know about jihadist types, whether they're from al-Qaeda or one of the other groups, these dudes aren't famous for either their subtlety *or* their sense of humor."

"And the zoo angle hasn't led anywhere, either," Libby said.

"It hasn't led us to the perps, if that's what you mean. Dale and I got a look at the local police reports in both cases. We told them we were looking into some kind of multi-state Satanist conspiracy, and they gave us access to anything we wanted. Local law can vary a great deal in quality, Libby, but the guys working these are pretty good. They haven't missed anything, far as we can tell."

"Maybe they haven't missed stuff because magic covered it up so well."

"Entirely possible," Colleen said. "The magic angle is intriguing – but of course we couldn't say anything to the cops in Michigan or Indiana about that aspect, or ask the wrong kinds of questions, either."

"Were you able to sniff out the remains of any black magic?"

"No, but I didn't get on either scene until several weeks after the break-ins. The residue, if there was any, had faded away long before I arrived."

"Well, I'll keep an eye out for internet reports of any new attacks on lions. And that reminds me – there's some kind of specialized database that you FBI types use, isn't there?"

"I think you mean NCIC – the National Crime Information Center. It keeps track of reported crimes nationwide, at all levels of government."

"That's the one – I read an article about it someplace. Is it possible for you to put, I don't know the proper term, something like an e-mail alert on this thing, so that any zoo invasions will be brought to your attention as soon as they're reported?"

"Yeah, it *is* possible," Colleen said. "And I'll set one

up as soon as we get off the phone. You think there's gonna be more?"

"I don't know, but my spider sense is tingling."

"Your *what*?"

"Sorry, I've always wanted to say that," Libby said. "But here's the thing – all my research supports the notion that an afreet doesn't *need* to eat. These lion hearts are more in the nature of a tasty snack, an indulgence."

"Yeah, so?"

"You've never had kids, have you?"

"No, and neither have you, unless you've been hiding something," Colleen said.

"I haven't – but what I *do* have is a bunch of nieces and nephews. Some of them are adorable, but my sister Rhonda's kids are total brats."

"Are you going somewhere with this, Libby?"

"Yes, I am. Do you know what happens when you indulge a bratty kid by giving him treats?

"What?"

"The little bastard wants more."

Thirty-Six

"*ANOTHER* ONE?" DR. Abdul Nasiri slammed his hand down on the table. "This is outrageous!"

The table was in a back room of The Souk, one of Dearborn's better Syrian restaurants. Nasiri had reserved the private room for his "business meeting"; they would neither be observed nor disturbed. He had thus allowed himself the indulgence of showing his quite genuine anger.

"You are perhaps unwise in allowing our friend out of his confinement, my brother," Jawad Tamwar said to Uthman, the wizard. "He could not make such unreasonable requests of you – of *us* – if he could not speak to you."

Uthman showed an attitude of patience that he did not feel. Between the afreet and these idiots he had to work with (always excepting Dr. Nasiri, of course), he sometimes felt as if his head was caught in a vice and each day the screw was turned a little tighter.

"As I have said before, my brother," he said to Tamwar, "it is necessary for me to have regular interaction with Rashid, to ensure that he will obey me when the great day comes."

"Then why don't you tell him to stick his cock up his

own ass, and see if he obeys you then," Rahim said, and laughed. No one else at the table joined in.

"My brother," Nasiri said to Uthman, "can you not persuade our friend to a little more patience? We leave in two weeks, and soon thereafter he can let loose his fury at thousands of infidel targets, to burn as he has never burned before."

"He understands this, brother," Uthman said. "He even says he looks forward to it. But if we deny him this last time, he may prove uncooperative on the great day, and what a loss that would be to our cause."

"I thought the whole point of having a bit of Suleiman's Seal was to *compel* him to obedience." Nasiri said.

"It is a powerful force, to be sure," Uthman said. "But it is not all-powerful. The last time we had this discussion, I made a comparison of myself to a lion tamer –"

"Enough! Tamwar said angrily. "I have heard all that I wish to hear about you and the lion tamer."

Nasiri laid a hand on Tamwar's arm. "Peace, brother. Let us not blame our magician friend for forces that are outside his control." *If they really are outside the old fool's control*, he thought.

"So, this means another visit to one of their 'zoos'?" Rahim said. "More risks? More butchery?"

Nasiri took in a big breath and let it out, forcing himself to calmness. "This is the last time, my brothers – this I promise you. The day of vengeance is nearly here – and I promise you *that*, as well."

With a sigh, Tamwar said, "Have you determined where we must go – this 'one last time'?"

Nasiri gave his number two man a hard look. Their long sojourn in the House of War was taking its toll on them all. Tamwar would never have dreamed of such insolence when they were still in Paris together.

He turned to Uthman. "I assume you brought your book of maps along with the bad news, brother?"

"The Rand McNally," Uthman said, reaching underneath his chair. "A most wondrous book. Yes, I have it right here."

"Let me take a look."

Thirty-Seven

ELEVEN DAYS LATER, Libby Chastain was awakened by the bubbly sound of the *Bewitched* theme, and came close to throwing her phone through a window. Instead, after some muttered obscenities, she answered it.

"'Lo."

"Libby?"

"Yeah. Who's this?"

"It's Colleen, Libby. Did I wake you up? It's almost a quarter to ten, girlfriend."

"Late night, I guess."

"Oh, really? Hot date?"

"They don't get any hotter," Libby muttered.

"What?"

"Forget it. What's up, Colleen?"

"Well, I hope you've got it together enough to process this, because I bring news of great import."

"Small words, Colleen. Use small words."

"They did it again. There – were those small enough for you?"

"Who did what?"

"I dunno, Libby. If I explain, I may have to use some big words."

"Colleen..." It was a difficult name to say through

clenched teeth, but Libby managed it.

"The lion killers. They struck again last night. A zoo in Ohio."

Libby's eyes snapped open. "Ohio, you said?"

"Yeah – Ohio."

"Whereabouts in Ohio?"

"Some hole in the wall called Berlin Center."

"Um. Is that anywhere near Toledo?"

"Why, Libby? Are you all hot to see Toledo, or something?"

"Just check, will you?"

"Toledo's in the northwest part of the state, right?"

"Yeah."

"This place is in the northeast, between Akron and Youngstown. Closer to Youngstown. Couple of hundred miles from Toledo, anyway. Sorry to disappoint."

"It's okay."

"Don't you want to hear the news of great import?"

"I thought that was it – that they hit a third zoo."

"No, that isn't it."

"Well, what, then?"

"This time, they made a mistake."

Thirty-Eight

THE LAW ENFORCEMENT needs of the good people living in Berlin Center, Ohio are met by the Ellsworth Township Post II Sheriff's Office, located some sixteen miles away.

On their way to Ellsworth – in a gray Buick rented at the Youngstown airport – were Special Agent Dale Fenton of the FBI (driving), Special Agent Colleen O'Donnell of the FBI (riding shotgun), and Ms. Elizabeth Chastain from New York City (in back) whom the agents planned to describe, if asked, as a "special consultant."

Fenton and O'Donnell, who had met Libby's flight in Youngstown, took turns briefing her during their forty-minute ride to the metropolis that is Ellsworth Center.

"It's the original one-horse town," Fenton said, "although I'm not sure the Sheriff Department's budget would allow them to *feed* a horse. Maybe if it was real small – you know, one of those miniature horses."

"I'm more interested in lions," Libby said. "Especially the one that got cut open. What kind of a zoo can they support out here in the sticks, anyway?"

"It's not so much a zoo as a rescue operation," Colleen said. "They take in large animals that the real zoos and the circuses don't want anymore. And when some idiot who lives in a state where it's legal to keep 'exotic pets' decides he's tired of paying to feed his Bengal tiger, he calls someplace like Noah's Lost Ark."

"Hell, they've got tigers, leopards, cougars, bears, wolves – everything you can think of," Fenton said. "Including twenty lions."

"Nineteen now," Colleen said.

Fenton nodded. "Point taken."

"It sounds like that place that got hit in Indiana last month," Libby said.

"Very similar," Fenton said. "They broke into a real zoo the first time out, but then they got smart."

"Smart in what way?" Libby asked.

"From the perp's perspective, one of these rescue places is a piece of cake to get into and do stuff in," he said. "No high walls, no guards worth a damn, probably no security cameras – and a shitload of lions to pick from, most of them old and slow."

"They got smart," Colleen said, "but still found a way to be careless."

"Yeah, it was nice of them to leave that little souvenir behind, wasn't it?" Libby said. "I don't suppose it could be a deliberate plant, to throw us off the trail?"

Colleen looked at Libby over her shoulder. "Throw us off *what* trail?"

"Point taken," Libby said, with a smile. "Have you been out to the crime scene yet?"

"We took a walk through the place yesterday," Colleen said.

"Any residue of black magic?"

"Fuck, yeah," she said. "Clear as day – or maybe I should say, dark as night."

"Are you sure you can make this hocus-pocus work with a computer screen?" Fenton asked.

"Yes – I practiced for a couple of hours yesterday. I also put a spell on my laptop, to make things easier. I even brought a grease pencil, so we can make marks on the screen."

"Outstanding," Colleen said. "I'd try it myself, but my Talent doesn't run in that direction. I've never been any good at the psychic location stuff."

"Every cobbler to her last, to coin a phrase," Libby said. "By the way, how come you guys didn't ask Quincey to come with me? He's still in New York, you know."

"Didn't see much point in having him fly out to the boonies – and us paying for it – for a few hours, when you're the one we really need," Fenton said. "If you turn up anything useful, then we'll bring him in for the follow-up."

"Bet your ass you will."

The Ellsworth Township Sheriff's Office occupies a one-story red brick building at the end of Pine Street. Six blocks away, Fenton had to stop, as a crossing guard made way for a bunch of grade-schoolers to cross the street.

"Are the kids back in school already?" Libby said.

"Yeah, Labor Day was last Monday," Fenton said. "Didn't you notice?"

Libby shrugged. "When you don't work a nine-to-five job, minor holidays can slip by. Besides, I've been busy."

Colleen half turned in her seat, looked at Libby for a couple of seconds, then faced front again. But as the crossing guard waved them forward, she said, "You're still fucking Ashley, aren't you?"

"Leave it alone, Colleen," Libby said, in a voice that most people would have heeded. But Colleen O'Donnell was not most people – she was Libby's Sister in witchcraft.

"I'm only asking, because I –"

"*Leave it the fuck alone, Colleen.*"

Colleen lapsed into silence. Fenton kept his eyes on the road and his mouth shut; his mother had raised no fools.

Five minutes later, they were turning into the small parking lot adjoining the Sheriff's Office. In her normal tone of voice, Libby said, "I don't see any media – not that I'm complaining."

Fenton grinned at her in the mirror. "*What* media?"

"There was a crew from one of the Youngstown TV stations out here yesterday," Colleen said. "They shot some footage at the scene and spent five minutes interviewing the Sheriff. Then they put together a 'God, ain't it awful what people will do' story that got shown last night just before the weather report."

"Nobody's made a connection to the other zoo invasions," Libby said. "Good."

"They did have a twelve-second sound bite of Sheriff Welles saying that the investigation is ongoing," Colleen told her.

"He's got *that* right," Fenton said, and turned off the engine. "Come on, let's go."

The single desk in the reception area was occupied by Jane Landingham, a pleasant, fortyish blonde who was the Sheriff's secretary, clerk, and receptionist.

"Good morning, Mrs. Landingham," Colleen said. "Is he in?"

"Sure," the woman said with a smile. "Just give me a second."

She went to the door marked "Sheriff," rapped twice on the frosted glass covering the upper half, and went inside without awaiting an invitation.

A few seconds later, she walked back out, leaving the door open behind her. "You folks go on in," she said.

Sheriff Desmond Welles looked to be about two years

from retirement. He still had most of his hair, although it had gone iron-gray some time back and matched his mustache, which could have used a trim. His plain blue suit had some mileage on it, not unlike the Sheriff himself. Watery brown eyes viewed the world through a set of horn-rimmed glasses, perched on a nose that appeared never to have been broken. He had a nervous smile that came and went like a flashing caution light, its brightness due to the nightly bath that his dentures received, in a solution of water and Polident.

Welles was out of his depth, and had enough sense to realize it. He had spent the last sixteen years arresting drunks, teenage vandals, and the occasional abusive husband. There had been one murder in his jurisdiction five years ago, but the State Police had taken over that investigation almost from the get-go, much to the Sheriff's private relief.

The killing and mutilation of a lion out at Noah's Lost Ark had befuddled him, and the arrival of the FBI both confused and intimidated him. Although he would have died rather than admit it, the presence of real law enforcement people always made him feel like an asshole. At least the two FBI agents, whom Welles had met for the first time yesterday, had been courteous and respectful.

The colored man (as Welles thought of Agent Fenton) had explained that there was a possible link between his local crime and a group of Satanists from out of state who might have killed Jimbo the lion as a sacrifice to their dark god. They'd said they were bringing in some outside consultant to look at the evidence left behind at the scene, and here she was – a nice-looking woman in her thirties with kind gray eyes but a face that bore the pinched look of someone under a lot of stress. Her name, the FBI agents had said, was Elizabeth Chastain, and she had come all the way from New York City, just to examine the odd-looking knife that had been found in Jimbo's pen.

Welles opened a drawer in his filing cabinet and removed the object in question, which was being preserved in a Ziploc freezer bag that Welles called an "evidence envelope."

"The thing is," he said, "some fellas from the State Police Crime Lab are comin' over this afternoon, and they're gonna want to take a look at this thing. A real close look."

"Not to worry, Sheriff," said the other FBI agent, a buxom, freckled redhead named O'Donnell. "We won't do anything to degrade what you've got here."

Welles raised his gaze from O'Donnell's chest to her face. "Sorry... degrade?"

"We won't do anything to destroy its value as evidence," the colored FBI agent told him. He was already pulling on a pair of those thin plastic gloves that CSI people always wore on TV. That made Welles feel a little more relaxed.

"I don't suppose you have wi-fi here, Sheriff?" Welles's confused expression apparently answered the Chastain woman's question; she went on, "Then we'll need an internet connection for this." She held up the laptop computer she'd carried in with her. "And a quiet place to work."

"We only got two computer jacks," Welles told her. "One is out next to Janie's desk, and the other one's in here." He shrugged. "Since you folks want some privacy to do... whatever it is you do, I guess you might as well use my office."

"We'd hate to inconvenience you, Sheriff," the redhead said.

"No inconvenience at all," Welles said, picking his fedora off the coat rack. "I'll go get a cup of coffee over at Luanne's, and take a look through the paper. Then I'll take a turn around town, see what's goin' on. Any calls come in, Janie can take a message."

"Thank you, Sheriff," the Chastain woman said with a smile. "We really appreciate it."

"Happy to cooperate with the federal government," Welles said. "About two hours give you folks enough time?"

The two FBIs looked to Chastain, who said, "That should be plenty of time, Sheriff. Thanks again."

"My pleasure," Welles said. He donned his hat and left the office, closing the door behind him.

After waiting a few seconds to be sure the Sheriff was out of earshot, Fenton said, "Okay – let's get this clairvoyance show on the road."

Thirty-Nine

WHILE HER LAPTOP was booting up, Libby picked up the freezer bag containing the knife she was going to be working with. Well," she said, turning it over in her hand, "whoever owned this, it's a safe bet he didn't get it at Sears."

The knife was about a foot long. About two-thirds of its length came from the curved blade, which had a blood groove running down the center. The handle was carved from some kind of horn, decorated with cheap-looking gemstones of various sizes.

Libby was not a Sensitive, but she could not suppress a shudder at the thought of how many throats had been slashed with this wicked-looking thing.

"It's called a *janbia*," Fenton told her. "I took a couple of pictures of it with my phone camera yesterday, and sent 'em to Quantico. Whoever they've got in Edged Weapons these days was really on the ball – found the name for me in a couple of hours."

"It looks... vaguely Arabic," Libby said. "Or am I letting my expectations rule my perceptions?"

"Not this time," Fenton said. "Once I had the right name for the blade, it wasn't hard to find info about it on the Internet. The *janbia* originated in Yemen, centuries ago – although I gather it eventually spread to other Arab countries, as well. In Yemen, men wear 'em on their belts as a kind of clothing accessory, like we wear neckties over here. And like designer neckties, some of these things can get pretty damn pricey – although I wouldn't say that this specimen here is what you'd call high-end."

"Apparently, these days," said Colleen, "the *janbia* mainly serves a symbolic function, and is rarely used for business. But I gather there used to be a tradition in Yemen – you never took your *janbia* out of its sheath unless you were planning to cut somebody with it. And if you pulled it, you couldn't put it back until it had drawn blood."

"The Arabs do love their knives," Libby said. "Or so I've heard."

"Is holding it with a glove on gonna interfere with the... I don't know – psychic vibrations?" Fenton asked her.

"I don't think so," Libby said. "But let's give it a go, and find out."

"Where do you want to start?" Colleen asked. "Map of the United States?"

Libby shook her head. "We've had zoos that were hit in Michigan, Indiana, and now Ohio. Let's start with those individual states – it might save us some time."

Libby worked the keyboard for a minute or two, and then a detailed map of Ohio nearly filled her computer's monitor.

"Okay," she said, "let's turn the computer so that the screen is lying flat. And I'll need one of you to hold it in place for me. The half with the keyboard's a lot heavier, and I don't want this thing flipping over on me while I'm working."

"I'll do it," Fenton said.

"And you better give me a glove for my left hand

before I pick up that knife," Libby said. "I sure wouldn't want to degrade any of the evidence."

Soon, dagger in one hand and pendulum in the other, Libby was bent over her computer.

Pendulum gently swinging, she traversed the image of Ohio from west to east. When that failed to produce results, she had Fenton turn the computer sideways, then did the same thing from south to north.

"Nothing,' she said as she straightened up. "Okay, one down, two to go. Let's take a look at Indiana now."

Libby slowly repeated the procedure over a digital image of the Hoosier state. East to west first, then south to north.

"Nada," she said finally. "Okay, bring up Michigan. Let's hope the third time's the charm, so to speak."

Libby sent the pendulum swinging over the map of Michigan and began slowly moving it to the right. Then, after half a minute or so, she softly said, "Hmmm. Let's go again, just to be sure."

She brought the pendulum back to the western border of the state, and slowly began moving east once more. In a little while she said, without looking up, "Lady and gentleman, I believe we have a winner. Grab the grease pencil, Colleen, and see if Sheriff Welles has got a ruler in one of his desk drawers."

A ruler was duly found. Libby held the pendulum over the Detroit area now, and set it swinging.

A moment later, she said, "Mark it." Colleen leaned carefully in with the ruler and grease pencil. "Got it," she said.

"Okay, Dale," Libby said. "Let's rotate the computer a little – about thirty degrees, or so."

Fenton turned the computer slightly to the right and then held it in place.

"Mark it," Libby said, a few seconds later. "Good. Now turn it another thirty degrees."

Once six intersecting lines had been drawn, the three of them peered at the screen.

"Dearborn," Colleen said. "Well, I can't say that I'm surprised."

"Isn't that the town with, like, the greatest concentration of Arabs in the country?" Libby asked.

"That's the one," Fenton told her. "Can you say, 'protective coloration,' boys and girls?"

"All right, then," Libby said. "Let's see if we can find us a city map of Dearborn online."

Forty

THE MOON HAD just risen over the cornfields as Peters slowly drove the rental car toward the turnoff on Route 25 that led to the North American home of the Knights Templar.

"Outside Toledo" covers a lot of territory, and it had taken Ashley and Peters almost a week to pinpoint the location. Ironically, they had done it with publicly available satellite photo images. The Knights were not the only ones who could use Google Maps and Bing.

"I still don't like the idea of you going in there alone," Peters said.

"What do you imagine is going to happen to me?" Ashley said, a trifle impatiently. "I'm going to be invisible, remember? And you might also bear in mind that I am Ashur Badaktu, Demon of the Fourth Rank, former resident of the bowels of Hell."

"Yeah, but these guys are all priests, as well as being killers," Peters said.

"So what? Do you think I'm going to cower in front of a fucking priest, like a vampire in some old horror movie?"

"No, it's just that –"

"Remember Finlay – the guy we worked with in New

York last year? He was a priest, too. Shit, he was a damn *exorcist*. But I bothered *him* a hell of a lot more than he bothered *me* – especially when I let him take a quick look at my true nature. You saw it – you were there."

"Yeah, I know. I know."

"Anyway, this is just a reconnaissance operation, sweet pea. Considering the power that Solomon's Seal is supposed to have over demons, I shouldn't have any trouble sniffing it out. I'll slip in, find out where they keep it, and sneak back out again. Then we'll put our heads together and figure out the best way for me to go back and swipe the damn thing."

"Okay, sure, whatever."

"When we get to the turnoff, don't come to a complete stop. Just slow down to about twenty, and I'll jump out. No sense in calling attention to the car. I'll be waiting in the same spot at 5:00."

"Just be careful in there, okay?"

She turned in her seat and looked at him. "Peters, you're not getting all mushy about me, are you? A demon from Hell?"

"Well, aren't we here because *you're* getting all mushy about *Libby*? You, Ashur Badaktu – a fucking demon from fucking Hell?"

She turned away and faced front again. "Peters?"

"Yes, Ashley?"

"Shut the fuck up."

"Yes, Ashley."

Forty-One

The man they were looking for lived in a third-floor apartment at 288 Leonard Street in Dearborn, out near the highway. Although Libby had been able to pinpoint the building in which the *janbia's* owner now stayed, she had been unable to determine the specific apartment number. Magic will only take you so far.

A conversation with the landlady, Mrs. Shadid, had solved that problem. There had been only four new rentals in that building over the past year, she'd told the FBI agents. Three had been to families with children. Only one had been to a single male – one Sofian Zakkout, a man in his late twenties. Mister Zakkout, whose English was halting, according to his landlady, had claimed to be a recent immigrant from Yemen. He kept to himself, paid his rent on time, and didn't cause trouble. More than that, Mrs. Shadid didn't know, or want to know.

Any doubts that Agents Fenton and O'Donnell might have had about whether they had found the right apartment were erased when a phone call to INS determined that no immigrant named Sofian Zakkout had entered the United States legally anytime in the past three years.

Now they had the name (probably an alias) and

address of the man who had almost certainly left the dagger behind at Noah's Lost Ark.

Fenton and O'Donnell had a name and address. What they did not have was probable cause for an arrest, or even a search warrant.

There had been fingerprints on the *janbia* all right, but they had not matched any of the seventy million sets on file with IAFIS, the Bureau's automated fingerprint ID system. There was probably some DNA material on the knife, as well – but Fenton and O'Donnell had nothing of Zakkout's to match it to.

Claiming to a judge that Sofian Zakkout had been identified as a felony suspect based on witchcraft (even of the white variety) was likely to be unpersuasive – even in post-9/11 America, where civil liberties were being accorded somewhat less consideration than they had formerly enjoyed.

But officers of the law did not need probable cause to *question* someone about his possible knowledge of a crime. A conversation with the man known as Sofian Zakkout could well be fruitful, especially with FBI "consultant" Libby Chastain sitting in to determine whether Zakkout was speaking truthfully. If nothing else, the FBI's attention might panic the man, or his associates, into doing something stupid – something that *would* provide probable cause for a search or arrest.

Mrs. Shadid had said she believed that Zakkout worked during the day, so the two FBI agents and their "consultant" called on him at 5:50 that evening – or, rather, they tried to. Mister Zakkout was not home, or at least was not answering the door.

After getting no response to his repeated knocking, Fenton sighed and nodded at his partner. Colleen had prepared the proper spell in advance; a few seconds later the door to Zakkout's apartment clicked open. What they were about to do constituted illegal entry, and anything the agents found or learned would not be admissible in a court of law. But they went inside anyway, for the same reason the bear went over the mountain – to see what they could see.

And what they saw was a whole lot of emptiness. Not only was Sofian Zakkout not at home – the man had apparently left for good, and taken his stuff with him. The apartment wasn't exactly clean – it seemed that Zakkout had been something of a slob – but there wasn't anything left behind that mattered.

"Well, fuck," Libby said.

Colleen nodded. "You can say that again, girlfriend."

"He didn't waste any time," Fenton said. "The bastard was in Ohio just four days ago, and now he's in the fuckin' wind."

"You know, in the movies," Colleen said, "this would be the point where the cops find half a bus ticket, or maybe an open phone book with an airline's number circled."

"Could be Zakkout's seen the same movies," Fenton said. "But we might as well find out for sure."

They split up and went through the apartment, looking for something – anything – that would provide a clue as to where Zakkout had gone. They were about to call it a night when Colleen called from the bathroom, "Hey, check this out!"

Libby and Fenton found her holding a blue toothbrush. "How'd we miss that the first time through?" Fenton said. "And the second?"

Colleen pointed. "There's a three-inch gap between the vanity and the wall. See? It must've rolled down there, and the dude forgot about it. Shit, I almost missed it myself."

Libby took the toothbrush from Colleen and looked at it. "I don't mean to rain on your parade, kiddo, but it occurs to me this thing could have fallen down there last year, or five years ago. Just because we found it today doesn't mean it belongs to the guy who lived here yesterday."

"That crossed my mind, too," Colleen said, but she was smiling as she did. "Run your finger over the bristles, slowly."

Libby did as directed, and she began to smile, too. "Still moist." Then the smile melted. "Unless he just spilled some water over the edge of the sink, or there's a leak from the base of the vanity..."

"I thought of that, and checked," Colleen said. "It's dry as a bone down there."

"Maybe I'm being slow," Fenton said, "but I don't see what the excitement's all about. Even if that thing is covered with the guy's fingerprints and DNA material, it's still the fruit of an illegal search. It's useless as evidence."

"As evidence, yes," Libby said, weighing the toothbrush in her hand. "But still not *entirely* useless."

"Okay, stop dragging it out," Fenton said. "Get to the punchline, so I can stop feeling stupid."

"As far as belongings go, you can't get much more personal than a toothbrush, can you?" Libby said.

Fenton's eyebrows went up as he figured out where she was going.

"That's right, Dale," Colleen said. "For us, it's as good as the knife, probably better." She looked toward Libby. "If she can find the bastard once, she can find him again."

"Hell," Fenton said, "this sucker's *better* than a bus ticket."

Forty-Two

Ashley squinted at her watch. It was just past 2:00 a.m.

"It ought to be a piece of cake," she said.

"Uh-huh. I think that expression is indexed in *Bartlett's Familiar Quotations*," Peters said.

"Is it?"

"Yeah – under 'Custer, George A.'"

Their rental car was parked on some high ground that overlooked the Knights Templar complex from about a mile away. The trunk contained a couple of items that the folks at Avis would not have considered standard equipment, including two black market RPG launchers that Peters had purchased the day before from an Ohio gun nut he'd become friendly with online.

"I met Custer in Hell," Ashley said. "He was an asshole there, too. Still couldn't figure out what he'd done wrong at Little Big Horn."

"The mistake he made was attacking a vastly superior force," Peters said. "Kind of like what we're about to do."

"We're not attacking anybody, dummy. This is subterfuge – like a commando raid."

"And commandos never get captured or killed," he said. "That's never been known to happen."

"Peters –"

"Are you sure you can't just carry the damn Seal out while you're invisible?"

"I'd be invisible, but the Seal wouldn't – I already explained that. Having a chunk of the Great Seal of Solomon floating through the air, apparently under its own power, would draw the kind of attention we don't want."

"And what we're gonna do won't draw attention – much," Peters said.

"It will draw attention where we *want* it to go. That's called misdirection."

"Misdirection. Right."

"I go in invisible, and half an hour later you blow a hole in the rear fence with one of the rocket launchers. Everybody runs to the hole, expecting an attack, but none comes. Then you hit the front gate with the other rocket launcher. The Knights decide *that's* the main attack and run to the gate, leaving me and the Seal to go out through the hole in the fence."

"They'll leave guards at the fence, honey. These guys aren't stupid."

"Then I give the guards a look at my true nature, they fall to the ground screaming, and I just keep on truckin'."

"It's a great plan, Ashley. There's only about twelve things that can go – what the fuck is *that*?"

A stream of fire had appeared in the night sky, shooting downward. Whatever that was, Peters was damn sure it wasn't lightning. Almost immediately, the quiet around them was shattered, as a huge explosion came from inside the Knights Templar compound. While Peters and Ashley watched, dumbfounded, it happened again – a streak of incandescence from above and an eruption of smoke and fire, with the roar of its detonation reaching them a second later.

Then quiet returned to the car – Ashley and Peters were too far away from the Knights' compound to hear any screams or sounds of burning.

After a few seconds, Ashley said, "If I didn't know better, I'd say we just witnessed the Wrath of You-Know-Who. But I'm reasonably certain that He doesn't work that way, anymore."

"No, not since Sodom and Gomorrah," Peters said. "But I figure it's the next best – or worst – thing: the wrath of the CIA."

"You think?"

"I've been catching up with the developments in covert warfare technology that occurred while I was... away. You never know when the knowledge will come in handy. And I'm pretty sure we just saw a Predator drone firing a couple of Hellfire missiles right into the lap of the Knights Templar."

"I saw in the *Times* that the government had started to use drones domestically, but it's supposed to be just for surveillance," she said.

"Looks like at least one of them's been equipped for more than reconnaissance, doesn't it?"

"I guess the Knights made a miscalculation, based on what Libby told me," Ashley said. "They figured the CIA wouldn't be interested in payback for that raid, and that the spooks couldn't find the Knights even if revenge *was* on the agenda."

"Uh-huh. Sounds like a good example of what the gamer dudes call an *epic fail*."

"Oh, that concept is lots older than videogames," Ashley said. "'*Pride goeth before destruction, and haughtiness before a fall.*' Proverbs 16:18."

"It still cracks me up that you read the Bible," he said.

"We all have our little vices, Peters."

They sat silent for a while and watched the flames down below.

"Well," Peters said, "this changes everything."

"It sure as shit does," Ashley said. "But not necessarily for the worse."

Forty-Three

"Got him!" Libby Chastain said.

In her room at the Dearborn Holiday Inn, Libby, with Felton and Colleen's help, had been searching digital maps for the elusive Sofian Zakkout. The map of Michigan had failed to yield any joy; Zakkout, it seemed, had left the state. Libby had then checked Indiana – nothing. Illinois – nothing. Ohio – nothing. But the passage of the pendulum over the map of Pennsylvania had produced that familiar tingle that told Libby she was on to something promising.

"Grab the grease pencil," Libby told Colleen. "Ready? Mark it."

The six converging lines that eventually appeared on the monitor came together just off Interstate Route 80, at Lewisberg.

"Lewisberg?" Fenton said. "What the fuck's in Lewisberg – another zoo?"

"There's got to be some closer than Lewisberg," Libby said. "Pittsburgh's got a big zoo – I know that."

"Maybe if we can find out just where in Lewisberg he is," Colleen said, "we can figure out what the fuck he's doing there."

"Okay," Libby said. "Back to work, kids. We need a map of the city."

Using an online map of Lewisberg, Libby was able to pinpoint Sofian Zakkout's location to the part of town closest to the interstate – but that was as far as the map could take them.

"Satellite images," Libby said. "Now that we know what part of town he's in, I might be able to pinpoint the building, if we can get a clear satellite picture."

It took them nearly an hour to find a satellite photo of northern Lewisberg. That allowed Libby to identify the building where Sofian Zakkout was staying, but it didn't show what the building *was*.

Twenty minutes later, they found a shot that allowed them to see written on the building, in big letters, "Hampton Inn."

"Okay, so the dude got himself a hotel room for the night," Fenton said, and checked his watch. "It's just after ten. He's probably in his room, eating room service and watching porn flicks on the pay-per-view."

"Which means he's having more fun than we are," Libby said.

Colleen was staring into space. "What?" Fenton asked her.

"Let's get this computer right-side up again, and look up the phone number for that Hampton Inn," she said. "I'd use 411 on my phone, but I don't know the area code out there. The computer's quicker."

Google gave them the hotel's website. Colleen clicked on it, and soon had the phone number.

"What are you gonna do?" Fenton asked. "*Call* the guy?"

"Gonna try," she said, and picked up her phone.

While the call went through, she riffled through the pages of her notebook.

"Hi," she said into the phone. "Could you please ring the room of Mister Sofian Zakkout?" She checked her notes. "That's Z-A-K-K-O-U-T." A few seconds went by, then she said, "Really? Okay, thanks, anyway."

Ending the call, she told Fenton and Libby, "Nobody by that name registered. And if he checked out, I'm pretty sure they would have said so."

"What if they'd put the call through, and the guy answered?" Fenton asked.

Colleen shrugged. "*So sorry. Wrong number.*"

"Doesn't sound like a big deal," Libby said. "Just means he's using another alias."

Colleen sat on the edge of the bed. "Maybe – but why would he? The guy's got no reason to believe his current ID is compromised. He sure as hell doesn't know *we're* looking for him."

"So, what're you saying?" Fenton asked her. "That Libby messed up and picked the wrong building?"

"Possible, but in due deference to the abilities of my Sister witch here" – she nodded toward Libby – "I don't think it's likely. Another possibility is the one Libby just raised. Even if he doesn't know we're on his trail, he might have gone to a new alias, simply as a matter of security. Maybe it's standard procedure for his cell."

Colleen leaned forward a little. "But there's a third option, and frankly my money's on this one – that he's travelling with somebody, most likely his controller, and the hotel registration is in the other guy's name."

"Fuck," Fenton said softly.

Libby looked from Colleen to Fenton, and back again. "All this spy stuff is new to me, guys – so spell it out, will you? Why is this cause for concern, assuming it's even true?"

"A suspected terrorist is suddenly on the move, and he's not alone," Colleen said.

"Means he's going operational," Fenton added.

"You mean," Libby said, "he's getting ready to turn the afreet loose."

Both of the FBI agents nodded.

"Well, *fuck*." Libby said it like she meant it – because she did.

Forty-Four

QUINCEY MORRIS WAS so tired, he didn't even know what day it was anymore. Libby had given him the use of her condo while she was off making magic in Ohio, and he had tried to make good use of the time until she returned.

It seemed to him that the key to this whole plot – if there was a plot – was "midnight at the oasis," the phrase that U.S. intelligence kept finding in jihadist chatter. If you assumed it had nothing to do with a '70s pop song, maybe the best way to approach the problem was to break it into its component parts – "midnight" and "oasis."

He started with "midnight," wondering whether the word had any consistent usage in terrorist-speak. His quest led him to newspaper stories, scholarly journal articles on jihadism, and web sites (some of which had been set up by people who possessed many more opinions than they did facts) and discussion boards dealing with such diverse topics as Islamic fundamentalism, the work of the National Security Agency, psycholinguistics, and Arab culture.

He spent almost thirteen hours on it, stopping only for a couple of meals microwaved out of Libby's freezer, bathroom breaks, and a few brief walks around the condo just to stretch his legs. Morris had made a lot of notes on a legal pad as he worked, but most of what he'd written down seemed of dubious value now. But he had found three different sources that said terrorist code often operated on a mirror system when it came to time. If somebody said 9:00 a.m., it often meant 9:00 p.m. Three in the morning could well refer to three in the afternoon.

Apply that logic to "midnight," and you get "noon."

But what if the terrorist wannabees going on about "midnight at the oasis" didn't follow common practice? Perhaps they were smart enough to realize that western eavesdroppers might well be on to the "twelve-hour difference" formula, and had gone with something less predictable.

Well, he had a small fragment of something as a result of all his work – whether it would prove to be a gold nugget or a fly-covered piece of shit remained to be seen.

He checked his watch and saw that it was just past 2:00 a.m. Where had the damn day gone – and with only this to show for it?

All right then – what about "oasis?" He knew what the word meant, of course – anybody who'd ever seen *Lawrence of Arabia* could tell you what an oasis was. But did America even have any real estate that could be reasonably labeled an oasis? Why would a bunch of terrorists attack America in the middle of the Mojave Desert, or some such? And what if the term wasn't meant literally, anyway? Morris cleared his search history and began again.

He actually found a couple of interesting items, and scrawled notes about them on his pad. But the urgency of the matter was dubious, Morris had already put in a long day, and the high-back leather chair that Libby used at her computer was extremely comfortable. He had found that it tilted back about forty-five degrees if you shifted your weight just a little in that direction.

Eventually, Quincey Morris fell asleep. His dreams were not peaceful.

Forty-Five

"What we need to do is keep those guys in Lewisberg under surveillance when they leave that damn hotel," Fenton said. "Otherwise, everything we've done up to now is worth shit."

"Where's the closest FBI field office?" Libby asked. "Would they handle it for you?"

"Based on what we've got right now?" Colleen said. "Not a chance. The Special Agent in Charge of Harrisburg is going to want something better than 'a friendly witch told us' if a couple of Bureau agents he's never heard of call up and ask him for help."

Fenton sat slumped in his chair, his face covered by one big hand. Then he dropped the hand, sat up straighter and said to Libby, "Hand me that phone book over there, will you?"

"Got an idea?" Colleen asked.

"Maybe, maybe not. I need to think this through and maybe make a couple of phone calls." He stood up, took the phone book from Libby, and turned toward the door. "I'll let you know if it pans out. Meantime, either of you comes up with something half-decent, give me a shout. I'll be in my room." He went out the door of Libby's room and let it swing shut behind him.

Libby turned to Colleen. "What was *that* about?"

"I guess if it works, he'll tell us. If not, it doesn't much matter."

The two women tried to come up with solutions of their own, but they kept running into the barriers posed by time, distance, and the inability to seek help from the rest of the FBI.

About fifteen minutes later, there was a knock on the door, and Fenton's voice said, "It's me."

When Libby let him in, he said, "Good thing I've got plenty of slack on my Visa card, because this is gonna cost a lot of coin, which I may or may not get reimbursed for."

He turned to Colleen. "Better pack, and quick. We're on a charter flight to Harrisburg that leaves out of Detroit, as soon as we can get to the hangar."

Colleen stood and walked to the door connecting Libby's room with hers. "I'm on it," she said. At the door she paused and said to Fenton, "Good work, by the way."

Fenton showed no signs of leaving, so Libby said, "Aren't you going to pack?"

"Already have. I didn't really unpack yet, so it didn't take too long."

"So you've chartered a plane to Harrisburg," she said. "Then what?"

"We rent a car and drive north to Lewisburg. Just over sixty miles. Even if Zakkout and his friend – or friends – are early risers, we should be there before they leave the hotel."

"And then you'll follow them in your car."

"The technical term is 'tail,'" he said. "But, yeah."

Libby nodded slowly. "Not bad," she said. "But how will you know Zakkout and company when you get there?"

"I plan to wave my badge at whoever's behind the front desk," he said, "and explain how it is an urgent matter of national security for me to find out if any Middle Eastern gentlemen checked in the day before. If the answer's 'Yes,' my next questions will be about the make, model, and license number of their vehicle."

"And what if the answer's 'No?'"

"Then I am gonna feel really, *really* stupid."

"I notice that you didn't invite me along on this jaunt," Libby said. "Not that I'm complaining, mind you."

"Apart from the hellish expense for the charter, there's no real need for a third person on a tail job, Libby. Colleen and I can switch off driving."

"What would you like me to do instead?"

"Go home, fill Morris in, and get your pit-throwing weapons ready. Once Zakkout and his pals light somewhere, I'll call and let you know."

"Then what?"

"Then you and Morris can come on over and kill us an afreet."

"I thought you'd never ask," Libby said.

Forty-Six

MUJAB RAHIM, WHO was known in some parts of Dearborn, Michigan as Sofian Zakkout, arose at 5:00 for the *fajr*, the pre-dawn prayer – the first of five occasions for prayer that a devout Muslim observes every day. He had brought his own small alarm clock with him, since he did not trust the infidels working in this hotel to wake him on time. Most of these Americans knew little of the True Faith and cared even less, more shame to them.

Rahim unrolled his *sajjada*, making sure that it faced toward Mecca – a direction that Dr. Nasiri had helped him determine before retiring last night. Then he walked to the bathroom, to perform his morning ablutions before prostrating himself on the mat to pray.

He had been invited, along with Uthman and Tamwar, to break his fast with Dr. Nasiri at 6:00, the earliest that room service could be induced to deliver food, or so he had been told. Rahim wondered if the hotel's infidel guests would receive their breakfasts earlier than that, had they wished to.

As he dressed, Rahim automatically reached for his *janbia*, normally carried in its sheath within his right side pocket – he would have preferred to wear it on his belt, as was proper, but had been told it was unwise in this country.

Then he remembered – the *janbia* had been lost, sometime during their last expedition to butcher a lion, to feed its heart to their greedy afreet. Rahim was uncertain exactly when he and his knife had become separated, but suspected he had left it in the pen in Ohio where they had cut open the old lion, once Uthman's magic had rendered the creature unconscious.

The realization had, at first, caused him some anxiety. But he soon realized that there was no way the infidel policemen could tie the knife to him, even if they had found it. Rahim knew about fingerprints, but he was also aware that he had never allowed his own prints to be copied, by anyone. There was no way the knife could be used to identify him. He had not endangered Dr. Nasiri's great act of jihad, in which he would be privileged to participate very soon now.

In Dr. Nasiri's room, which was twice as large as his own, Rahim and the others breakfasted on toast, cereal, hard-boiled eggs, the variety of strained yogurt that the Americans labeled Greek, and strong coffee. Dr. Nasiri had even purchased some of the chocolate-hazelnut spread, known in this country as Nutella, for their toast. But the vacuum-sealed jar had resisted his efforts to open it. Rather than asking one of the others to try turning the lid, he said to Rahim, "Lend me your knife for a moment, brother. If I can get a little air past this misbegotten seal, the problem will be solved."

Rahim cleared his throat. "I regret, brother, that I was forced to discard it. The handle had cracked, and it no longer held the blade securely."

Nasiri looked at him. "You did not leave it behind in your apartment, did you?"

Rahim forced a smile that he hoped looked convincing. "Of course not, brother. I dropped it in a public waste can several blocks away, at night when none could see me."

Nasiri held the searching look for a moment longer, then found a fork on the room service tray which worked well enough in breaking the jar's vacuum seal. The matter was forgotten – almost.

A few moments later, Rahim caught Tamwar looking at him, a slight smirk on the man's pockmarked face. Clearly he found it amusing that Rahim, who so loved to use the knife, was now without one of his own. Rahim had been ashamed to admit that he had lost his *janbia*, but he decided to replace it at the first opportunity. Perhaps one day soon he and the new knife would teach Tamwar how unwise it was to mock him, even silently.

Forty minutes later, they were done eating, checked out of the hotel, and on the road heading east, toward their destiny. Rahim had once asked Dr. Nasiri why they did not enter the City of Lies a day or more in advance of their attack. He had explained, "Their police and intelligence agencies are very vigilant, especially in that city. The less time we spend near the target, the more we reduce our chances of discovery."

It was some thirty minutes later that Nasiri, who was driving the big car, glanced in his mirror toward the back seat and said to Uthman, "Is something troubling you, brother? Did you find your breakfast disagreeable?"

"No, brother, the breakfast was excellent," the wizard said. "But for several minutes now I have had a feeling of... unease."

"What is causing your concern?" Nasiri asked.

"I do not know. But I sense the presence of a rival magician, someone whose purpose is inimical to my own."

"A magician? In this vehicle?"

"No, brother, it is not so close as that." Uthman shrugged. "Perhaps it was some enemy living in a house we have passed close to on our drive. If such was the case, my troubled feeling will pass soon enough."

Nasiri pursed his lips. "Inform me later if it has not passed. Then we shall seek its cause."

"Of course, brother, I will. But it is probably of no consequence."

"That has yet to be determined," Nasiri said.

Forty-Seven

AT 7:30 THAT morning, Libby Chastain found herself at Detroit Metro airport – sitting in the passengers' lounge adjoining Gate 34, and waiting for the Delta clerk to call boarding on her flight to New York. She wondered if it was too early to call Morris, then remembered that he was usually an early riser. Her big purse was on the empty seat next to her. She pulled it toward her and began digging for her phone.

In Libby's New York City condo, Morris's phone began playing its ringtone – a banjo and guitar version of "The Yellow Rose of Texas" recorded years ago by Lester Flatt and Earl Scruggs. The telephone, volume set to 2, was in a pocket of Morris's suit jacket, hanging in a closet near the condo's door. Meanwhile, in Libby's comfortable office chair fifty-some feet away, Morris slept on.

"*Howdy. You have reached Quincey Morris Investigation. If you've got this number, then you know what I do. If you want me to do it for you, wait for the beep and leave a detailed message. I'll get back to you as soon as possible. Y'all take care, now.*"

Libby frowned. Even if Morris hadn't gotten up yet, he usually kept his phone near the bed – in this case, Libby's bed. Well, maybe he was in the shower.

"Hi, Tex, it's me. I'm in Detroit – it's kind of a long story. Anyway, my flight home is due to leave in twenty minutes, which is supposed to put me at JFK around nine. Give me a call, when you get the chance. Bye."

Forty-Eight

In the Denny's restaurant half a mile from Toledo Express Airport, Mal Peters put down his cup of surprisingly good coffee and said, "I bet Libby is just about going to fall over when you hand this to her."

He patted the briefcase on the bench seat next to him. Inside, carefully wrapped in a towel that the Sheraton was probably going to bill him for, was a piece of very old iron about half the size of a dinner plate. To Peters it was just an interesting artifact from the distant past, but Ashley said she could feel the power coming off it, like heat from a furnace. She had assured him that this was the fragment of Solomon's Seal that the Knights Templar had been hoarding since the Middle Ages. Where they had obtained it was anybody's guess, but there was a good chance that someone in their Order had looted it from Jerusalem during one of the Crusades.

"Yes, I think she'll be pleased," Ashley said with a satisfied-looking smile. They both kept their voices down, out of long habit.

Some farmer living within sight of the Knights Templar complex must have heard the Hellfire missiles (a name that amused Ashley no end) exploding, gotten up to see the distant flames, and called 911. Fire trucks had arrived about twenty minutes later, and three State Police cars had shown up shortly thereafter. One of them must have summoned the ambulances, which had begun arriving at the compound just as dawn's first light revealed the full extent of the carnage. The removal of the dead and wounded had gone on all morning and into the afternoon.

Peters and Ashley had observed this activity through binoculars from their high vantage point a mile away. They had passed the time by using Peters's iPhone to locate a place in Bowling Green that rented construction equipment, and to ensure that the John Deere backhoe loader they wanted was available and would be ready for them to pick up later that day.

The last of the ambulances had departed by 1:00 in the afternoon. The State Police crime lab people had finished their preliminary investigation and left by 3:15. The last State Police officers to depart had put up a bunch of yellow "Crime Scene – Do Not Cross" tape across both the front gate of the Templar complex and the entrance to the turn-off on Route 25. They were gone by 3:40. Ashley and Peters were excavating the rubble by 4:30.

Since Ashley had determined during her covert visit to the compound exactly where the fragment of Solomon's Seal had been kept, she and Peters had not wasted time in fruitless searching. They had found the Seal, and were exchanging triumphant high-fives, by a little after 6:00 in the evening.

And now it was 8:15 the next morning, after a night of celebratory sex in their hotel room, and the two of them were eating Denny's scrambled eggs prior to catching the 9:30 plane back to New York.

"It's been an interesting trip," Peters said, "but I'm

still not a hundred percent clear why we went to the trouble. I mean, you said Libby had already started fucking you again, right?"

Ashley gave him one raised eyebrow. "What's the matter, Peters, jealous? Or are you just pissed because Libby won't let you join us? I already asked her, I told you that – it's not my fault she doesn't do three-ways."

"I'm not jealous *or* pissed," Peters said. "I'm just wondering about your motives. This isn't altruism, is it? Not from Ashur Badaktu, Demon of the Fourth Rank, straight from the pits of Hell."

Ashley stirred cream into her second cup of coffee. "Libby's pretty cool, as well as being a great fuck," she said. "I like her. I like Morris, too." She sipped coffee and put the cup down. "Hell, I even like *you*, Peters, when you're not pissing me off with annoying questions."

"So that's it? You went through all this trouble to swipe a piece of Solomon's Seal for Libby, just because you *like* her?

Ashley shrugged her elegant shoulders, perhaps a trifle defensively. "Yeah, I suppose so."

Peters grinned at her. "Sounds like the kind of thing one of us sentimental humans would do."

"Shut up, Peters."

Forty-Nine

Uthman leaned forward in the back seat and said, "I regret to say that my feeling of disquiet persists, my brother."

Nasiri looked sharply at the man's image in the rear-view mirror. "Have you been able to ascertain its cause?"

"Not with precision, but I believe it comes from somewhere behind us."

Nasiri glanced at the side-view mirror and said, "There is a white car that has been a quarter-mile behind us ever since we left the hotel. Many people travel this road, but still..."

Rahim, sitting in the rear seat next to Uthman, turned and stared through the back window. He saw nothing remarkable. "As you say, brother, there are many who use this highway. Perhaps the white car is there by chance."

"Perhaps," Nasiri said. "Let us see if we can find out."

He had been driving at a steady sixty-five, the legal limit. Even though they had nothing with them that could be considered incriminating – unless one were knowledgeable in the ways of magic, of course – he wanted to avoid the attention of the authorities if at all possible. But traffic was light on this part of the highway right now, and Nasiri decided to take a small risk.

He slowly brought the speed up to seventy, then seventy-five, and then to eighty. The white car behind them maintained the same quarter-mile distance. Nasiri came back down to sixty-five and said to Uthman, "I fear your feelings of unease were justified, my brother. The white car appears to be following us, a situation that we cannot tolerate. Is there anything your magic can do to remove these misbegotten fleas from our tail?"

Uthman reached for his bag of tricks, which sat on the floor between his feet. "Most certainly. Do you wish for me to smite them, my brother?"

Nasiri considered. "Enjoyable as that would be to observe, I fear it might bring us unwanted scrutiny. I would prefer it if you could find a way for them to smite *themselves*."

"A most ingenious solution, my brother," Uthman said. "And I believe I know just how to accomplish it."

He opened the canvas bag, removed several vials and a small brazier. "This should take only a few minutes, and then we will be rid of them."

"Excellent," Nasiri said. "Excellent."

Fifty

DALE FENTON WAS biting the inside of his mouth in an effort to stay awake. He had thought to catch a few z's on the plane ride from Detroit to Harrisburg, but the seats in the chartered fan jet were uncomfortable and the noise of the engines would have kept Rip Van Winkle from dozing off. Colleen hadn't gotten any sleep either, although she was snoring softly now in the passenger seat next to Fenton.

They'd played rock-paper-scissors to see who was going to drive the first leg – "first leg" in this case being defined as "until the bastards in the Continental stop for some reason," which meant it was likely to be a long one – and Fenton had lost.

He was no chauvinist – especially around Colleen, who'd have belted him at the first sign of his going easy on her because she was female. If he'd won the brief contest, he would have happily handed her the keys. But her scissors had cut his paper, and that was that.

He hoped things wouldn't get so bad that he'd have to wake Colleen and tell her that he was pulling over to the side of the highway, just long enough for them to trade places. She needed to rest as badly as he did. But fairness was one thing; crashing the car because you fell asleep behind the wheel was another matter entirely.

Fenton had once read that some academic types had figured out that, for an experienced driver, highway driving in good weather usually took up about forty percent of available concentration. How exactly the professors had made that determination, Fenton couldn't recall. But maybe if he could find a way to keep the other sixty percent occupied somehow, it would help him stay awake.

He was trying to do the times tables backwards – and had, in fact, got as far as "eleven elevens is one hundred and twenty-one" – when the twenty-foot-high red brick wall appeared in the middle of the highway, three hundred feet in front of the car and closing fast.

The wall wasn't moving, of course – the car was. Fenton had no time to reason out that there was no way in hell somebody could/would/did build a wall there, and consequently he must be viewing a hallucination. He did what anyone would have – jammed on the brakes, and twisted the wheel hard right in a desperate effort to get around the barrier.

Their rental Ford Focus shot off the highway, smashed through a guardrail as if it were made of balsa wood, and slid down an incline of perhaps thirty degrees. That was enough to roll the car. It made two complete revolutions, then half of another one, so that the Focus ended up on its right side. The two powerless tires on top kept spinning for a while, like the legs of a dog who dreams of chasing rabbits. The gas tank, miraculously, did not rupture; there was no fire.

The two spinning tires slowly ran down to a stop, and then there was no movement at all – not from the car, nor from the two Special Agents for the Federal Bureau of Investigation who had been inside it.

Fifty-One

It was November 22, 1963 – another one of those dates that will live in infamy. Morris was Lee Harvey Oswald, kneeling next to that open window at the Texas Schoolbook Repository, waiting for the target to come into range of his rifle.

He didn't *want* to kill JFK, but he had no choice. The President was evil – he was sure of it. If allowed to live, he would set loose an afreet that would destroy –

"Quincey? Quincey? Come on, cowboy, time to wake up now." Someone was gently shaking him, and the voice in his ear, that voice was...

Libby Chastain gave Morris's shoulder another mild shake, and kept saying his name. He must really be down in the sub-basement of dreamland. She wondered for a moment if he'd been drinking, but there was no evidence of alcohol in the room, and no telltale odor on Morris's breath or skin.

Morris opened his eyes, then immediately squinted against the bright sunlight coming in through the window of Libby's small office. "Libby?" Morris rubbed a hand vigorously over his face. "Shit, what time is it?"

"Just about 10:20," Libby said. "In the morning, that would be." She stepped back to give him some room.

"Gosh, Quincey, why didn't you use my bed? It's a lot better for your back than the chair."

Morris yawned. "I was planning to – use your bed, I mean. But I guess I spent so much time online yesterday that I must've just conked out. Sorry. I found a few interesting tidbits, though."

"No apologies needed, although I was wondering why you didn't answer your phone."

"Phone – *shit*. I think it's still in my jacket, which is –"

"– hanging up in the front closet. Yes, I saw it when I came in." She smiled at him. "I hope your internet time wasn't all spent at sites like 'Lesbian Schoolgirls in Bondage.'"

"Hmm. Never came across that one. Have you got the URL?"

"What I've *got* is coffee brewing, and it smells like it might be ready. I'll be right back."

She was true to her word, returning shortly with a couple of stoneware mugs full of her own special blend of java. She gave him one, and sat down in the room's extra chair.

"I've learned a few things too, in my travels," she said. "You want to go first, or shall I?"

"You start. I'm still waiting for my brain to get firing on all cylinders."

Libby gave him a quick summary of what she had been up to, in the company of their two favorite FBI agents. When she finished, Morris sat frowning.

"So, these presumed jihadists," he said, "are headed east, with Fenton and O'Donnell on their tail?"

"That was the plan," she said. "The second part, I mean."

"And Fenton thinks they're getting ready to send up the big balloon."

"That's the assumption he and Colleen are operating under. I can't say that it's supported by a ton of facts, but it's probably the best conclusion given the limited evidence available."

"Have they checked in with you?"

"No," she said. "I haven't heard from them since they left for the airport last night."

Morris's frown remained in place. If anything, it grew deeper. He reached for the legal pad on which he'd made his notes.

"Speaking of conclusions based on limited evidence," he said, "here's one for you." He told her about the "midnight really means noon" hypothesis that a few jihadist experts bought into.

"It seems rather simplistic," she said. "On the other hand, 'the simplest explanation that fits the known facts is often true.'"

"William of Occam and his famous razor may take a bow," Morris said. He scratched his cheek. "There was something else I turned up, kind of late. Hold on."

He flipped yellow pages, then stopped. "One of things I did was a search of print news sources, using the word 'oasis.' I wanted to see what words it was most often associated with."

"Sounds like a good approach," Libby said.

"A lot of the connections I found were what you'd expect – stuff relating to the desert. 'Camel,' 'sand,' 'palm trees,' stuff like that. But there were six instances when the word was used in connection with something called the Freedom Tower."

Libby blinked, but her voice was flat when she said "Really."

"Yeah, I didn't bother to write 'em all down, but there was one from the President – Leffingwell's predecessor, I mean, who said the Freedom Tower had a big garden that 'would be an oasis of tranquility in the midst of urban intensity,' or something like that." He looked at Libby, not noticing that she had grown pale. "What is this Freedom Tower, anyway – some kind of monument?"

She stared at him. "You're *serious*? You don't fucking *know*?"

He looked back at her curiously. "What's the matter? Who cares about another hunk of marble someplace?"

"Don't you watch the *news*?

"Not much, since I got out of jail. I kind of lost the habit, inside. What's wrong with you?"

Libby shook her head, then told him, "Quincey, the Freedom Tower is the nickname for a building – brand new, only opened three months ago. It's official name is *One World Trade Center*!"

Morris looked at her, as his jaw slowly dropped toward his chest.

"It's the central building in a whole new complex," she said. "Taller than all the others, built right on the site of one of the towers that were destroyed on –"

Libby's eyes grew wider than Morris had ever seen them. Then she said, very fast, "Oh, my Goddess, Quincey – what's today's date?"

He shrugged. "Hell, I'm not sure what day of the week it is."

Libby had bought a copy of the *Detroit Free Press* before boarding her plane, then stuffed it in her purse when she'd finished reading. She practically knocked the chair over as she sprang to her feet and ran out of the room.

Morris sat there, staring at the doorway as a ball of ice big enough to bowl with seemed to form in his stomach.

Libby was back within seconds, the newspaper clutched in her hand. She thrust the front page out at Morris, pointing to the dateline near the top.

By now, Morris didn't even have to look, but he did, anyway.

September 11th. The anniversary of the terrible jihadist attacks on America in 2001. *Today was 9/11*.

The terrorists, last seen heading east on Interstate 80, were headed for New York – hell, they were probably here already. They were going to turn an afreet loose to destroy the central building of new World Trade Center, which had been built as a symbol of American resilience in the face of the worst possible kind of adversity.

They were going to turn a fucking fire djinn loose on the Freedom Tower. And they were going to do it in less than ninety minutes.

Fifty-Two

The subway was not crowded at this hour, and the four men had no trouble finding seats together. Nasiri had said they must not leave their car too close to the target, lest they be caught up in the immense traffic jam that was sure to follow their strike. They had parked at the Port Authority building and would return there, either by subway or on foot, once their glorious task was completed. He wanted to get out of New York before the whole city was closed down.

Nasiri had already written their statement, explaining to the stupid Americans that there would be no safety for any of them as long as their government continued to oppress and murder the people of the Middle East, and to offend Allah by their continued military presence in the Land of the Prophet.

The brief manifesto was in the form of a text message already typed into Nasiri's phone. Once the tower was in flames, he would press "Send" and the statement would be delivered instantaneously to all the major media markets in the city, along with the Mayor's Office.

Timing was important – he knew that many groups would try to take credit for this action as soon as they heard of it. But Nasiri's message, sent in the name of

"The Brothers of the Sheik," would arrive within seconds after the afreet had set the immense building ablaze. There would be no doubt in the world's mind as to who was responsible for this great act of jihad.

He glanced toward Uthman, who sat across from him, and let his gaze linger on the canvas bag resting between the wizard's feet. So much power in such a small object. So much fury, waiting to be unleashed on Uthman's command.

As the subway car began to slow, a metallic voice informed them that the next stop would be the World Trade Center complex. Nasiri felt his heart racing, and he reveled in the sensation.

It was going to be a wonderful day.

Fifty-Three

"I NEED A rifle, a good one," Morris said.

Libby's face showed her confusion.

"A dream I was having when you woke me up," Morris said. "Something – or someone – was trying to tell me that a real rifle, not something shooting just cherry pits, was what would stop these bastards. I should have realized it before – if you kill the wizard, you don't have to worry about the fucking afreet. As long as you get him in time."

"Get him from where?"

"You said there was more than one tower?"

"Yes – seven of them."

"We need to get on the roof of one of those towers, with binoculars and a rifle, along with our fruit stone weapons. We have to command the high ground, Libby."

"But where are you going to get a rifle in time? There's a sporting goods store one block over –"

"Even if they had what I need, there's no time to sight it in – and this is most likely going to call for precision marksmanship. I wish I was as good with a rifle as–"

He stopped talking for a second, then said, "Shit, we know a guy who used to do this stuff for a living."

"You mean Peters?"

"That's the fella."

Morris jumped to his feet and headed rapidly for the door. Over his shoulder he said, "I need a phone. Meantime, you get online and figure out which of those buildings offers a good view of the central tower."

"They all do, Quincey. They built it that way."

"Then *pick* one, dammit!" Morris yanked open the door of the closet, found his jacket, and extracted his cell phone. "I need to know, so I can tell Peters where to meet us – assuming he's even in town."

Libby headed back toward her office, then stopped and turned back to Morris. But what if he's not?"

"Then we're fucked – but not as bad as the people in that building. Now go!"

Fifty-Four

The Delta flight from Toledo kissed the tarmac at JFK, bounced once, then settled down and began to slow as the pilot applied reverse thrust. When the plane reached taxiing speed, one of the flight attendants spoke over the PA system. "Ladies and gentlemen, please remain in your seats until the aircraft has come to a complete stop at the gate. The use of cell phones and other electronic devices is now permitted."

Mal Peters reached inside his jacket and removed his Android phone. Next to him, Ashley pulled out his briefcase from where it had been stowed under the seat in front of her. The object in the case, which had seemed so innocuous to the TSA screeners in Detroit, was too valuable to risk being lost by careless baggage handlers.

Peters began checking his messages. "Quincey Morris called," he told Ashley. "Just a couple of minutes ago, looks like."

"Don't tell him about Solly's Seal," she said. "I want Libby to be surprised."

"She sure as hell ought to be," said, then looked sideways at her. "No pun intended."

"Yeah, I bet," she said. "Just see what Morris wants, will you?"

"Yes, dear."

Peters pressed an icon on the phone and brought it to his ear. Ashley watched his facial expression slide from happy to serious to grim, all within the space of half a minute.

As he was closing down his voicemail, Ashley said, "What?" She was sounding pretty grim herself.

"It's today – at noon. The main World Trade Center tower."

"Oh, fuck," Ashley said softly.

Peters grimaced as he scrolled through his phone directory in search of Morris's number. "I should have known."

"Why?"

"Check the date."

Ashley glanced at her watch, saw the "11" in the date window. She was swearing under her breath as Peters found Morris's number and called it.

"Quincey? It's Peters. Yeah – we're in a plane, but should be in the terminal building within ten minutes."

Peters listened, then said, "Yeah, I've got what you need at the apartment." He looked at his own watch then said, "It's gonna be tight, but I might make it if we get lucky with the traffic. Where you gonna be?"

Peters listened a few seconds longer, then said "I'll do my best, buddy," and ended the call.

He turned to Ashley. "Four World Trade Center. On the roof. He needs a rifle."

"You've gotta be a much better shot than he is, especially with your own gun."

"Yeah, I know. I was planning to volunteer my services – assuming I get there in time to do anything useful."

"Why didn't you tell him about the Seal?"

"You said not to."

"*Idiot* – that was before I knew the shit was gonna hit the fan today."

"Want me to call him back?"

"No – if I don't get it to Libby in time, it doesn't matter whether he knows or not."

A line of concentration appeared on Ashley's forehead.

"All right. Fuck the other baggage for now – we've got what we need right here." She rested a hand on the briefcase. "So we take separate cabs – you go home, get what Morris needs, and haul ass for the building. I'll head there directly with our little artifact and try to get it to Libby."

"Hopefully one of us will get there in time to do something useful."

"A consummation devoutly to be fucking wished."

They still had not reached the gate, but a glance out the window showed they were close now. Ashley let her eyes drift around the cabin. "I'm glad we always fly first class," she said.

"How come?"

"Fewer people between us and the door to knock over."

Fifty-Five

THE SKYSCRAPER KNOWN as Four World Trade Center stands seventy-two stories over the city of Manhattan. Its roof is not supposed to be accessible to the public – that's why the stairs leading up there are behind a locked steel door that reads, "Authorized Personnel Only." But the lock has not been invented that could withstand Libby Chastain's magic.

Normally anyone walking into the building carrying a rifle case, as Morris was, would be challenged by building security before he could even reach the elevators. But Libby had a solution to that problem, too. She cast a spell that temporarily conferred on Morris the Tarnhelm Effect, which meant he was not noticed as they hustled from their taxi into the building and across the lobby. Morris was not invisible, as such, but nobody's eye would be drawn to him – which was the next best thing.

So Morris and Libby reached the roof without interference, closed the steel door behind them, and took a look around. They were not made happy by what they saw.

One problem was the distance between the tower buildings. Seven were planned for the complex, but so far only WTC buildings One (the "Freedom Tower"), Three, Four, and Seven were open for business, with the other three still in various stages of construction.

Morris estimated that the Freedom Tower was about eight hundred feet from where he and Libby now stood. The building next door, WTC 3 (which, Libby said, was fifty-eight stories tall) was closer, but only by three hundred feet or so. Five hundred feet was just too damn far for either the air rifle or Libby's slingshot to have any hope of hitting something – and that was for the *closest* building.

The other perturbing factor was the wind. At street level, they had encountered nothing more than a gentle breeze. But seventy-two stories up in the sky was a different matter. Morris was no expert at measuring these things, but he would have wagered a great deal of money that the wind atop WTC 3 was blowing at least twenty-five miles an hour.

Using a powerful, sighted-in rifle with a good telescopic sight, Morris figured he'd have a good chance of hitting anything man-sized on the roof of the adjoining building, and might even have a chance of hitting someone on one of the other buildings, at least twelve hundred feet away. The wind would still be a problem, but you can compensate for it – maybe.

However, Morris had no rifle – at the moment, anyway. Peters had promised to bring one as soon as he could, but the time/distance equation was not promising. Moving quickly through the city was hard to do without access to flashing red lights and a siren, and Peters had neither.

Morris stood with his hands resting on the brick ledge surrounding the roof area, staring at the Freedom Tower. When Libby joined him, he said, "Unless Peters gets here in time with a long gun for us, we are pretty much screwed."

"Yes," she said. "I was just thinking that myself."

"The distances between buildings are just too damn far – even without the fucking wind."

"I know." Libby ran a hand nervously through her hair and said, "I've got kind of an idea about that, actually. But I'm reluctant even to suggest it."

Morris looked at her. "How come?"

"Because it might get us killed."

"Oh, hell, is that all?" Morris snorted. "Let's hear it."

"I could put together a summoning spell – I've got the gear with me to do it, I already checked. If they turn that afreet loose, the spell might get his attention and prompt him to head over here. That way, we might have a chance with our pit-propellers."

"Pit-propellers," Morris said with a weak grin. "That's pretty good. But I thought your magic was useless against any species of djinn."

"It is, in the sense that I can't compel it to do anything – not without a piece of Solomon's Seal, anyway, and we know how *that* worked out. But I can put something out there which the afreet will almost certainly notice. Whether it chooses to do anything about it is anybody's guess."

"So you magically ask the afreet to come over and say, 'Hi.' And if it does, we let fly with our weapons, such as they are."

"Something like that, yes," she said.

"And if the pits don't work, the afreet might decide to burn us to cinders, just because we pissed it off."

"I did say we could die, Quincey."

"But you're willing to try the spell anyway?"

It took her a few seconds to answer. "Yes, I am. I've been thinking about all the people who work in the

Freedom Tower, and what's going to happen to them when the afreet's turned loose on the building. If I didn't do everything in my power to stop it, I'm pretty sure their dying screams would haunt me for the rest of my life."

"Yeah, I hear you." Morris looked over at the Freedom Tower a little longer, then said, "Well, shit, Libby – if you're willing to invite the damn thing over, the least I can do is shoot some cherry pits at him by way of welcome."

"I was hoping you'd say that. Well, I'd best get started on the spell."

Morris had a pair of binoculars slung around his neck, which Libby had dug out of a closet in her condo. "You gonna take a look around with those?" She asked.

"Might as well."

"Sing out if you see anything interesting."

"You'll be the first to know," he said.

Fifty-Six

The taxi fare from JFK to Peters's apartment building was $38.50. He gave the driver a fifty and said, "Keep the change – and wait for me. I won't be more than ten minutes."

Not long afterward, he was unlocking the apartment that he shared with Ashley. He walked swiftly to the spare bedroom, opened a closet, and surveyed the four rifle cases stacked on the floor. They were different colors for easy identification, and Peters grabbed the black one without hesitation. He opened it to reveal a Remington XM 2010, the standard sniper rifle of the U.S. Army, with an attached Leupold Mark 4 telescopic sight. He unlocked a nearby file cabinet and found a box of .300 Winchester Magnum ammunition, which he placed inside the rifle case before relocking it.

Minutes later, he walked rapidly out of his building – to find no cab waiting in front. The bastard must have taken off, despite the promise of another good tip from Peters. Muttering speculations about the cab driver's probable lineage, physical endowment, and relationships with female family members, Peters jogged to the curb and began looking for another cab to flag down.

Not only were taxis sparse in this neighborhood during mid-day, but quite a few cab drivers are reluctant to stop for a large, clearly pissed-off man carrying a gun case. By the time Peters finally got somebody to pick him up, it was 11:48.

The deadline was noon, and he already knew he wasn't going to make it – but he tried, anyway. Waving two fifties near the cabbie's face, he said, "These are for you if you can get me to the World Trade Center Plaza before noon."

The driver stared at the bills, then at Peters. "You pay for any tickets I get?"

"Yeah," Peters said. "I'll take care of 'em."

"Then I suggest you find something to hang on to."

Fifty-Seven

Morris kept busy with the binoculars, scanning the nearby roofs and the streets below for anything suspicious. It was 11:53 when he said to Libby, "Looks like we've got company."

"Where?" Libby was on her knees ten feet behind him, still busy conjuring the spell that might or might not attract an afreet to their rooftop. Morris wasn't sure whether he hoped she would succeed or fail.

"Right next door – Building Three." Four World Trade Center, where Morris and Libby were, stood fourteen stories taller than the adjoining skyscraper, some five hundred feet away.

"What have we got?" Libby asked.

"Four guys. I'd say they look Arab to me. One of them's got some kind of big carpet bag with him."

"Let me know if they do anything interesting," she said. "I'll be ready in a minute."

"Right." Morris brought the binoculars back up to his eyes. "*Where the hell is fucking Peters?*"

Fifty-Eight

NASIRI STARED WITH loathing at the immense building the Americans had put up – so big and new and shiny. It was as if the great act of vengeance had never happened, on this date those years ago. They thought they could forget what the Sheik had done.

Nasiri was about to remind them.

He posted Tamwar on the roof door, with instructions to kill anyone who tried to interfere. Tamwar carried the big automatic that Nasiri had got for him, and he knew how to use it. He was the only one of the group who was armed.

Then Nasiri saw what Uthman was bringing out of his bag, and could not suppress a face-splitting grin. He had been wrong; Tamwar was not the only one of them who was armed, and the weapon that Uthman had brought was more deadly than any gun ever invented.

Fifty-Nine

"LIBBY?" MORRIS DID not lower the binoculars as he spoke.

"Almost there."

"You won't believe what this old dude just brought out of the bag."

"Try me."

"It's a *lamp* – one of those old fucking oil lamps that looks kinda like a flattened teapot. I swear, it's straight out of the *Arabian Nights*."

"Nice to hear that somebody's keeping up the traditions," she said. "Okay, I'm set. Let me know when the afreet appears."

"What's it gonna look like?"

"Trust me, Quincey – you'll know it when you see it."

Sixty

Nasiri watched with fascination as Uthman waved his hands slowly over the lamp and began to chant. He had never seen the afreet, only heard Uthman's description of the creature. He was beside himself with eagerness.

"What would you have me do to assist, my brother?" Rahim asked him. With no throats to cut or lions to butcher, he seemed at a loss."

"Pray to Allah for our success!"

Nasiri's eyes widened as red smoke began to issue from the spout of the lamp.

"Come forth, great Rashid," Uthman called, in ancient Arabic. Nasiri had studied enough of the dialect to follow what was being said. "The great day is at hand!" Uthman held in his right hand an irregularly-shaped piece of metal the approximate size of a silver dollar.

The scarlet smoke continued to billow, and now it began to take coherent shape. It looked vaguely humanoid, with identifiable arms, legs, and head. As Nasiri watched, it slowly grew to a height of twenty feet, and now more detailed features could be seen.

The afreet, red as the smoke coming from the lamp, had horns like a bull and hands that ended in long, vicious-looking claws. Unlike some of the old illustrations, which Nasiri now realized had been modified for the sake of decency, the creature was not clothed – and its gender was obviously, emphatically male.

When the creature spoke, its voice was so loud that Nasiri had to fight the urge to cover his ears.

"Rashid is here, o wizard!" the afreet thundered. **"I have come forth, as bidden by the ancient words. What dost thou want of me?"**

Uthman pointed. "Behold the great tower of the infidels! There it stands, a testament to the vanity of man, and an affront to Allah, whom all men must obey. I bid you, mighty Rashid, destroy it with your fire! Show the infidels thy power, and let them know thy wrath!"

The creature was silent long enough for Uthman to wonder whether he had made a huge mistake. Then the voice shook the air again. **"I hear, and obey."**

As the men on the rooftop watched, it began to grow.

Sixty-One

"LIBBY!" MORRIS CALLED, without turning away from the awful spectacle unfolding just five hundred feet away. "It's show time!"

Morris let go of the binoculars, letting them dangle from the lanyard around his neck. He didn't think he would need the glasses from this point to see what was going on. He watched the human-looking red cloud from the archaic lamp enlarge, as it began to drift in the direction of the Freedom Tower.

Behind him, Libby was chanting in ancient Aramaic – a language that Morris recognized, although he did not speak it. Her voice grew louder, and Morris told himself that he did not hear a note of desperation in it.

He bent down and picked up the air rifle. He had three shots, and no more. Even if bringing the scuba tank they'd bought had been practical, he knew from experience that the rifle took twelve minutes to charge. He was pretty sure that, once he began to fire his pathetic cherry pits at this terrifying creature – even assuming he got the chance – he would not be given twelve minutes' grace to reload. Twelve seconds would be optimistic.

Sixty-Two

On the rooftop of Three World Trade Center, Nasiri was ecstatic. He began to clap his hands together rapidly in excitement, his dignity temporarily forgotten. He, Abdul Nasiri, had made this wondrous thing happen. His leadership, and his alone, was responsible for bringing this great act of jihad into being.

Then he noticed a strange voice.

Unlike the reedy tone of Uthman, or the afreet's earth-shaking bass, this was the voice of a woman. Going from his expression, Uthman had heard it, too.

"What is that?" Nasiri demanded. "*Who* is that?"

The wizard's voice was a study in confusion. "Truly, brother, I do not –"

"There!" Rahim's voice came like a whipcrack. He was pointing at the nearest building, which towered over Building Three by perhaps two hundred feet. There was a dark-haired man standing there, looking down at them. Clearly the voice did not belong to him, but it seemed to be coming from the same direction.

Nasiri snorted dismissively. If the man had a weapon, he would have used it by now. Some infidel from Building Four had simply been on the roof when the great event began, and he had a woman with him, who was already keening over the loss of life that was imminent in the main tower. Then he heard Uthman say, "Brother, something... something is amiss!"

He turned. The wizard was pointing toward the afreet, which was already halfway to the so-called Freedom Tower.

But now the creature had changed direction, and was moving slowly toward the other building – the one where the woman's voice was coming from.

"*Why is this happening?*" he screamed at the wizard.

Uthman shook his head helplessly. "I do not know what transpires."

"*Then fix it! Get the afreet back on course – now!*"

Uthman nodded humbly. Then, facing in the direction the afreet had gone, he began to chant anew.

Sixty-Three

Quincey Morris tried to control the panic that wanted to overtake him at the sight of the great humanoid cloud, now over a hundred feet tall, heading in their direction. Libby was by his side now, and she had brought the slingshot and a pocket full of artichoke pits, ready to fire.

"Nice work," Morris said, unable to take his eyes off the approaching monstrosity. "I think."

"Thanks," she said, flexing the elastic of the slingshot nervously. "I think."

"Remember the wind," Morris told her. "It's blowing left to right, so if you fire directly at our friend over there, the breeze is gonna carry your pit way to the right before it gets to him. Our point of aim has got to be to his *left*."

"I understand," Libby said. "But how *much* to the left?"

"That," Morris said, "is something of a crapshoot. Figure twenty feet for a start. If your first shot misses, you can readjust your aiming point. I'll do the same."

"Assuming either of us gets a second shot."

"Well, yeah, there's always that."

When it was perhaps a hundred and fifty feet away, the creature spoke. Morris had heard its voice from a greater distance, and knew that it was loud. But even he was not prepared for the assault on his eardrums that followed.

"Thou hast summoned me," the afreet said, "and Rashid would know why. Dost thou think to compel me, like that other worm whose bidding I must do? Thou hast no power over me, daughter of Eve."

Libby had studied several ancient languages as part of her magical studies, since spellcasting must be done in an archaic tongue. She knew she was being addressed in ancient Arabic, but could not respond in kind. *What the hell*, Libby thought. *Let's see if he's bilingual.*

"We have begged audience of thee, o mighty one, to urge thy mercy," she said in ancient Aramaic.

Apparently Rashid was familiar with more than one of the old tongues. He replied, in the language Libby had used, "Mercy? When have any of the children of man been worthy of great Rashid's mercy?"

Libby said to Morris, without turning her head, "I think he's about as close as he's likely to get."

"Okay, here goes everything," Morris said, and raised the air rifle to his shoulder. Libby brought up the sling and pulled the elastic band as far back as she could.

They both let fly at the same moment – with the same result.

The wind carried their ammunition away long before it got to the afreet – neither projectile had even come near the point where he was hovering. The range was just too great.

"Well, shit," Morris said. He adjusted his Kentucky windage and fired again, with the same result. The cherry pit from his rifle never got anywhere near the creature.

It had gotten his attention, though.

"Thinkest thou to smite great Rashid with those puny things? Such folly will cost thee dearly."

"Here," said a female voice directly behind them. "Try this."

Libby turned, and Ashley held out to her something wrapped in a white towel that, incongruously, said "Sheraton" on it. Libby opened the bundle, and saw that she now held a piece of very old metal about half the size of a dinner plate, albeit uneven around the edges.

She looked at Ashley with widened eyes "Is it..?"

"Solomon's Seal," she said. "But I think what you need right now is a diversion."

She moved her arm as if pitching a baseball into the sky, and an orb of fire left her fingertips and flew into the air, to burst like fireworks. It did not touch the afteet, but then she had not meant it to.

Rashid stared in wonderment for a few seconds. As he turned back to their rooftop, Ashley spoke, in ancient Arabic. Her voice was every bit as loud as the afreet's had been.

"Hold, o great djinn! Stay thy wrath, and learn of the great gift we have brought thee!"

"Gift! What could such as thee have to offer the mighty Rashid?"

"Thy freedom!" Ashley thundered. **"By the power of the great Suleiman, we shall free thee from bondage, and bid thee go on thy way, in peace!"**

To Libby, Ashley said in a normal voice, "You're on, kid."

Holding the fragment of Solomon's Seal raised in both hands, Libby began to chant the invocation in ancient Chaldean that she had memorized. She did not know exactly what it said, but her parsing of the words suggested, as had the book where they'd been found, that this was a spell designed to break any control that someone would have over the afreet.

Fortunately for the limitations of Libby's memory, the obscure ritual was not very long. Within a minute, Libby was finished. She slowly lowered the fragment of Solomon's Seal and said, in ancient Aramaic, "Thou art free from the control of men, o mighty afreet. I would bid thee depart this place, and return to thine own kind, with the blessings of the Great King!"

The afreet stared at her, and Libby thought, *I blew it. Maybe I mispronounced the words, or the spell was no good to start with. He's gonna fry us like catfish, and then do the same to all those people...*

Then Rashid said, **"I thank thee for my freedom, and shall do as thou hast bid. But first..."**

The great, human-looking red cloud made a slow hundred-and-eighty-degree turn, so that Rashid was facing the rooftop whence he had come. When he spoke, his voice, if possible, seemed even louder than before.

"Miserable wretches! Thou wouldst bend the great Rashid to thy will? Well, learn now what my will is for thee! A small gift – in parting."

The afreet waved one giant arm toward Building Three, and at once its roof was engulfed in flame. Even from the distance between the towers, Libby and her companions could hear the agonized screams of the four men who had been gathered there. Then, after perhaps five seconds, the fire was extinguished, and the afreet was gone.

Libby, Morris and Ashley stared at the charred roof of Three World Trade Center and the four still forms that lay there – or what was left of them.

Finally Morris said to Ashley, "Where's Peters? Not that I'm complaining, you understand."

"He had to go home and get the rifle you wanted," she said. But I came directly here from the airport."

"Where –" Libby tried, failed, and tried again. "Where did you *get* this?" she said, hefting the fragment of the Great Seal.

"It's kind of an interesting story," Ashley said. "But let me tell you about it over some lunch. I'm starving."

"Sounds good to me," Morris said. He began to pack the air rifle back in its case.

"Me, too," Libby said. "I'm buying."

The End

About the Author

Justin Gustainis is a college professor living in upstate New York. In earlier incarnations, he was an Army officer, garment worker, speechwriter, and professional bodyguard. In addition to many short stories, he is author of the *Haunted Scranton* series (consisting of *Hard Spell* and *Evil Dark*) and the *Morris & Chastain Investigations* series (consisting of *Black Magic Woman*, *Evil Ways*, and *Sympathy for the Devil*), as well as a standalone novel, *The Hades Project.*

Acknowledgements

In working out the plots for both these novellas, I received a great deal of valuable advice and counsel from Jeanne Cavelos, sole proprietor of Jeanne Cavelos Editorial Services and Director of the Odyssey Writing Workshop. Jeanne understands the mechanics of story better than anyone I've ever met.

David Moore and Jonathan Oliver of Solaris Books deserve thanks – David for his editorial skills, and Jon for his patience in the face of my notorious deadline issues.

The people of the City of New York deserve apologies (if any of them care) for my opening most of the buildings at One World Trade Center a year or more ahead of schedule. Call that literary license.

Jackie Kessler, C.J. Henderson, Lili Saintcrow, Rachel Caine, and Julie Kenner all offered valuable suggestions to help me with a particularly thorny plot problem – you guys are the best!

Linda Kingston continued her outstanding work of morale maintenance and spiritual upkeep. I love you, Linda.

Terry Bear contributed his usual nutritional advice. Thanks to Linda, I was able to ignore most of it.

BLOOD
AND
FEATHERS
'A hell of a ride, but heaven to read: eerie, compelling and very funny.'
MICHAEL MARSHALL SMITH
LOU MORGAN